D1289201

The Works of

SIGRID UNDSET

Winner of the Nobel Prize for Literature in 1928

NOVELS

Jenny

Kristin Lavransdatter
  A Trilogy
  The Bridal Wreath
  The Mistress of Husaby
  The Cross

The Master of Hestviken
  A Tetralogy:
  The Axe
  The Snake Pit
  In the Wilderness
  The Son Avenger

The Winding Road
  which comprises:
  The Wild Orchid
  The Burning Bush

Ida Elisabeth

The Longest Years

Gunnar's Daughter

The Faithful Wife

Images in a Mirror

Madame Dorthea

ESSAYS

Stages on the Road   *Men, Women, and Places*

A BOOK OF WARTIME EXPERIENCES

Return to the Future

BOOKS FOR CHILDREN

Happy Times in Norway   *True and Untrue*

Sigurd and His Brave Companions

These are BORZOI BOOKS
published in New York by ALFRED A. KNOPF

Kristin Lavransdatter

VOLUME II

THE MISTRESS OF HUSABY

Kristin Labransdatter

SIGRID UNDSET

VOLUME II
THE MISTRESS OF HUSABY

TRANSLATED FROM THE NORWEGIAN
BY CHARLES ARCHER

ALFRED A. KNOPF : 1946 NEW YORK

Original title: HUSFRUE. Copyright 1921 by H. Aschehoug & Company, Olso, Norway.

Published March, 1925, and reprinted three times.

Reprinted as Volume II of the Lillehammer Edition (three volumes) of *Kristin Lavransdatter* June, 1927.

Included in one-volume edition of *Kristin Lavransdatter* February, 1929, and reprinted nine times in that form.

Reset as in the present volume February, 1935 and included in a one-volume edition of *Kristin Lavransdatter*. Reprinted four times in that form.

Reprinted separately as Volume II of a three-volume edition of *Kristin Lavransdatter* January, 1946.

MANUFACTURED IN THE UNITED STATES OF AMERICA

Kristin Lavransdatter

VOLUME II

THE MISTRESS OF HUSABY

THE MISTRESS OF HUSABY

PART ONE

THE FRUIT OF SIN

THE FRUIT OF SIN

I

THE EVENING before Simon's Mass,* Baard Peterssön's galleass lay in to the landing-place at Birgsi. Abbot Olav of Nidarholm had himself ridden down to the strand to greet his kinsman, Erlend Nikulaussön, and bid welcome to the young wife he was bringing with him home. The pair were to be the Abbot's guests, and to sleep at Vigg that night.

It was a deathly pale, woebegone young wife that Erlend led shoreward from the pier. The Abbot spoke jestingly of the pains of the sea-voyage; Erlend laughed and said he well believed his wife longed for nothing so much as to lie once more in a bed well fixed into a house-wall. And Kristin strove to smile; but within herself she thought that never, so long as she lived, would she willingly set foot on shipboard again. She turned sick if Erlend so much as came near her, he smelt so of the ship and of the sea — his hair was all matted and sticky with sea-water. He had been crazy with joy all the time on board — and Sir Baard had laughed: at his home in Möre, where Erlend had grown up, the boys had been out in the boats sailing or rowing late and early. 'Twas true they had been a little sorry for her, Erlend and Sir Baard, but not so sorry, Kristin thought, as her wretchedness deserved. They kept on saying the sea-sickness would pass when she grew used to being aboard ship. But from first to last her misery had not abated.

Even the next morning she felt as if she were still sailing, as she rode up through the settled lands. Uphill and downhill, their road led over great, steep clay ridges, and when she tried to fix her eyes on some spot on the hills far ahead, it was as though the whole country-side were dipping, then rising, in waves cast up against the shining, blue-white winter-morning sky.

A whole troop of Erlend's friends and neighbors had come to Vigg in the early morning to attend the bridal pair, so that they

* 28th October.

rode in a great company. The ground sounded hollow under the horses' hoofs, for the earth was as hard as iron with the black frost. The air was full of steam from the men and horses; the bodies of the beasts and the men's hair and furs were white with rime. Erlend seemed as white-haired as the Abbot; his face glowed from his morning draught and the biting wind. He wore his bridegroom's dress to-day; youth and gladness seemed to shine out of him, and joy and wantonness welled out in the tones of his mellow, supple voice as he rode, shouting and laughing, amidst his guests.

Kristin's heart began to tremble strangely — with sorrow, with tenderness and with fear. She was still sick from the voyage; she had the burning pain at her breast that came now whenever she had eaten or drunk never so little; she was bitterly cold; and deep down in her mind was a dull, dumb spot of anger with Erlend, that he could be so gay and care-free. . . . And yet, now that she saw his childlike pride and sparkling happiness in bringing her home as his wife, a bitter regret welled up in her; her breast ached with pity for him. She wished now that she had not hearkened to the counsel of her own self-will, but had let Erlend know when he was at her home last summer — let him know what made it most unfit that their wedding should be held with too great pomp. She saw now that she had wished he should be made to feel — he too — that they could not escape unhumbled from what they had done.

— And she had been afraid of her father, too. And she had thought in her mind: when once their bride-ale had been drunk, they were to journey so far off; 'twas like she would not see her home-country again for a long, long time — not till all talk about her had had good time to die away. . . .

Now she saw that things here would be much worse than she had deemed. True, Erlend had spoken of the great house-warming he would hold at Husaby, but she had not thought it would be like a second wedding-feast. And the guests here were the folk that Erlend and she were to live among — it was their respect and friendship they had need to win. It was these folk that had had Erlend's folly and evil fortunes before their eyes all these years. Now he himself believed that he had redeemed himself in their judgment, that now he could take the place among his fellows that was due to his birth and fortune. And now 'twas like he would be a laughing-stock through this whole country-side when it came out that he had done amiss with his own betrothed bride.

The Abbot leant over towards her from his horse:

" You look so sad, Kristin Lavransdatter; are you not quit of your sea-sickness yet? Or is it, perhaps, that you are home-sick for your mother? "

" Even so, sir," said Kristin softly; " 'tis of my mother I am thinking."

They had come up into Skaun, and were riding high on a hill-side. Below them in the valley bottom the woods stood white and shaggy with rime; everywhere the sunlight glittered, and a small lake in the midst flashed blue. Then all at once the troop passed out from a little pinewood, and Erlend pointed ahead:

" There lies Husaby,* Kristin. God grant you many happy days there, my own wife! " he said, with a thrill in his voice.

Before them stretched broad plough-lands, white with rime. The manor stood, as it were, on a broad shelf midway on the hill-side — nearest them lay a small church of light-coloured stone, and just south of it were the clustered houses; they were many and great; the smoke whirled up from their smoke-vents. Bells began ringing from the church, and many folk came streaming from the courtyard to meet them, with shouts of greeting. The young men in the bridal trains clashed their weapons one on another — and with a great clattering and the thunder of hoofs and joyous uproar the troop swept forward towards the new-married man's abode.

They stopped before the church. Erlend lifted his bride from her horse, and led her forward to the church-door, where a little crowd of priests and clerks stood waiting to welcome them. Within, it was bitterly cold, and the daylight, sifting in through the small round-arched windows of the nave, dulled the shine of the tapers burning in the choir.

Kristin felt lost and afraid when Erlend loosed her hand and went over to the men's side, while she herself took her place among the throng of strange women, all in festal dress. The service was most goodly. But Kristin was very cold, and it seemed as though her prayers were blown back upon her when she tried to free her heart and lift it upwards. She thought maybe it was no good omen that this should be St. Simon's day — the guardian saint of the man by whom she had done so ill.

* See Note 1.

From the church all the people went in procession down to the manor, the priests first, then Kristin and Erlend hand in hand, then their guests pair by pair. Kristin was not enough herself to see much of the manor buildings. The courtyard was long and narrow; the houses lay in two rows, south and north of it. They were big and built close together; but they looked old and ill-tended.

The procession halted at the door of the hall-house, and the priests blessed it with holy water. Then Erlend led her through a dark outer room. On her right a door was thrown open, letting out a flood of light. She bent, passing through the doorway, and stood with Erlend in his hall.

It was the greatest room * she had ever seen in any man's dwelling-house. There was a hearth-place in the midst of the floor, and it was so long that there were two fires on it, one at each end; and the room was so broad that the cross-beams were borne up on carven pillars — it seemed to her more like the body of a church or a king's hall than a room in a manor-house. Up by the eastern gable-end, where the high-seat stood in the middle of the wall-bench, closed box-beds were built in between the timber pillars.

And what a mass of lights were burning in the hall — on the tables, that groaned with costly cups and vessels, and on sconces fastened to the walls! After the fashion of the old age, weapons and shields hung amidst the stretched-out tapestries. Behind the high-seat the wall was covered with a velvet hanging, and against it a man was even now fastening up Erlend's gold-mounted sword and his white shield with the red lion saiient.

Serving-men and women had taken the guests' outer garments from them. Erlend took his wife by the hand and led her forward to the hearth, the guests standing in a half-ring just behind them. A fat lady with a gentle face came forward and shook out Kristin's head-linen, where it had been crumpled by the hood of her cloak. As she stepped back into her place, she nodded to the young couple and smiled; Erlend nodded and smiled back to her, and looked down at his wife — his face, as he looked, was beautiful. And again Kristin felt her heart sink — with pity for him. She knew what he was thinking now, as he saw her standing there in his hall with the long snow-white linen coif over her scarlet bridal dress. And this morning she had had to wind a long woven belt tight around her waist under her clothes before she could get the

* See Note 2.

dress to fit upon her, and she had rubbed upon her cheeks some of a red salve that Lady Aashild had given her; and while she thus bedecked herself, she had thought in sorrow and bitterness that Erlend must look but little upon her, now that he had her safely his own — since he still saw and knew nothing. Bitterly she repented now that she had not told him.

While the married pair stood thus, hand in hand, the priests were walking the round of the hall, blessing house and hearth and bed and board.

Next a serving-woman bore forth the keys of the house to Erlend. He hooked the heavy bunch on Kristin's belt — and looked, as he did so, as though he had been fain to kiss her where she stood. A man brought a great horn ringed about with golden rings — Erlend set it to his lips and drank to her:

" Hail, and welcome to thy house, Lady of Husaby! "

And the guests shouted and laughed while she drank with her husband and poured out the rest of the wine on the hearth-fire.

Then the minstrels struck up their music, as Erlend Nikulaussön led his wedded wife to the high-seat, and the wedding guests took their seats at the board.

On the third day the guests began to break up, and by the hour of nones on the fifth day the last of them were gone, and Kristin was alone with her husband at Husaby.

The first thing she did was to bid the serving-folk take all the bed-gear out of the bed, wash it and the walls round about it with lye, and carry out and burn up the straw. Then she had the bedstead filled with fresh straw, and above it made up the bed with bed-clothes from the store she had brought with her. It was late in the night before this work was at an end. But Kristin gave order that the same should be done with all the beds on the place, and that the skin rugs should be well baked in the bath-house — the maids must set to the work in the morning the first thing, and get as much done towards it as they could before the Sunday holiday. Erlend shook his head and laughed — she was a housewife indeed! But he was not a little ashamed.

For Kristin had not had much sleep the first night, even though the priests had blessed her bed. 'Twas spread above with silken pillows, with sheets of linen and the bravest rugs and furs; but beneath was dirty, mouldy straw, and there were lice in the bed-clothes and in the splendid black bearskin that was spread over all.

Many things had she seen already in these few days. Behind the costly tapestry hangings, the unwashed walls were black with dirt and soot. At the feast there had been masses of food, but much of it spoilt with ill dressing and ill service. And to make up the fires they had had naught but green and wet logs, that would scarce catch fire, and that filled the hall with smoke.

Everywhere she had seen ill husbandry, when on the second day she went round with Erlend and looked over the manor and farm. By the time the feasting was over, little would be left in barn and storehouse; the corn-bins were all but swept clean. And she could not understand how Erlend could think to keep all the horses and so many cattle through the winter on the little hay and straw that was in the barns — of leaf-fodder there was not enough even for the sheep and goats.

But there was a loft half full of flax that had been left lying unused — there must have been the greatest part of many years' harvest. And then a storehouse full of old, old unwashed and stinking wool, some in sacks and some lying loose in heaps. When Kristin took up a handful, a shower of little brown eggs fell from it — moth and maggots had got into it.

The cattle were wretched, lean, galled and scabby; and never had she seen so many aged beasts together, in one place. Only the horses were comely and well-tended. But, even so, there was no one of them that was the equal of Guldsveinen or of Ringdrotten, the stallion her father had now. Slöngvanbauge, the horse he had given her to take along with her from home, was the fairest beast in the Husaby stables. When she came to him, she had to go and throw her arms round his neck and press her face against his cheek.

She thought on her father's face, when the time came for her to ride away with Erlend and he lifted her to the saddle. He had put on an air of gladness, for many folk were standing round them; but she had seen his eyes. He stroked her arm downwards, and held her hand in his for farewell. At the moment, it might be, she had thought most how glad she was that she was to get away at last. But now it seemed to her that as long as she lived her soul would be wrung with pain when she remembered her father's eyes at that hour.

And so Kristin Lavransdatter began to guide and order all things in her house. She was up at cock-crow every morning, though

Erlend raised his voice against it, and made as though he would keep her in bed by force — surely no one expected a newly-married wife to rush about from house to house long before 'twas daylight.

When she saw in what an ill way all things were here, and how much there was for to set her hand to, a thought shot through her clear and hard; if she had burdened her soul with sin that she might come hither, let it even be so — but 'twas no less sin to deal with God's gifts as they had been dealt with here. Shame upon the folk that had had the guidance of things here, and on all them that had let Erlend's goods go so to waste! There had been no fit steward at Husaby for the last two years; Erlend himself had been much away from home in that time, and besides, he understood but little of the management of the estate. 'Twas no more than was to be looked for, then, that his bailiffs in the outlying parishes should cheat him, as she was sure they did, and that the serving-folk at Husaby should work only as much as they pleased, and when and how it chanced to suit them. 'Twould be no light task for her to put things right again.

One day she talked of these things with Ulf Haldorssön, Erlend's own henchman. They ought to have had the threshing done by now, at least of the corn from the home farm —and there was none too much of it either — before the time came to slaughter for winter meat. Ulf said:

" You know, Kristin, that I am not a farm-hand. It has been our place to be Erlend's arms-bearers — Haftor's and mine — and I have no skill in husbandry any longer."

" I know it," said the mistress of the house. " But so it is, Ulf, that 'twill be no easy task for me to guide things here this winter, a newcomer as I am here north of Dovre, and with no knowledge of our folks. 'Twould be a friend's turn of you if you would help and counsel me."

" I can well believe it, Kristin — that you will have no easy task this winter," said the man, looking at her with a little smile — the strange smile that was always on his face when he spoke with her or with Erlend. It was bold and mocking, and yet there were both kindness and a sort of respect for her in his bearing. Nor, it seemed to her, had she a right to take offence that Ulf should bear himself more forwardly towards her than might have been seemly otherwise. She herself and Erlend had made this serving-man a party to their wanton and deceitful doings; and she could see that he knew, too, how things stood with her now. She must let this pass — and indeed she saw that Erlend put up with anything Ulf might say or do, and that the man showed but little reverence for his master. True, they had been friends from childhood; Ulf came from Möre, and was son to a small farmer that lived near Baard Petersson's manor. He called Erlend by his name; and her, too, now — it was true that this way of speech was commoner here north of Dovre than in her own country.

Ulf Haldorssön was a proper man, tall and dark, with sightly eyes; but his mouth was ugly and coarse. Kristin had heard ugly tales of him from the maids on the place — when he was in at the city he drank beyond measure and spent his time in revel and roistering in the lowest houses of call — but at home at Husaby he was the best man to have at one's beck, the fittest, the hardest worker, and the shrewdest. Kristin had come to like him well.

" 'Twere no easy thing for any woman," he went on, " to come hither to this house — after all that has come and gone. And yet, Mistress Kristin, I deem that you will win through it better than most could have done. You are not the woman to sit down and moan and whimper; but you will set your thoughts on saving your children's inheritance yourself, since none else here takes thought for such things. And methinks you know that you can trust me, and that I will help you as far as in me lies. You must bear in mind that I am unused to farm work. But if you will take counsel with me and let me come to you for counsel, I trow we will tide over this winter none so ill."

Kristin thanked Ulf, and went into the house.

She was heavy at heart with unrest and fear, but she tried to forget it in work. One thing was that she understood not Erlend — even now he seemed to suspect nothing. But another and a worse trouble was that she could feel no life in the child she bore within her. At twenty weeks it should quicken, she knew — and now more than three weeks over the twenty had gone by. She lay awake at night and felt the burden within her that grew greater and heavier, but was still as dull and lifeless as ever. And there floated through her mind all she had heard of children that were born crippled, with sinews stiff as stone, of births that had come to the light without limbs — with scarce a semblance of human shape. Before her tight-shut eyes would pass pictures of little infants, dreadfully misshapen; one shape of horror melting into another still worse. Southward in the dale at home, at Lidstad, the folks had a child — nay, it must be grown up now. Her father had seen it, but would never speak of it; she had marked that he grew ill at ease if anyone but named aught of it. What did it look like? — Oh, no! Holy Saint Olav, pray for me! — She must needs trust firmly on the holy King's tender mercy; had she not placed her child under His ward? She would suffer for her sins in meekness, and with her whole heart have faith that there would be help and mercy for the child. It must be the Enemy himself that tempted her with these ugly visions, to drive her to despair. But her nights were evil. . . . If a child had no limbs, if it were palsied, like enough the mother would feel no sign of life within her. . . . Erlend, half waking, marked that his wife was restless, drew her closer into his arms, and laid his face against the hollow of her throat.

But by day she showed no sign of trouble. And every morning she dressed her body with care so as to hide from the house-folk yet a little longer that she bore another life about with her.

It was the custom at Husaby that after the evening meal the serving-folk went off to the houses where they slept; so that she and Erlend were left alone in the hall. Altogether the ways of this manor were more as they had been in the ancient days, when folks kept thralls and bondswomen for the household work. There was no fixed table in the hall, but morning and evening the meals were spread on a great board that was laid on trestles, and after the meal it was hung up again on the wall. At the other meals folks took their food over to the benches and sat and ate it there. Kristin knew such had been the custom in former times. But nowadays, when 'twas hard to find men to serve at table, and all folks had to content them with maids for indoor work, it fitted the times no longer — the women were loath to break their backs lifting the heavy tables. Kristin remembered her mother telling how at Sundbu they had put a fixed table into the hall when she was but eight winters old, and that the women thought it in every way the greatest boon — they need no longer take all their sewing out to the women's house, but could sit in the hall and clip and cut out — and it made such a goodly show to have candlesticks and a few costly vessels standing out in view. Kristin thought: next summer she would pray Erlend to have a fixed table set up along the northern wall.

So it was at her home, and there her father had his high seat at the board's end — but then the beds there were by the entrance wall. At home her mother sat highest up on the outer bench, so that she could go to and fro and keep an eye on the service of the food. Only when there was a feast did Ragnfrid sit by her husband's side. But here the high seat stood in the middle of the eastern gable-end, and Erlend would have her always sit in it with him. At home her father always placed God's servants in the high seat, if any such were guests at the manor, and he himself and Ragnfrid served them while they ate and drank. But Erlend would have none of this, unless they were high of station. He was no great lover of priests and monks — they were costly friends, he was used to say. Kristin could not but think of what her father and Sira Eirik always said, when folk complained of the churchmen's greed of money: men forgot the sinful joys they had snatched for themselves when the time came to pay for them.

She questioned Erlend about the life here at Husaby in ancient days. But he knew strangely little. Things were thus and thus, he had heard; but he could not remember so nicely. King Skule had owned the manor and built on it — 'twas said he had meant to make Husaby his dwelling-place, when he gave away Rein for a nunnery. Erlend was right proud of his descent from the Duke, whom he always called King, and from Bishop Nikulaus; the Bishop was the father of his grandfather, Munan Bishopsson. But it seemed to Kristin that he knew no more of these men than she herself knew already from her father's tales. At home it was otherwise. Neither her father nor her mother was overproud of the power of their forbears and the high esteem they had enjoyed. But they spoke often of them; held up the good that they knew of them as a pattern, and told of their faults and the evil that had come of them as a warning. And they had little tales of mirth too — of Ivar Gjesling the Old and his quarrel with King Sverre; of Ivar Provst's quick and witty sallies; of Haavard Gjesling's huge bulk; and of Ivar Gjesling the Young's wonderful luck in the chase. Lavrans told of his grandfather's brother that carried off the Folkunga maid from Vreta cloister; of his grandfather's mother Ramborg Sunesdatter, who longed always for her home in Wester Gothland and at last went through the ice and was lost, when driving on Lake Vener one time she was staying with her brother at Solberga. He told of his father's prowess in arms, and of his unspeakable sorrow

over his young first wife, Kristin Sigurdsdatter, that died in childbirth when Lavrans was born. And he read, from a book, of his
ancestress the holy Lady Elin of Skövde, who was given grace to
be one of God's blood-witnesses. Her father had often spoken of
making a pilgrimage with Kristin to the grave of this holy widow.
But it had never come to pass.

In her fear and distress, Kristin tried to pray to this saint that she
herself was linked to by the tie of blood. She prayed to St. Elin
for her child, kissing the reliquary that she had had of her father;
in it was a shred of the holy lady's shroud. But Kristin was afraid
of St. Elin, now when she had brought such shame on her race.
When she prayed to St. Olav and St. Thomas for their intercession,
she often felt that her complaints found a way to living ears and
merciful hearts. These two martyrs for righteousness her father
loved above all other saints; above even St. Laurentius himself,
though this was the saint he was called after, and in honour of
whose day in the late summer he always held a great drinking-
feast and gave richly in alms. St. Thomas her father had himself
seen in his dreams one night when he lay wounded outside Baagahus. No tongue could tell how lovely and venerable he was to
look on, and Lavrans himself had been able to say naught but
" Lord! Lord! " But the radiant figure in the Bishop's raiment had
gently touched his wounds and promised that he should have his
life and the use of his limbs, so that he should see again his wife and
his daughter, according to his prayer. But at that time no man had
believed that Lavrans Björgulfsön could live the night through.

Aye, said Erlend. One heard of such things. Naught of the kind
had ever befallen him, and to be sure 'twas not like that it should —
for he had never been a pious man, such as Lavrans was.

Then Kristin asked of all the folk who had been at their home-
coming feast. Erlend had not much to say of them either. It seemed
to Kristin that her husband was not much like the folks of this
country-side. They were comely folk, many of them, fair and
ruddy of hue, with round hard heads and bodies strong and heavily
built — many of the older folks were hugely fat. Erlend looked like
a strange bird among his guests. He was a head taller than most
of the men, slim and lean, with slender limbs and fine joints. And
he had black silky hair and was pale brown of hue — but with light-
blue eyes under coal-black brows and long black eyelashes. His
forehead was high and narrow, the temples hollow, the nose some-

what too great and the mouth something too small and weak for a man — but he was comely none the less; she had seen no man that was half so fair as Erlend. Even his mellow, quiet voice was unlike the others' thick full-fed utterance.

Erlend laughed and said his forbears were not of these parts either — only his grandfather's mother, Ragnfrid Skulesdatter. Folks said he was much like his mother's father, Gaute Erlendssön of Skogheim. Kristin asked what he knew about this grandfather. But it proved to be almost nothing.

One night Erlend and Kristin were undressing in the hall. Erlend could not get his shoe-latchet unloosed; as he cut it, the knife slipped and gashed his hand. He bled much and swore savagely. Kristin fetched a piece of linen from her chest. She was in her shift. As she was binding up his hand, Erlend passed his other arm around her waist.

Of a sudden he looked down into her face with fear and confusion in his eyes, and his face grew red as fire. Kristin bowed her head. Erlend took away his arm, saying nothing — then Kristin went off in silence and crept into the bed. Her heart beat with hard dull strokes against her ribs. Now and again she looked over at her husband. He had turned his back to her, and was slowly drawing off one garment after another. At last he came to the bed and lay down.

Kristin waited for him to speak. She waited so, that at times 'twas as though her heart no longer beat, but only stood still and quivered in her breast.

But Erlend said no word. Nor did he take her in his arms. At last, falteringly, he laid a hand across her breast and pressed his chin down on her shoulder so strongly that the stubble of his beard pricked her skin. As he still spoke not a word, Kristin turned to the wall.

It was as though she were sinking, sinking. Not a word could he find to give her — now when he knew that she had borne his child within her all this long weary time. She clenched her teeth hard in the dark. Never would she beg and beseech — if he chose to be silent, she would be silent too, even, if need be, till the day she bore his child. Bitterness surged through her heart; but she lay stock-still against the wall. And Erlend too lay still in the dark. Hour after hour they lay thus, and each knew that the other was

not sleeping. At last she heard by his even breathing that he had
fallen asleep; and then she let the tears flow as they would, in sorrow and bitterness and shame. Never, it seemed to her, could she
forgive him this.

For three days Erlend and Kristin went about thus — he like a
wet dog, the young wife thought. She was hot and hard with
wrath — she grew wild with rage when she marked that he would
look searchingly at her and then hastily look away again if she
turned her eyes towards him.

On the morning of the fourth day, as she sat in the hall, Erlend
came in through the doorway, dressed for riding. He said he was
going westward to Medalby; maybe she would come with him and
see the place; it was one of the farms that fell under her morning-
gift. Kristin said yes; and Erlend helped her himself to put on her
long shaggy boots and the black sleeve-cloak with the silver
clasps.

In the courtyard were four horses ready saddled, but Erlend
said now that Haftor and Egil might stay at home and help with
the threshing. Then he helped his wife up into the saddle. Kristin
felt that 'twas in Erlend's mind to speak now of what lay between
them unuttered. Yet he said naught as they rode slowly southward
towards the woods.

It was far on now in the early winter, but no snow had yet fallen
in this country-side. The day was fresh and fair, the sun just risen,
and the white rime glittered in silver and gold everywhere, on the
fields and on the trees. They were riding over the Husaby lands.
Kristin saw that there was little sown or stubble land, but mostly
fallows left for grass, and old meadow-land, uneven, moss-grown,
and choked with alder-shoots. She spoke of this.

Her husband answered jauntily:

" Know you not, Kristin, you that have such skill in guiding
goods and gear, that it profits not to raise corn so near to a great
market? — a man does better by bartering his wool and butter for
the outland merchants' corn and flour — "

" Then should you have bartered away all that wool that lies
now in your lofts and is long since spoiled," said Kristin. " But so
much I know, that the law says every man that leases land shall
sow corn on three parts of it, and let the fourth part lie fallow

for grass. And 'tis not fit that the landlord's manor should be worse cared for than the tenants' farms — so my father always said."

Erlend laughed a little, and answered:

" I have never searched out the law in that matter — so long as I have my dues, my tenants can till their farms as likes them best, and, for Husaby, I manage it as seems to me best and fittest."

" Would you be wiser, then," asked Kristin, " than our fathers that went before us, and St. Olav and King Magnus that made these laws? "

Erlend laughed again and said:

" 'Tis a matter I have never thought on — but the devil and all must be in it, Kristin, that you have the laws of the land so at your finger-ends — "

" I know a little of these things," said Kristin, " because my father often prayed Sigurd of Loptsgaard to say over the laws to us when he came to visit us and we sat at home of an evening. Father deemed it profitable for the servants and the young folk to learn somewhat of such things; and so Sigurd would repeat one passage or another."

" Sigurd — " said Erlend. " Aye, now I remember seeing him at our wedding. He was that long-nosed toothless old fellow that wept and drivelled and patted you on the breast — he was drunk as an owl even the next morning, when the folks came up to see me set the linen coif on your head — "

" He has known me from before I can remember," said Kristin angrily. " He used to take me on his lap and play with me when I was a little maid — "

Erlend laughed again:

" Well, 'twas a strange pastime enough — for you all to sit there and listen to that old fellow chanting out the laws, part by part. Sure Lavrans is in all ways unlike other men — others are used to say that if the peasant knew the laws of the land in full, and the stallion knew his strength, 'twould take the devil to be a knight."

Suddenly, with a cry, Kristin struck her horse on the quarter and dashed on, leaving Erlend gazing after his wife in wonderment and anger.

Of a sudden he put spurs to his horse. Christ — the fjord — there was no crossing over it now — the clay bank had slipped in the autumn.

Slöngvanbauge stretched himself to gallop the harder when he heard the other horse behind him. Erlend was in deadly fear — how she was dashing down the steep hill-sides too! At last he tore past her through the undergrowth, then swung into the road where it ran level for a little way, and stood so that she must needs stop. When he came alongside her, he saw that she seemed a little frightened herself now.

Erlend leant forward towards his wife and struck her a ringing blow under the ear — so that Slöngvanbauge leapt aside and reared in fright.

" Aye, and you deserved it," said Erlend in a shaken voice, when the horses had quieted down and they were riding side by side again. " To carry on so — clean crazy with rage. You frighted me — "

Kristin held her head so that he could not see her face. Erlend was wishing that he had not struck her. But he said again:

" You made me afraid, Kristin — to behave so! And of all times, now — " he added in a low voice.

Kristin neither answered nor looked at him. But Erlend could feel that she was less angry now than before, when he had mocked at her home. He wondered much at this — but he saw that so it was.

They came to Medalby, and Erlend's tenant came out and would have them into the dwelling-house. But Erlend said 'twere well they should look round the farm-buildings first — and Kristin must come with them. " The farm is hers now — and she understands these things better than I, Stein," he said, laughing. There were some other farmers there, come to act as witnesses — some of them too were Erlend's tenants.

Stein had come to the farm last term-day, and ever since he had been praying that the landlord would come up and see the state of the houses when he took them over, or would send men to act for him. The other farmers bore witness that not one of the houses had been weather-tight, and that those which now were tumbledown had been no better when Stein came. Kristin saw that it was a good farm, but that it had been ill cared for. She could see that this Stein was a hard-working man. Erlend, too, was reasonable and promised him some relief in his rents, till such time as he had got the houses mended.

Then they went into the hall, and found the board set out with good food and strong ale. The farmer's wife begged Kristin to forgive that she had not come out to meet her. She said her husband would not suffer her to go out under open sky till she had been churched after her childbed. Kristin greeted the woman kindly, and had her take her over to the cradle to look at the child. It was these people's first-born: a son twelve days old, and big and sturdy.

Next Erlend and Kristin were led to the high-seat, and all the folks sat down, and ate and drank a good while. Kristin was the one that talked most during the meal; Erlend said little, and the peasants not much; but Kristin thought she could mark that they liked her well.

Then the child awoke, and began first to whimper, and then to shriek so fearfully that the mother had to fetch it and give it the breast to stop its cries. Kristin looked more than once across at the two, and when the boy was full-fed and quiet, she took him from the woman and laid him on her arm.

" Look, husband! " she said. " Is not this a fair and lusty knave? "

" Doubtless it is," said her husband, not looking towards them.

Kristin sat holding the child a little before she gave it back to the mother.

" I will send over a gift for this little son of yours, Arndis," she said, " for that he is the first child I have held in my arms since I came hither north of Dovre."

Hot and defiant, with a little smile, she looked at her husband and then along the row of peasants on the bench. There was the least little twitching at the corners of the mouths of one or two of them; but immediately they stared before them, stiff with solemnity. Then stood up a very old fellow who had drunk well already. He took the ladle out of the ale-bowl, laid it on the table and lifted the heavy vessel aloft:

" Then will we pledge you, mistress, on a wish: that the next child you hold in your arms may be the new master of Husaby! "

Kristin rose up and took the heavy bowl. First she held it out to her husband. Erlend but touched it with his lips, but Kristin drank deep and long.

" Thanks for that good wish, Jon o' the Woods," she said, nodding to him, her face shining and gleeful. Then she passed on the bowl.

Erlend sat there darkly flushed and, Kristin could see, in great wrath. She herself felt naught now but an unthinking need to laugh and be glad. Some time after, Erlend gave the sign for breaking up, and they set out on their homeward way.

They had ridden a good way in silence, when Erlend broke out of a sudden:

"Think you it was needful to let our very peasants know you were with child when you were wedded? You may stake your soul that 'twill be no time now ere the tale about us two is all over every parish by the Trondheim Fjord. . . ."

Kristin made no answer at first. She looked straight forth over her horse's head, and her face grew so white that Erlend was afraid.

"As long as I live, I shall not forget," she said at last, without looking at him, "that this was your first greeting to your young son that is beneath my girdle."

"Kristin!" said Erlend beseechingly. "My Kristin," he implored, when she answered not, nor looked at him. "Kristin!"

"Sir?" she said in cold, measured tones, without turning her head.

Erlend swore furiously, set spurs to his horse and dashed forward along the road. But, a little after, he came riding back to meet her.

"Now had you vexed me so sorely," he said, "that *I* was nigh riding off and leaving *you*."

"And if you had," answered Kristin quietly, "it might have been that you had had long and long to wait ere I came after you to Husaby."

"How you talk!" said the man despairingly.

Again they rode for a space without speaking. In a while they came to a place where a bridle-path led off over a ridge. Erlend said to his wife:

"I had meant that we should ride home by this way over the hill — 'tis a little farther, but I had a mind to take you up here with me some time."

Kristin nodded listlessly.

In a little, Erlend said it would be better they should go on foot. He tied their horses to a tree.

"Gunnulf and I had a fort on the hill-top here," he said. "I would like well to see if any of our castle is left —"

He took her hand. She let him hold it, but walked with her eyes cast down, looking to her footing. It was not long before they reached the top. Over the rime-covered woods in the gorge of the little stream they saw Husaby on the hill-side right over against them, lying wide-stretched and brave, with its stone church and the many great houses, wide plough-lands around it and dark pine-clad ridges behind.

"Mother," said Erlend in a low voice, "she would come with us up here — often. But always she sat gazing south, up towards the Dovrefjeld. I trow she longed both early and late to be gone from Husaby. Or sometimes she would turn to the north and look towards the hill-glen where you see the far-off blue — the hills beyond the fjord. Never did she look across at Husaby."

His voice was soft and beseeching. But Kristin neither spoke nor looked at him. Soon he went off and began kicking the frozen heather:

"No, I can see there's naught left here of Gunnulf's and my stronghold. True enough, 'tis many a long day since we played about here, Gunnulf and I — "

There was no answer. — Right below where they stood lay a little frozen pool — Erlend took up a stone and threw it down on to the ice. The pool was frozen to the bottom, so the stone did but make a small white star on the black mirror. Erlend took another stone and threw harder — then another and yet another, till at last he was showering down stones furiously, bent on splintering the ice to shards. Then he caught sight of his wife's face — she stood there with eyes dark with scorn, smiling disdainfully at his child-ishness.

Erlend turned sharp round — but at the same moment Kristin grew deadly pale, and her eyelids closed. She stood clutching in the air with her hands, swaying as if about to fall — then caught the trunk of a tree and held to it.

"Kristin — what is it?" he asked fearfully.

She made no answer, but stood as if she were listening for something. Her eyes were far away and strange.

Now she felt it again. Deep down within her she felt as though a fish moved its tail. And again it was as if the whole earth swayed around her, and she grew dizzy and weak, but less now than at first.

"What is amiss with you?" said Erlend once again.

She had waited so for this — hardly daring to acknowledge to herself the anguish of her waiting. She could not speak of it —

now, when they had been unfriends this whole day. But then *he* said it:

"Was it the child that grew quick within you?" he asked in a low voice, touching her shoulder.

At that she cast from her all her wrath against him, and clung to her child's father and hid her face in his breast.

Soon after, they went down again to the place where their horses were tied. The short day was nearly done; behind them in the southwest the sun went down behind the tree-tops, a blurred red ball in the frost-haze.

Erlend tried his wife's saddle-girths and buckles with care before he lifted her up to the saddle. Then he went and untied his own horse. He felt under his belt for his gloves, which he had stuck in there, and found but one. He began to look about on the hill-side.

Kristin could not forbear saying:

"'Tis of no use seeking here for your glove, Erlend."

"You might as lief have told me, if you saw me lose it — though you were never so wroth with me," he said. The gloves were those Kristin had sewn for him and given him with her betrothal-gifts.

"It fell from your belt when you struck me," said Kristin very low, and with downcast eyes.

Erlend stood by his horse's shoulder, with his hand on the saddle-bow. He looked abashed and unhappy; but of a sudden he burst out laughing:

"Never had I dreamed, Kristin — in those days when I was wooing you, running around beseeching my kinsmen to speak for me, and making me so supple-jointed and so humble to win you — that you could ever be such a troll!"

Then Kristin, too, laughed:

"No — for if you had, doubtless you had given up that quest long before — and doubtless that had been best for you."

Erlend took a couple of strides across to her and laid his hand upon her knee:

"Jesus help us, Kristin — when have you ever heard tell of me that I did the thing that was best for me — ?"

He laid his head down on her lap and looked with shining eyes up in his wife's face. Flushed and happy, Kristin bent her head and tried to hide from him her smile and her eyes.

He took her horse by the bit and let his own follow after them; so he led her till they were come down from the hill-side. Every time he looked at her, he laughed; and she turned away her head from him to hide that she was laughing too.

"Now," he said gaily when they were down again on the road, "now will we ride home to Husaby, my Kristin, and be as happy as two thieves!"

2

ON Yule Eve it blew and rained in torrents. 'Twas no fit weather for sleighing, so Kristin had to stay at home when Erlend and the house-folk rode off to midnight mass at Birgsi church.

She stood in the doorway of the hall and looked after them. The fir-root torches they bore shone red on the murky old house-walls, and were mirrored in the watery glaze of the courtyard. The wind took the flames and blew them flat out sidewise. Kristin stood till the noise of their going died away in the night.

Within, in the hall, tapers burned on the board. It was littered with the leavings of the supper — slabs of porridge in platters, half-eaten bread-slices and fishbones in puddles of spilt ale. The serving-maids who were to stay at home had lain down already in their resting-places on the floor-straw. Kristin was alone on the manor with them and one old man that they called Aan. He had served at Husaby since the days of Erlend's grandfather; he lived now in a little hut down by the lake, but often came up to the manor in the day-time, and went pottering about, doing, as he thought, a deal of work. Aan had fallen asleep at the board to-night, and Erlend and Ulf had borne him off to a corner, laughing, and laid him there, covered with a rug.

By now, the floor would be strewn thick with rushes at home at Jörundgaard; for all the house-folk slept in the hall together the holy nights of Yule-tide. Ere they set forth to the church, it was their use to clear away the broken food of the fast supper, and her mother and the wenches set out the board as fairly as they could, with butter and cheeses, piles of thin, light-brown bread-slices shining white bacon and the thickest of smoked knuckles of mutton. The silver flagons and mead-horns stood shining on the board; and her father had himself put the ale-cask up on the bench.

Kristin turned her chair round to the hearth — she would look no longer at the sluttish table. One of the girls was snoring — the sound was horrible to hear.

'Twas one of the things she could not like in Erlend — at home in his own house he ate in such a slovenly fashion, raked about in the dishes for tit-bits, and would scarce so much as wash his hands before he went to meat. And then he would let his dogs get up on his lap and snatch at bits of food while people were eating. So 'twas only what might have been looked for that the serving-folk had no manners at the board. . . .

At home she had been taught to eat daintily — and slowly. For 'twas not seemly, her mother said, that the folk of the house should sit waiting while the servants ate — and those who swinked and toiled must be given time to eat well and be filled.

" Gunna," Kristin called softly to the great yellow bitch that lay with a whole litter of whelps up against the stone border of the hearth. She was so snappish that Erlend had called her after the ill-tempered old lady of the house at Raasvold.

" Poor old barebones! " whispered Kristin, patting the beast, as it came and laid its head on her knee. She was sharp as a scythe along the backbone, and her dugs almost swept the floor. The whelps were eating their mother quite up. " So, so, my poor old barebones! "

Kristin laid her head back against the chair and looked up at the sooty rafters. She was weary. . . .

Oh, no — no easy time had she had, these months she had been at Husaby. She had had some talk with Erlend in the evening of the day they had been at Medalby; and had seen that he believed she was bitter against him because he had brought this upon her.

" I mind me well," he said in a whisper, " the day in the spring when we went in the woods north of the church. I mind well you prayed me to let you be — "

Kristin was glad because he said this. For at other times she had often wondered to see how many things Erlend seemed to have forgotten. But now he said:

" Yet had I not believed of you, Kristin, that you could go about thus, bearing a hidden grudge against me, and yet seeming kind and joyous as ever. For you must have known long since how things were with you. I had thought you were as clear and open as the sun in heaven — "

" Ah, Erlend," she said sadly, " you should know best of any in this world that I have followed secret ways and been false to them that trusted me most." But she was fain that he should understand. " I know not if you remember now, my dearest, that, long before that, your deeds towards me had been such as none would call fair. And yet God and Mary Virgin know that I bore you no grudge, nor loved you any less — "

Erlend's face grew tender.

" So thought I," he said low. " But this too I trow you know — through all those years I strove to set up again what I had broken down. I took comfort in the thought that things would go in the end so that I could reward you for being so long-suffering and so true."

Then she had asked him:

" You have heard of my grandfather's brother and the Lady Bengta, who fled together from Sweden against the will of her kin. God punished them by giving them no child. Have you never been afraid, in these last years, that He would punish us in like wise — ? "

And she had said to him, softly and trembling:

" You may well believe, my Erlend, that small joy was mine last summer, when first I grew ware of this. And yet methought — methought if you should die and leave me before we were wedded, I had liefer you left me with a child of yours than all alone. And I thought, if *I* should die in bearing you a child — 'twould be better than that you should have no true-born son to mount into the high-seat in your place when you have to part from this earthly home."

Erlend answered hotly:

" For me, I would deem my son all too dear bought if he should cost you your life. Speak not so, Kristin. . . . So dear to me Husaby is not," he said in a while. " And least of all since I have been sure that Orm can never inherit after me — "

" Care you more for *her* son than for mine? " asked Kristin then.

" *Your* son — " Erlend laughed a little. " Of him, see you, I know but this, that he comes hither a half-year or so too soon. Orm I have loved for twelve years — "

A while after, Kristin asked:

" These children of yours — you miss them sometimes? "

" Aye," said the man. " Before, I would often go inland to Österdal, where they are, to see them."

" You could go there this Advent," said Kristin in a low voice.

" Would it not mislike you if I went? " asked Erlend eagerly.

Kristin had answered that she would think it but right. Then he had asked whether 'twould be against her liking if he brought the children home with him for Yule. " Soon or late, look you, you must see them." And again she had answered that this seemed to her but right.

While Erlend was gone to Österdal, Kristin had worked hard making things ready for Yule. It irked her much to go about now amidst these strange henchmen and serving-women — she had much ado to force herself to dress and undress in the presence of the two maids, who Erlend had said were to sleep near her in the hall. She had to remind herself that she could never have borne to lie alone in that great house — where another before her had slept with Erlend.

The serving-women of the manor were no better than one might have looked they should be. Such peasants as took good heed of their daughters had had no mind to send them to service in a house where the master lived in open adultery with a wedded woman, and had set her to rule his house. The maids were idle and unused to obey a mistress. But some of them soon began to like the new order that Kristin brought in, and that she took a hand herself in their tasks. They grew full of talk and cheer, since the mistress hearkened to them and answered them kindly and cheerily. And Kristin showed the house-folk daily a calm and gentle face. She rebuked none harshly, but if any serving-maid should gainsay her bidding, the mistress seemed to think the girl knew not what to do, and quietly showed her how she would have the work done. It was thus Kristin had seen her father take things with new serving-men who grumbled — and no man at Jörundgaard had ever offered to gainsay Lavrans a second time.

Thus they might get through this winter well enough. Later she must contrive to get rid of the women that she could not come to like, or that she could not bring into shape.

One piece of work there was that 'twas beyond her to take in hand, except when she was free from the eyes of these strangers. But in the mornings when she sat alone in the hall, she sewed on clothes for her child — swaddling-clothes of soft wadmal, bands of bought stuff, red and green, and white linen for the christening-gown. While she sat sewing on her seam, her mind was tossed about between fear and trust in the holy friends of mankind she had prayed to intercede for her. True, the child lived and moved within her now, so that she had no rest night or day. But she had heard of children born with a belly where their face should have been, or with heads turned backwards, or toes where the heels should be. And she could see before her eyes Svein, who was bluish-red over half his face, because his mother had taken fright at a fire. . . .

Then she would throw down her seam, go and bend the knee before the picture of the Virgin Mary, and say seven Aves. Brother Edvin had said that God's Mother was filled with exceeding great joy each time she heard the Angel's greeting, even if it were in the mouth of the vilest sinner. And 'twas the words *Dominus tecum* that most rejoiced Mary's heart; therefore must she ever say them three times over.

It helped her always for a while.

One evening when she was sitting at the table with the house-folk, one of the women, a young maid that helped in the indoor work, had said:

"Methinks, mistress, 'twere better we should begin sewing swaddling-bands and baby-clothes now, before we set up this web you speak of — "

Kristin made as though she had not heard, and went on speaking of the dyeing of the web. Then the girl began again:

"But maybe you brought baby-clothes with you from home?"

Kristin smiled a little and turned again towards the others. When, a little while after, she glanced round, the wench was sitting, fiery-red in the face, peeping fearfully across at her mistress. Kristin smiled again and began speaking to Ulf across the table. Then of a sudden the girl burst out crying. Kristin laughed a little, and the girl wept more and more, till she was snivelling and sobbing.

"Nay, Frida — let us have no more of this," said Kristin at last, quietly. "You came hither as a grown serving-maid; try now not to behave like a baby girl."

The maid whimpered — she had not meant to be saucy — Kristin must not be wroth.

"No," said Kristin, still smiling. "Eat your supper now and weep no more. We have none of us more wit than God hath been pleased to grant us."

Frida jumped up and ran out, sobbing bitterly.

Afterwards, when Ulf Haldorssön stood talking with Kristin of the work to be done next day, he said with a laugh:

"Erlend should have betrothed him to you ten years agone, Kristin. Then had things stood better with him now in every wise."

"Think you so?" said she, smiling as before. "In those days I was but nine winters old. Think you Erlend was the man to go around waiting long years for a child-bride?"

Ulf laughed and went out.

But that night Kristin lay awake, weeping tears of loneliness and shame.

Then Erlend had come home, the week before Yule, with Orm, his son, riding at his father's side. A stab of pain went through Kristin's heart when he led the boy up to her and bade him greet his stepmother.

He was a most comely child. 'Twas thus she had thought *he* might look, the son she was to bear. Sometimes when she dared to be glad, to trust that her child would be born sound and shapely, to dream ahead of the boy that should grow up by her knee, it was thus he looked in her dream — so like his father.

He was, maybe, somewhat small of his age, and slight, but well-shaped, fine-limbed and fair of face, dark of skin and hair, but with great blue eyes and red, soft mouth. He greeted his stepmother in seemly wise, but his face was hard and cold. Kristin had had no chance to speak much with the boy. But she felt his eyes upon her, wherever she went, and she felt as though she grew yet more heavy and awkward of body and gait when she knew that the lad was gazing at her.

She saw not that Erlend spoke much with his son, but she could see that of the two it was the boy that held back. Kristin spoke to her husband of Orm, saying that he was a comely lad and seemed of a good wit. His daughter Erlend had not brought with him; he deemed Margret was too small to make such a long journey in winter-time. She was fairer still than her brother, he said proudly when Kristin asked of the little maid — and much quicker of wit; she could turn her foster-father and mother round her little finger. She had gold-yellow, curling locks and brown eyes.

Then must she be like her mother, thought Kristin. In spite of herself, jealousy gnawed her heart. Did Erlend love this daughter of his as her father had loved her? His voice had been so soft and warm when he spoke of Margret.

Kristin stood up now and went to the outer doorway. It was so dark without and so heavy with rain that neither moon nor stars were seen. She thought, though, it must be nigh on midnight now. She brought in the lantern from the outer room and lighted it. Then she threw her cloak around her and went out into the rain.

"In Jesu name," she whispered, crossing herself thrice, as she stepped out into the night.

At the top of the courtyard stood the priest's house. It was empty now. Though Erlend had long since been freed from the ban, no priest had yet come to dwell at Husaby; now and then one of the chaplains from Orkedal would come over and say mass; but the new priest appointed to the church was in foreign parts with Master Gunnulf; it seemed they had been school-friends. They had been looked for home the last summer — but now Erlend said they could scarce be there before the late spring. Gunnulf had had the lung-sickness in his youth — he would scarce travel in the winter-time.

Kristin let herself into the cold, empty house, and found the church-key. Then she paused awhile. The ground was a slippery glaze — there was pitch-darkness, and wind, and rain. 'Twas a parlous thing for her, as she was now, to go out at night-time, and most of all on Yule Eve, when all evil spirits are in the air. But she could not give it up — she must come into the church.

"In the name of God the Almighty I go forth here," she whispered out into the storm. Lighting herself with the lantern, she set her feet with care where grass-tufts and stones showed above the ice-crust. In the dark the road to the church seemed long; but at last she stood on the threshold-stone.

Inside, it was bitter cold, much colder than outside in the rain. Kristin went forward to the chancel and knelt down before the crucifix, which gleamed dimly in the darkness above her.

When she had said her prayers and risen up, she stood still a little. It was as though she had looked that something should befall her. But there happened nothing. She was cold and afraid in the dark, desolate church.

She crept up to the altar and turned her light on the pictures. They were old, harsh and ugly. The altar-table was of naked stone

— altar-cloths, books and vessels she knew were locked away in a chest.

In the nave was a bench running along the wall. Kristin went down and sat on it, placing her lantern on the floor. Her cloak was wet, and her feet were wet and cold. She tried to draw up one foot under her, but it hurt her to sit so. So she wrapped her cloak well about her, and strove to gather and fix her thoughts on this one thing, that now was come again the holy midnight hour, when Christ had Himself born of Mary Virgin in Bethlehem.

*Verbum caro factum est et habitavit in nobis.**

She remembered Sira Eirik's deep, clear voice. And Audun, the old deacon, that was never to be aught but deacon. And their church at home where she had stood by her mother's side and heard the Christmas mass. Every single year she had heard it. She tried to remember more of the holy words, but she could think of naught but the church and all the well-known faces. Farthest in front, on the men's side, stood her father and gazed with far-off eyes into the blaze of light from the choir.

'Twas so unbelievable that their church was no more. It was burnt down. She burst into tears at the thought. And here was she sitting all alone this night, when all Christian folk were gathered together in joy and gladness in God's house. But 'twas like this was as it should be — that she was barred out to-night from the rejoicings for the birth of God's Son by a pure and stainless maid. — Her father and mother were surely at Sundbu this Christmas. But there would be no mass to-night in the chapel there; she knew on Yule Eve the Sundbu folk ever rode over to mass in the head church at Ladalm.

It was the first time, as far back as she could remember, that she had not been at Christ's Mass. She must have been quite small the first time her father and mother took her with them. For she could remember that they had stuffed her into a sheepskin bag with the wool inside, and her father had borne her in his arms. It was a night of fearful cold, and they rode through a forest — the light of the fir-root torches gleamed on snow-laden pines. Her father's face was purple-red in the glare, and the furred rim of his hood was snow-white with rime. Now and again he bent his head a little and bit the tip of her nose, asking her if she felt the bite; then called laughing over his shoulder to her mother that Kristin's nose

* St. John's Gospel, i. 14.

was not frozen off yet. It must have been while they still dwelt at Skog — belike when she was three winters old. In those days her father and mother were quite young folk. She remembered now her mother's voice that night — high and glad and full of laughter as she called out to her husband and asked about the child. Aye, her mother's voice had been young and fresh then. . . .

— Bethlehem — it betokens in Norse the place of heavy bread. For there was given to men the bread that nourisheth unto life ever-lasting. . . .

'Twas at the day mass that Sira Eirik stepped up into the lectern and set forth the evangel in the people's own tongue.

Between the masses the folks sat in the guest-shed northward of the church. They had drink with them and the cups went round. Betweenwhiles the men would go out to the stalls and see to the horses. But on vigil nights in the summer-time the congregation sat out on the church-green, and between the services the young folks danced.

— And the blessed maid, Mary, herself wrapped her son in the swaddling-clothes. And she laid him in the manger from which oxen and asses were wont to eat. . . .

Kristin pressed her hands strongly against her sides.

Little son, sweetest son, son of mine, God will have mercy on us for His blessed Mother's sake. Blessed Mary, thou brightest star of the sea, thou dawn of life eternal, who didst bring forth the sun of all the world — help us! Little child, what ails thee to-night, that thou art so unquiet — canst thou feel, even beneath my heart, that I am so bitter cold — ? "

On Childermas Day last Yule-tide Sira Eirik had set forth the gospel concerning the innocent children whom the cruel soldiers slaughtered in their mothers' arms. But so it was, he said, that God had chosen out these young children to enter into the hall of heaven before all the other blood-witnesses. And this was for a sign that the Kingdom of Heaven is of such as these. And He took a little lad and set him in the midst of them. Except ye make your-selves over in the likeness of these, dear brothers and sisters, ye cannot enter into the halls of the heavenly kingdom. And let this be for a comfort for everyone, man or woman, that mourneth the death of a young child. . . . At that Kristin had seen her father's and mother's eyes meet across the church; and she looked away quickly, for she knew that in this she had no part. . . .

This had been last year. The first Yule-tide after Ulvhild's death. Oh — but not *my* child! Jesus, Mary! Let me keep my son!

Her father had been loath to go for the St. Stephen's riding last year — but all the men had begged and prayed him till at last he joined them. The ride set out from the church-green at home and galloped down to the riversmeet by Loptsgaard; there they met the men from Ottadal. She remembered her father dashing past on his golden-chestnut stallion — he stood in his stirrups and leaned forward along his horse's neck, whooping and cheering on the beast, the whole ride thundering after.

But last year he had been home early, and he came quite sober. Other years the men were used to come home late that day, and beyond measure drunken. For they had to call in at all the farmyards by the way and drink the healths brought out to them, to Christ and to St. Stephen, who was the first to see the Star in the East as he was riding King Herod's colts to water them in Jordan river. The horses, too, were given ale to drink that day, to make them wild and fiery. On Stephen's day it was ever so that the farmers must be busy with horse-games even till the time of evensong — scarce could the men be got to think of aught or speak of aught but horses. . . .

She could remember one Yule-tide when they had had the great common drinking-feast at Jörundgaard, and her father had promised a priest that was among the guests that he should have a young chestnut colt, a son of Guldsveinen, if he could catch it and back it, as it ran, loose and bare-backed, in the courtyard.

'Twas a long time since — before the mishap to Ulvhild. Their mother stood before the house-door with the little sister on her arm, and Kristin stood holding to her skirt — a little afraid.

The priest ran after the horse, seized the halter, leapt from the ground so that his long gown flew out on all sides; but had to loose the rearing fiery beast again. "So — coltie, coltie — heia, coltie, heia, sonny!" he sang out, hopping and dancing like a billy-goat. Her father and an old farmer that was there stood helpless, holding each other up, their features all drawn awry with laughter and strong drink.

Either the priest must have earned and won the colt, or Lavrans must have given it him unearned, for Kristin remembered that he was riding it when he left the manor. Then were they all sober enough; as he mounted, Lavrans held the stirrup for him with great reverence, and he blessed them with three fingers as he said farewell. 'Twas like he had been a priest of some dignity. . . .

Aye, her home was often right merry at Yule-tide. There was the coming of the guisers, too. Her father tossed her up on to his back, and she felt his coat all icy and his hair wet. To clear their heads before they went to Vespers, the men went off to the well and poured icy water over each other. They laughed when the women scolded about this. Her father took her little cold hands and pressed them against his forehead, which was red and burning-hot still. This was out in the courtyard, in the evening — a young white sliver of moon hung over the mountain ridge in the sea-green sky. When he was bearing her into the hall, he hit her head by mischance against the door-lintel, so that a great bump rose up on her forehead. Afterwards she sat on his lap at the board. He held the hilt of his dagger against the bump, and fed her with tit-bits, and let her drink mead from his beaker. And, sitting there, she felt no fear of the noisy guisers that were ramping about the hall.

— O father, O father — my kind, dear father!

Sobbing aloud, Kristin hid her face in her hands. Oh, if her father knew how things were with her this Christmas Eve!

As she went back to the hall, she saw sparks flying up above the kitchen-house roof. The maids were getting ready food for the churchgoers.

It was dark in the hall. The candles on the table were burnt out, and the hearth was almost black. Kristin laid on more wood, and blew up the embers. Then she saw that Orm was sitting in her chair. He rose up as soon as she caught sight of him.

" Orm! " said Kristin. " Went you not to the mass with your father and the others? "

Orm swallowed once or twice:

" He must have forgot to wake me, methinks. He bade me lie down awhile on the south bed. He said he would wake me — "

" 'Twas pity, Orm," said Kristin.

The boy made no answer. In a little while he said:

" I thought you were gone with them after all -- I woke up all alone in the hall."

" I was over awhile in the church," said Kristin.

" Dare you go out on Yule night, then? " asked the lad. " Know you not that the Asgards-ride might have come by and taken you — ? "

" I trow 'tis not only the evil spirits that are abroad this night," she answered. " On Yule night they say all spirits — I knew a monk once, that is now dead — I trust well he stands before God's face, for there was naught in him but good. He told me once — heard you ever of the beasts in their stalls, how they spoke together on Christmas night? They could talk Latin in those days. So the cock crowed: *Christus natus est* — nay, I remember not the whole. But the other beasts asked: Where? and the goat bleated: *Betlem, Betlem* — and the sheep said: *Eamus, eamus* — "

Orm smiled scornfully:

" Think you I am such a babe you can comfort me with nurses' tales — ? Why offer you not to take me in your lap and give me suck — ? "

" Methinks I said it most to comfort my own self, Orm," said Kristin, quietly. " I too had been fain to go with them to the mass."

She felt now that she could not bear to look at the dirty, littered table any longer. She went over, swept all the leavings on to a platter, and set it on the floor for the dogs. Then she took out the mop of sedge-grass from beneath the bench and wiped the table-top dry with it.

" Will you come with me to the west storehouse, Orm, to fetch bread and salt meat? " asked Kristin. " Then will we set out the table for Christmas morning."

" Why bid you not your serving-women to do all this? " asked the boy.

" 'Twas taught me at home in my father's and mother's house," said the young wife, " that at Yule-tide none should ask another for aught, but each should strive to do the most. He was most blest that most could serve the others throughout the holy days."

" Yet you ask me," said Orm.

" 'Tis another thing to ask you — that are the son of the house."

Orm took the lantern, and they went together across the court-yard. In the storehouse Kristin filled two great platters with Christmas fare. She took, too, a bundle of great tallow candles. While they were about this, the boy said:

" I trow 'tis farmer's fashion that you spoke of but now. For I have heard he is but a wadmal-farmer, Lavrans Björgulfsön."

" Of whom have you heard this? " asked Kristin.

" Of mother," said Orm. " Many a time I heard her say to father, when we lived at Husaby before, that he might see now, not
even a grey-clad farmer would give his daughter to him in marriage."

" A pleasant home was Husaby in those days," said Kristin,
shortly.

The boy made no answer. His mouth quivered a little.

Kristin and Orm bore the laden platters back to the hall, and
she set the table for the meal. But some things were still lacking,
to be fetched from the storehouse. Orm took a platter and said,
a little bashfully:

" I will go for you, Kristin; 'tis so slippery in the yard."

She stood outside the door, and waited till he came back.

Afterward they sat them down by the hearth — she in the arm-
chair and the boy on a joint-stool near her. In a while Orm Erlendssön said in a low voice:

" Tell me something more, while we sit waiting here, stepmother."

" Tell you — ? " asked Kristin in the same tone.

" Aye — a story or the like — something fitting for Christmas
night," said the boy, shyly.

Kristin leaned back in her chair, grasping in her thin hands the
carven beasts' heads at the arm-ends.

" That monk I named but now, he had been in England, too.
And he used to tell that there is a place there where grow thorn-
bushes that bloom with white blossoms each Christmas night. St.
Joseph of Arimathea came to land in that country-side, when he
fled before the heathen, and there he thrust his staff into the earth,
and it took root and blossomed — he was the first that brought the
Christian faith to Bretland. Glastonborg that place is called — I
mind me now. Brother Edvin had seen those bushes himself. . . .
'Twas there in Glastonborg that he was buried, along with his
Queen, that King Arthur that you will have heard tell of — he that
was one of the Seven Champions of Christendom.

" They say in England that Christ's Cross was made of alder-
wood. But we at home used to burn ash in the holy days; for 'twas
ash-wood he made up the fire with, St. Joseph, Christ's stepfather,
when he was to light a fire to comfort Mary Virgin and the new-
born Son of God. Father heard that too of Brother Edvin — "

" But there's little ash grows here north of Dovre," said the boy. " They used it up in the old times for spear-shafts, you know. I know not of one other ash on all the lands of Husaby but the one that stands by the eastern yard-gate, and that one father cannot cut, for the Brownie of the Yard dwells under it. — But, Kristin, I wot they have the Holy Rood itself at Romaborg; surely they can find out if 'tis true that it is made of alder-wood — "

" Aye," said Kristin, " I know not if it be true. For you know 'tis said that the Cross was made of a shoot from the Tree of Life, that Seth was given grace to fetch from the Garden of Eden and bear home to Adam before he died — "

" Aye," said Orm. " But tell it to me."

A while after, Kristin said to the boy:

" 'Twere well you lay down now, kinsman, and slept awhile. It will be long yet till the church-folk are back."

Orm stood up.

" We have not pledged each other yet as kin, Kristin Lavransdatter."

He went and brought over a drinking-horn from the table, drank to his stepmother, and handed her the horn.

She felt as though an icy stream ran down her back. She could not but remember that hour when Orm's mother would have drunk with her. And the child in her womb moved unquietly. How is it with him to-night? thought the mother. It was as though the unborn babe felt all that she felt, was cold when she was cold, shrank in fear when she was afraid. But since 'tis so, I must not be so weak, thought Kristin. She took the horn and drank to her stepson.

As she gave it back to Orm, she passed her hand lightly over his black mane of hair. No, she thought, to thee I shall be no hard step-dame, be sure — thou fair, fair young son of Erlend's. . . .

She had fallen asleep in her chair when Erlend came in and flung his frozen mittens on the table.

" Are you come back already? " asked Kristin, wondering. " I deemed you would have stayed for the morning mass."

" Oh, two masses will serve my turn for a long time," said Erlend. The cloak that Kristin took from him was heavy with ice. " Aye, now 'tis clear again, and freezing hard — "

" 'Twas pity you should have forgot to wake Orm," said his wife.

" Was he vexed about it? " asked the father. " 'Twas not that I forgot, either," he said in a low voice. " But he was sleeping so sound that I thought — You may be sure the good folk gaped at me enough in church, for that I came there without you — I had no mind, on the top of that, to go forward with the boy at my side."

Kristin said naught; but the words hurt her. She could not think this well done of Erlend.

3

THEY saw not much of outside folk at Husaby that Yule-tide. Erlend would not go abroad to any place where he was bidden, but stayed at home on the manor, in no pleasant mood.

The thing was that this misadventure galled him more nearly than his wife could know. He had boasted not a little of his betrothed ever since his kinsmen had gone to Jörundgaard and won her father's consent. It was the last thing he had wished, that any should believe he held her or her kin of less account than his own kindred. No — all men should know that he held himself honoured and uplifted again to worship by Lavrans Björgulfsön's betrothing his daughter to him. Now would all folks say he could scarce have held the maid much better than a peasant's child, since he had dared to do her father such despite as to sleep with his daughter before she was given him in wedlock. At his wedding Erlend had pressed his bride's parents strongly to come to Husaby the next summer and see how things were with him there. Not alone was he fain to show them it was no mean condition he had brought their daughter to; but he had been glad, too, at the thought of going about and showing himself in the company of these comely and stately new kinsfolk, for he knew that Lavrans and Ragnfrid could hold their own with the foremost, wherever they might come. And he had deemed, since the time he was at Jörundgaard when the church burned down, that, in spite of all, Lavrans liked him none so ill. But now there was small reason to think that the next meeting between him and his wife's kin would bring joy to either part.

It vexed Kristin that Erlend vented his ill-humour so often upon Orm. The boy had no playfellows of his own age, and so it came that he was often troublesome and in the way. He did his share of mischief, too. One day he had taken his father's French cross-bow without leave, and had broken something in the lock. Erlend was in great wrath; he struck Orm a box on the ear, and swore that the boy should never more touch a bow at Husaby.

" 'Twas not Orm's fault," said Kristin without turning. She was sitting sewing with her back to the two. " The spring was out of gear when he took the bow, and he tried to put it right. You should not be so unfair as to deny a great boy like your son the use of one from among all the bows you have in this house. Rather give him one of the bows that are up in the armoury."

" You can give him a bow yourself, if you have a mind," said Erlend, wrathfully.

" That will I gladly," answered Kristin as before. " I will speak of it to Ulf, next time he goes in to the city."

" You must go and thank your kind stepmother, Orm," said Erlend, in a voice of anger and scorn.

Orm did as he was bid, and then flew out of the room as swiftly as he might. Erlend stood still awhile.

" 'Twas most to vex me you did this, Kristin," he said.

" Aye, I know I am a troll. You have told me that already," she replied.

" But mind you too, my sweet," said Erlend sorrowfully, " that I spoke not in earnest when I said that word? "

Kristin made no answer, nor looked up from her seam. Soon he went out, and when he was gone she sat there weeping. She had come to care for Orm, and she deemed that Erlend was often unjust to his son. But then, too, her husband's silence and unjoyous looks were tormenting her so that she lay weeping half the night; and then her head would ache all the day after. Her hands were grown so thin now that she had to thrust on some small silver rings she had had since childhood above her betrothal ring and her wedding-ring, to keep them from falling off while she slept.

The Sunday before the beginning of the fast, late in the afternoon, Sir Baard Peterssön with his daughter, the widow, and Sir Munan Baardssön with his lady came to Husaby as unlooked-for guests. Erlend and Kristin went out into the courtyard to bid the strangers welcome.

The moment Sir Munan set eyes on Kristin, he clapped his hand on Erlend's shoulder:

"I see well, kinsman, you have known how to care so for your wife that she hath thriven in your house. You are nowise so thin and peaked, now, Kristin, as you were at your wedding — and far fresher of hue are you too," said he, laughing, for Kristin had flushed red as a berry.

Erlend made no answer. Sir Baard's face was clouded; but the two ladies seemed neither to hear nor see aught; they greeted their hosts seemly and quietly.

Kristin had ale and mead brought forth to them by the hearth while they waited for the meal. Munan Baardssön talked without cease. He had letters with him for Erlend from the Duchess — she had asked what was become of him and his bride; and was the maid he had wedded now the same that he would have carried off to Sweden? 'Twas the devil's own journey in midwinter that he had made — up through the dales and by ship to Nidaros. But he journeyed on the King's errand, and it booted not to murmur. He had looked in on his mother at Haugen, and he brought her greetings.

"Were you at Jörundgaard?" asked Kristin, in a low voice.

No; for he had come to know they were gone from home to the grave-ale at Blakarsarv. There had been a grievous mischance. The mistress of the house, Tora, Ragnfrid's cousin — she had fallen down from the storehouse balcony and broken her back — and 'twas her husband coming against her unawares that had pushed her over — it was one of those old storehouses where there was no right balcony, but only a few boards laid on the beam-ends of the upper story. He heard they had had to bind Rolf and watch him night and day since the mishap befell — to keep him from laying hands on himself.

The listeners sat very still, shuddering. Kristin knew but little of these kinsfolk, but they had been at her wedding. Suddenly she felt strange and faint — there was a blackness before her eyes. Munan, who sat over against her, leapt up and came to her. When he stood by her with his arm around her shoulders, he looked kind — Kristin thought, 'twas maybe not so strange that this cousin of Erlend's was dear to him.

"I knew him, Rolf, when we were young," he said now. "Folk were used to pity Tora Guttormsdatter — they said he was wild and hard-hearted. Yet one can see now that he held her dear. Aye, aye — many a man blusters and talks big about how glad he would be to be quit of his wedlock, but most men know well that a wife is the worst loss they can have — "

Baard Peterssön rose suddenly and went over to the bench by the wall.

" Beshrew my mouth," said Sir Munan softly. " To think I can never remember to watch my tongue — "

Kristin understood not what was amiss. The dizziness had passed now, but she had a feeling of discomfort — they seemed all so strange. She was glad when the serving-folk brought in the meal.

Munan looked at the table and rubbed his hands:

" Sure I was that we should do well to look in on you, Kristin, before we settle down to munching Lenten fare. Where have you gotten savoury dishes like these from in such a little while? A man might go nigh to think you had learned witchcraft of my mother. But I see well you are quick to bring forth all things that a house-wife should gladden her husband withal."

They sat down to the table. Velvet cushions had been laid for the guests on the wall-bench on either side of the high seat. The serving-folk sat on the outer bench, Ulf Haldorssön in the midst, over against his master.

Kristin talked a little, quietly, with the strange ladies, striving to hide how ill at ease she was. Time and again Munan Baardssön broke in with would-be playful words, ever harping on Kristin's state. She made as though she did not hear.

Munan was a man fatter than the common. His small well-formed ears were sunk right into the flesh of his thick red neck, and his belly got in his way when sitting down to table.

" Aye, often have I wondered about that matter of the resurrection of the body," he said; " whether I shall be raised up with all this blubber I have laid on around my bones, when that day comes. *You* will soon enough be slim-waisted again now, Kristin — but with me 'tis no such easy matter. You will scarce believe it, but my belt was no wider than Erlend's there when I was twenty winters old — "

" Be still now, Munan," Erlend begged, in a low voice. " You are plaguing Kristin — "

" I shall be so, since so you say," the other took him up. " You are a proud man now, I dare swear — sitting at your own table with your wedded wife by you in the high-seat. Aye, and God that's over all knows that 'twas none too soon either — you are old enough, boy! Surely I will hold my tongue, since you bid me. But never did any tell you when you should speak or be silent, in days gone by when *you* sat at *my* table. Often and long were you my guest, and I deem not you marked at any time that you were not welcome.

" But much I wonder whether indeed it likes Kristin so ill that I jest a little with her — what say you, fair wife of my kinsman? — you were not wont to be so startlish in days gone by. I have known Erlend since he was as high as my knee, and methinks I can say I have wished the boy well all his days. Mettlesome and manful are you, Erlend, with a sword in your hand, either a-horseback or a-shipboard. But I will pray to St. Olav to cleave me in two halves with his axe the day I see you stand up on those long legs of yours, look man or woman straight in the face, and answer for the mischief you have wrought in your light-mindedness. No, dear kinsman of mine, then do you hang your head like a bird in the snare, and wait upon God and your kindred to help you out of the pinch. Aye, and so clear-witted a woman are you, Kristin, that I trow you know this — and methinks you may well have need to laugh a little now; for I wager you have seen enough this winter past of shamefaced looks and sorrow and repentance — "

Kristin sat with face darkly flushed. Her hands were shaking, and she dared not look towards Erlend. Anger seethed within her — here sat the strange ladies and Orm and her serving-folk. So these were the courtly ways of Erlend's rich kinsmen. . . .

Then said Sir Baard, in a low voice that only those who sat next him were meant to hear:

" I see not that 'tis aught to jest about — that Erlend should have behaved him thus before his wedding. I pledged my word for you, Erlend, with Lavrans Björgulfsön."

" Aye, devil knows 'twas unwisely done of you, foster-father," said Erlend, loud and hotly. " And I marvel how you could be so foolish. For you — I trow you know me too — "

But now was there no checking Munan any longer:

" Aye, but now will I say why this seems to me a merry jest. Mind you what answer you made me, Baard, when I came to you and said we must needs help Erlend to make this marriage — nay, now I *will* tell of it; Erlend shall know what you believed of me — thus and thus it stands between them, said I, and if he wins not Kristin Lavransdatter to wife, God and Mary Virgin alone know

what mad doings we shall next hear of. Then it was you asked me,
was I so fain to have him wedded to the maid he had betrayed because I thought belike she was barren, since after so long she had
yet shown no sign? But I trow you know me, you others — you
know me for a trusty kinsman to my kin — " Quite overcome, he
burst out weeping. " God and all holy men be my witness — never
have I coveted your goods, kinsman — and then, to be sure, there
is Gunnulf besides between me and Husaby. And I answered you,
Baard, well you know it — the first son that Kristin bore, I would
give him my gold-mounted dagger with the ivory sheath — and
you can have it now! " he shouted through his tears, throwing the
costly weapon along the table to her. " If it be not a son this time,
'tis like there will come one next year — "

Tears of shame and wrath rolled down on Kristin's cheeks. She
had a hard struggle not to give way altogether. But the two
stranger ladies sat eating as calmly as if they were well used to
such scenes. And Erlend whispered to her to take the dagger: " Or
Munan will keep on with this all night."

" Aye, and I deny not, Kristin," went on Munan, " that I am not
so ill pleased your father should be made to see he was too rash
when he answered for your mind. So haughty was Lavrans — we
were not good enough for him, forsooth — and you were all too
fine and pure to suffer a man like Erlend for your bedfellow. He
spoke as if he deemed you could not bear to do aught of nights
but sing in a nunnery choir. I said to him: ' Dear Lavrans,' I said,
' your daughter is a fair and fresh and sprightly young maid, and
the winter nights are long and cold in this our land — ' "

Kristin drew the linen of her coif across her face. She sobbed
aloud, and would have risen, but Erlend drew her down again into
her seat.

" Be still," he said vehemently. " Pay no heed to Munan — surely
you can see he is raving drunk — ? "

She felt that Lady Katrin and Lady Vilborg deemed that 'twas
poor-spirited of her not to be better mistress of herself. But she
could not stay her weeping.

Baard Peterssön said in fury:

" Hold your rotten tongue. A swine have you been all your days
— yet might you well leave a sick woman in peace from your filthy
talk — "

" Said you ' swine ' — ? Aye, true it is, I have more bastards than you. But one thing have I never done — nor Erlend either — bought another man to be called our child's father in our place — "

" Munan! " shouted Erlend, springing up. " Now call I for peace in my hall! "

" Oh, call for peace in your tail! — *Our* children call father him that got them — in swinish living, as you call it! " Munan smote the board so that cups and platters leapt in the air. " *Our* sons dwell not as serving-men in the house of their kindred. But here sits son of yours at the board with you, and he sits on the varlets' bench. Now should I deem that the worst shame of all — "

Baard sprang up and drove a flagon into the other's face. The two men grappled, half upsetting the table-top, so that food and vessels went sliding down into the laps of those on the outer bench.

Kristin sat deadly white, with mouth half opened. Once she glanced across at Ulf — the man was laughing aloud, with a coarse, evil laughter. Then, taking hold of the table-top, he heaved it into place and thrust it against the two struggling men.

Erlend leapt on to the table. Kneeling on it amid the litter of the feast, he caught Munan round the arms below his shoulders and dragged him bodily up beside himself — his own face purpling with the strain. Munan kicked out at the old man, drawing blood from his mouth, but the next moment Erlend had flung him clean across the table on to the open floor. He himself leapt after him — and stood panting like a bellows.

Munan scrambled to his feet and rushed at Erlend, who slipped clear of his grasp once or twice, then suddenly leapt upon him and held him tightly grappled with his long sinewy legs and arms. Erlend was lithe as a cat, but Munan, solid and heavy, kept his footing and would not be thrown. They swayed struggling about the hall, while the serving-women shrieked and screamed, and none of the men moved a hand to part them.

Then Lady Katrin, fat, heavy and slow-moving as ever, arose from her seat and stepped over the table as calmly as though she were mounting her storehouse-steps.

" Have done, now, " she said in her thick, dragging voice. " Loose him, Erlend! This was ill done of you, husband — to speak thus to an old man and a near kinsman — "

The men obeyed her. Munan stood meekly and let his wife stanch the blood from his nose with the hem of her coif. She bade him go to bed, and he followed obediently when she led him over to the southern box-bed. His wife and one of his men pulled the clothes off him, rolled him into the bed, and shut the bed-doors on him.

Erlend had gone over to the table. He leant across it beside Ulf, who had not stirred from his place.

" Foster-father! " he said in an unhappy voice. He seemed quite to have forgotten his wife. Sir Baard sat rocking with his head, the tears trickling down his cheeks.

" There had been no need, either, for Ulf to serve," he brought out, through the weeping that made him gasp and sob. " You could have had the farm when Haldor died — you know well 'twas my intent you should."

" The farm you gave to Haldor was none so brave — you bought a husband for your wife's maid good cheap," said Ulf. " He cleared and tilled and bettered it — methought, for one thing, it was but reason that my brothers should have it after their father. And besides, little was I minded to sit down and be a farmer — and least of all up on yonder hill-side, gaping down into the Hestnes court-yard — meseemed I could hear every day up there the voices of Paal and Vilborg, cursing that you had given all too rich a gift to your bastard son — "

" I proffered you help, Ulf," said Baard, still weeping, " when you were bent on faring forth with Erlend. I told you all the truth of this matter, as soon as you were of age to understand. I prayed you to turn to your father — "

" I call him my father who fostered me when I was a child. And that man's name was Haldor. He was good to mother and to me. He taught me to ride a horse and to handle a sword — as a churl doth his cudgel, I mind me Paal once said."

Ulf hurled from him the knife he had in his hand, so that it flew ringing across the table. He rose and picked it up again, wiped it on the back of his thigh, and stuck it in its sheath. Then he turned to Erlend:

" Make an end now with this feast of yours, and send your people to bed! See you not your wife is unused as yet to the fair fashions of our kindred in their feasting? "

And with that he was gone from the hall.

Sir Baard looked after him — he seemed of a sudden wretchedly old and feeble, as he sat there, huddled together among the velvet cushions. His daughter, Vilborg, and one of his men helped him to his feet and led him out.

Kristin sat alone on the high-seat, weeping and weeping. When

Erlend tried to take hold on her, she struck his hand aside vehemently. She swayed about on her feet once or twice when she walked across the floor; but she answered curtly: " No," when her husband asked if she were sick.

She liked not these shut-up box-beds. At home the beds were only curtained off from the hall by hangings, so that the air inside was less hot and stifling. And to-night it was worse in there than ever — for at best she could scarce draw breath. The hard lump she felt pressing right up under her breast-bone she thought must be the child's head — she fancied that it lay with its little head bored in amongst the roots of her heart — it choked her breathing as Erlend had done in old days, when he pressed his dark-haired head against her breast. But to-night there was no sweetness in the thought. . . .

" Will you never make an end of weeping? " asked her husband, trying to pass his arm beneath her shoulders.

He was quite sober. He could bear much liquor, and for the most part he drank but little. Kristin was thinking — never in the world could aught like this have befallen in her home. Never had she heard folk there revile each other, or rake up in their talk things that were best left unnamed. Often as she had seen her father reeling in drunkenness, and the hall full of drunken guests, not once had it befallen even then that he had not been fit to keep order in his house — peace and goodwill had ever ruled, even till the folks dropped off the benches to the floor, and fell asleep together in joy and harmony.

" Dearest one, take not this so hardly," Erlend begged.

" And Sir Baard," she broke out through her tears. " Fie on such doings — he that talked to my father as if he bore a message from God himself — aye, Munan told me of it at our betrothal-feast — "

Erlend answered softly:

" Well enough I know it, Kristin, that I have cause to cast down my eyes before your father. He is a good man — but my foster-father is no worse than he. Inga — Paal and Vilborg's mother — she lay crippled and sick for six years before she died. 'Twas before I came to Hestnes, but I have heard all the story, and never has a husband cherished a sick wife more truly and lovingly. But 'twas at that time Ulf was born — "

" All the more the shame, then — with his sick wife's maid — "

" You show you so childish sometimes, a man can scarce talk

with you," said Erlend in despair. " God help us, Kristin, you will be twenty come next spring — and more winters than one are gone by since you must needs be accounted a grown woman — "

" Aye, 'tis true *you* have the right to scorn me for it — "

Erlend groaned aloud:

" You know yourself that I meant it not so. — But you have lived there at Jörundgaard and hearkened to Lavrans — and for all he is a bold man and a manful, he talks oft-times as if he had been a monk and not a whole grown man — "

" Heard you ever of any monk that had six children? " she said angrily.

" I have heard of one, Skurda-Grim, that had seven," said Erlend, desperately. " The Abbot of Holm that was — Nay, Kristin, Kristin, weep not so, in God's name! Methinks you have lost your wits — "

Munan was passing meek the next morning. " I could never have thought you would take my drunken pratings so much to heart, Kristin, girl," he said gravely, patting her cheek. " Else had I kept a better watch on my tongue, be sure."

He spoke to Erlend of Orm, saying it must be irksome for Kristin now to see this boy about. 'Twould be best to send him out of the way at this time — he offered to take the boy for a while. Erlend liked the proffer well — and Orm was glad to go with Munan. But Kristin missed the child much — she had come to hold her stepson dear.

Again now in the evenings she was left alone with Erlend, and he was no great company for her. He sat by the hearth, said a word now and then, or took a draught from the ale-bowl, and played a little with his dogs. Then he would go and stretch himself on the bench — then go to bed — would ask once or twice if she should not go to rest soon, and then fall asleep.

Kristin sat and sewed. Her breaths came short and so heavy they could be heard. But there was not long to wait now. She could scarce remember, it seemed, what 'twas like to be free and supple in the waist, to be able to tie her shoe without pain and labour.

Now that Erlend slept, she need not even try to keep back the tears. There was no sound in the hall, save when a crumbling brand would drop on the hearth, or a dog would move in its sleep. Sometimes she would wonder — what had they spoken of in the days that were gone — Erlend and she? Like enough they had not spoken much — they had other pastime in their short, stolen trysts. . . .

This was the time of year when her mother and the serving-maids were wont to sit of evenings in the weaving-house. And her father and the men too would come in and sit down by the women with their own tasks — mending leather gear and farm tools, and carving in wood. The little house was filled full of folk, and talk ran on quietly and easily amongst them. When one had gone over to get him a drink from the ale-tub, he asked ever, before he hung up the ladle again, if any other had a mind to drink — 'twas a firm, fixed rule.

Then would there be someone who could say forth a snatch of some saga — of champions in the old age that had fought with mound-dwellers and giantesses of the hills. Or her father would tell them, as he sat at his wood-carving, tales of knighthood, such as he had heard read aloud in his Lord's hall, when he was a page to Duke Haakon in his youth. Fair outlandish names — King Osantrix, Sir Titurel the knight — and Sisibe, Guniver, Gloriana and Isood were the Queens' names. . . . But other evenings they would tell cock-and-bull stories and merry tales, till the menfolk guffawed with laughter, and her mother and the maids shook their heads and tittered.

Ulvhild and Astrid would sing. Her mother had the sweetest voice of all, but it took much praying before they could bring her to sing to them. Her father was not so backward — and he could play so tunably on his harp.

Then Ulvhild would lay from her wheel and spindle and press her hands to her back.

" Is your back weary now, little Ulvhild? " her father would ask, and would take her up in his lap. Someone would bring the draughtboard, and father and Ulvhild would play till bedtime came. She remembered her little sister's yellow locks flowing down over her father's greenish-brown wadmal sleeve. He held up the weak little back so tenderly with the circle of his arm.

Father's long slender hands, with a heavy gold ring on each little finger. The rings had been his mother's. The one with the red stone, her bridal-ring, he had said that Kristin should have after him. But the one on his right hand, with a stone that was half blue and half white like the device of his shield, that had Sir Björgulf had made for his wife when she went with child of Lavrans — she was to be given it when she had borne him a son. Three nights had Kristin Sigurdsdatter worn the ring; then she tied it round her boy's neck; and Lavrans said he would take it with him to his grave.

Oh, what would her father say when he heard this of her? When 'twas noised abroad all over the country-side at home, and he could not but know, wherever he might fare, to church, to Thing, or to meetings, that all men were laughing at him behind his back, that he had let him be so fooled. At Jörundgaard they had decked out a wanton with the Sundbu bridal crown above the flowing hair of maidenhood —

" Folk say of me, I know well, that I cannot rule my children." She remembered her father's look when he said it — he would fain have been sad and stern of face, but his eyes were merry. She had done amiss in some little matter — spoken to him, unspoken to, before strangers, or the like. " Aye, Kristin, sooth it is you go not much in fear of your father." Then a laugh broke out, and she laughed too. " Aye, but 'tis an ill thing, Kristin." And neither of them knew what it was that was so ill a thing — that she stood not in seemly awe of him; or that he could in no wise keep a sad brow when he had to chide her.

It was as though the unbearable dread that there should be somewhat amiss with the child grew fainter and farther off as Kristin's pains and bodily trouble grew. She tried to send her thoughts forward — in a month — she would have had her boy for a while then already. But she could not make it seem true. She could only long and long for her home.

Once Erlend had asked if she would he should send for her mother. But she said: No — she deemed not her mother was fit to journey so far in winter-time. Now she repented this. And she repented that she had said: No, to Tordis of Laugarbru, who had been so fain to come north with her and help her through her first winter as the mistress of a house. But she had thought shame to have Tordis by. Tordis had been Ragnfrid's maid at her home at Sundbu, and had followed her mistress to Skog and back again to the Dale. When she married, Lavrans had made her husband steward at Jörundgaard, since Ragnfrid could not bear to be parted from her dear hand-maiden. Kristin had no mind to have with her any woman from her home.

But now it seemed to her a fearful thing that she should not have a single known face to look upon when her time came to lie in the straw. She was afraid — she knew so little of the bringing to bed of women. Her mother had never spoken to her of it, and would never have young maids with her when she helped women in their labour — it would but frighten the young things, she said. But Kristin knew it must sometimes be fearful — she remembered the time Ulvhild was born. That, though, Ragnfrid had said was because she had forgot herself and crept under a fence-rail — her other children she had borne easily. But Kristin remembered now that she herself had been thoughtless, and passed under a rope on the ship. . . .

Yet this did not always bring heavy labour — she had heard her mother and other women talk of such things. Ragnfrid had the name in their country-side of the best midwife far around, and never would she deny her help, not if it was to a beggar woman or the poorest man's daughter that had fallen in trouble, nor if the weather was such that three men must go with her on ski and take turns at bearing her on their backs. . . .

But surely, it came to Kristin in a flash, 'twas not to be believed that a women of such skill in these things as her mother had, should not have seen what was amiss with her last summer, when she was so ailing. But then — sure it was that her mother would come, even though they had not sent to call her. Ragnfrid would never suffer that her daughter should go through that struggle in a stranger's arms. Her mother would come — surely she was even now on her way thither. . . . Oh, and then she could pray her mother's forgiveness for all that she had sinned against her — her own mother would hold her up, she would kneel at her mother's knee when she bore her child. Mother comes, mother comes. . . . Kristin sobbed behind her hands from a lightened heart. O mother — forgive me, mother.

The thought that her mother was on her way up to her grew so fixed in Kristin that one day she deemed she could feel within herself: Mother will come to-day. And on in the morning she took her cloak about her and went out to meet her on the road that leads from Gauldal over to Skaun. None marked her as she left the manor.

Erlend had had timber driven down from the woods for the mending and bettering of the houses, so that the road was well trodden; but 'twas heavy going for her none the less — she lost her breath, her heart beat hard, and sharp pain came in her sides — it felt as though the over-stretched flesh would break asunder when she had walked a little while. And most of the way was through thick forest. She was afraid indeed — but there had been no word of wolves in the country-side this winter. And surely God would guard her that went forth to meet her mother, fall at her feet, and pray her for forgiveness — and she could not but go on and on.

She came by and by to a little lake, where there lay some small farmsteads. Where the road led on to the ice, she sat down upon a log — and sometimes sitting, sometimes walking to keep warm, stayed waiting there many hours. But at last she must needs turn home again.

The day after, she strayed out again by the same road. But as she crossed the yard of one of the small farms by the lake, the woman of the house came running after her.

"In God's name, mistress, what is this you do?"

No sooner had she spoke than Kristin herself grew so afraid that she could not move from the spot — trembling, with eyes wild with fear, she gazed at the peasant woman.

"Through the woods — think but if the wolf got scent of you! And other ill things too might well come upon you — how can you bear you so witlessly?"

The goodwife threw her arms around the young lady of the manor to hold her up — and looked into her thin face, all yellowish-white and flecked with brown:

"You must come into our house and rest awhile — and then we will take you home — someone from here," she said, as she led Kristin away with her.

It was a little and a poor house, and within all was in much disorder, for there were many small children playing on the floor. The mother sent them out to the kitchen-house, took her guest's cloak, led her to a seat on the bench, and drew off her snowy shoes. Then she wrapped a sheepskin round her feet.

For all Kristin prayed the other not to put herself about, her hostess was not to be hindered from serving her with food and with ale from the Yule-cask. And she was thinking the while — a rare rule must they keep at Husaby! She herself was but a poor man's wife; little help had they had on their farm, and often none at all; but never would Öistein suffer her to go alone without the farm-yard fence when she was with child — nay, if she but went across to the byre after dark had fallen, someone must ever keep an eye on her. But the richest lady in all the country-side might stray out and run the risk of the most dreadful death, and not a Christian soul to take care of her — though the serving-folk at Husaby were tumbling over each other and doing naught. 'Twas like, then, the folks said sooth that said Erlend Nikulaussön was weary of his marriage already, and cared not for his wife. . . .

But she chatted away to Kristin all the time, and forced her to eat and drink. And Kristin was much ashamed — but she had such a stomach to her meat as she had not felt — not since the last spring; the kind woman's food tasted so good. And the woman laughed and said 'twas like great folks' womankind were made no otherwise than poor. 'Twas often so that when a body could not bear to look at food at home, one would be right greedy for strangers' fare even if 'twere coarse and poor.

Her name was Audfinna Andunsdatter, and she was from Updal, she said. When she marked that it cheered her guest, she took to telling of her home and her country. And before Kristin was aware, *her* tongue too was loosed — and she was talking of *her* home and her parents and her own country-side. Audfinna saw well that the young wife's heart was near breaking with homesickness — so she tempted and beguiled Kristin into going on. And Kristin, hot and dizzy with the strong ale, went on talking till she was laughing and crying in the same breath. All that she had tried in vain to sob away from her heart in the lonesome evening hours at Husaby, seemed to melt now little by little as she told her tale to this kind peasant wife.

It was quite dark now above the smoke-vent, but Audfinna would have Kristin stay till Öistein or their sons came home from the wood and could take her home. Kristin grew silent and drowsy, but she sat smiling, with shining eyes — so happy she had not felt since she came to Husaby.

Suddenly the door was flung open, and a man shouted in to ask if they had seen aught of the mistress — then caught sight of her sitting there and rushed out again. A minute after, Erlend's long shape came stooping low through the doorway. He set from him the axe he bore, and staggered back against the wall — he had to prop himself with hands thrust behind him, and he could not speak.

" You have been afraid for your lady? " asked Audfinna, going over to him.

" Aye — I take no shame to say it." He passed his hand up under his hair. " So frighted has man scarce ever been, I trow, as I have been this night. When I heard she had gone off into the woods — "

Audfinna told how it was Kristin had come thither. Erlend took the woman's hand.

" Never will I forget what I owe you and your husband for this," he said.

Then he went across to where his wife sat, and, standing beside her, laid a hand upon her neck. He spoke not a word to her, but stood still thus as long as they were in the house.

Now came crowding in henchmen from Husaby and men from the nearest farms. All looked as though they needed a heartening draught, so Audfinna bore round the ale-bowl before they set forth again.

The men went off on ski across the fields, but Erlend had given his to one of his followers; he walked down the hill holding Kristin inside his cloak. It was quite dark now, and the stars shone bright.

Then came a sound from the woods behind them — a long-drawn howl that mounted higher and higher in the night. It was wolves — and there were many. Erlend stopped short, shivering, loosed his hold on her, and Kristin knew that he crossed himself, while he gripped the axe in his other hand. " Had you now been — oh, no — " He crushed her to him so fiercely that she moaned with pain.

The ski-runners in the fields turned sharp about, and toiled back to the pair as fast as they could climb. Then they flung the ski over their shoulders, and made a close ring around her with their spears and axes. The wolves followed them all the way to Husaby — so near that now and then they could see a glimpse of them through the darkness.

When they came into the lighted hall, many of the men's faces showed grey and white. One said: " This was the grimmest — " and straightway fell a-vomiting into the hearth-fire. The frightened maids brought their mistress to her bed. Eat she could not. But now that the sick, awful dread was overpast, it yet seemed to her comforting after a fashion to see that all had been so affrighted for her sake.

When they were left alone in the hall, Erlend came across and sat himself down on the edge of her bed.

" Why did you this? " he whispered. And when she made no answer, he said, yet lower:

" Is it such grief to you that you have come into my house — ? "

It was a little while before she understood what he meant:

" Jesus, Maria! How can you think such a thought? "

" What had you in mind that time you said — when we had been at Medalby, when I would have ridden from you — that I might have had long to wait ere you came after me to Husaby? " he asked in the same low tone.

" Oh, I spoke but in wrath," said Kristin, bashfully, in a low voice. And she told him now what it was that had taken her out these days. Erlend sat very still and listened.

" Much do I wonder when the day will come that my house of Husaby will seem home to you," said he, bending over her in the dark.

" Oh — in not much more than a week now, maybe," whispered Kristin, with a wavering laugh. When he laid his face down against hers, she threw her arms round his neck and gave back his kiss eagerly.

" 'Tis the first time you have laid your arms about my neck of your own accord since I struck you," said Erlend in a low voice. " You are slow to forgive, my Kristin — "

It came into her mind that this was the first time since the night when he had learned she was with child, that she had had courage to offer him a caress unasked.

But after this day Erlend showed such kindness towards her that Kristin repented each hour she had felt anger against him.

4

Gregory's Mass * came and went by. Kristin had believed so surely that her time must come then, at the latest. But now it would soon be Mary's Mass in Lent,† and still she was about on her feet.

Erlend was forced to go to Nidaros for the mid-fast Thing; he said he would surely be home Monday night, but now it was

* 13th February.   † 25th March.

Wednesday morning and he was not yet come. Kristin sat in the hall, scarce knowing what to be about — it was as though she had no power to begin upon any work.

The sunlight streamed in through the smoke-vent — she felt that without it must be like spring to-day. She rose up and threw a cloak about her.

One of the maids had told her that folk said if a woman went beyond her due time, a good way was for her to let the horse she rode at her bridal eat corn from her lap. Kristin stood a little while in the hall-door — in the blinding sunlight the yard lay all brown, but glittering rills of water ran in bright frozen runnels through the horse-dung and litter. The skies were spread bright and silky-blue above the old houses — on the two figure-heads fixed to the beams of the east storehouse, the traces of their old-time gilding shone out to-day in the clear air. Water dribbled and ran from the roofs, and the smoke whirled and danced in little mild puffs of wind.

She went to the stables and in, and filled the lap of her skirt with oats from the corn-bin. The stable smell, and the sound of the horses stirring in there in the dark, did her good. But some of the folks were in the stable; and she was ashamed to do what she had come to do.

She went out and threw the grain to the hens that were scratch-ing around and sunning themselves in the yard. Her thoughts far off, she looked at Tore, the stable-man, currying and brushing down the grey gelding — it was fast shedding its winter coat. Now and then she shut her eyes, and turned her face, faded and pale with the indoor air, up to the sunshine.

So she was standing when three men rode into the court-yard. The foremost of them was a young priest whom she did not know. As soon as he was aware of her, he leapt from his horse and came straight up to her with outstretched hand.

" You had not meant me this great honour, I trow — that you, the lady of the house, should come forth to welcome me," said he, smiling. " But I must thank you for it, none the less. For I wot well you must be my brother's wife, Kristin Lavransdatter? "

" Then must you be Master Gunnulf, my brother-in-law," she answered, flushing red. " Well met, sir! And welcome home to Husaby! "

" Thanks for a fair welcome," said the priest; and he stooped

and kissed her cheek, after the fashion she knew was used in foreign lands, when kinsfolk met. " Happy be your coming hither,
Erlend's wife! "

Ulf Haldorssön came out, and bade a groom take the strangers'
horses. Gunnulf greeted Ulf right heartily:

" Are you here, kinsman? — I had looked to hear that you were a
wedded man and a householder by now."

" Nay, no wedding for me, till I must choose between a wife and
the gallows," said Ulf, with a laugh; and the priest laughed too.
" I have pledged me to the devil to live unwed as firmly as you have
promised it to God."

" Aye, then should you be scatheless whichever way you turn
you, Ulf," answered Master Gunnulf, laughing. " For you will
do well the day you break your promise to yonder man; and yet
'tis said also that a man should keep his word, were it to the fiend
himself. . . . Is Erlend not at home? " he asked in wonder. He
proffered Kristin his hand, as they turned to go into the hall.

To hide her bashfulness, Kristin moved about among the serving-women, and saw to the spreading of the board. She bade Erlend's learned brother sit in the high-seat, but, when she would
not sit there with him, he moved down to the bench beside her.

Now she was sitting at his side, she saw that Master Gunnulf
must be shorter than Erlend by half a head at the least — but he
seemed to bulk larger. He was stronger-built and more thickset in
body and limbs, and his broad shoulders were quite straight — Erlend's slouched a little. He was clad in dark raiment, most seemly
for a priest, but the long cassock, reaching to his feet, and upward
almost to the band of his linen shirt, was fastened with buttons of
enamel, and from his woven belt his eating-gear hung in a silver
sheath.

She looked up into the priest's countenance. He had a round
strong head and a round but thin face, with broad low forehead,
cheek-bones a little large, and a fine rounded chin. The nose was
straight and the ears small and comely, but his mouth was wide and
thin-lipped, and the upper lip came forward never so little and
overshadowed the lower lip's little splash of red. Only his hair
was like Erlend's — the close-cropped ring round the priest's ton-
sure was black, with a dry, sooty gleam, and looked as though
'twere as silky-soft as Erlend's mane. For the rest he was not unlike his cousin Munan Baardssön — she could see now it might

be true that Munan had been comely in his youth. Nay, 'twas Aashild, his mother's sister, that he favoured — now she saw that he had the same eyes as Lady Aashild — amber-yellow eyes, shining under narrow straight black brows.

At first Kristin was a little shy of this brother-in-law of hers that had laid up such store of learning at the great schools in Paris and Valland.* But little by little she forgot her bashfulness. It was so easy to talk to Master Gunnulf. It seemed not as though he talked of himself — far less that he was fain to flaunt his learning. But when she had time to bethink herself a little, she found he had told her so much that Kristin thought she never had known before how great a world there was outside Norway. She forgot herself and all her affairs, as she sat looking up in the priest's round large-boned face, with its subtile sprightly smile. He had laid one leg over the knee of the other under his cassock, and sat with his white sinewy hands clasped round his ankle.

When, late in the afternoon, he joined her in the hall, he asked if they should play draughts. Kristin could but answer that she thought not there was any draught-board in the house.

" Is there not? " asked the priest in wonder. He went over to Ulf:

" Know you, Ulf, what Erlend has done with mother's gilded draught-set? — The things for pastime that she left behind her here — surely he has not let any other have them? "

" They are in a chest above in the armoury," said Ulf. " 'Twas in his mind, methinks, that they should not come into the hands of others — that were on the manor heretofore," he added low. " Would you have me fetch the chest, Gunnulf? "

" Aye — Erlend cannot, surely, have aught against it now," said the priest.

A little after, the two came back bearing a great carven chest. The key was in it, and Gunnulf opened it. On top lay a cithern and another stringed instrument whose like Kristin had never seen before. Gunnulf called it a salterion — he let his fingers stray over the strings, but it was untuned. There were rolls of ribands, reels of silk, broidered gloves, and silken hoods, and three books with clasps. At length the priest found the draught-board; the squares were in white and gold, and the men were of narwhal ivory, white and golden.

* A general name for the Latin countries.

Kristin had to own now to her brother-in-law that she was slow-witted at the draughts and had no great skill of stringed music. But the books she was eager to look into.

" Aye — belike you have learnt to read in books, Kristin? " the priest asked; and now she could answer, a little proudly, that so much she had indeed learned while she was yet a child. And in the cloister she had been praised for her skill in reading and writing.

The priest stood over her with a smile on his face while she turned the leaves of the books. One was a knightly saga of Tristan and Isolde, and the other held histories of holy men — she opened it at St. Martin's saga. The third book was in Latin, and was in a passing fair script with great capital letters painted in many hues.

" This one belonged to our ancestor, Bishop Nikulaus," said Gunnulf.

Kristin read, half aloud:

> *Averte faciam tuam a peccatis meis —*
> *et omnes iniquitates meas dele.*
> *Cor mundum crea in me, Deus —*
> *et spiritum rectum innova in visceribus meis.*
> *Ne projicias me a facie tua —*
> *et Spiritum Sanctum tuum ne auferas a me.*[*]

" Understand you this? " asked Gunnulf, and Kristin nodded and said she understood a little. She knew enough of the words' meaning to be strangely moved that her eyes should fall on them just now. Her face quivered a little, and she could not keep back her tears. Then Gunnulf took the psaltery on his lap, and said he would try if he could not mend it.

While they sat thus, they heard the trampling of horses in the court-yard — and straightway after Erlend burst into the hall, beaming with gladness — he had heard who it was that was come. The brothers stood with their hands on each other's shoulders, Erlend asking questions and not waiting for the answers. Gunnulf had been in Nidaros two days, so it was pure chance that they had not met there.

" 'Tis strange too," said Erlend. " Methought that all the priesthood of Christ's Church would have gone forth in procession to meet you, when you came home — so wise and stuffed with learning as you must be now — "

" And know you so surely that they did not? " asked his

[*] Psalm li. 9-11.

brother, laughing. " You come not over nigh to Christ's Church when you are in the city, I have heard tell."

" True, boy — I draw not nigh to my Lord Archbishop when I can steer clear of him — he hath singed my hide for me once already," Erlend laughed unrepentantly. " How like you your brother-in-law, my sweet? — I see you have made friends with Kristin already, brother — she cares not much for our other kindred. . . ."

It was not till they were sitting down to the supper-board that Erlend marked that he still had his fur cap and his cloak on and the sword at his belt.

It was the merriest evening Kristin had yet had at Husaby. Erlend forced his brother to sit with her in the high-seat; he himself carved for him and filled his cup. The first time he drank to Gunnulf, he kneeled down on one knee, and made as though to kiss his brother's hand.

" All hail, Lord! We must use us, Kristin, to show the Archbishop all seemly honour — nay, for Archbishop you surely will be one day, Gunnulf! "

It was late before the house-folk left the hall, but the two brothers and Kristin sat on over their drink. Erlend had set himself on the table facing his brother.

" Aye, this gear I had thought on at our bridal," said he, pointing to his mother's chest, " and thought that Kristin should have it. But 'tis so easy for me to forget; and you, brother — you forget nothing. But the ring my mother left hath found its way on to a fair hand, methinks? " He laid Kristin's hand on his knee and turned round her betrothal-ring.

Gunnulf nodded. He laid the psaltery in Erlend's lap:

" Sing now, brother; you were wont to sing so sweetly and play so well in old days — "

" 'Tis many years since," said Erlend, more gravely. Then he ran his fingers over the strings:

> Good King Olav, Harald's son,
>   Rode in the thick woods' shade;
> Found in the earth a footprint small,
>   — Here be tidings great!
>
> Out spoke he then, Finn Arnessön,
>   — Rode of the meiny foremost:
> "Fair would show such a little foot,
>   All in scarlet hosen. . . ."

Erlend smiled as he sang, and Kristin looked up at the priest a little timidly — not knowing but he might mislike this ditty of St. Olav and Álvhild. But Gunnulf sat smiling — yet she felt sure, of a sudden, that 'twas not at the song, but at Erlend.

"Kristin need not sing to-night. I trow you are short of breath now, my dearest," said Erlend, stroking her cheek. "But now 'tis your turn —" He gave the psaltery to his brother.

One could tell from the priest's playing and singing that he had been well schooled:

> The King rode northward into the hills —
>
> He heard a dove that made her moan,
> Lamenting that her mate was gone:
>
> > *Lully, lulley! lully lulley!*
> > *The falcon hath borne my mate away!*
>
> After the hawk he is fain to ride;
> It flies through the wild hills far and wide.
>
> It led him up, it led him down,
> It led him into an orchard brown.
>
> In that orchard there was an hall
> That was hangèd with purple and pall.
>
> There lieth a fair knight in his blood —
> He is the Lord so brave and good.
>
> At his bed's head there standeth a stone,
> *Corpus Domini* written thereon.
>
> > *Lully, lulley! lully lulley!*
> > *The falcon hath borne my mate away!* *

"Where learned you that song?" asked Erlend.

"Oh — some boys sang it outside the hostel where I lodged in Kanterborg," said Gunnulf. "And methought I would try to turn it into our Norse tongue. But it goes not so well in Norse." He sat playing snatches of the tune on the strings.

"Well, brother — 'tis long past midnight. Like enough, Kristin needs to come to her bed now — are you weary, my wife?"

Kristin looked up at the men in fear; she was very pale:

* See Note 3.

" I know not. . . . Methinks 'twere best now I should not lie in the bed in here — "

" Are you sick? " they both asked, bending over her.

" I know not," she said as before. She pressed her hands behind her hips. " My back feels so strange — "

Erlend sprang up and went towards the door. Gunnulf followed him:

" 'Tis an ill chance that you brought them not here before this, the ladies that are to help her," he said. " Is it come much before she looked for it — ? "

Erlend flushed a burning red.

" Kristin deemed she would need none other but her own maids — they have borne children themselves, some of them — " He tried to laugh.

" Are you beside yourself! " Gunnulf gazed at him. " Hath not every cottar's wife skilled women and neighbours' wives * to help her when she is brought to bed — and shall your wife creep off and hide herself in a hole, like a tib-cat kittening? Nay, brother — so much of a man I would have you be as to fetch the foremost ladies of the country-side to Kristin — "

Erlend bent his face, flushed with shame:

" You say truly, brother. I will ride myself to Raasvold — I must send men to the other manors. And do you bide here with Kristin! "

" Are you going forth? " asked Kristin fearfully, when she saw Erlend put on his riding-cloak.

He came across and threw his arms around her.

" I go to fetch the best women in the country-side for you, my Kristin. Gunnulf will stay by you, while the maids make ready for you in the little hall," he said, kissing her.

" Could you not send one to Audfinna Andunsdatter? " she begged. " But not before daylight — I would not have her waked from sleep for my sake — she has so much on her hands, I know — "

Gunnulf asked his brother who Audfinna was.

" It seems not to me over-seemly," said the priest. " The wife of one of your tenants — "

" Kristin shall have it as she will," said Erlend. And as the priest went out with him and he stood waiting for his horse, he told the

* See Note 4.

other how Kristin had come to know the farmer's wife. Gunnulf bit his lip and stood deep in thought.

There was noise and commotion now throughout the manor; men rode away into the night, and serving-women came running in to ask how it fared with their mistress. Kristin said there was not much amiss as yet, but they must make all things ready for her in the little hall. She would send word when she would be brought in there.

Then she was left alone again with the priest. She strove to speak evenly and cheerily with him as before.

" *You* are not afraid," he said with a little smile.

" Nay, but I *am* afraid! " She looked up into his eyes — her own were dark and frightened. " Know you, brother-in-law — were they born here at Husaby, Erlend's other children? "

" No," said the priest, quickly. " The boy was born at Hunehals, and the little maid up in Strind — on a farm he once owned there. — Is it," he asked in a little, " that it has troubled you to remember that this other woman lived here with Erlend before? "

" Aye," said Kristin.

" 'Tis hard for you to judge justly of Erlend's doings in this matter of Eline," said the priest gravely. " It was no easy thing for Erlend to rule himself — never has it been easy for Erlend to know what right was. For, ever since we were little children, so has it been, that whatever Erlend did, mother thought it was well done, and father that it was ill. Aye, he has told you, doubtless, so much of our mother, that you know of all this — "

" For all I can remember, he has named her but twice or thrice," said Kristin. " But I have seen well enough that he loved her."

Gunnulf said softly:

" Surely there has never been such love between a mother and her son. Mother was much younger than my father. Then there befell this mischance of her sister, Aashild — Baard, our father's brother, died, and 'twas said — aye, doubtless you know of that? Father believed the worst, and he said to mother — Erlend flung his knife at father once, when he was yet a boy — he flew at father's throat more than once for mother's sake, when he was half-grown. . . .

" When mother fell sick, he parted him from Eline Ormsdatter. Mother fell sick with sores and scabs on her flesh, and father said 'twas leprosy. He sent her from him — would have forced her to dwell as a commoner * with the Sisters at the spital. Then Erlend fetched mother away and bore her with him to Oslo — they went, on the way, to Aashild, who is skilled in leechcraft, and she, and the King's French leech too, said that she was no leper. King Haakon welcomed Erlend kindly then, and bade him try the virtue of the holy Erik Valdemarssön's grave — the King's mother's father. Many had there found healing for skin-sicknesses.

" Erlend set forth for Denmark with mother, but she died aboard his ship, south of Stad. When Erlend came home with her — aye, you must bear in mind that father was stricken in years, and Erlend had been an unruly son all his days — when Erlend came to Nidaros with mother's body — father was in our town dwelling then, and he would not take Erlend in — before he saw whether the boy had taken the sickness, he said. Erlend took horse and rode off, and rested not till he came to the farm where Eline was with her son. And after that he held fast to her, in despite of all, despite that he himself was weary of her; and so it came about that he brought her to Husaby and set her to rule his house, when he was once master here. She had this hold on him, that she said if he failed her after this, he were worthy to be smitten down himself with leprosy. — But now 'tis time, I trow, for your women to see to you, Kristin — " he said, looking down at her young face, grown grey and stiff with horror and torment. But when he would have gone to the door, she cried aloud after him:

" No, no, go not from me — "

" 'Twill be all the sooner over," the priest said to comfort her, " since you are so sick already."

" 'Tis not that! " She gripped his arm hard. " Gunnulf — " It seemed to him he had never seen such terror in a human face.

" Kristin — remember — you must remember, this is no worse for you than for other women! "

" Yes. Yes." She pressed her face down on the priest's arm. " For now I know that Eline and her children should be sitting in my place. For he had pledged her his faith and wedded troth, ere ever I came to be his paramour — "

" Know you that? " said Gunnulf calmly. " Erlend knew no better himself then. But you know that that word of his he could not keep — never had the Archbishop given his leave that they two

* See Note 13 to *The Bridal Wreath* (*The Garland*).

should wed. Think not it can be that your marriage holds not good. You are Erlend's true wife — "

" Oh, I had thrown away all right to tread the earth long before he wed me. And 'twas yet worse than I knew — oh, would I might die, and this child never be born — I dare not see what 'tis I have borne within me — "

" God forgive you, Kristin — you know not what you say! Would you wish that your child die unborn and unchristened — ? "

" Aye, for, whatever befall, what I bear beneath my heart must be the devil's. It cannot be saved. Oh, had I but drunk the draught Eline proffered me — it had mayhap been some atonement for all we had sinned, Erlend and I. — Then had this child never been gotten — oh, Gunnulf, all the time have I known it — that when I should see the thing I had nourished within me, then would I know full well it had been better for me to drink the draught of leprosy that she proffered me, than to drive her to death, to whom Erlend had first bound himself — "

" Kristin," said the priest, " you speak you know not what. 'Twas not you that drove that hapless woman to her death. Erlend *could* not keep the word he had pledged her when he was young and knew little of law or of right. Never could he have lived with her but in sin. And she had let herself be led astray by another too, and Erlend would have wed her to that other when he heard it. 'Twas not your doing that she took her life — "

" Would you know how it came to pass that she took her life? " Kristin was so hopeless now that she spoke quite calmly. " We were at Haugen together, Erlend and I, and she came thither. She had a horn with her, she would have had me drink with her — 'twas for Erlend she had meant it, I can see now, but when she found me there with him, she would have had me — I knew that there was treachery — I saw that she drank no drop herself when she set her lips to the horn. But I would as lief have drunk — I cared not whether I lived or died, since I had come to know he had had her with him at Husaby all the time. Then came Erlend in — he threatened her with his knife, to make her drink first. She begged and prayed, and he would have let her go. Then the devil took hold on me — I took the horn. — ' One of us two, your paramours,' said I — I egged Erlend on — ' you cannot keep us both,' said I. So it was that she slew herself with Erlend's knife — but Björn and Aashild found a device to hide how it had come about — "

"So, Moster * Aashild was of this counsel!" said Gunnulf grimly. "I understand — she had beguiled you into Erlend's hands — "

"No," said Kristin vehemently. "Lady Aashild prayed us — she prayed Erlend and she prayed me, in such wise that I know not how I could hold out against her — that we should deal honourably, so far as that yet might be — fall at my father's feet and pray him to forgive us our misdeeds. But I dared not. I made pretence that I was fearful lest father should slay Erlend — oh, though I knew well father would never have harmed a man who yielded himself and his cause into his hands. I made pretence that I feared to bring on him such sorrow that he could never hold up his head again. Oh, but I have shown since, I feared not so much to bring my father sorrow — You cannot believe, Gunnulf, how good a man my father is — none could know, that knows not my father, how good he has been to me all my days. Ever has father loved me so. 'Twas that I could not bear he should know I had borne me so shamelessly, that while he deemed I was sitting among the Sisters at Oslo, learning all that was good and right — aye, for I bore the novices' weed while I was lying with Erlend in barns and in lofts down in the city — "

She looked up at Gunnulf. His face was white and hard as stone. "See you now why I am afraid? She that took him to her, when he came tainted with leprosy — "

"Would *you* not have done it?" asked the priest, in a still voice.

"Yes, yes, yes." A shadow of the wild smile of former days flew over the woman's ravaged face.

"And, besides, Erlend was not tainted," said Gunnulf. "None but father ever believed that mother died of leprosy."

"But surely *I* must be as a leper in the sight of God," said Kristin. She laid her face down on the priest's arm, to which she was clinging. "Such as I am now, tainted with all sin — "

"My sister," said the priest softly, laying his other hand on her linen coif, "so sinful sure you cannot be, you young child, that you have forgotten that as sure as God can cleanse a man in the flesh from leprosy, so surely can He cleanse your soul from sin — "

"Oh, I know not," she sobbed, her face still hidden in his arm. "I know not — and I repent not either, Gunnulf. Frighted am I, but yet — frighted was I when I stood before the church-door

* Moster = mother's sister.

with Erlend and the priest joined us together — frighted was I
when I went with him in to the bride's mass — with golden crown
on flowing hair, for I dared not speak of my shame to my father —
with all my sins unatoned, aye, I dared not confess the truth to my
own parish priest. But when I went about here at Husaby in the
winter, and saw myself grow fouler with each day that passed —
then was I yet more afraid, because Erlend was not towards me as
he once had been — I thought of the time when he came to me in
my bower at Skog of nights — "

"Kristin — " The priest tried to lift up her face. "You dare
not think of such things now! Think but that God sees now your
sorrow and your repentance. Turn you to the merciful maid,
Mary, that hath compassion on all that are sorrowful — "

"But understand you not? — I have driven another to cast away
her own life — "

"Kristin," said the priest sternly, "dare you think in your
wicked pride that sin of yours can be so great that God's loving-
kindness is not greater?"

He stroked and stroked her linen hood.

"Mind you not, my sister, how it was when the devil would
have tempted St. Martin? Did not the fiend ask if St. Martin dared
believe fully his own word when he promised all the sinners he
shrove God's mercy? But the Bishop answered: 'To thee also I
dare to promise God's forgiveness, in the hour that thou prayest
for it — wouldst thou but cast away thy pride and believe that His
love is greater than thy hate — '"

Gunnulf stood for a little space, still patting the weeping woman's head. And he thought the while — his mouth white-lipped and
hard-set — was it *so* that Erlend had dealt with his young bride!

Audfinna Andunsdatter was the first woman to come. She found
the lying-in woman in the little hall; Gunnulf sat by her, and a
couple of maids were busy in the room.

Audfinna greeted the priest with reverence, but Kristin rose up
and went toward her with outstretched hand:

"Have thanks, Audfinna, for your coming — I know 'tis no light
thing for your folks at home to do without you — ?"

Gunnulf had looked searchingly at the woman. Now he too
rose:

"'Twas bravely done of you to come so quick; there is need

that my brother's wife should have one with her she can trust — she is strange to this country-side, young and unaccustomed — "

" Jesus, she is white as her coif! " whispered Audfinna. " Think you, sir, I might give her a little sleeping-draught? — methinks she had need to win some rest before it comes on her more sorely."

She set about making ready busily but quietly; felt the couch that the serving-women had made up on the floor, and bade them bring more cushions and more straw. Next she placed small stone pots with herbs in them against the fire. Thereafter she set about loosing all bands and knots in Kristin's dress, and last of all drew out all the pins from the sick woman's hair.

" Never did I see fairer," said she, when the whole flood of gold-brown silky locks rolled down around the white visage. She could not forbear to laugh a little: " Methinks it can scarce have lost much either of strength or brightness, even if so be that you bore it uncovered a little longer than was right — "

She got Kristin softly bedded among the cushions on the floor and covered her well with rugs:

" Drink this now; then will you not feel the pains so sorely; and try to get a little sleep between-times."

It was time for Gunnulf to go. He went across and bent over Kristin.

" You will pray for me, Gunnulf," she asked, beseechingly.

" I will pray for you even till I see you with your child upon your arm — and after too," he said, and laid her hand back again under the coverlid.

Kristin lay and dozed. She felt almost well. The shooting pains across her loins came and went and came again — but it was so unlike all she had felt before, that each time they had passed she wondered almost if it were not but her fancy. After the torment and horror of the early morning hours she felt as though she were already happily over the worst dread and anguish. Audfinna went about so softly, hanging up child's clothing, rugs and furs to warm at the hearth — and stirring her pots a little, so that a spicy smell stole out into the room. At length Kristin fell half asleep between the fits of pain, and dreamed she was at home in the brewhouse at Jörundgaard, and was helping her mother with the dyeing of a great web of cloth — doubtless 'twas the steam from the ash-bark and nettles.

Then came the lady-midwives, one after another — ladies from the manors of their parish and of Birgsi. Audfinna drew back among the serving-women. And when evening was drawing on, Kristin felt the pains grew sore. The ladies said she should walk about the room as long as she could bear to do so. It was torture to her — the room was chock-full of women now, and she must pace about like a mare put up for sale. Between-whiles, too, she must let the strange ladies press and feel round about her body with their hands; and then they would talk together. At length Lady Gunna of Raasvold, who was to have the ordering of all things in the room, said that now she might lie down upon the floor. The lady divided the women in two parts, one to sleep while the other waked and watched: " Aye, 'twill not be quickly over, this — but scream all you will, Kristin, when you feel the pains sore — take no heed of the sleepers. We are all here for naught but to help you, poor child! " she said gently and kindly, patting the girl's cheek.

But Kristin lay gnawing her lips and crushing the edges of the coverlid in her sweat-bathed hands. It was stiflingly hot — but they said that so it should be. After every fit of pain the sweat poured from her.

Between-times she would lie thinking of the food for all these women. She was so fain they should deem that she had her house in good order. She had bidden Torbjörg, the cook, pour butter-milk into the water the fresh fish were boiled in. If only Gunnulf would not deem it a breach of the fast. Sira Eirik had said 'twas no breach, for buttermilk is not milk food, and, besides, the fish-broth is thrown away. The dried fish that Erlend had gotten for the house last autumn, they must nowise be let touch — spoiled and full of maggots as it was.

Mary, Blessed Lady of mine — will it be long, think you, till you will help me? — oh — now 'tis so hard, so hard — so hard —

She must try to hold out a little longer yet, before she gave way and screamed. . . .

Audfinna sat over by the hearth, tending the pots of hot water. Kristin wished so that she dared pray her to come to her and hold her hand. She knew not what she would have given now for the clasp of a friendly hand that she knew. But she was ashamed to ask it. . . .

All through the next forenoon a sort of bewildered stillness lay over Husaby. It was the eve of Mary's Mass, and all the work of the place should have been out of hand by the hour of nones; but the men were bemused and cast down, and the scared serving-wenches scrambled through the house-work in slovenly wise. The house-folk had grown fond of their young mistress — and things were going none too well with her, 'twas said.

Erlend stood out in the courtyard talking with his smith. He tried to keep his thoughts on what the man was saying. Then Lady Gunna came towards him swiftly:

"We can come no way with your wife, Erlend — now have we tried all shifts. You must come down — maybe 'twill help if she be set in your lap. Go in and put on you a short coat — but be hasty; she is hard bested, the poor young thing."

Erlend had grown red as blood. He remembered, he had heard — if a woman could no otherwise be delivered of a child she had conceived in secret, 'twas said it might help if she were set on the father's knee.

Kristin lay on the floor under some rugs; two women sat by her. As Erlend came in, he saw that she shrank together, bored her head into the lap of one of the women, and rolled it about here and there — but not a moan came from her.

When the fit was over, she looked up with wild, terrified eyes; the brown, cracked lips gasped open. Every trace of youth and comeliness was gone from the swollen, red, flaming face — even the hair was tangled up into a dirty mat, with bits of straw and wool from the sheepskins. She looked at Erlend as if she knew him not at first. But when she understood why the women had sent for him, she shook her head vehemently:

"'Tis not our use, where I come from — that men should be by when a woman bears a child — "

"They use it sometimes here north of Dovre," said Erlend softly. "If it might shorten the pain for you a little, my Kristin, you must suffer it — "

"Oh — !" As he knelt beside her, she threw her arms about his waist and crushed herself against him. Crouched together and shaking, she fought through the fit without a cry.

"Can I speak two words with my husband alone?" she said, swiftly, breathlessly, when it was past. The women drew back.

" Was it when she was in labour that you promised her what she said — that you would wed her when she was a widow — that night when Orm was born? " whispered Kristin.

Erlend gasped for breath, as though he had been struck a blow above the heart. Then he shook his head vehemently:

" I was at the castle that night — 'twas my troop that had the watch. 'Twas when I came home to our lodging in the morning and they laid the boy in my arms — Have you been lying here thinking of this, Kristin? "

" Aye — " Again she clung tight to him, while a wave of pain swept over her. Erlend dried away the sweat that poured down over her face.

" Now you know this," he asked when she was still again, " would you not I should bide with you as Lady Gunna says? "

But Kristin shook her head again. And at last the women were forced to let Erlend go.

But with that it seemed as if her strength to hold out were broken. She shrieked aloud in wild terror of the pangs she felt coming, and wailed out prayers for help. Yet when the women talked of fetching the husband in again, she screamed out: no — she had rather be tortured to death —

Gunnulf and the clerk that was with him went to the church to hold evensong. Every soul on the manor who was not with the lying-in woman went with them. But Erlend stole out of the church before the service was over, and went southward toward the houses.

In the west over the hill-tops on the farther side of the Dale the sky was yellowish red — dusk was beginning to fall in the clear mild spring evening. A star came forth here and there, white in the light-hued sky. A little flake of mist was drifting over the wood down by the lake — there were bare patches where the fields faced sunwards, and the smell of mould and melting snow was in the air.

The little hall lay westmost of the houses, out towards where the ground dipped to the valley. Erlend went over to it and stood awhile behind its wall. The timbers were still warm with the sun, when he leaned against them. Oh, her cries — ! He had heard a heifer once bellowing in the grip of a bear — it was up at their sæter, when he was a half-grown lad. Arnbjörn, the cowherd, and himself had run south through the woods. He remembered the

shaggy mass that stood up and turned into a bear with hot red
open maw. Arnbjörn's spear broke off in the bear's paws — then
the man snatched Erlend's from him, for he stood palsied with
horror. The heifer lay there still living, but udder and thighs were
eaten away —

Kristin mine — oh, Kristin mine — ! Lord, for Thy blessed
Mother's sake, have mercy —

He fled back to the church.

The maids came into the hall with the supper — the board was
not set up, but they put down the food by the hearth. The men
took bread and fish for themselves over to the benches, and sat in
their places silent; they ate a little, but none seemed to have a
stomach to his food. No one came to take away the dishes after
the meal, and none of the men got up to go to rest. They sat on,
gazing into the hearth-fire, and spoke not to each other.

Erlend had hidden himself in the corner by the bed — he could
not bear that any should see his face.

Master Gunnulf had lit a little hand-lamp and set it on an arm of
the high-seat. He set himself on the bench below it with a book in
his hands — and sat there, his lip just moving, soundlessly and without cease.

Once Ulf Haldorssön rose up, went over to the hearth and took
a slice of soft bread, then searched a little among the sticks of fire-
wood and picked out one. Then he went down the hall, to the
corner near the entrance-door, where old Aan sat. The two busied
themselves with the bread, hidden behind Ulf's cloak; and Aan
cut and carved at the stick. The other men glanced across at them
now and then. In a while Ulf and Aan stood up and left the hall.

Gunnulf looked after the two, but said no word. He went on
again with his prayers.

Once a young lad fell off the bench in his sleep and rolled out
on the floor. He rose up and looked about him bewildered. Then
he sighed a little and sat down again on the bench.

Ulf Haldorssön and Aan came in again quietly and went to the
places where they had sat before. The men looked over at them,
but none spoke.

Of a sudden Erlend sprang up. He went across the hall to his
house-folk. His face was grey as clay, and his eyes hollow.

" Is there none of you that knows a way? " said he. " You, Aan? " he whispered.

" It availed not," Ulf whispered back.

" Methinks 'tis written that she shall not have this child," said Aan, wiping his nose, " and then neither runes nor offerings avail. 'Tis pity of you, Erlend — to lose this kind young wife so soon — "

" Oh, speak not as though she were dead already," said Erlend, broken and despairing. He went back to his corner and threw himself down with his head within the bed-end.

Once a man went out and came in again. " The moon is up," he said. " 'Twill soon be morning."

A little while after, Lady Gunna came into the hall. She sank down on the beggars' bench by the door — her grey hair bunched out on all sides; her head-dress had slipped back on her shoulders.

The men rose — drew near to her slowly.

" One of you must come down there and hold her," she said, weeping. " We cannot, any more. You must go to her, Gunnulf — none can tell how it may end — "

Gunnulf stood up and thrust the prayer-book into the pouch at his belt.

" *You* must come too, Erlend," said the Lady.

The rough, hoarse crying met him in the doorway — Erlend stopped, trembling. He caught a glimpse of Kristin's distorted unknowable face in the midst of a group of weeping women — she was on her knees, they holding her up.

Near by the door some serving-women had flung themselves down with their faces hidden on the benches; they were praying aloud, unceasingly. He threw himself down beside them and hid his head in his arms. Shriek after shriek came from her, and each time it was as though an icy pang of unbelieving horror went through him. This thing *could* not be. . . .

Once he plucked up heart and looked across. Gunnulf was sitting now in front of her on a stool, holding her under the arms. Lady Gunna knelt by her side, and had her arms round Kristin's waist, but Kristin was struggling, in deadly terror, to thrust the other away.

" Oh, no — oh, no — loose me — I cannot bear — God, God, help me — "

" God will help you soon now, Kristin," said the priest each time. A woman stood by, holding a basin of water, and after every spasm she took a wet cloth and wiped the sick woman's face — the sweat from under her hair-roots and the slime from between her lips.

Then her head fell forward between Gunnulf's arms, and she slept for a moment — but the torments dragged her out of her sleep again, at once. And the priest went on saying:

"Now, Kristin, will you soon be helped — "

None thought any more what time of the night it might be. But through the smoke-vent already the dawn grinned greyly down.

Then, after a long frantic shriek of anguish, there came a sudden utter stillness. Erlend heard the women bustling about — he would have looked up; but he heard someone weeping aloud, and he shrank down again — he dared not know —

Then Kristin screamed again — a high wild scream of lamentation, unlike the mad inhuman animal cries that had gone before. Erlend started up.

Gunnulf stood bending over, holding Kristin, who still knelt. She was looking in deadly horror at something Lady Gunna was holding in a sheepskin — a raw, dark-red mass, like naught but the entrails of a slaughtered beast.

The priest drew her close to him:

"Kristin mine — you have borne as fine and fair a son as ever mother had need to thank God for — and he breathes!" he said vehemently to the weeping women. "He breathes — God will not be so cruel as not to hear us — "

Even while the priest was speaking, it came to pass. Through the mother's weary, bewildered head there flitted, half remembered, the vision of a bud she had once seen in the convent garden — something from out of which broke red crinkled silken petals — and spread themselves out into a flower.

The shapeless lump of flesh moved — sounds came from it — it stretched itself out and turned into a quite small wine-red child in human likeness — it had arms and legs and hands and feet, with full-formed fingers and toes on them — it struggled and wheezed a little. . . .

"So little, so little, so little he is — " she cried aloud in a thin hoarse voice, and sank down, helpless between laughter and weeping. The women round about burst into laughter and dried their tears, and Gunnulf passed her over into their arms.

"Roll him in a trough, that he may scream the better," said the

priest, following the women who bore the new-born boy away
to the hearth-place.

When Kristin waked from her long swoon, she was lying in her
bed. Someone had taken off the dreadful sweat-drenched clothes,
and a blessed sense of warmth and healing was streaming into her
body — they had laid small bags of hot nettle-porridge upon her,
and packed her in with heated rugs and skins.

One bade her hush when she would have spoken. There was a
great stillness in the room. And through the stillness came a voice
that she could scarce call to mind:

" — Nikulaus, in the name of the Father, the Son and the Holy
Ghost — "

There was a trickling of water.

Kristin rose a little on her elbow and looked out. Out there by
the hearth stood a priest in white vestments, and Ulf Haldorssön
lifted a red, sprawling naked child up out of the great brazen cauldron, gave it to the godmother, and took from her the lighted
taper.

She had her child — it was he that was shrieking now so as almost
to drown the priest's words. But she was so weary — she cared but
little, and only wished to sleep —

Then she heard Erlend's voice, saying hastily and in fear:

"His head — his head is so strange."

"'Tis swollen up," said a woman calmly. "That is nothing
strange — he has had to fight hard, this lad, for his life."

Kristin cried out something. It was as though she grew awake
right into her inmost heart — this was her son, and he had striven
for his life even as had she.

Gunnulf turned quickly, laughing — caught the little bundle
of swaddling-clothes from Lady Gunna's lap and bore it over to
the bed. He laid the boy in his mother's arms. Sick with tenderness
and joy, she rubbed her face against the little glimpse of a red
silky-soft face within the linen cloths.

She looked up at Erlend. She knew that once before she had
seen him with a grey, ravaged face like this — she could not remember when, she was so strange and dizzy in the head — but she knew
that it was well that she need not remember. And it was good to
see him stand thus by his brother — the priest had laid a hand upon
his shoulder. A sense of measureless peace and safety came upon

her, as she looked up at the tall man in alb and stole; the round, lean face under the black ring of hair was so strong, but his smile was comely and kind.

Erlend drove his dagger deep into the timber wall-post behind the mother and child.

" 'Tis needless now," said the priest, laughing, " for the boy is baptised."

Kristin came to think of somewhat Brother Edvin had once said. A new-christened child, he said, was as holy as the holy angels in heaven. 'Twas washed clean from the sins of its parents, and as yet it had done no sin itself. Timidly and warily she kissed the little face.

Lady Gunna came over to them. She was worn out and weary, and wroth with the father, who had not had wit enough to say a word of thanks to the lady helpers. And the priest had taken the child from her and borne it to the mother — she should have done that, for she had delivered the woman, and, besides that, she was godmother to the boy.

" You have not greeted your son yet, Erlend, or taken him in your arms," she said angrily.

Erlend lifted the babe out of its mother's arms, and laid his face against it for a moment.

" I doubt I shall scarce come to like you from my heart, Naakkve, till I have forgotten that you tormented your mother so cruelly," he said, and laid the boy down again by Kristin.

" Aye, blame *him* for it, do," said the old lady wrathfully. Master Gunnulf laughed, and then Lady Gunna laughed too. She would have taken the child and laid it in the cradle, but Kristin begged hard to keep him with her a little longer. Soon after, she fell asleep, with her son close in by her — knew dimly that Erlend touched her, warily, as if he feared to hurt her by a touch, and then slept again.

5

THE TENTH day after the child's birth, Master Gunnulf said to his brother, when they were alone in the hall in the morning:

" Methinks 'tis full time now, Erlend, that you send word to your wife's kin of how things stand with her."

"I see not that there is such haste," answered Erlend. "They will scarce be overjoyful at Jörundgaard when they hear that there is a son in our house already."

"Can you believe," said Gunnulf, "that Kristin's mother knew not in the autumn that her daughter was ailing? And if she knew, then must she now be going in fear — "

Erlend made no answer.

But a little later in the day, as Gunnulf sat in the little hall talking with Kristin, Erlend came in. He had a skin-cap on his head, a short and thick outer coat of wadmal, long breeches and shaggy boots. He bent over his wife and patted her cheek:

"Tell me, Kristin mine — would you have me bear any greeting from you to Jörundgaard? — for now am I bound southward to tell them of our son."

Kristin flushed deeply — she looked both affrighted and glad.

"'Tis no more than your father has a right to crave of me," said Erlend gravely, "that I come myself with these tidings."

Kristin lay still a little.

"Tell them at home," she said softly, "that I have longed every day, since I left my home, to fall at my father's and mother's feet and pray them for forgiveness."

Soon after, Erlend left her. Kristin did not think to ask him how he was journeying. But Gunnulf went with his brother out into the courtyard. Outside the hall-door stood Erlend's ski and a spear-headed staff.

"You go on ski?" said Gunnulf. "Who goes with you?"

"None," said Erlend, laughing. "You should know best, Gunnulf, that 'tis no easy thing for any to bear me company on ski."

"Methinks 'tis folly and rashness," said the priest. "There are many wolves in the Höiland woods this year, they say — "

Erlend only laughed and began to fasten on his ski.

"I shall be up by the Gjeitskar sæters, I trow, before 'tis dark. There is long light already. By evening the third day I should be at Jörundgaard — "

"'Tis ill going from Gjeitskar on to the beaten road — and there are bad fog-pockets to pass through. And you know that those sæters are ill places in winter-time."

"You can give me your flint and steel," said the other, still laughing, "lest by chance I should have to cast away my own — at some elf-woman if she should crave such *kurteisi* of me as beseems not a wedded man. Come, brother; now am I to do as you would have me — betake me to Kristin's father and bid him crave such amends from me as he deems fair and right — so far you can sure let me guide myself, as to choose how I shall journey."

With this Master Gunnulf was forced to be content. But he warned the house-folk strictly to keep it hidden from Kristin that Erlend had gone forth alone.

The southern sky stretched pale-yellow over the deepening blue of the mountain snowfields, the evening that Erlend rushed down past the Sil churchyard, the snow-crust hissing and crunching under his ski. High up rode a half-moon, shining misty-white in the evening twilight.

At Jörundgaard dark smoke was whirling up from the vent-holes towards the pale clear sky. The strokes of an axe rang out, measured and cold through the stillness.

From the gateway a pack of farm-dogs rushed out barking at the new-comer. Inside the courtyard a flock of shaggy goats were picking their way about, dark in the clear dusk — they were tugging at a heap of pine-branches in the midst of the yard. Three little children in thick winter clothes ran about amongst them.

The homely peace of this place took hold on Erlend strangely. He stood uneasily and waited for Lavrans, who came out to meet the stranger — he had been standing down by the woodshed talking to a man who was splitting fence-staves. He stopped short when he saw it was his son-in-law — thrust the spear he bore in his hand hard down into the snow.

" Is it *you?* " he asked in a low voice. " Alone — ? Is there — is aught — ? How is it that you come in this wise? " he added in a moment.

"Thus it is." Erlend pulled himself together and looked his father-in-law in the face. " Methought that less I could not do than come myself to bear you these tidings: Kristin bore a son on Mary's Mass in the morning. — Aye, she does well now," he added quickly.

Lavrans stood still awhile. He set his teeth hard in his under lip — his chin shook and quivered a little.

" These were tidings! " he said at last.

Little Ramborg had come up, and stood at her father's side. She looked up, her face glowing red.

" Be still," said Lavrans harshly, though the little maid had not said a word, but only blushed. " Stand not here — begone — "

He said no more. Erlend stood, bent forward, leaning on the staff clenched in his left hand. He looked down at the snow. His right hand was thrust into his breast. Lavrans pointed:

" Are you hurt? "

" A little," said Erlend. " I came over some bare rocks last night in the dark."

Lavrans took hold of the wrist and felt it warily: " No bone is broken, methinks," he said. — " You must tell her mother yourself — " He went off towards the hall as Ragnfrid came into the yard. She looked in wonderment after her husband — then she knew Erlend and went swiftly towards him.

She hearkened without a word, while Erlend for the second time had to bring forth his tidings. But her eyes shone with moisture when he said at the end:

" Methought that you had maybe seen somewhat before she left you last autumn — and that you might be fearful now for her — "

" 'Twas kindly done of you, Erlend," said she, in a voice that shook, " to think of this. True it is that I have been afraid for her every day since you took her from us."

Lavrans came back:

" Here is fox's fat — I see your cheek is frozen, son-in-law. You must bide awhile in the outer room while Ragnfrid dresses it with this and gets you thawed — how stands it with your feet? — you must take off your boots that we may see — "

When the house-folk came in to supper, Lavrans told them the tidings, and bade that strong ale be brought in for them to make merry on. But there was no right merriment over the ale-drinking — the master himself sat there with a cup of water. He prayed Erlend to forgive this — 'twas a vow he had made while yet a boy, to drink naught but water in fast-time. And so the folks sat somewhat soberly, and the talk went but tardily over the good ale. The children would come round to Lavrans now and then — he put an arm round them when they came close to his knee, but he answered absently when they spoke to him. Ramborg answered short and sharply when Erlend tried to jest with her — bent, it seemed, on showing that she misliked this brother-in-law of hers. She was in her eighth winter now; lively and comely, but bearing no like-ness to her sisters.

Erlend asked who the other children might be. Lavrans an-swered that the boy was Haavard Trondssön, the youngest of the Sundbu children. 'Twas dull for him there amid his grown-up brothers and sisters; and last Yule he had set his heart on coming home with Ragnfrid, his father's sister. The little maid was Helga Rolfsdatter of Blakarsarv — there had been naught for it but for the kinsfolk to take the children away home with them after the grave-ale there — 'twere pity they should see their father as he was now. For Ramborg it was a happy thing to have this foster-brother and sister. "We begin to grow old now, Ragnfrid and I," said Lavrans, "and this little one is more frolicsome and fond of play than Kristin was" — he stroked his daughter's curly hair.

Erlend went and sat by his mother-in-law, and she asked him of Kristin's childbed. He saw that Lavrans was listening to what they said. But soon he stood up, crossed the room, and put on hat and cloak. He had a mind to go over to the parsonage, he said — he would pray Sira Eirik to come and drink with them.

Lavrans went by the well-trodden path over the fields to Ro-mundgaard. The moon was dipping behind the hills now — but thousands of stars glittered above the white mountains. — He hoped that the priest might be at home — he could bear no longer to sit alone with the others.

But when he was come in between the fences near the farm, he saw a little taper coming towards him. Old Audun was bearing it — when he marked that there was someone on his path, he rang his little silver bell. Lavrans Björgulfsön threw himself on his knees in the snow-drift by the path.

Audun went by bearing the taper, and the bell that still tinkled gently. Behind him came Sira Eirik a-horseback. He lifted the pyx high in his hands when he came by the kneeling man — looked not to right or left, but rode calmly past, while Lavrans bowed himself down and stretched his two hands up in greeting towards his Saviour.

— 'Twas Einar Hnufa's son, the man that was with the priest — so 'twas drawing to an end with the old man now — ! Aye, aye. Lavrans said the prayers for the dying before he rose from the snow and went homewards. Even so, this meeting with God in the night had strengthened and comforted him much.

When they had gone to rest, he asked his wife:

"Knew you aught of this — that 'twas *so* with Kristin?"

"Did you not know?" said Ragnfrid.

"No," answered her husband, so shortly that she understood it must none the less have been in his thought at times.

"'Tis true I was afraid one while this last summer," said the mother, haltingly. "I saw that she had no joy in her food. But as time wore on, I deemed I must have been deceived. She seemed so joyous all the time we were making ready for the wedding —"

"Aye, for *that* she had good reason," said the father somewhat grimly. "But that she said naught to you — you that are her mother —"

"Aye, you can remember that, now she has done amiss," answered Ragnfrid bitterly. "You know full well, never has Kristin been used to turn to me —"

Lavrans said no more. In a little while he gently bade his wife sleep well, and lay quiet beside her. He felt that sleep would scarce come to him for a long time yet.

Kristin — Kristin — his little maid —

— Never had he touched with a single word on what Ragnfrid had confessed to him that night of the bridal. And she could not with reason think that he had let her feel he thought of it. He had not changed in his bearing towards her — rather had he striven to show her yet more friendliness and love. But 'twas not the first time this winter that he had marked this bitterness in Ragnfrid, or seen her search for some hidden offence in innocent words of his. He understood it not, and he knew of no remedy — he must let it be.

Our Father which art in heaven — He prayed for Kristin and her child. Then he prayed for his wife and himself. Last of all he prayed for strength to bear with Erlend Nikulaussön in patience of spirit, for so long as he needs must have his son-in-law dwelling on this, his manor.

Lavrans would not have his daughter's husband set forth for home till it was seen what turn things would take with his wrist. And he would not hear of Erlend's going back alone.

" Kristin would be joyful if you bore me company," said Erlend, one day.

Lavrans was silent awhile. Then he brought forward many lets and hindrances. Ragnfrid would like little to be left alone here on the manor. And should he fare so far north, he could scarce hope to be back for the spring sowings. But the end was that he set out with Erlend. He took no man with him — he would come back by ship to Raumsdal; he could hire horses to bring him thence down the Dale — he had acquaintance everywhere along that road.

They spoke not much together on their way, but they journeyed in good accord. It tasked Lavrans' strength to keep up with Erlend, for he would not own that the other went too fast for him. But Erlend soon marked this, and suited his pace to his father-in-law's. He gave himself great pains to please his wife's father — he had this quiet compliant way with him when he wished to win the friendship of any.

The third night they took shelter in a stone hut. They had had foul weather, with mist, but Erlend seemed to find the way as surely as ever. Lavrans had marked that Erlend had a marvellous sure eye for all signs and marks in the air and on the earth, and for the nature and ways of beasts — and he ever knew where he was. All that he himself, used as he was to the hills, had taught himself by looking and marking and remembering, the other seemed to know blindly. Erlend laughed himself about it — he did but feel it all within him.

They found the hut in the pitch-darkness, at the very hour Erlend had foretold. Lavrans thought to himself of a night like this when he had made a bed for himself in the snow but a bow-shot from his own horse-camp. The snow was drifted high around the hut, so that they had to break in through the smoke-hole. Erlend covered over the opening with a horse-hide that was lying in the hut, and fastened it with slats of wood which he pressed in under the rafters. He scraped away with a ski the snow that had sifted in, and managed to make up a fire in the fire-place with the frozen wood that lay there. He drew out three or four ptarmigan from under the bench — he had hid them away there on his way south — plastered them round with clay from the floor by the fire-place where it had thawed, and threw the lumps into the glowing embers.

Lavrans lay on the earthen bench, where Erlend had made a couch for him as well as he could with their wallets and cloaks.

"'Tis the fashion the soldiers use with stolen fowls, Erlend," said he, laughing.

"Aye, for I learned one thing and another when I was serving the Count," said Erlend, in the same tone.

He was as brisk now and full of life as he had been quiet and almost sluggish at most times his father-in-law had seen him. He began to tell tales, as he sat on the ground in front of the other, of the years when he had served Count Jacob of Halland. He had been troop-leader in the Castle, and he had cruised about with three small ships to guard the coast. Erlend's eyes were like a child's now — he did not brag, he but let his tongue run on. Lavrans lay looking down at him. . . .

He had prayed God to grant him patience with this husband of his daughter — and now he was well-nigh angry with himself that he liked Erlend so much better than he had a mind to. He remembered, too, that that night when their church burned down he had liked his son-in-law well. 'Twas not in that long carcass of his that Erlend lacked manhood. A stab of pain went through the father's heart — 'twas pity of Erlend, he might have been fit for better things than beguiling of women. But, as things were, little more had come of all the rest of him than boyish pranks. Had the times been such that a chieftain could have taken this man in hand and used him — but as the world now was, when each man must trust to his own judgment in many things — and a man in Erlend's place had in his hands not his own welfare only, but so many others' — And this was Kristin's husband. . . .

Erlend looked up at his father-in-law. He too grew grave. Then he said:

"One thing would I pray you, Lavrans — before we come home to my house — that you would say to me what you must needs have on your heart."

Lavrans was silent.

"You know well," said Erlend, as before, "that I will willingly submit me to you in any fashion you may wish, and make such amends as you deem may be a fitting punishment for me."

Lavrans looked down into the young man's face — then he smiled strangely:

" That might be a hard matter, Erlend — for me to say and for
you to do. — But at the least you must give fitting gifts to the
church at Sundbu and to the priests whom you two fooled along
with other folk," he said vehemently. " I will speak of it no more.
You cannot blame it on your youth either. More honour had it
been to you, Erlend, had you confessed and made submission before I made your bridal — ”

" Aye," said Erlend. " But I knew not then that things stood so
that the wrong I had done you must come to light."

Lavrans sat up.

" Knew you not, when you were wedded, that Kristin — ? "

" No," said Erlend, with a crestfallen look. " We had been
wedded nigh on two months before I knew it."

Lavrans looked at him with some wonder, but he said naught.
Then Erlend went on, haltingly and weakly:

" Glad am I that you came with me, father-in-law. Kristin has
been all this winter so heavy of mood — she has scarce cared to
speak a word to me. Many a time has it seemed to me as though
she found but little happiness either at Husaby or with me."

Lavrans answered somewhat coldly:

" 'Tis the same, I trow, with all young wives. Now she is well
once more, doubtless you will soon be as good friends again as
you were before," he added, smiling a little mockingly.

But Erlend sat gazing into the heap of embers. It came over
him so surely, of a sudden — though truly he had felt it ever since
he first saw the little red baby face against Kristin's white shoulder
— things would nevermore be between them as once they had
been.

When her father came into the little hall where Kristin lay, she
sat up in bed and stretched out towards him. She threw her arms
around him, and wept and wept so sorely that Lavrans was afraid.

She had been up for a time, but then she came to know that
Erlend had gone south over the hills alone, and when time dragged
on and he returned not, she grew so fearful that fever came on her
and she must needs lie abed again.

It was plain to see that she was weak still — weeping came on
her for never so little things. — The new chaplain, Sira Eiliv Serkssön, had come to the manor while Erlend was away. He had taken

it on him to go now and then to sit by the lady of the house and read to her — but she wept at the least thing so causelessly that he scarce knew what he dared let her hear.

One day when her father sat with her, Kristin had set her heart on swaddling the child herself, so that he might see rightly how fair and well-shaped the boy was. As he lay sprawling amidst his swaddling-clothes on the coverlid in front of his mother:

" What is yonder mark he has on his breast? " asked Lavrans.

Right over his heart the boy had some small blood-red spots — it looked as though a bloody hand had touched him there. Kristin had herself been troubled when first she saw this mark. But she had tried to comfort herself with the reason she now gave:

" 'Tis but a fire-mark, belike — I caught at my breast when I saw the church burning."

Her father started. Aye — true it was that he knew not how long — or how much — she had kept hidden. And he could not understand how it had been possible for her — his own child — from him. . . .

" Methinks you have no right liking for my son," Kristin said to her father many times; and Lavrans laughed and said: nay, that he liked him right well. He had brought rich gifts, too, to lay both in the cradle and in the lying-in woman's bed. But Kristin deemed that no one truly thought enough of her son — Erlend least of all. " Look on him, Father," she begged; " see you, he is laughing — did you ever see so fair a babe as Naakkve, Father? "

She asked this, time and again. Once Lavrans said, as though in thought:

" Haavard, your brother — our second son — was a passing fair child."

In a little Kristin asked, in a weak voice:

" 'Twas he that lived the longest of my brothers? "

" Aye, he lived to be two winters old. . . . Nay, now, my Kristin, you must not weep again," he prayed her gently.

Neither Lavrans nor Gunnulf Nikulaussön liked the boy to be called Naakkve; he was christened Nikulaus. Erlend would have it that 'twas the same name; but Gunnulf said: no; sagas told of men called Naakkve back in heathen times. But naught could bring

Erlend to use the name his father had borne; and Kristin ever called the boy the name by which Erlend had first greeted their son.

So to Kristin's mind there was but one at Husaby besides herself who fully understood how noble and hopeful a child Naakkve was. This was the new priest, Sira Eiliv. — In this matter his judgment was scarce less sound than the mother's own.

Sira Eiliv was a short spare-limbed man with a little round belly, and this gave him a somewhat laughable look. His presence was unremarkable — folks who had spoken with him more than once still found it hard to know the priest again, so common was his face. His hair and skin were of the same hue — like reddish-yellow sand — and his round watery-blue eyes were flat with his head. In his bearing he was quiet and retiring; but Master Gunnulf said that Sira Eiliv was so learned that he, too, could have passed through all the degrees, had he but had more forwardness. But much more than by learning was he adorned with purity of life, humility and devout love towards Christ and His Church.

He was of low kindred, and though he was but little older than Gunnulf Nikulaussön, he seemed already not far from an old man. Gunnulf had known him since they went to school together at Nidaros, and he spoke always with great love of Eiliv Serkssön. Erlend deemed 'twas no great matter of a priest they had gotten for Husaby, but Kristin soon looked on him with trust and love.

Kristin still lived down in the little hall with the child, even after she had been churched. 'Twas a heavy day for Kristin that — Sira Eiliv led her within the church-door, but he dared not give her the Lord's body. She had confessed herself to him, but for the sin she had committed, as partner in the guilt of another's unblessed death, she must seek absolution from the Archbishop. That morning when Gunnulf had sat with her in her soul's agony, he had strictly charged her that, as soon as she was free from danger of bodily death, she must haste to seek healing for her soul. So soon as health and strength enough were hers, she must fulfil her vow to St. Olav. Now that he by his intercession had saved her son and brought him alive and whole to the light and to cleansing baptism, she must walk barefoot to his grave and lay down upon it the golden garland of maidenhood, which she had guarded so ill and borne so wrongfully. And Gunnulf counselled her to prepare herself for this pilgrimage by solitary life, prayers, reading and meditation, also by fasting, but this with due measure, for the sake of the child at her breast.

The evening of her churching, when she was sitting sorrowful, Gunnulf had come to her and given her a rosary. He said that in foreign lands 'twas not only cloister-folk and priests that used such bead-rolls for a help in their pious exercises. This rosary was a most fair one; the beads were of a sort of yellow wood that came from India, and smelt so sweet and delicate that they were well fitted to bring to mind that which a good prayer should be — the heart's sacrifice and yearning for help to live righteously before God. Some among the beads were of amber and gold, and the cross was of a fair enamel.

This spring Erlend Nikulaussön busied himself much with setting his estate in order. This year all fences were mended and gates set up in due time, the ploughing and spring-sowing well and early gotten out of hand, and Erlend bought some right good horned cattle. He had had to slaughter many at the new year, and 'twas no great loss, so many old and wretched beasts as there had been in his herd. He got together folk for tar-burning and birch-bark-peeling, and the houses of the manor were timbered up and their roofs repaired. There had not been such order at Husaby, folks said, since old Sir Nikulaus was in his full strength. Aye, and 'twas known, too, that the master sought counsel and help from his wife's father. With him and with his brother, the priest, Erlend went about and visited friends and kinsfolk in the country round when he had leisure from his work. But now he went around in seemly wise, with a few brisk and likely serving-men. In former days Erlend had used to ride about with a whole troop of unruly hotheads. And so the talk of the countryside, which so long had seethed with wrath over Erlend Nikulaussön's shameless evil life and shiftless and ruinous husbandry at Husaby, died away now into good-humoured jesting. Folks smiled and said that the young housewife Erlend had gotten had brought much to pass in six months.

A while before Botolph's Mass, Lavrans Björgulfsön set forth for Nidaros in Master Gunnulf's company. He was to be the priest's guest for some days, while he sought out the shrine of St. Olav and the other churches in the city, before he journeyed south to his home again. He parted from his daughter and her husband in all love and kindness.

6

KRISTIN was to set out on her walk to Nidaros three days after the mass of the Seljemen * — later on in the month the city would be full of bustle and commotion making ready for the Olav's Mass † festival; and earlier the Archbishop would not be in the town.

The evening before, Master Gunnulf had come to Husaby, and early in the morning he went with Sira Eiliv to the church to sing Matins. The grass was as a grey fur coverlid with the heavy dew, as Kristin walked to the church; but the sunlight was golden on the woods that topped the ridge, and the cuckoo called from the hill-side — it looked as though she would have fair weather for her pilgrimage.

There was none in the church save Erlend and his wife, and the two priests in the lighted choir. Erlend looked across at Kristin's naked feet. Ice-cold must it be for her, standing on the stone floor. She was to walk the twenty miles with no other company than their prayers. He strove to lift up his heart to God, so as he had not striven for many a year.

She was clad in an ashen-grey kirtle, and had a rope about her waist. Underneath, he knew, she wore a shift of sackcloth. A tightly bound wadmal cloth hid her hair.

When they stepped from the church out into the morning sunshine, a maid met them with the child. Kristin set herself down on some logs of wood. With her back to her husband she sat and let the boy suck his fill, that he might be full-fed when she set out. Erlend stood, unmoving, a little space away from her — he was white and cold in the face with the strain.

The priests came out a little later — they had taken off their vestments in the sacristy. They stopped by Kristin. Then Sira Eiliv went on down towards the manor, but Gunnulf stayed and helped her to get the child securely bound on her back. In a bag that hung from her neck she had the golden garland, money and a little bread and salt. She took her staff in her hand, bowed deeply

* 8th July.   † 29th July.

before the priest, and began to walk quietly northwards up the path that led to the woods.

Erlend was left standing — deadly white of face. Of a sudden he began to run. North of the church were some small hillocks covered with scanty grass and close-cropped juniper and birch — goats were used to graze there. Erlend ran up them — from there he could see her yet a little way on — till she was swallowed up in the woods.

Gunnulf walked slowly up after his brother. The priest looked tall and dark in the bright morning light. He, too, was very pale.

Erlend stood with mouth half open, the tears running down over his white cheeks. Of a sudden he fell on his knees — then threw himself forward headlong on the short grass, and lay, sobbing, sobbing, and tearing at the heather with his long brown fingers.

Gunnulf stood motionless. He looked down at the weeping man — then out towards the woods where the woman had vanished.

Erlend lifted his head a little.

" Gunnulf, was it needful that you should lay this upon her? — Was it needful? " he asked again. " Could not *you* have absolved her? "

The other made no answer; and he went on again:

" Had not I confessed and done penance? " He sat up. " I bought *her* thirty days' masses and vigils and a yearly mass on her death-day for ever and a grave in hallowed ground — I confessed the sin to Bishop Helge, and made pilgrimage to the Holy Blood at Schwerin — could not all this help a little for Kristin — ? "

" If you have done this," said the priest quietly, " laid before God a contrite heart and won His full forgiveness — you sure must know that the marks left by your sin here on earth you must yet strive, year in, year out, to wipe away. What you brought on her that is now your wife, when you first dragged her down into unclean living and after into manslaughter — that cannot you amend for her, but only God. Pray that He may hold His hand over her on this journey, where you cannot bear her company and guard her. And forget not, brother, so long as you two live, that you saw your wife go forth from your house in this wise — by reason of your sins, more than of her own."

Erlend said in a little:

" I had sworn by God and my Christian faith, before I took her honour, that I would never have another to wife; and she promised that never would she have another to husband, so long as we lived on the earth. You have said yourself, Gunnulf, that they that vow thus are bound in wedlock before God; any of them who there-after wedded another would be living in adultery in His eyes. But if so it be, then was it not unclean living, I trow, for Kristin to be mine — "

" The sin was not in that you lived with her," said the priest in a while, " had that been possible without your transgressing other laws — but you had led this child away into sinful revolt against all whom God had set over her — and at last you brought blood-guiltiness upon her. I told you this also, that time when we spoke of the matter: therefore hath the Church ordained laws concern-ing marriage, that banns be published forth to the world, and that we priests shall not wed man and maid against the will of the kin-dred." He sat down, clasped one knee with his hands, and gazed out over the country-side bright with summer, with the little lake gleaming blue in the valley-bottom. " You must have known it yourself, Erlend — a thicket of briers and thorns and nettles had you sowed around you — how could you draw a young maid in to your side and she not be torn and wounded and bleeding — "

" You stood my friend more than once, brother, in the days when it was Eline and I," said Erlend, low. " I have ever been thankful for it — "

" I scarce deem that I had done it," said Gunnulf in a voice that shook, " could I have believed of you that you had the heart to deal as you have done with a fine and pure young maid — a child in years beside you."

Erlend made no answer. Gunnulf asked in a low voice:

" That time in Oslo — thought you never of how it would have gone with Kristin, if she had been found with child — while dwelling in a cloister of nuns? — and was the betrothed of another — her father a proud man, jealous of his honour — all her kindred high-born folk, unused to suffer shame — "

" You may well believe I thought of it — " Erlend had turned his head aside. " I had Munan's word to stand by her — I told her, too, of this — "

" Munan! Could you find in your heart to talk to a man like Munan of Kristin's honour? "

" He is not what you think him," said Erlend, shortly.

" And how of his wife, our kinswoman, Lady Katrin? For 'twas not your meaning, I trow, that he should carry her to one of those other places of his where he keeps his paramours — ? "

Erlend smote the ground with his fist till the knuckles grew bloody:

" Aye, 'tis the devil's own business for a man, when his wife goes to shrift with his brother! "

" She hath not confessed her to me," said the priest. " And I am not her parish priest. She made her moan to me in her bitter agony and fear — and I strove to help her and to give her such counsel and such comfort as seemed best."

" Well," Erlend threw back his head and looked at his brother, " I know it myself — I should not have done it — have had her come to me in Brynhild's house — "

The priest sat speechless a moment.

" In Brynhild Fluga's — ? "

" Aye; told she not of that, when she told the rest — ? "

" 'Twould be hard enough, methinks, for Kristin to tell such things of her own husband in confession," said the priest in a while. " I think that she would rather die than tell them any other place." He sat awhile, and then said with a harsh vehemency:

" If so it were, Erlend, that you deemed you were her husband before God, he that should protect and guard her — then do your doings seem yet worse to me. You tempted her astray in groves and hay-lofts, you led her over a harlot's threshold — and, last of all, you brought her to Björn Gunnarssön and Lady Aashild. . . . "

" You shall not speak so of Moster Aashild," said Erlend softly.

" You have said yourself, before now, that you believed her guilty of our uncle's death — she and this man Björn — "

" I care naught for that," said Erlend vehemently. " Moster Aashild is dear to me — "

" Aye, I understood as much," said the priest. His mouth twisted into a little crooked scornful smile. " Since you grudged it not to her that she should meet Lavrans Björgulfsön after you had borne away his daughter. 'Twould seem, indeed, Erlend, that you deem your friendship can scarce be bought too dear — "

" Jesus! " Erlend hid his face in his hands. But the priest went on:

" Had you seen your wife's anguish of soul, as she shuddered with horror of her sins, unshriven and helpless — and she sat there and was to bear your child, and death stood at her door — so young a child herself, and so unhappy — "

" I know, I know! " Erlend trembled. " I know that she lay thinking of it, in her torment. For Jesu sake, Gunnulf, be still now — I am your brother after all! "

But the priest went on without mercy:

" Had I been a man like you and not a priest — and had I led so young and good a maid astray — I had freed me from the other — God help me, rather would I have done as Moster Aashild did with her husband and burned in hell for it world without end, than I would have borne that she should suffer such things as you have brought down on the head of your innocent love — "

Erlend sat awhile, trembling.

" You call yourself a priest," he said in a low voice. " Are you *so* good a priest that you have never sinned — with a woman? "

Gunnulf looked not at his brother. A wave of red flooded his face:

" You have no right to ask such things — but yet I will answer you. He knows that died for us upon the Cross what bitter need I have of His mercy. But I say to you, Erlend — had He on all the earth's round not one single servant that was pure and unstained by sin, and were there not in His holy Church one single priest more faithful and worthy than I, wretched traitor to my Lord that I am — yet is it the Lord's laws and commandments that are taught in it. Never can His Word be polluted by the mouth of an unclean priest, it will but burn and consume our lips — but this, maybe, you cannot understand. Yet this you know as well as I and every other filthy thrall of Satan whom He hath bought with His blood — God's law cannot be shaken nor His honour diminished. As surely as His sun is alike mighty, whether it shine upon the barren sea and waste grey mountain or upon these fair and fertile lands — "

Erlend had hidden his face in his hands. He sat long silent, and when he spoke his voice was dry and hard:

" Priest or no priest — since you are not so absolute in saintly living — understand you not — ? Could you do to a woman who had slept in your arms — borne you two children — could you do to her as Aashild did to her husband? "

The priest was silent a little. Then he said, a little mockingly:

" You were not wont to judge Moster Aashild so hardly — "

" It cannot be the same for a man, I trow, as for a woman. I mind me the last time they were here at Husaby, and Sir Björn was with them. We were sitting by the hearth, mother and Aashild, and Sir Björn was playing his harp and singing to them — I was standing by his knee. Then Baard called her — he was in bed, and he would have her go to rest at once — he used words so shameless and immodest — Moster Aashild rose, and Sir Björn too; he left the hall, but first they looked at each other — Aye, afterwards I thought, when I grew old enough to understand — it may well be it is true — I had begged leave to light Sir Björn across to the house he was to sleep in, but I dared not, and I dared not lie in the hall. I ran out and laid me down by the men in the servants' house. By Jesus, Gunnulf — for a man it can never be as it was for Aashild that night —

" No, Gunnulf — kill a woman that — except I took her with another — "

Yet had he done that very thing. But *this* Gunnulf could not say to his brother. So he asked coldly:

" Was it not true, then, either, that Eline had been untrue to you? "

" Untrue? " Erlend turned on his brother, suddenly afire. " Mean you that I should have laid it to her charge that she had given herself to Gissur — after I had made plain to her again and yet again that betwixt us all must be at an end? "

Gunnulf bowed his head.

" No, like enough you are right," he said wearily, in a low voice. But under this little breath of approval Erlend flamed up — he threw back his head and looked at the priest.

" You are so tender of Kristin, Gunnulf. Strange how you have hung over her all the spring — almost more than is seemly for a brother and a priest. Almost it might seem you grudged her to me — Were it not that things were with her as they were when you first saw her, folks might deem — "

Gunnulf looked at him. Beside himself under his brother's look, Erlend sprang up — and Gunnulf, too, rose. He did not withdraw his look, and Erlend struck out at him with his clenched fist. The priest caught and gripped his wrist. Erlend tried to close with his brother, but Gunnulf stood immovable, holding him off.

Erlend grew quiet straightway. " I should have remembered you were a priest," he said low.

" You see that on that score you have no need to repent," said Gunnulf, with a little smile. — Erlend stood chafing his wrist.

" Aye, you ever had the devil's own strength in your hands — "

" This is like the days when we were boys." Gunnulf's voice had grown strangely soft and mild. " I have thought of it often all these years I have been from home — the times when we were boys. Often were we unfriends then, but never did it last long, Erlend."

" But now, Gunnulf," said the other sorrowfully, " it can nevermore be as when we were boys."

" No," answered the priest quietly, " 'tis like it cannot — "

They stood still a long time. At last Gunnulf said:

" I leave you now, Erlend. I will go now down to Eiliv, and bid him farewell, and then I shall set out. Aye, 'tis to the priest in Orkedal that I go; I shall not come to Nidaros while *she* is there." He smiled a little.

" Gunnulf! I meant it not so — go not from me like this — "

Gunnulf stood still. He drew one or two deep breaths, then said:

" One thing I would have you know of me, Erlend — since you know that I have knowledge of all this concerning you. — Sit down."

The priest sat himself down as before. Erlend stretched himself on the ground before him, and, hand under chin, looked up into his brother's strangely stiff and strained face. Then he smiled a little:

" What is it, Gunnulf — would you make confession to me? "

" Aye," said his brother, softly. Yet then he sat a long time silent. Erlend saw his lips move once, and he clenched his folded hands tightly round his knee.

" What is it? " A smile flickered over Erlend's face. " Sure it cannot be so — that some fair lady, far off in southern lands — "

" No," said the priest. His voice grew rough and hoarse. " 'Tis not of love —

" Know you, Erlend, how it came about that I was vowed to be a priest? "

" Aye. When our brothers died, and they feared they would lose us too — "

" No," said Gunnulf. " Munan they thought was well again,

and Gaute had not taken the sickness — 'twas not till the winter after that he died. But you were lying, choking to death, and mother vowed me to the service of St. Olav if he would save your life — "

"Who has told you this?" asked Erlend in a while.

"Ingrid, my foster-mother."

"Aye, 'tis true, indeed, that *I* had been a strange gift to give St. Olav," said Erlend, laughing a little. "He had been ill-served with me. — But you have said yourself, Gunnulf, you were well content that you had been called to the priesthood from childhood up — "

"Aye," said the priest. "But 'twas not always so. I mind me well the day you rode from Husaby with Munan Baardssön, to fare to the King, our kinsman, and become his man. Your horse danced under you; your new arms glittered and shone. *I* was never to bear arms. — Fair were you, my brother — you were but sixteen winters old; and already I had seen, for many a day past, that you were well loved of dames and damsels — "

"That glory endured not long," said Erlend. "I learned to cut my nails straight across, swear by Jesus at each second word, and use my dagger to ward with while I struck with my sword. Then was I sent north, and met *her* — and was hunted from the bodyguard with shame, and my father shut his doors against me — "

"And you fled forth from the land with a fair lady," said Gunnulf, quietly as before. "And we heard at home that you were Captain of Count Jacob's castle."

"Aye, that was no such great matter as it sounded here at home," said Erlend, laughing.

"Father and you were not friends — me he thought not enough of to care to be unfriends with me. Mother held me dear, I know — but how little she deemed me worth, weighed against you — that marked I best when you had fled from the land. You, brother, were the only one that loved me truly. And God knows that you were my dearest friend on earth. But in those days when I was young and witless, times have been when I deemed you had been given all too much more than I. This it was that I would have told you, Erlend."

Erlend lay face downwards on the hill-side.

"Leave us not, Gunnulf," he begged.

"Yes," said the priest, "I go. Too much have we said now one to the other. God and Mary Virgin grant that we may meet again in a better hour. Farewell, Erlend — "

" Farewell," said Erlend, not looking up.

When Gunnulf, some hours after, came forth from the priest's house, ready for his journey, he saw a man riding over the fields towards the southern woods. He had a bow slung across his back, and three hounds ran by his horse's side. It was Erlend.

Meanwhile Kristin was walking swiftly on her way, by the forest path that led over the hills. The sun stood high in the heavens now, and the pine-tops shone against the summer sky, but within the woods was still the cool and freshness of morning. The air was full of the balmy scent of pine-needles and peaty soil, and of the twinflower that sprinkled all the knolls with its small pink bells; and the grassy pathway was damp and soft and comforting to her feet. Kristin walked, saying over her prayers, and now and then she looked up at the little white fair-weather clouds that swam in the blue above the tree-tops.

All the time she could not but think of Brother Edvin. So had he walked and walked, year in, year out, from early spring to deepest winter. Over the mountain paths, under black scaurs and white snow-fields. He had rested him at the sæters, drunk of the beck, and eaten of the bread that sæter-girls and horse-herds bore out to him — then had he bidden farewell and called down God's peace and benison on fold and cattle. Down through the sighing woods of the hill-sides he had passed, down into the Dale; tall and stoop-shouldered, with head bent forward, he had wandered along the high-road past the well-tilled farms and the dwelling-places — and everywhere, wheresoever he passed, his loving intercessions for all men left, as it were, fair weather in his track.

She met not a living thing, save now and then a few cattle — there were sæters on these hill-tops. But the path was well-trodden, and over the marshy grounds were cordwood bridgeways. Kristin was unafraid — she felt as though the monk walked invisibly by her side. Brother Edvin, if in truth thou art a holy saint, if thou standest before the face of God, pray for me now!

Lord Jesus Christ, holy Mary, St. Olav — She longed to reach the goal of her pilgrimage — she longed to cast from her the burden of the hidden sins of years, the weight of masses and offices that she had filched unlawfully while yet unshriven and unrepentant — she longed to be free and cleansed, yet more keenly than she had yearned to be delivered of her burden in the spring before the boy was born. . . .

He slept so soundly and securely on his mother's back. He waked not till she had passed through the woods and come down to the Snow-bird farms, and could look out over Budvik and the Saltnes arm of the fjord. She sat down in a pasture off the path, slung the bundle with the babe in it round into her lap, and opened the breast of her kirtle. It was sweet to feel him against her breast; sweet to be able to sit awhile; a blessed sweetness through all her body to feel the stone-hard, milk-swollen breasts grow soft as he sucked.

The country-side lay still below her, baking in the sunshine — with green meadows and bright cornfields amid dark woods. Here and there a little smoke went up above the house-roofs. In some places the hay-harvest had begun.

She had leave to cross from Saltnes-sand over to Steine by boat. Once across, she had come to a quite unknown country. The road she must follow across the Bynes led up for a while among farms, then she came into woods again, but here she never had to go for long out of sight of human dwellings. She was passing weary. But she thought of her parents — had they not walked barefoot all the way from Jörundgaard in Sil, over Dovre and down to Nidaros, bearing Ulvhild between them on a litter? She must not think how heavy Naakkve was upon her back.

— Worse was the dreadful itching in her head from the thick sweat-drenched wadmal hood. And round her waist, where the rope pressed her garments against her body, her shift had gnawed at the flesh till there must be raw places on it.

Other wayfarers began to pass her on the road. Now and again folk would ride by her, going one way or the other. She overtook a peasant cart bound for the city with wares — the heavy solid wheels bumped and jolted over roots and stones, creaking and squeaking. Two men were dragging along a beast for the slaughter-house. They looked a little at the young pilgrim woman, for her comeliness' sake — but such wayfarers were a common sight in this country-side. At one place some men were busy putting up a house a little off the road; they called out to her, and an oldish man came running up and proffered her a drink of ale. Kristin curtsied, drank, and gave thanks in words such as poor folks were wont to say to her when she gave alms.

Soon after she must needs rest again. She found a little green slope near by the road, with a stream running by it. Kristin laid her child in the grass; he wakened and began to shriek piteously, so that she hastened with a wandering mind through the prayers she should have said. Then she took Naakkve in her lap and unwound his swaddling-clothes. He had fouled his cloths, and she had but little with her to put in their stead; so she washed out the cloths and laid them on a warm smooth rock to dry in the sun. The outer clothes she wrapped loosely round the boy. He liked this well, for he could kick and sprawl now, as he drank from his mother's breast. Kristin looked with joy at his fine rosy-white limbs, and pressed down one of his hands between her breasts as she suckled him.

Two horsemen rode by at a sharp trot. Kristin glanced up — 'twas a master and his man; but suddenly the master reined up his horse, sprang from the saddle, and came back on foot to where she sat. It was Simon Andressön.

" Maybe you had liefer I should not greet you? " he asked. He stood holding his horse and looking down at her. He was clad as for a journey, in a sleeveless leather jerkin over a light-blue linen coat — a silk cap was on his head, and his face was red and shone with sweat. " 'Tis strange to see you — but maybe you have no mind to talk with me — ? "

" Surely you must know — how is it with you, Simon? " Kristin drew up her bare feet under her skirt, and tried to take the child away from her breast. But the boy screamed and gulped and groped about so that she was forced to lay him to it again. She gathered her kirtle over the breast as well as she could, and sat with eyes downcast.

" Is it yours? " asked Simon, pointing to the child. " Nay, that was a foolish question! " he said, laughing. " 'Tis a son, I warrant? Erlend Nikulaussön has fortune with him." He had bound his horse to a tree, and now he sat down on a stone a little way from Kristin. He brought his sword forward between his knees, and sat with his hands on the hilt, turning up the earth with the scabbard-end.

" I looked not to meet you here, north of Dovre, Simon," said Kristin, that she might say something.

" No," said Simon. " I have had no errands in this part of the land before."

Kristin called to mind that she had heard somewhat — at her

home-coming feast — of the youngest son of Arne Gjavvaldssön of Ranheim being to wed Andres Darre's youngest daughter. — Had he been at Ranheim, she asked.

" You know of it? " said Simon. " Aye, it has got about already in this country-side, I can well believe."

" It is so, then," said Kristin, " that Gjavvald is to wed Sigrid? " Simon looked up sharply, pressing his lips together:

" I see you know *not* of it yet."

" I have not set foot outside Husaby courtyard all the winter," said Kristin. " And few folks have I seen. I heard there was talk of this wedding — "

" Aye — as well that you hear it from my lips, I trow — it must needs get abroad up here." He sat silent a little. " Gjavvald died three days before winter-night * — he fell with his horse and broke his back. Mind you, just before you come to Dyfrin, where the road runs east of the river, and the ground falls sheer — oh, no, you would scarce remember. We were on our way to their be-trothal-ale; Arne and his sons had come by sea to Oslo — " Simon stopped short.

" Maybe she loved Gjavvald — Sigrid — and had been joyful that she was to wed him? " asked Kristin, shyly and fearfully.

" Aye," said Simon. " And she bore a son to him — at Apostles' Mass last spring — " '

" Oh, Simon! "

Sigrid Andresdatter, with the brown curls about her little round face. When she laughed there came deep pits in her cheeks. Dim-ples and little childish white teeth — Simon had these too. Kristin remembered that when she was in her less gentle moods towards her betrothed, this had seemed to her unmanly — most of all after she had come to know Erlend. They were much alike, Sigrid and Simon; but that she was so plump and laughing made *her* but the fairer. She was fourteen winters old then. — Such joyful laughter as Sigrid's Kristin had never heard. Simon was ever teasing and jesting with his youngest sister — Kristin had felt that he held her dearest of them all.

" You know that father was fondest of Sigrid," said Simon. " So he was fain that she and Gjavvald should see if they could like one another, before he clinched the bargain with Arne. And they did — methought a little more than seemed good — they must ever be

* Winter-night = 14th October, the beginning of the winter half-year.

flinging at each other when they met and glancing and laughing —
this was last summer at Dyfrin. But they were so young — none
could have thought of this. And Astrid — you know she was betrothed when you and I — Aye, she said naught against it; and Torgrim, you know, has great wealth, and is kind, too, after a fashion
— but nothing, nor no one, can please him, and he thinks ever he
has all the hurts and ailments that folks ever heard tell of. So we
were glad, all of us, that Sigrid was so joyful in the match that had
been made for her. . . .

"And when we brought Gjavvald home like this — Halfrid, my
wife, managed things so that she went home with us to Mandvik.
And then, afterward, it came to light that Gjavvald had not left
her — alone — "

They were silent awhile. Then Kristin said, softly:

"This has been no joyous journey for you, then, Simon?"

"Oh, no." Then he laughed a little. "But soon I shall be used
now to riding on woeful errands, Kristin. And for this one, you
see, I was the properest — father had not the strength, and 'tis
with me at Mandvik that Sigrid and the boy are. Now have we
ordered things so that he will take his father's place among the
Ranheim kindred, and I could see on them all, I trow, that unwel-
come he will not be, the poor little lad, when presently he is sent
thither — "

"And your sister," asked Kristin, catching her breath, "where
will she be?"

Simon looked down at the ground.

"Father will have her home to Dyfrin now," he said in a low
voice.

"Simon! Oh, have you the heart to let this be — ?"

"You sure can see," he answered, without looking up, "how
great a gain it is for the boy to be taken into his father's kindred
from the very first. Halfrid and I would gladly have them both
with us. No sister could have been more faithful and loving
towards another than Halfrid was to Sigrid. None of her kindred
have been hard to her — believe not that of us. Not even father —
though this thing has made of him a broken man. But see you not?
— unrighteous had it been if any of us had set ourselves against
that which gives the innocent boy his father's name and heritage."

Kristin's babe let go the breast. The mother drew the clothes
quickly over her bosom, and pressed the little one to her, trem-

bling. He gulped contentedly a couple of times, and slobbered over himself and his mother's hands.

Simon glanced over at the two, and said with a sort of smile:

" You had better fortune, Kristin, than befell my sister."

" Aye — surely it must seem to you no righteous fate," said Kristin softly, " that I am called wife and my son is true-born. For had I been left with a fatherless bastard, I had been rightly served — "

" I had deemed that the worst tidings I could hear," said Simon. " I wish you naught but good, Kristin," he said in a lower voice.

Soon after, he asked her of the road. Northward he had journeyed by ship from Tunsberg, he said, " I must ride on now and see to it that I overtake my man — "

" Is it Finn that you have with you? " asked Kristin.

" No, Finn is wedded now; he is with me no longer. Do you remember him still? " asked Simon, with a little gladness in his voice.

" Is he a fair child, Sigrid's boy? " asked Kristin, looking at Naakkve.

" I hear them say so. To me one babe in arms looks much like all others," answered Simon.

" Then I trow you have no children yourself," said Kristin, and could not forbear to smile.

" No," he answered shortly. And thereupon he bade farewell and rode away.

When Kristin set out again, she had the child on her back no longer. She bore it in her arms, pressing its face into the hollow of her neck. She could think of naught else but Sigrid Andresdatter.

But *her* father could never have done it. Lavrans Björgulfsön ride out to beg for his daughter's base-born child part and lot with its father's kindred! — never could he have done it. And never, never would he have had the heart to take her babe from her — tear a little being out of his mother's arms, tear him from her breast, with her milk still on his innocent lips. My Naakkve, no, *he* would never have had the heart — if 'twas righteous ten times over, my father would never have done it. . . .

But she could not drive a picture from her mind. A troop of riders vanishing northward through the gorge, where the Dale grows narrow and the mountains crowd together, black with pinewoods. Cold gusts come from the river that rushes thundering over the great rocks, ice-green, foaming, with here and there black pools. He that should fall over there would be hurled from rock to rock and crushed straightway — Jesus, Maria —

Then she saw the fields at home at Jörundgaard of a clear summer night — saw herself running down the path to the little green clearing in the alder-brake by the river — where they were used to wash clothes. The river ran with a changeless harsh roar among the great stones of its shelving bed — Lord Christ, I cannot do aught else —

Oh, but father had never had the heart to do it. Not if it were never so right. When I prayed, prayed on my bare bended knees: Father, you must not take my child from me —

Kristin stood on Feginsbrekka and saw the city lying below her in the golden sunlight. Beyond the river's broad shining curves lay brown houses with green turfed roofs, dark domes of leaves in the gardens, light-hued stone houses with pointed gables, churches that heaved up black shingled backs, and churches with dully gleaming leaden roofs. But above the green land, above the fair city, rose Christ's Church,* so mighty, so gloriously shining, 'twas as though all things else lay prostrate at its feet. With the evening sun blazing full upon its breast and on the shining glass of its windows, with towers and giddy spires and golden vanes, it stood pointing up into the bright summer heavens.

Around lay a country-side green with summer, bearing worshipful great manors on its slopes. Outside again the fjord stretched wide and bright, with shadows drifting upon it from the great summer clouds that rose over the shining blue hills beyond. The cloister-holm, low among plashing wavelets, lay like a green garland, white-flowered with its stone houses. So many ships' masts out in the roadstead, so many fairest houses —

Quite overcome, sobbing, the young woman flung herself down before the cross by the wayside, where thousands of pilgrims had lain before her, thanking God for that helping hands were stretched out towards human souls on their journey through this fair and perilous world.

The bells were ringing to Vespers in churches and cloisters when Kristin came into Christ's churchyard. She dared to glance for a

* See Note 5.

moment up at the church's west front — then, blinded, she cast down her eyes.

Human beings had never compassed this work of their own strength — God's spirit had worked in holy Öistein, and the builders of this house that came after him. Thy Kingdom come, Thy will be done on earth as it is in heaven — now she understood the words. A reflection of the glory of God's kingdom witnessed in these stones that His will was all that was fair. Kristin trembled. Aye, well might God turn in wrath from all that was foul — from sin and shame and uncleanness.

In the galleries of the heavenly dwelling stood holy men and women, so fair that she dared not look upon them. Lovely unwithering tendrils of eternity wound silently upwards — broke into leaf on tower and spire, and blossomed in stone monstrances. Over the midmost door hung Christ upon His cross, Mary and John the Evangelist stood by His side, and they were white as though fashioned out of snow, and gold glinted on the white.

Three times she walked around the church, praying. The mighty wall-masses with bewildering riches of pillars and arches and windows, the glimpses of the huge slopes of the roof, the tower, the gold of the spire far up in the skyey spaces — Kristin sank under her load of sin.

She trembled when she kissed the hewn stone of the portal. In a lightning flash she saw the dark carven wood round the church-door at home — that she had kissed with childish lips after her father and mother. . . .

She sprinkled holy water over the child and herself — and thought of the time her father used to do this, when she was small. With the child pressed tight in her arms, she went forward up the church.

She went as through a forest — the columns were furrowed like ancient trees, and in through the forest flowed the light, many-hued and clear as song, from the pictured windows. High up above her, beasts and men sported among the stone leafage, and angels played — and yet far, dizzily far higher, the vaulting soared, lifting the church towards God. In a hall that lay to one side, worship was being held at an altar. Kristin sank down on her knees by a pillar. The singing cut into her like a too strong light. Now she saw how low she lay in the dust. . . .

Pater noster. Credo in unum Deum. Ave Maria, gratia plena. She had learnt her prayers by saying them after her father and mother before she understood a word — longer since than she could remember. Lord Jesus Christ! Was there ever woman so sinful as she — ?

High under the triumphal arch, uplifted over the people, hung Christ the Crucified. The stainless Virgin that was His mother stood gazing in deathly anguish up at her innocent Son, suffering a death of torment like an evil-doer.

And here knelt she, with the fruit of sin in her arms. She pressed the child to her — he was fresh as an apple, red and white as a rose — he was awake now, and lay looking up at her with his clear sweet eyes. . . .

Conceived in sin. Borne under her hard evil heart. Drawn from her sin-polluted body, so fair, so whole, so unspeakably lovely and fresh and pure. The undeserved mercy broke her heart asunder; she knelt, crushed with penitence, and the weeping welled up out of her soul as blood flows from a death-wound.

Naakkve, Naakkve, child of mine — God visiteth the sins of the fathers upon the children. Knew I not that? — Ah, yes, I knew it. But I had no mercy in my heart for the innocent life that might be wakened in my womb — to be accursed and condemned to torment for my sin —

Repented I my sin, when I bore you within me, my beloved, beloved son? Oh, no, 'twas not repentance. — My heart was hard with anger and evil thoughts in the hour when I first felt thee move, so little and so defenceless. — *Magnificat anima mea Dominum. Et exaltavit spiritus meus in Deo salutari meo* — thus she sang, the gentle Queen of all women, when she was chosen out to bear Him that was to die for our sins. — I called not to mind Him that had power to take away the burden of my sin and my child's sin — oh, no, 'twas not repentance, I but feigned me lowly and wretched, and begged and begged that the commands of righteousness be broken; for that I could not bear it if God upheld His law and chastened me according to the Word that I had known all my days —

Oh, aye, now she knew it. She had thought that God was such an one as her own father, that St. Olav was as her father. She had thought all the time, deep in her heart, that when her punishment grew to be heavier than she could bear, then would she meet, not with justice, but with compassion. . . .

She was weeping so that she could not rise when the people stood up during the worship. She lay on, crouched in a heap over her child. Near her there were other folk that did not rise — two well-dressed peasant women with a young boy between them.

She looked up towards the choir. Behind the golden grated doors St. Olav's shrine gleamed in the darkness, towering high behind the altar. An icy-cold shuddering ran through her. There lay his holy body awaiting the day of resurrection. Then would the lid fly open, and he would arise. With his axe in hand he would stride down this mighty church; and up from the paven floor, up from the earth outside, up from every graveyard in Norway's land would the dead yellow skeletons arise. — They would be clothed upon with flesh and would muster themselves round their King. They that had striven to tread in his blood-marked footsteps, and they that had only sought him that he might help them with the burdens of sin and sorrow and sickness that here in life they had bound on themselves and their children. Now they throng around their lord and pray him to lay their needs before God. Lord, hearken to my prayer for this folk, which I held so dear that I would rather suffer outlawry and need and hatred and death, than that man or maid should grow up in Norway and not know that Thou diedst to save all sinners. Lord, Thou who didst bid us go out and make all the peoples Thy disciples — with my blood did I, Olav Haraldssön, write Thy Evangel in the Norse tongue, for these my poor freedmen. . . .

Kristin shut her eyes, sick and dizzy. The King's countenance was before her — his flaming eyes saw to the bottom of her soul — she trembled under St. Olav's glance.

Understand you now, Kristin, that you need help?

Aye, Lord King, now I understand it. Sore need is mine that thou support me, that I may not turn me from God again. Be with me, thou Chief of His people, when I bear forth my prayers, and pray thou that I be granted mercy. Holy Olav, pray for me!

Cor mundum crea in me, Deus, et spiritum rectum innova in visceribus meis.

Ne projicias me a facie tua —

Libera me de sanguinibus, Deus, Deus salutis meæ —

The worship was at an end. Folks were leaving the church. The two peasant women, who had knelt near Kristin, rose up. But the boy between them did not rise; he began to move over the pavement by pressing the knuckles of his clenched hands on the flags and jerking himself along like a young unfledged crow. He had tiny legs, twisted up close under his body. The women walked so as to hide him as well as they could with their garments.

When they were out of sight, Kristin threw herself down and kissed the church-floor where they had passed by her.

Somewhat doubtful and at a loss, she stood by the entrance to the choir, when a young priest came out of the grated door. He stopped before the red-eyed young woman, and Kristin told him her errand, as well as she might. At first he scarce understood. She brought out the golden garland and held it toward him.

"Oh, are you Kristin Lavransdatter, Erlend's wife, of Husaby — ? " He looked at her with a little wonder; her face was all swollen with weeping. "Aye, aye, your brother-in-law, Master Gunnulf, spoke of this, aye — "

He led her out into the sacristy, took the wreath, and unwrapped the linen cloth from around it and looked at it; then he smiled a little.

"Aye, you will understand, I trow — there must be witnesses and such-like by — you cannot give away such a precious thing, mistress, as though 'twere a piece of buttered bread — but I can take it in charge, meanwhile — 'tis like you would not choose to bear it about with you in the city. — Oh, pray Canon Arne to be so good as to come hither," he said to a church-servant.

"Your husband should be with you too, I trow, rightly. But it may be Gunnulf has some letter from him. . . .

"You are to be brought before the Archbishop himself — was it not so? Else 'tis Hauk Tomassön who is Pœnitentiarius — I know not whether Gunnulf has talked with Lord Eiliv — but you must come hither to matins to-morrow, and you can ask for me after lauds; I am called Paal Aslakssön. Him " — he pointed to the child — " you must leave in the hostel. You are to sleep in the Sisters' hostel at Bakke, I mind me your brother-in-law said."

Another priest came in, and the two spoke together awhile. The first opened a little locker in the wall, took out a pair of scales, and weighed the wreath, while the other wrote in a book. Then they laid the wreath away in the press and locked it.

Canon Paal was about to lead her out — but he asked first if she wished he should lift her son up to St. Olav's shrine.

He took the boy with the sure, somewhat careless deftness of a priest used to holding babies at baptism. Kristin went with him into the church, and he asked if she, too, would not fain kiss the shrine.

I dare not, thought Kristin; but she followed the priest up the steps to the high platform whereon the shrine was set. There came, as it were, a great blinding white light before her eyes when she approached her lips to the golden tabernacle.

The priest looked at her a moment, fearing she might fall down in a swoon. But she rose again to her feet. Then he let the child's forehead touch the sacred shrine.

Canon Paal went with her to the church-door and asked if she were sure she could find her way to the ferry. Then he bade her good-night — he had spoken all the time in smooth, dry fashion, like any other mannerly young courtier.

— It had begun to rain a little, and a breathing of sweet scents came balmily from the gardens and from the street, which was fresh and green like a country courtyard, save for the strips worn bare by the coming and going of people and carts.

Kristin sheltered the boy from the rain as best she could; he was so heavy now, so heavy that her arms were numb and dead from bearing him. And he whimpered and cried unceasingly — like enough he was hungry again.

His mother was deadly tired — from the day-long walking, and from all the weeping and the vehemency of her emotion in the church. She was cold — and the rain grew heavier; the leaves of the trees glanced and shivered under the spattering drops. She threaded her way through the lanes and came out on an open place, where she could see ahead to where the river ran broad and grey, its surface pitted like a sieve by the falling drops.

There was no ferry-boat. Kristin spoke to two men who had taken shelter under the floor of a warehouse that stood on piles at the water's edge. They said she must go out to the landing-place — the nuns had a house there, and there was a ferry-man.

Kristin dragged herself up again across the open place, footsore and wet and weary. She came to a little grey stone church — behind it lay some houses inside a fence. Naakkve was shrieking wildly, so that she could not go into the church. But the sound of singing came to her through the unglazed window-openings, and she knew the antiphon: *Lætare Regina Cæli* — Rejoice, thou Queen of Heaven — for He whom thou wert chosen to bear — is arisen even as He said. Alleluja!

It was the song the Minorites sang after complin. Brother Edvin had taught her this hymn to the Lord's Mother when she watched by his bed those nights when he lay in mortal sickness at home with them at Jörundgaard. — She stole into the churchyard, and, standing by the wall with her child upon her arm, she said it softly over to herself.

— Nothing, Kristin, that you could do could turn your father's heart from you. 'Tis therefore you must give him no more cause for sorrow. . . .

— Even as Thy nail-pierced hands were outstretched upon the Cross, O dear Lord of heaven — howsoever far away a soul had strayed from the straight path, yet were the nail-pierced hands stretched out towards it yearningly. Naught was needful save this one thing: that the sinful souls should turn them to those open arms, freely, as a child goes to its father, not like thralls hunted home to their cruel master. Now she understood how hateful sin was. Again there came that pain in her breast; as though her heart would break asunder in penitence and in shame at her unworthiness of the mercy shown her. . . .

Close in to the church-wall there was a little shelter from the rain. She sat down upon a grave-stone and began to still the child's hunger. Now and then she bent forward and kissed the little down-covered head.

She must have fallen asleep. Someone touched her shoulder. A monk in orders and an old lay brother with a sexton's spade in his hand stood before her. The barefoot friar asked if she sought lodging for the night.

It flashed across her — she would far rather abide here to-night with the Minorites, Brother Edvin's brethren. And it was so far to Bakke — and she was sinking with weariness. Then the monk bade the lay brother bring this woman to the women's hostel — " and give her a little calamus-wash for her feet — she is footsore, I see."

It was close and dark in the women's hostel — it stood without the fence, out by the lane. The lay brother brought her water to wash with and a little food, and she sat by the hearth and tried to quiet the child. 'Twas plain that Naakkve felt it in his food that his mother was worn out and had fasted that day; he wept and whimpered between-times while sucking at her exhausted breasts. Kristin took mouthfuls of the milk the lay brother had brought her; she tried to spirt it from her mouth into the child's — but the little knave clamoured loudly against this new fashion of taking in food, and the old man laughed and shook his head. She must drink it herself, he said, then the boy would soon get the good of it. . . .

At last he went away. Kristin crept up into one of the uppermost box-beds, close under the roof. From it she could reach up to open a trap in the roof — and there was need, for there was a sickening smell in the hostel. Kristin opened the trap — the rain-washed air of the bright cool summer night streamed in about her. She sat in the short bed with her head and neck propped against the wall-timbers — there were so few pillows in the bed. The boy slept on her lap. She had meant to shut the trap again in a while, but she fell asleep unawares.

Far on in the night she awoke. The summer moon shone in, pale and honey-yellow, across the child and her, and lit up the wall over against them. And she was ware of a figure in the midst of the stream of moonlight, hovering between floor and roof-tree.

He was clad in an ashen-grey frock — he was tall and stoop-backed. Now he turned his old, old furrowed face towards her. It was Brother Edvin. He smiled, and his smile was unspeakably tender — a little roguishly merry, just as when he lived on earth.

Kristin wondered not at all. Humble, happy, full of hope and trust, she looked at him, awaiting that which he might say or do.

The monk laughed and held up an old, heavy fur mitten towards her — then he hung it on the moonbeam and left it hanging there. And then he smiled still more, nodded to her, and melted away.

THE MISTRESS OF HUSABY

PART TWO

HUSABY

HUSABY

I

ON a day early in the new year, there came to Husaby some unlooked-for guests. They were Lavrans Björgulfsön and old Smid Gudleikssön from Dovre, and with them were two gentlemen whom Kristin knew not. And Erlend wondered much to see his father-in-law come in their company — they were Sir Erling Vidkunssön of Giske and Haftor Graut of Godöy — he had not deemed that Lavrans knew these men. But Sir Erling made things clear, telling how they had met together at Nes of Raumsdal, where he had sat with Lavrans and Smid on the Court of Six * that had at last set at rest the dispute between Sir Jon Haukssön's distant heirs. Lavrans and he had fallen into talk of Erlend, and the thought came to Sir Erling that, since he had an errand to Nidaros, he would like well to wait upon the folks at Husaby, if Lavrans would join him and sail north with him. Smid Gudleikssön said, laughing, that he had all but bidden himself to come along with them:

" For I was fain to see our Kristin again — the fairest rose of the Norddal. And then, methought my kinswoman, Ragnfrid, would be beholden to me if I kept an eye on her husband, to mark what weighty counsels he may be hatching with wise and mighty men like these. Aye, your father has other gear to guide this winter, my Kristin, than making the rounds of the manors with us, drinking out Yule till the Fast comes in. Now have we sat at home on our lands in peace and quiet all these years, and looked, each man of us, to his own affairs. But now would Lavrans have all us King's-men of the Dale ride in a troop to Oslo at hardest midwinter — now are we to counsel the great lords of the King's council in the King's behoof — they are ruling things so ill for the poor boy in his nonage, says Lavrans — " †

Sir Erling looked somewhat ill at ease. Erlend raised his eyebrows.

* See Note 6.   † See Note 7.

" Are you of these counsels, father-in-law — the calling of the great meeting of King's-men? "

" No, no," said Lavrans. " I but ride to the meeting like the other King's-men in the Dale, since we have been summoned thither — "

But Smid Gudleikssön took up his tale again: 'Twas Lavrans that had talked him over — and Herstein of Kruke, and Trond Gjesling and Guttorm Sneis and others that had had no mind to go. . . .

" Nay but — is it not your wont in these parts to bid stranger folk step into the house? " asked Lavrans. " Let us try now whether Kristin brews as good ale as her mother! " . . .

Erlend looked doubtfully, and Kristin wondered greatly.

" What is this, father? " she asked a little later, when he was with her in the little hall, whither she had brought the child to be out of the strangers' way.

Lavrans sat dancing his grandson on his knee. Naakkve was ten months old now, a great child and comely. Already, at Yule-tide, he had been put into short coats and hose.

" Never before, father, have I known you put in your word in matters such as this," went on his daughter. " I have ever heard you say that for the welfare of the land in peace and war and of his subjects 'twas best the King should take order, and the men whom he called to his side. Erlend says that this venture is the work of the nobles in the south — they would set aside Lady Ingebjörg and the men her father gave her for councillors — and seize again for themselves such power as they had when King Haakon and his brother were children. But you yourself were used to say that the kingdom suffered great scathe from their rule — "

Lavrans whispered to her to send away the child's nurse. When they were alone, he asked:

" Whence came these tidings to Erlend — was it from Munan? "

Kristin told him that Orm had brought with him a letter from Sir Munan when he came home in the autumn. She did not tell that she herself had read it to Erlend — he had no great skill in making out writing. But in the letter Munan had made bitter complaint that every man in Norway that bore arms on his shield deemed now that he understood the governing of the realm better than the men who had stood at King Haakon's side when he lived; and they held that they knew better what was for the young King's welfare than the high-born lady, his own mother. He had warned Erlend that should there be signs that the Norwegian nobles had a mind to copy what the Swedes had done at Skara in the summer — hatch plots against Lady Ingebjörg and her old and tried councillors — the lady's kinsmen must hold them ready, and Erlend should come south and meet Munan at Hamar.

"Said he not, too," said Lavrans, pushing his finger in under Naakkve's fat chin, "that I was one of the men that set their faces against the unlawful call to arms that Munan brought with him up the Dale — in our King's name?"

"You!" said Kristin. "Met *you* Munan Baardssön in the autumn?"

"I did so," answered Lavrans. "And we agreed not over-well together."

"Spoke you of me?" asked Kristin, quickly.

"No, little Kristin," said her father, laughing a little. "I cannot call to mind that at that meeting your name came up between us. — Know you if it is so that your husband has a mind to fare south and seek out Munan Baardssön?"

"I believe it," said Kristin. "Sira Eiliv drew up a letter for Erlend not long since — and he spoke of having soon to journey south."

Lavrans sat silent a little, looking at the child groping with its fingers about his dagger-hilt and trying to bite the rock-crystal set in it.

"Is it true that they would take away the rule of the realm from Lady Ingebjörg?" asked Kristin.

"The lady is as old as you, or thereabouts," answered her father, still smiling a little. "None would take from the King's mother the honour or the power whereto she is born. But the Archbishop, and certain of the friends and kinsmen of our King that is gone, have called a meeting to take counsel how the lady's power and honour and the good of the people of the land can best be guarded."

Kristin said low:

"I can see well, father, that you are not come to Husaby this time only to see Naakkve and me."

"Not only for that," said Lavrans. Then he laughed: "And I can see, my daughter, that this likes you but little!"

He laid one of his hands over her face and stroked it up and down. 'Twas so he had been used to do, ever since she was a little girl, whenever he had been scolding or teasing her.

Meantime Sir Erling and Erlend sat up in the armoury — so was called the great storehouse that lay north-east of the courtyard, near by the main gate. It was high as a tower, having three stories; in the uppermost was a chamber with loopholed walls, and there were kept all the arms that were not in daily use on the manor. King Skule had built this house.

Sir Erling and Erlend had fur cloaks on, for it was bitter cold in the room. The guest walked about, looking at the many fair weapons and suits of armour that Erlend had inherited from his mother's father, Gaute Erlendssön.

Erling Vidkunssön was a somewhat short man, slightly built, though a little plump, but he bore himself lightly and with grace. Fair of face he was not, though his features were well formed — but his hair was of a light reddish hue, and his eyelashes and brows were white — the eyes themselves, too, were of the palest blue. That Sir Erling was deemed, none the less, to be a well-looking man may have been because all knew he was the richest knight in Norway. But 'twas true he had a rarely winning, quiet way with him. He was of excellent understanding, well-taught and rich in knowledge, and since he never strove to show off his learning, but always was found ready to hearken to others, he had gotten him the name of one of the wisest men in the land. He was much of the same age as Erlend Nikulaussön, and they were of kin to each other, though far off, through their kinship to the Stovreim house. They had known each other long, but there had been no close friendship between the two men.

Erlend sat on a great chest, talking of the ship he had built him last summer; 'twas a thirty-two-oar ship, and he deemed that she would prove a rarely swift sailer and easy steerer. He had had two shipwrights down from the Nordland, and had himself overseen the work along with them.

"Ships are among the few things whereof I know a little, Erling," said he; "and you shall see, 'twill be a fair sight to watch *Margygren* cleave the sea-surges — "

"*Margygren** — 'tis a fearsome, heathenish name you have

* *Margygren* = the *Sea-Ogress*.

given your ship, kinsman," said Sir Erling, laughing a little. " You mean to sail south in her, then? "

" You are as holy as my wife, I see — she too says 'tis a heathenish name. Aye, she likes not the ship either; but she is inland-bred — she cannot endure the sea."

" Aye, she seems right holy and fine and gracious, your lady," said Sir Erling, courteously. " As one might look she should be, seeing the kindred she comes of."

" Aye — " Erlend laughed a little. " There goes by no day when she hears not mass. And Sira Eiliv, our priest whom you saw, reads aloud for us from godly books — 'tis what he likes best, next to ale and dainty dishes, to read aloud. And poor folk come hither to Kristin for counsel and help — they would be fain to kiss the hem of her garment, I well believe — my men I scarce know again any more. She is likest one of the ladies of whom there is record in the holy sagas that King Haakon forced us to sit and hear the priest read aloud — mind you? — when we were pages together. Much is changed at Husaby since last you were my guest, Erling. — I marvel, indeed, that you would come to me as things were then," he said, a little after.

" You spoke of the time when we were pages together," said Erling Vidkunssön, with a smile that became him well. " We were friends then, were we not? In those days all of us, Erlend, deemed that you would go far in this land of ours — "

But Erlend only laughed: " Aye, so did I deem too."

" Can you not sail southward along with me, Erlend? " asked Sir Erling.

" My purpose is to journey by land," answered the other.

" A toilsome journey for you — over the mountains in mid-winter," said Sir Erling. " 'Twould be pleasant if you would bear Haftor and me company."

" I have given my promise to certain other folks to go with them," answered Erlend.

" Doubtless you go along with your father-in-law — aye — that is but reason."

" No, not so — I know so little of these men from the Dale he is to ride with." Erlend sat silent a little. " No, I have promised to look in on Munan at Stange," he brought out hurriedly.

" You can spare yourself the pains," answered the other. " Munan is gone down to his estates in Hising, and it may well be that 'twill be long ere he come north again. Is it long since you heard from him? "

" 'Twas at Michaelmastide — he wrote to me from Ringabu."

" Aye — but you know what befell in the Dale this last autumn? " asked Erling. " You know it not? Sure you must know that he rode round himself to the Wardens, all about Mjös and up the Dale, with letters, bearing that the farmers should bring forth full levies of horses and supplies — one horse to every six farmers — and the nobles and freeholders should send horses, but might stay at home themselves? *Have* you not heard of this? And that the men of the northern Dale denied to furnish this levy when Munan came with Eirik Topp to the Thing at Vaage? Moreover, 'twas Lavrans Björgulfsön that led the opposers — he challenged Eirik, if there were aught outstanding from the lawful levies, to gather it in in lawful wise; but he called it high-handed oppression on the people to crave war-taxes from the farmers only to help a Danish man to wage war on the Danish King. And, should our King call for service from his King's-men, said Lavrans, he should find them ready enough to come to tryst with good weapons and horses and men-at-arms — but *he* sent not from Jörundgaard so much as a he-goat in a hempen halter, except the King craved he should ride it himself to the muster. Nay, now, know you not this? Smid Gudleiksson says that Lavrans had promised his farmers he would pay their levy-fines * for them, if need should be — "

Erlend sat in wonderment:

" Did Lavrans so? Never have I heard before that my wife's father meddled in aught but what might touch his own estates, or his friends' — "

" 'Tis not often he does so, like enough," said Sir Erling. " But so much I could see, when I was in at Nes with him, that when Lavrans Björgulfsön speaks his mind in a matter, he lacks not followers in plenty — for he speaks not except he know the business so well that his word can hardly be overthrown. Now, touching these supplies, 'tis said he has changed letters with his kin in Sweden — as you know, Lady Ramborg, his father's mother, and Sir Erngisle's grandfather were cousins, so that his kinsfolk there are many and worshipful. Quiet a man as he is, your father-in-law, he has no little power in the country-side where folks know him — though he use it not often."

* See Note 8.

" Aye, then do I understand why you seek his company, Erling,"
said Erlend, laughing. " I marvelled that you were grown such
hot friends."

" Marvel you at that? " answered Erling, unmoved. " A strange
man must be he that would not be fain to call Lavrans of Jörundgaard his friend. You, kinsman, would serve your turn better by
hearkening to him than to Munan."

" Munan has been like an elder brother to me ever since the day
I first went forth from my home," said Erlend, a little hotly.
" Never did he fail me when the pinch came. And if, now, a pinch
be come for him — "

" Munan will be safe enough," said Erling Vidkunssön, calmly
as before. " The letters he bore around were sealed with the Great
Seal of Norway — unlawfully, but that touches not him. True,
there is more — that which he was privy to, and attested with his
seal, when he was witness to the Lady Eufemia's betrothal — but
that can scarce be brought to light without touching one whom
we would not — Truth to tell, Erlend — I trow Munan can save
his own skin without your help — but you may harm yourself — "

" 'Tis the Lady Ingebjörg you aim at, I see well," said Erlend.
' I have promised our kinswoman to serve her both here and in
foreign lands — "

" And even so have I promised," answered Erling. " And I mean
to keep that promise — and so, I trow, does every Norseman that
served and loved our lord and kinsman, King Haakon. And the
best service that can be shown her is to part her from those councillors who counsel so young a lady to her own hurt and her son's."

" Believe you," asked Erlend in a low voice, " that you can compass *that?* "

" Aye," said Erling Vidkunssön firmly. " I believe it. And I trow
all believe it who hearken not to " — he shrugged his shoulders —
" evil-minded — and loose — talk. And that should we, the lady's
kinsmen, be the last of all to do."

A serving-maid lifted the trap-door in the floor, and asked if it
would suit them now that the mistress have the supper borne into
the hall. . . .

While the house-folk were still at the board, the talk ever and
anon kept glancing towards these weighty matters that were in
question. Kristin marked that both her father and Sir Erling tried

to hinder this; they turned the talk with news of wedding-bargains and deaths, strife among heirs, and dealings in farms. She was uneasy, though she scarce herself knew why. They had some errand of weight to Erlend, she could see. And though she would not own it to herself, she knew her husband so well now as to feel that, headstrong as he was, he might mayhap easily enough be turned aside by one who had a firm hand in a soft glove, as the saying went.

After the meal, the men moved over to the hearth and sat there drinking. Kristin settled down on the bench, took her broidery frame into her lap, and began plaiting the fringes. Soon after, Haftor Graut came across to her, laid a cushion on the floor, and sat on it at her feet. He had found Erlend's cithern, and he held it on his knee and sat thrumming on it and prattling. Haftor was a quite young man with yellow ringleted hair; most comely of face, but freckled beyond measure. Kristin soon marked that he was a most heedless talker. He had but just wedded richly; but he had grown weary at home on his estates, he said; 'twas therefore that he was going now to the meeting of the King's-men.

"But 'tis no more than reason that Erlend Nikulaussön bide at home," he said, and laid his head back on Kristin's lap. She drew a little aside, laughed, and said, if she mistook not, her husband too was minded to journey south — "whatever the cause may be" — she said, with an air of innocence. "There is so much unrest in the land these days; 'tis no easy thing for a simple woman to judge of such things."

"Yet 'tis a woman's simplicity that is most to blame for it," answered Haftor, laughing, and shifting nearer again. "Aye, so at least say Erling and Lavrans Björgulfsön — I would be fain to know what they mean by it. What think you, Mistress Kristin? Lady Ingebjörg is a good, simple woman — maybe she is sitting now, even as you are, plaiting silk with her snow-white fingers and thinking: hard-hearted would it be to deny her departed husband's trusty vassal a little matter of help towards bettering his fortunes — "

Erlend came over and sat by his wife; Haftor had to move a little to make room.

"'Tis such trumpery tales the dames hatch out in their lodging when their husbands are fools enough to take them with them to the assemblies — "

" Folks say, where I am from," said Haftor, " that there is no smoke without fire — "

" Aye, we have that byword too," said Lavrans — he and Erling had joined them — " yet was I cheated, Haftor, last winter — when I would have lit my lantern with a piece of fresh horse-dung." He sat himself down on the edge of the table. Straightway Sir Erling fetched Lavrans' beaker across and proffered it to him with a bow, then sat down near him on the bench.

" 'Tis not possible, Haftor," said Erlend, " that you can know, away north in Haalogaland, what Lady Ingebjörg and her councillors know of the purposes and undertakings of the Danes. I know not if you were not short-sighted when you set you up against the King's call for help. Sir Knut — aye, we may as lief call him by his name, 'tis he we all have in our thoughts — he seemed not to me to be the man to let himself be caught dozing on his perch. You folk dwell too far away from the great cauldrons to smell what is cooking in them. And, better timely ware than after yare, say I — "

" Aye," said Sir Erling. " Almost a man might say, they cook for us now in our neighbour's manor — soon will we Norsemen be most like folk living on a pittance from their heirs; they send us in at the door the porridge they have cooked in Sweden — eat it, if you would have meat! I deem that 'twas an error of our Lord, King Haakon — that, as it were, he moved the kitchen to an outskirt of the farm, when he made Oslo the first city of the land. Before, it lay midway of the farmplace, if we may keep to this way of speech — Björgvin * or Nidaros — but now there is none to rule in these parts but the Archbishop and chapter. — Aye, what say you, Erlend — you that are a Trönder, with all your goods and all your lordship in Trondheim here — "

" Aye, God's blood, Erling — if 'tis that you would be at — carry home the pot and hang it up at the right hearth-stone once again — "

" Aye," said Haftor. " All too long have we here in the north had to be content with a smell of singeing and a gulp of cold broth — "

Lavrans broke in:

" Thus it stands, Erlend — I had not taken it on me to be spokesman for the folk of our country-side at home, but that I had in my

* Bergen.

keeping letters from my kinsman, Sir Erngisle. So I knew none o
the men who bear rightful rule either in the Dane-King's or i
our King's realms have any thought of breaking the peace and
friendship between our lands."

"If you know who bears rule in Denmark now, father-in-law
I wot you know more than do most other men," said Erlend.

"One thing I know. There is *one* man whom none would se
bear rule, neither here nor in Sweden, nor in Denmark. And tha
was the drift of the Swedes' doings at Skara last summer, and tha
is the drift of the meeting we would now hold at Oslo — to mak
clear to all who have not yet understood it, that on this all pruden
men are at one."

By now they had all drunk so much that they were grown some
what loud-voiced — all but old Smid Gudleikssön, who sat nodding
in his chair by the hearth. Erlend cried out:

"Aye, you folks are so prudent that the devil himself canno
trick you! 'Tis no marvel you should be afeard of Knut Porse
You cannot understand him, you good gentry — he is not the ma
to be content to sit mumchance watching the days slip by and th
grass grow as God wills it. Fain would I be to meet that knigh
again; I knew him when I was in Halland. And naught would
have against it if I stood in Knut Porse's shoes."

"So much dared not *I* have said where my wife could hear me,"
said Haftor Graut.

But Erling Vidkunssön, too, was now well on in drink. He trie
to keep a hold on his courtly ways, but they slipped from hi
grasp:

"You!" said he, bursting into a great laughter. "You, kinsman
— Nay, Erlend!" He slapped the other on the shoulder and laughe
and laughed.

"Nay, Erlend," said Lavrans, bluntly; "there needs more fo
that than beguiling of fair ladies. Were there no more in Knu
Porse than that he can play the fox in the goose-pen, I trow w
gentlefolk of Norway were all too slothful to turn out of ou
houses to hunt him off — even were the goose our King's mothe
But whomsoever Sir Knut can beguile to play the fool for hi
sake, he himself plays no tricks that have not a meaning in them
He has his goal, and be sure that he takes not his eyes from it —

There was a pause in the talk. Then Erlend said, his eyes glit
tering:

" Then I would that Sir Knut were a Norseman."

The others sat silent a little. Sir Erling took a draught from his goblet, then said:

" God forbid — had we such a man among us here in Norway, I fear me there would quickly be an end of peace in the land."

" Peace in the land! " said Erlend scornfully.

" Aye, peace in the land," answered Erling Vidkunssön. " Bear in mind, Erlend — 'tis not we of the knighthood alone that own this land and live in it. To you 'twould mayhap seem sport if there should arise here a man greedy of adventure and of power like Knut Porse. So it was in bygone days that when a man raised revolt in this our land, 'twas ever easy for him to find followers from among the nobles. Either they would gain the upper hand and win titles and fiefs, or their kinsmen won and they were given grace for life and goods — aye, the record tells who lost their lives, but the more part saved their skins, whether things went so or so — the more part of *our* fathers, mark you. But the mass of the common farmers and the townsmen, Erlend — the working-folk that many a time had their dues wrung from them twice over in one year, and might be joyful, moreover, each time a troop had passed through the country-side without burning their farms and slaughtering their cattle — the common folk that had to suffer such unbearable burdens and oppressions — *they*, I trow, thank God and St. Olav for old King Haakon and King Magnus and his sons, who strengthened the laws and made the peace sure." . . .

" Aye, I well believe that you believe 'tis so." — Erlend threw back his head. Lavrans sat looking at the younger man — he was wide awake enough now, was Erlend. His dark vehement countenance was flushed red, his throat seemed to swell into an arch in the slender brown neck. Then Lavrans looked at his daughter. Kristin had let her work fall on her lap and was following the men's talk intently.

" Are you so sure that the peasants and the common folk think thus and praise so much the new order of things? 'Tis true they had hard times often — in the old days when kings and rival kings warred with each other through all the land. I know that they remember still the time when they must often take to the hills with cattle and wives and children, while their farms went up in flames all down the valleys. I have heard them speak of it. But I know that they remember somewhat else as well — that their own fathers were in the armies; not we alone played for power, Erling, the peasants' sons played too — and time and again they won our lands from us. 'Tis not when law rules in a land that the son of a Skidan * trull, that knows not his own father's name, wins a Baron's widow with her lands and goods, as did Reidar Darre — you deemed a son of his house a good enough match for your daughter, Lavrans, and now hath he wedded your lady's niece, Erling! But now law and justice rule; and — I know not how it comes, but I know that 'tis so — the peasants' land comes into our hands more and more, and that *with* the law — the more law and right rule, the quicker it goes, the quicker their power in the kingdom's affairs and their own slips from their hands. And, Erling, the common farmers know it too! Oh, no! be not too sure, good sirs, that the common folk have no yearnings back to that time when they might lose their farms by fire and by rapine — but they might also win by arms more than they can win by law."

Lavrans nodded:

" There is some truth in what Erlend says," he said in a low voice.

But Erling Vidkunssön rose:

" I can well believe it — that the common folk remember better the few men that rose from nothing and came to might and mastery in the time of the sword, than the numberless men that went under in black poverty and misery. And yet none were harder masters to the small folks than these first — I trow 'tis of them the byword was first made: none more unkind than kin. If a man be not born to mastery, he is ever a hard master — but if he have grown up in childhood amid serving-men and serving-women, 'tis far easier for him to understand that without the common folk we are in many a wise as helpless as children all our days, and that not only for the love of God, but quite as much for our own sake we should serve them on our part with our knowledge and guard them with our knighthood. Never yet has a kingdom stood except there were in it great men with the strength and the will to use their power to make sure the lesser folk's rights — "

" You could preach against my brother for a wager, Erling," said Erlend, laughing. " But my belief is that these stubborn Trönders liked us great folk better in the old days when we led thei

* The modern Skien.

sons to battle and foray, let our blood flow out over the deck-
planks mixed with theirs, and hewed rings in sunder and shared
the booty with our house-carls. — Aye, you see, Kristin, sometimes I sleep with one ear open when Sira Eiliv reads from his
great books."

"Goods that are won by unright come not down to the third
heir," said Lavrans Björgulfsön. "Have you not heard this, Erlend?"

"Surely have I heard it!" Erlend laughed aloud. "But seen it
I have not —"

Erling Vidkunssön said:

"So it is, Erlend, that few are born to be masters, but all are
born to serve; the right lord is the servant of his servants —"

Erlend clasped his hands together behind his neck and stretched
himself, smiling:

"Thereon have I never thought. And I deem not that my
tenants have any service to thank me for. And yet, strange though
it be, I trow they like me well." — He rubbed his cheek against
Kristin's black kitten, which had sprung up on his shoulder, and
now, arching its back, was walking, purring, around his neck.
"But my wife here — she is the most serviceable of ladies to all —
though in faith you have no cause to believe it — for our cans and
flagons are empty, Kristin mine!"

Orm, who had sat silent, following the men's talk, got up at once
and went out.

"The lady grew so weary she fell asleep," said Haftor smiling,
"and the fault is yours — 'twere liker you had left her in peace to
speak with me that have the wit to know how to talk to ladies."

"Aye, this talk has run on too long for you, I fear, mistress,"
began Sir Erling, in excuse; but Kristin answered with a smile:

"So indeed it is, sir, that I have not understood all that has been
said here to-night; but I bear it well in mind, and I shall have good
time to think over it hereafter." . . .

Orm came back with some maids bearing in more liquor. He
went round filling the cups. Lavrans looked sorrowfully at the
comely boy. He had tried to have some speech with Orm Erlendssön, but the boy was of few words, though his bearing was
mannerly and courteous.

One of the maids whispered to Kristin that Naakkve was awake
down in the little hall and was screaming terribly. On this the lady

of the house bade her guests good-night, and left the hall with her maids.

The men turned to the ale-cup again. Sir Erling and Lavrans changed glances now and again, and at last the knight said:

" There is a matter, Erlend, that I had a mind to speak of with you. 'Tis sure that a levy of ships will be called out from the lands around the fjord here and from Möre — folks in the north dread that the Russians will come again in strength in the summer and that without help they will not be strong enough to guard the land. This Russian feud is the first profit we have drawn from our sharing a King with Sweden — 'twould not be just that the Haalogalanders should be left to enjoy it all alone. Now, it so falls out that Arne Gjavvaldssön is too old and sickly — and there has been talk of naming you as chief of all the ships from this side of the fjord! How would that like you — ? "

Erlend smote one fist into the palm of the other hand — his whole face shone: " How would it like me — ! "

" 'Twill scarce be possible to raise any great force," said Erling, as though to sober him. " But we thought that, if you will, 'twere well you should set things in train with the wardens round about. — You know all this country well — and 'twas said among the Lords of the Council that mayhap you were the man best fitted to make somewhat of this matter. There are they that still remember that you won no small honour when you were warden of the Halland coast under Count Jacob — I mind myself that I heard him say to King Haakon he had been unwise to deal so harshly with a likely young fellow; he said there was the stuff in you for a trusty servant to your King — "

Erlend snapped his fingers. " Nay, now, never tell me *you* are to be our King, Erling Vidkunssön! Is this the plot you are hatching," he said, laughing loudly, " to make Erling King? "

Erling said, testily:

" Nay, Erlend, see you not that I speak now in all sadness — "

" God help us — were you jesting before, then? Methought you had spoken in sadness enough all the night. — Aye, aye, let us speak in sadness, then, kinsman — tell me all concerning this affair."

Kristin lay sleeping with the child by her breast when Erlend came down to the little hall. He lit a fir-root brand at the embers on the hearth, and looked at the two for a little while by its light.

So fair she was — and a fair child was he, too, their son. She was always so sleepy in the evenings now, Kristin — the moment she had laid her down and drawn her child close to her, both of them fell asleep. Erlend laughed a little and threw the stick back on to the hearth. Slowly he drew off his garments.

Northward in the spring with *Margygren* and three or four warships. Haftor Graut with three ships from Haalogaland — but Haftor was new and untried in such work, him 'twas like he could manage as seemed good to him. Aye, he saw well he could have things as he would, up there; for this Haftor looked not as though he were a coward or half-hearted. Erlend stretched himself out and smiled in the dark. He had thought to raise a crew for *Margygren* from Möre, outside the fjord. But both this country-side and Birgsi swarmed with stout bold young fellows — the finest choice of men was his. . . .

Not much more than a year since he was wedded. Child-bearing, penance and fasting, and now the boy first and the boy last, both day and night. Yet — she was the same young sweet Kristin — when he could get her to forget the prating priests and her greeding suckling for a little while. . . .

He kissed her shoulder, but she marked it not. Poor child, let her sleep — he had so much to think on to-night. Erlend turned him away from her and gazed out into the room at the little glowing spark on the hearth. Aye, maybe he should get up and cover up the embers — but he had no mind to. . . .

Memories of his youth came in shreds and snatches. A quivering ship's-stem standing as 'twere waiting a second for the oncoming wave — and the sea that came washing inboard. The mighty clamour of storm and waves. The whole vessel groaned in the press of the seas — the mast-head cut its wild curve on the flying clouds. 'Twas somewhere off the Halland coast. — Erlend lay overwhelmed — feeling the tears fill his eyes. He had not known, himself, how these years of idleness had irked him.

The next morning Lavrans Björgulfsön and Sir Erling stood at the upper end of the courtyard, looking at some of Erlend's horses that ran loose without the fence.

" — Methinks," said Lavrans, " should Erlend appear in this assembly, such rank and birth are his — since he is kinsman to the

King and the King's mother — that he must needs come forth among the foremost. Now I know not, Sir Erling, whether you deem you can be sure that his judgment in these affairs will not rather lead him to the other side. If Ivar Ogmundssön should try a countermove — Erlend has near ties, too, with the men who will follow Sir Ivar — "

"I have little thought that Sir Ivar will do aught," said Erling Vidkussön. "And Munan" — his lip curled a little — "*he* will be wise enough, I trow, to stay away — he knows that else it might well be made clear to all men how much or how little Munan Baardssön counts for." They both laughed. "And there is this to be thought on — aye, you know yet better than I, Lavrans Lagmandssön,* you who have kith and kin there, that the Swedish lords are loath to count our knighthood as the equals of theirs. It might seem needful, then, that we should let no man be lacking from among those we have richest and of highest birth — we can ill afford to let a man like Erlend have leave to sit at home, dallying with his wife and tending his farms — tend he them well or ill," he added, as he saw Lavrans' look.

Lavrans smiled slightly.

"But should you deem it unwise to press Erlend to come with us, I will let it be."

"Methinks, dear sir," said Lavrans, "that Erlend would do better service here, in his own country. As you said yourself — we look for no goodwill towards this levy in the parishes south of Namdalseid — whose folk deem they have naught to fear from the Russians. It might be that Erlend would be the very man to change folks' thoughts of the matter in some measure — "

"He hath such a cursed loose tongue," Sir Erling burst out.

Lavrans answered with a little smile:

"Maybe his kind of talk will be understood by many better than — more clear-headed people's speech — " They looked at each other again, and both laughed. "Howsoever that may be — he could sure do greater hurt should he go to the meeting and talk too loudly there."

"Aye, if so be that you cannot stay him."

"That can I at no rate do, when once he meets with birds of the flock he has been wont to fly with — my son-in-law and I are too unlike."

Erlend came up to them:

* See *The Bridal Wreath* (*The Garland*), p. 13.

"Have you had so much profit of the mass that you have no need of breakfast?"

"I heard not aught of breakfast — I am hollow as a wolf — and thirsty —" Lavrans caressed a dirty white horse he had been handling as he stood there. "The man that tends your farm-horses, son-in-law, I would drive off the place before I sat down to table, were he *my* man."

"I dare not, for fear of Kristin," said Erlend. "One of her maids is with child by him —"

"Nay, but count you that so great a deed in this country-side," said Lavrans, raising his eyebrows a little, "that you deem, because of it, you cannot be lacking him — ?"

"No, but see you," said Erlend, laughing, "Kristin and the priest will have them wed — and they will have me put him in the way of earning a living for himself and her. The girl would not, and her guardian would not, and Tore himself is none too willing — but they will not let me turn him out; she fears he would fly the parish. Then, too, there is Ulf Haldorssön to oversee him — when Ulf is at home —"

Erling Vidkunssön went to meet Smid Gudleiksson. Lavrans said to his son-in-law:

"Methinks Kristin looks somewhat pale in the day-time —"

"Aye," said Erlend, eagerly. "Can you not speak to her, father-in-law? — that boy of hers is sucking the very marrow out of her. I trow she will keep him at the breast till the third fast comes round, like any cottar woman —"

"Aye, she loves her son much," said Lavrans, with a little smile.

"Aye," Erlend shook his head. "They will sit for three hours — she and Sira Eiliv — and talk of it, should a little rash show on him here or there; and for every tooth he cuts, it seems to them a great miracle has come to pass. I have never known aught else but that children were apt to cut teeth; and methinks it had been a greater marvel if our Naakkve had had none."

2

THE YEAR after, one evening at the end of the Yule-tide festival, Kristin Lavransdatter and Orm Erlendssön came, quite unlooked-for guests, to Master Gunnulf's house in the city.

It had blown and sleeted the whole day since before noon, and now in the late evening a heavy snowstorm had come on. The two were thick with snow when they came into the room where the priest sat at the supper-board with his household.

Gunnulf asked, in some fear, whether there was aught amiss at home on the manor. But Kristin shook her head. Erlend was away from home, at a feast in Gelmin, she answered when the priest questioned; but she had been so tired, she could not go with him.

The priest thought how she had now ridden all the way into the city — her horse and Orm's were quite worn out, the last of the way they had scarce had strength to struggle through the snow-drifts. Gunnulf sent the two women of his household with Kristin — they were to get dry garments for her. They were his foster-mother and her sister — other women there were none in the priest's house. He himself cared for his brother's son. Meantime Orm was speaking:

" Kristin is sick, I trow. I said it to father, but he grew angry — "

She had been quite unlike herself in these last days, said the boy. He knew not what it was. He could not remember whether 'twas she or himself that had first thought of coming hither — oh, yes, 'twas she that had first spoken of how much she longed to come in to Christ's Church, and he had said that if that were so, he would go with her. So this morning, straightway after his father had ridden off, Kristin had said that now they would go. Orm had let her have her way, though he saw the weather was threatening — but he liked not the look in her eyes.

Gunnulf thought that neither did he like it, when Kristin now came in. Sorely thin she looked in Ingrid's black habit; her face was wan as bast, and the eyes were sunken, with blue-black rings beneath them — their glance was dark and strange.

It was more than three months since he had seen her — when he was at Husaby for the christening-feast. She had looked well then, as she lay in state in her bed, and she had said that she felt strong — it had been an easy delivery. So he had spoken against it when Ragnfrid Ivarsdatter and Erlend would have the child given to a foster-mother — while Kristin wept and begged that she might nurse Björgulf herself — the second son was called after Lavrans' father.

The priest asked, therefore, first after Björgulf — for he knew too that Kristin had not liked the nurse they gave the child to.

But she said that he was thriving well and Frida was fond of him, and tended him much better than any could have deemed she would. And Nikulaus? asked the uncle; was he as bonny as ever? A little smile came to the mother's face. Naakkve grew comelier and comelier every day. No, he spoke not much; but else he was ahead of his age in every wise, and so big — no one would believe he was in his second winter — Lady Gunna said so too.

Then she sat lost again. Master Gunnulf looked at the two, his brother's wife and his brother's son, sitting one on each side of him. They looked so weary and sorrowful, he grew sad at heart to see them.

Orm, indeed, seemed ever heavy of mood. The boy was fifteen years old now; he would have been the comeliest of youths, had he not looked so weak and ailing. He was well-nigh as tall as his father, but his form was all too slender and narrow of shoulder. In face, too, he favoured Erlend, but his eyes were a much darker blue, and the mouth under its first short black down was yet smaller and softer than his father's, and ever, when it was closed, a sad little furrow showed at its corners. Even Orm's narrow brown neck under his black curled hair looked strangely unhappy as he sat, stooping a little over his food.

Kristin had not sat at the board with her brother-in-law before in his own hall. The year before, she had been with Erlend in the city at the spring-tide Thing,* and then they lodged in this house, which Gunnulf had from his father — but the priest himself had lived then in the house of the Crossed Friars, as vicar for one of the canons. Now was Master Gunnulf parish priest of Steine; but he kept a chaplain in his charge, and himself oversaw the work of engrossing books for the churches of the Archbishopric, while the precentor, Eirik Finssön, was sick. Thus he lived for the time in his own house.

The hall was unlike the rooms Kristin was used to see. 'Twas a timber house, but in the midst of the eastern gable-wall Gunnulf had had built a great stone fire-place, such as he had seen in the southlands; a log fire burned between cast-iron dogs. The table stood along one of the long walls, and by the wall over against it were benches with writing-desks; before a picture of Mary Virgin burned a lamp of yellow metal, and near by stood frames filled with books.

* See Note 9.

Strange seemed the room to her and strange her brother-in-law, now she saw him sitting here at his board with his household, clerks and serving-men with a strange half-priestly look. There were some poor folk too — old men and a young boy with film-like thin red eyelids clinging tightly over the empty sockets. On the women's bench with the two old women-servants sat a girl with a two years' child in her lap; she swallowed down the meat hungrily, and stuffed the child's mouth till its cheeks seemed like to burst.

So it was that all the priests of Christ's Church fed the poor at eventide. But Kristin had heard that to Gunnulf Nikulaussön came fewer beggars than to the other priests, although — or because — he made them sit with him in his own hall and welcomed every beggar man as an honoured guest. They were given food from his own dish and drink from the priest's own casks. Therefore they came hither when they felt the need of a meat-meal — but else they would liefer go to the other priests, where they were given porridge and small ale in the kitchen.

And as soon as the scribe had said grace after meat, the poor folk made ready to depart. Gunnulf talked kindly to each one, asked if they would not lodge here for the night, or whether there were aught else they desired; but only the blind boy stayed. The girl with the child in special the priest asked to stay, and not take the little one out into the night; but she muttered an excuse and hastened out. Gunnulf bade a serving-man see to it that blind Arnstein was given ale and a good bed in the guest-house. Then he rose and cast a hooded cloak about him: " You are weary, I trow, Orm and Kristin, and would go to rest. Audhild will see to you — belike you will be asleep when I come from the church."

But Kristin begged that she might go with him. " 'Tis for that I am come hither," she said, fixing desperate eyes on Gunnulf. He bade Ingrid lend her a dry cloak, and she and Orm went with the little company that followed him from the house.

The ringing of the bells sounded as though they were right above their heads in the black night sky — the church was not many paces off. They dragged heavily through deep wet new-fallen snow. The weather was still now — now and then single flakelets of snow still floated down, shining faintly in the dark.

In deadly weariness Kristin tried to lean against the pillar she stood by; but the stone chilled her through. She stood in the dark church and looked up towards the lights of the choir. She could

not see Gunnulf up there. But she knew he sat there amidst the
priests, with his taper by his book — no, after all she was sure she
could not speak to him. . . .

To-night it seemed as though there could be no help found for
her anywhere. Sira Eiliv at home reproved her, that she took her
everyday sins so hardly — he said 'twas the lure of spiritual pride:
let her but be diligent in prayer and good works, and she would
have no time to brood so much over such things. " The devil is
no such fool as not to see then that your soul must needs escape
him at last, and he will no longer care to tempt you so much — "

Oh, no! 'Twas like the devil was none so sure that he must lose
her soul — But when she had lain here before, crushed by sorrow
for her sins, for the hardness of her heart, her unclean life and her
soul's blindness — then had she felt that the sainted King had taken
her in beneath the sheltering hem of his cloak. She had felt the
clasp of his strong warm hand on hers, he had pointed out to her
the light that is the source of all strength and holiness. St. Olav
had turned her eyes toward Christ upon His Cross — see, Kristin,
God's loving-kindness. — Aye, she had begun to understand God's
long-suffering love. — But since then she had turned her again
from the light, and shut her heart against it, and now was there
naught else in her soul but disquiet and wrath and fear.

Wretched, wretched was she. She had seen it for herself: such
a woman as she was had need of hard trials ere she could be healed
of her unloving spirit. And yet so rebellious was she that it seemed
her heart must break under the trials that had been laid upon her.
They were but small trials — but they were so many — and she so
rebellious.

— She had a glimpse of her stepson's tall slender form over on
the men's side —

She *could* not help herself. Orm she loved like a child of her
own; but 'twas not possible for her to grow to love Margret. She
had striven and striven, and tried to force herself to like the child,
ever since the day last winter when Ulf Haldorssön had brought
her home to Husaby. She deemed herself it was a fearful thing —
could she feel such misliking and wrath towards a little maid of
nine years old! And well she knew that in part it was that the child
was so strangely like her mother — she understood not Erlend,
he showed naught but pride that his little brown-eyed daughter
was so fair; never did the child seem to wake discomforting memories in her father. 'Twas as though Erlend had forgotten all that

concerned these children's mother. — But it was not *only* because Margret favoured her mother that Kristin misliked her. Margret would not endure to be taught by any; she was haughty and harsh to the serving-folk; untruthful was she too, and, with her father, a flatterer. She loved him not, as did Orm — it was ever to gain something that she clung to Erlend with kisses and caresses. And Erlend poured out gifts upon her and humoured all the little maid's whims. Orm liked not his sister either, she had seen that. . . .

It was pain to her to feel herself so hard and cruel that she could not look on at Margret's doings without anger and harsh judgment. But 'twas much more pain to see and hear the endless bickerings between Erlend and his eldest son. The pain was the keener because she saw that Erlend in his inmost heart had a boundless love for the boy — and he was unjust and rough towards Orm because he was at his wit's end to know what he should do with his son or how he could make his future sure. He had given his bastard children lands and goods — but it seemed unthinkable that Orm could ever make a farmer. And Erlend grew desperate when he saw how weak and sinewless Orm was — he would call his son rotten; strive fiercely to harden him; practise him, hours after hour, in use of heavy weapons that 'twas impossible the boy could wield; force him to drink himself sick in the evenings, and bring him back half dead from perilous and toilsome huntings. Beneath all this Kristin could see the anguish of Erlend's heart — he was wild with sorrow often, she saw, that this fine-grained and comely son of his was fit but for one place — and from that his birth barred him out. And thus had Kristin come to understand how little patience Erlend had when he must fear for one that was dear to him or feel pity for him.

She saw that Orm understood it too. And she saw that the youth's heart was torn between love of his father and pride in him — and scorn for the man's unreason when Erlend made his child suffer because troubles lay before them for which he and not the boy was to blame. But Orm had drawn close to his young step-mother — it was as though with her he breathed freely and felt lighter of mood. When he was alone with her, he would jest and laugh by times — in his still fashion. But Erlend liked not this — 'twas as though he misdoubted that these two might sit in judgment on his doings.

Oh, no; 'twas no easy lot for Erlend — no marvel that he was

sore and hasty in all that touched the two children. And yet —
She winced with pain still when she thought on it.

They had had the manor full of guests the week before. Now
when Margret came home, Erlend had had the loft at the lower
end of the hall, over the outer room and the closet, set in order for
a sleeping-room — it should be her maiden bower, he said — and
there she slept, with the maid whom her father had set to tend
and serve her; Frida slept there too, with Björgulf. But now, in
this press of Yule-tide guests, Kristin had made this loft a sleeping-room for the young men, and the two maids and the babe
must sleep in the serving-women's house. But since she had thought
Erlend would maybe not like that she should send Margret to
sleep with the serving-folk, she had made up a bed for her on one
of the benches in the hall, where the ladies and maidens were sleeping. Margret was ever loath to rise in the mornings; that morning
Kristin had waked her many times, but she had turned over again,
and still lay sleeping after all the others were up. Kristin must
needs have the hall cleared and made ready — the guests must have
their morning meal — and at length she quite lost patience. She
pulled the down pillows from under Margret's head, and took
away the coverings from above her. But when she saw the child
lying there naked on the fur rug, she threw over her the cloak
from her own shoulders. It was a piece of plain undyed wadmal
— she wore it only when she went to and from the kitchen and
storehouses to see to the service of the food.

Erlend came in at that moment — he had slept in one of the storehouse lofts with some other men, for Lady Gunna lay with Kristin in the great bed. When he saw what was towards he had fallen
into a fury. He had grasped Kristin by the arm so hard that the
marks of his fingers still showed on her flesh.

" Think you it is fit that this daughter of mine lie in straw and
wadmal? Margit is mine, see you, even though she be not yours —
what is not too good for your own children is none too good for
her. But since you have held up the innocent little maid to scorn
before these women, you must even make it good again before
their eyes — spread over Margit again what you took off her — ! "

True it was that Erlend had drunk heavily the night before,
and when that was so he was ever fretful next morning. And he
might well have thought that there was talk among the women
when they saw Eline's children. And he was thin-skinned and sore

in all that touched the esteem they were held in. — And yet —

She had tried to speak of it with Sira Eiliv. But here he could not help her. Gunnulf had said the sins she had confessed and done penance for, before Eiliv Serkssön came to be her father confessor, she need not name to him unless she saw that he must know them in order that he might judge and counsel in her concerns. So there was much that she had never told him, though she felt herself that thus she had come to seem in Sira Eiliv's eyes a better woman than she was. But yet 'twas so comforting for her to have the friendship of this good and pure-hearted man. Erlend mocked — but she had so much comfort from Sira Eiliv. With him she could talk as much as she would of her children; all the little things that she wearied Erlend to death with, the priest was ready to talk over with her. He had a way with little children, and good skill in their little troubles and sicknesses. Erlend laughed at her when she went herself to the kitchen and cooked dainty dishes to send to the priest's house — for Sira Eiliv was fond of good food and drink, and it pleased her to busy herself with such things and try her hand with what she had learnt from her mother or seen in the cloister. Erlend cared not what he ate, if one but let him have flesh-meat at all times, when 'twas not a fast. But Sira Eiliv came and talked and thanked her and praised her skill when she had sent him a spitful of young ptarmigans in wrappings of fine bacon, or a dish of reindeer's tongues in French wine and honey. And he counselled her with her garden, and got her cuttings from Tautra, where his brother was a monk, and from Olav's Cloister, where the prior was his good friend. And then he read to her, and he could tell her so many fair things of the life out in the great world.

But for the very reason that he was so good and so simple-hearted a man, 'twas often hard to speak to him of the evil she saw in her own heart. When she confessed to him how wroth she had been with Erlend for his behaviour in this matter of Margret, he had enjoined on her her duty to bear with her husband. But he seemed to deem that 'twas Erlend alone that had offended in speaking so unjustly to his wife — and that in the hearing of strangers. And Kristin, indeed, thought the like. But in her inmost heart she felt that she shared in the guilt; she could not make it clear, but it troubled her heart sorely.

Kristin looked up at the shrine, gleaming faintly golden up in the twilight behind the high altar. She had looked so surely that when she stood here once more, something should again befall her — some deliverance of her spirit. Again would a living spring well up in her heart and wash away all the unrest and fear and bitterness and doubt that filled it.

But to-night there was none that had patience with her. Have you not learnt it once already, Kristin — to bring your self-right-eousness forth into the light of God's righteousness, to hold up your heathenish and selfish desire in the light of love? 'Tis that you *will* not learn it, Kristin. . . .

But when last she knelt there, she had had Naakkve in her arms. His little mouth against her breast sent such warmth into her heart that it grew even as soft wax, easy for the heavenly love to re-fashion. And still she *had* Naakkve — he ran about the hall at home, so fair and so sweet that her breast ached if she but thought of him. His soft curly hair began to darken now — he would be black-haired like his father. And he was so bursting with life and naughti-ness. — She made beasts for him out of old bits of fur rug, and he threw them away and ran after them, racing the young hounds. And 'twould often end with the bear falling into the hearth-fire, and burning up with much smoke and an evil smell, while Naakkve stood howling and jumping and stamping, and then buried his head in her lap — all his adventures ended there as yet. The maids fought for his favour, the men caught hold of him and threw him up to the roof, whenever they came into the hall. Did the boy see Ulf Haldorssön, he ran at once and clung to the man's leg — Ulf had taken him out into the farm-place now and then. Erlend snapped his fingers to his son and set him on his shoulder for a moment — but his father was the one at Husaby that paid least heed to the boy. Though he *was* fond of Naakkve. Erlend *was* glad that he had two true-born sons now.

The mother's heart turned in her:

Björgulf they had taken from her. He whimpered now when she would have held him; and Frida put him straightway to her breast — the foster-mother watched over the boy jealously. But the new child she would never give away from her. They had said, her mother and Erlend, that she must spare her strength now, and so they took her new-born son and gave him to another woman. 'Twas as though she had felt a sort of vengeful joy at the thought that all that had come of this was that now she looked to have yet a third child before Björgulf was full eleven months old.

She dared not speak of it with Sira Eiliv, he would maybe only think that she was vexed that already she must go through all this again. But it was not that. . . .

From her pilgrimage she had come home with a deep awe in her soul — nevermore should this madness overmaster her. All summer through she had sat alone with her child down in the old hall, weighed in her mind the Archbishop's words and Gunnulf's sayings, been vigilant in prayer and penance, diligent in working to restore the neglected manor and to win her house-folk by kindness and thought for their welfare, eager to help and serve all around her so far as her hands and her power might reach. There had sunk over her a calm delicious peace. She upheld herself with thoughts of her father, with prayers to the holy men and women Sira Eiliv read of, and meditation on their courage and steadfastness. And with a heart tender with happiness and thankfulness she remembered Brother Edvin, as he had appeared to her in the moonlight that night. She had understood full well his message, when he smiled so gently and hung his mitten on the beam of moonlight. Had she but faith enough, she could grow to be a good woman.

When the first year of marriage was at an end, she had to remove back to her husband. She comforted herself, when she felt herself unsure — the Archbishop himself had enjoined upon her that in the life in common with her husband she should show her new heart. And indeed she strove with an eager care for his welfare and his honour. Erlend himself had said it: " It has come to pass, after all, Kristin — you have brought back honour to Husaby." Folks showed her so much kindness and respect — all seemed willing to forget that she had begun her wedded life a little over-hastily. Where housewives came together, she was taken into council; they praised her ordering of her home; she was fetched to be brideswoman and to be helper at births on the great manors, none made her feel that she was young and unskilled, and a new-comer to the country. The serving-folk sat on in the hall through the evening, even as at Jörundgaard — all had somewhat to ask their mistress of. It came over her, in a glow of joy, how kind folks were to her and that Erlend was proud of her. . . .

Then Erlend had gone to work to take order for the ship-levy from the harbours south of the fjord. He journeyed about the country, riding or sailing, and was busy with folk who came to him, and letters that were to be sent off. He was so young and glad and comely — the sluggish unjoyous air she had often seen upon him in former days seemed blown clean away from the man. He glittered new-wakened like the morning. He had little time to spare for her now — but she grew dizzy and wild again when he came near her with his smiling face and his venture-loving eyes.

She had laughed with him over the letter that had come from Munan Baardssön. The knight had not been at the meeting of the King's-men himself, but he scoffed at the whole affair, and most of all at Erling Vidkunssön's being made Regent. It seemed, said Munan, his first task was to give himself new titles — he would have folk call him High Steward now, 'twas said. Munan wrote of her father, too:

" The hill-wolf from Sil crept under a rock and sat mum. That is to say, your father-in-law took lodging with the priests of St. Laurentius Church and raised not his honeyed voice in the parleys. There in his keeping had he letters under the seals of Sir Erngisle and Sir Karl Turessön; if they be not yet worn to shreds, then must the parchment be tougher than the devil's shoe-soles. This also you must know: that Lavrans gave eight marks, pure silver, to Nonneseter. Like enough the man hath got it in his head that Kristin had not so wearisome a life there as of rights she should — "

She had, indeed, felt a pang of shame and pain, but yet she could not help laughing with Erlend. The winter and spring had passed over her in a whirl of mirth and gladness. Now and then a storm on Orm's account — Erlend knew not if he should take the boy north with him. It ended with an outburst at Easter-tide — that night Erlend wept in her arms; he dared not take his son aboard with him; he feared that Orm must needs come short in war. She had comforted him and herself — and the lad — maybe the boy would grow stronger as he grew in years.

The day she rode down with Erlend to the haven at Birgsi, she could not feel aught of fear or sorrow at his going. She was drunken, as it were, with him and his overflowing gladness.

She had not known herself then that already she was with child again. She had thought when she felt sick, 'twas but with the bustle over Erlend's going, with the unquiet times and drinking-feasts at home, and that she was worn out with suckling Naakkve. When she felt new life quicken within her, she had been — She had so looked forward to the winter, to going about in city and country-side with her fair and gallant husband — while yet she, too, was fair and young. She was so sure that in his Russian warfare Erlend would show he was fit for other things than wasting his name and fame and goods. She had thought to wean the boy in autumn — 'twas troublesome to take him and his nurse with her wherever she might go. — And now — no, she had not been glad, and she had told this to Sira Eiliv. Then had the priest rebuked her most sharply for her unloving and worldly spirit. And the whole summer she had passed striving to be glad and to thank God for the new child she was to bear, and for the good tidings that came to her of Erlend's worthy deeds in the north.

Then he came home just before Michaelmas. She had seen well that *he* was not overglad when he saw what was at hand. And that night he said it:

" Methought that when once you were mine — 'twould be like drinking Yule-tide every day. But it looks as though most of the time would be long fasts."

Each time she remembered it, a wave of blood flooded her face, as hotly as that evening when she had turned her from him, darkly flushed and tearless. Erlend had tried to make amends with love and kindness. But she could not forget it. The fire in her that not all her tears of penitence had had power to quench, nor her anguish for her sin to choke — 'twas as though Erlend had trod it out with his foot when he said those words.

Late at night, the service over, they sat before the chimney-place in Gunnulf's hall, he and Kristin and Orm. A flagon of wine, with some small goblets, stood on the edge of the fire-place. Master Gunnulf had asked more than once if his guests would not to rest now. But Kristin begged that she might sit on.

" Mind you, brother-in-law," she asked, " I told you once that our priest at home counselled me to give myself to a cloister, should father not consent that Erlend and I should wed."

Gunnulf glanced swiftly across at Orm. But Kristin said with a little sick smile:

" Think you this grown youth knows not that I am a weak and sinful woman? "

Master Gunnulf answered softly:

" Had you a call to the life of the cloister, then, Kristin? "

" God might sure have opened my eyes, when once I was come into His service."

" Mayhap He deemed your eyes had need to be opened to understand that you should be in His service wheresoever you may be. Husband, children, house-folk at Husaby have surely need that a trusty and patient serving-woman of God go about among them and care for their welfare. . . .

" Surely that maid weds best who chooses Christ to her bride-groom and gives herself not into the power of any sinful man. But a child that hath already sinned — "

" ' I would have had you come to God, wearing your garland,' " whispered Kristin. " So said he to me, Brother Edvin Rikardssön, of whom I have often told you. Think you the same — ? "

Gunnulf Nikulaussön nodded:

" — Though many a woman has raised herself up out of a life of sin with such strength and steadfastness that we now may safely pray for her intercession. But this befell more often in the days gone by, when she was threatened with torture and the stake and red-hot pincers, if she avowed herself a Christian. I have oft-times thought, Kristin, that 'twas easier then to tear oneself free from the bonds of sin, when it could be done thus by might and main at a single wrench. Even though mankind is so corrupted — yet does courage still dwell by nature in many a breast — and 'tis cour-age that oftest drives on a soul to seek out God. And so 'tis like the tortures spurred on as many souls to steadfastness as they terrified to apostasy. But a young wildered child that is torn from the lusts of the flesh ere yet she has learned to understand what they bring upon her soul, is brought into sisterhood with holy maids who have given themselves up to watch and pray for them that sleep without in the world. . . .

" Would it might soon be summer! " he said of a sudden, rising up. The two others looked up at him in wonder.

" Aye — it came into my mind, the cuckoo's call from the hill-sides at Husaby of a morning. Always we heard it first from the eastward in the hills behind the houses, and then an answer came from far off in the woods round By — it sounded so sweet across the lake in the morning stillness. Think you not 'tis fair at Husaby, Kristin? "

" East-cuckoo is grief-cuckoo," said Orm Erlendssön in a low voice. " Methinks Husaby is the fairest place in all the world."

The priest laid his hands on his nephew's narrow shoulders for a moment:

" So thought I too, kinsman. 'Twas *my* father's home, too. The youngest son stands no nearer the heritage than do you, my Orm."

" When father lived with my mother, you were nearest heir," said the youth, softly as before.

" We cannot help it, I and my children, Orm," said Kristin, sorrowfully.

" I trow you will have marked, too, that I bear you no grudge," he answered quietly.

" 'Tis such a wide, open country-side," said Kristin in a little. " One sees so far around from Husaby — and the heaven is so — so wide. Where I am from, it lies like a roof right down upon the hill-tops. The Dale lies low in shelter, so hollow and green and fresh. The world is of so fit a size — not too great and not too narrow." She sighed and moved her hands in her lap.

" His home was there, the man your father would have wed you to? " asked the priest, and the woman nodded.

" Have you ever repented that you took him not? " he asked again, and she shook her head.

Gunnulf crossed the room and took a book from the case. He sat down again by the fire with it, opened its clasps, and turned over the leaves. He did not read from it, but sat with the book open in his lap.

" When Adam and his wife had defied the will of God, then felt they in their own flesh a power that defied their wills. God had created them, man and woman, young and fair, for that they should live in wedlock, and bring forth co-heirs with themselves of His bounteous gifts, the loveliness of the Garden of Paradise, the fruit of the tree of life and bliss everlasting. They needed not to feel shame of their bodies, for, as long as they obeyed God, their whole body and all their limbs were in the power of their will, even as are hand and foot."

Flushing red as blood, Kristin pressed her hands cross-wise under her breast. The priest bent towards her a little; she felt his strong yellow eyes on her bowed visage.

" Eve made spoil of that which belonged to God, and her husband received it, when she gave him that which by right was the possession of their Father and Creator. They would fain have made themselves His like — now they marked that they were like unto

Him first in this: as they had betrayed His lordship in the great world, so now was their lordship over the little world, the soul's house of flesh, betrayed. As they had played false to the Lord their God, so now would the body play false to its lord, the soul.

"Then did these bodies seem to them so ugly and hateful that they made them garments to hide them. First but a short apron of fig-leaves. But as they came to know more and more the inwardness of their own fleshly nature, they drew the garments up higher and higher, over the place of their hearts and over their backs so unwilling to bow. Until these last days when men clothe themselves in steel to the outermost joints of fingers and toes, and hide their faces behind the bars of the helm — so are strife and treachery spread abroad in the world."

"Help me, Gunnulf," prayed Kristin. She was white to the lips. "I — I know not my own will."

"Say then: 'Thy will be done,'" answered the priest softly. "You know that His will is that you should open your heart to His love, and that then must you love Him again with all your soul's might."

Kristin turned suddenly towards her brother-in-law:

"You know not — you — how dearly I loved Erlend. And my children — "

"My sister — all other love is but as an image of heaven in the water-puddles of a muddy road. Bemired must you needs be if you will dabble in them. But if you bear ever in mind that 'tis a mirroring of the light from yonder other home, then will you rejoice in its fairness, and will take good heed not to destroy it by stirring up the mud beneath — "

"Aye. But you, Gunnulf, are a priest — you have vowed to God to fly these — lures — "

"That have you too, Kristin — when you promised to forsake the devil and all his works. The devil's work is that which begins in sweet desire, and ends in them that work it stinging and biting each other like toad and asp. 'Twas that Eve learnt — that when she would have given her husband and her offspring that which was God's possession, then brought she them naught but outlawry and blood-guiltiness and death, that came into the world when brother slew brother on that first small field where thorns and thistles grew on the stone-heaps between the little plots — "

"Aye. But *you* are a priest," she said, as before. "You have not to strive every day to agree with another in your will " — she burst into tears — " to be patient — "

The priest said with a little smile:

" In that matter there is strife between soul and body in each mother's son. Therefore are bride-mass and wedlock appointed, that man and woman shall find help to live, wedded pair and parents and children and housemates, as trusty and helpful travelling companions on the journey towards the home of peace."

Kristin said low:

" Methinks it must be easier to watch and pray for them that sleep without in the world, than to strive against one's own sins — "

" It is so," said the priest sharply. " But think you, Kristin, there has lived one holy man that hath not had to defend *himself* against the enemy, at the same time as he strove to guard the lambs against the wolf — ? "

Kristin said, low and timidly:

" I had thought — they that move from holy place to holy place and have command of all prayers and words of power — "

Gunnulf leaned forward, mended the fire, and remained sitting with his elbows on his knees:

" 'Twas six years ago, about this time of year, that we came to Rome, Eiliv and I and two Scots priests that we had come to know in Avignon. We had gone afoot the whole way. . . .

" We came to the city just before the Fast. At that time the folk in the south-lands hold great feastings and banquets — they call it *carnevale*. Then does wine, both red and white, run like rivers in the tavern-houses, and folks dance at nights without doors, and have torches and bonfires in the open places. It is spring in Italia then, and the flowers are blooming in meadows and gardens, and the women deck themselves with these, and throw roses and violets to the passers-by in the streets — they sit up in the windows, and they have carpets of silk and gold brocade hanging from the sills down over the wallstones. For all the houses are of stone down there, and the knights have their castles and strong places in the midst of the cities. Belike there is no town-law or market-peace in that city — for they and their serving-men fight in the streets till the blood runs down —

" There stood such a castle in the street where we dwelt, and the lord who ruled there was named Ermes Malavolti. It shadowed all the narrow lane where we lodged, and our chamber was as dark

and cold as a dungeon in a stone fortress. Often when we went out,
we must needs press close to the wall while he rode by, with silver
bells on his garments and a whole troop of armed followers, while
filth and rottenness splashed up from under the horses' hoofs — for
in that land the people do but cast all filth and sweepings without
doors. The streets are cold and dark and strait as rock-clifts — little
like the green roadways of our towns. In those streets they hold
races when the time of *carnevale* comes — send out wild Arab
horses to race against each other — "

The priest paused a little, then he went on:

" This Sir Ermes had a kinswoman dwelling in his house. Isota
was her name, and she might well have been Isold the Fair herself.
Her skin and hair were of the hue of honey, but her eyes, I trow,
were black. I saw her time and again at a window —

" But outside the city the land is more waste than the most desolate uplands in our land, where nothing haunts but wolf and
reindeer, and the eagle screams. Yet are there towns and castles in
the mountains round about, and out on the green uplands a man
can see everywhere marks of folk who must have dwelt there in
days gone by; and great flocks of sheep and herds of white oxen
are grazing. Herdsmen armed with long spears follow them about
a-horseback, and these are perilous folk for wayfarers to meet, for
they murder and rob them and cast the bodies into holes in the
earth —

" But out upon these green plains lie the churches of pilgrimage."

Master Gunnulf was silent for a while:

" Maybe that land seems so unspeakably desolate because the
city lies in the midst of it, she that was queen over all the heathen
world and was chosen to be the bride of Christ. For now the
watchmen have forsaken the city, and in the whirl of feasting and
riot the town seems like a forsaken spouse. Ribalds have set up
their abode in the castle, where the husband is not at home, and
they have lured the lady on to wanton with them in their lust
and strife and bloodshed.* . . .

" But under the earth are treasures, dearer than all the treasures
the sun shines upon. There are the graves of the holy martyrs,
hewn out of the living rock beneath — and there are so many that
a man grows dizzy but to think of it. When one calls to mind how

* See Note 10.

many they are, the torture-witnesses that here have suffered death for the cause of Christ, one might deem that each grain of dust that whirls up from the hoofs of the ribalds' horses must be holy and worthy of worship." . . .

The priest drew a thin chain out from under his clothing, and opened the little silver cross that hung from it. Within was something black that looked like tinder, and a little green bone.

" Once we had been down in these passages all the day, and we had said our prayers in caves and oratories, where the first disciples of St. Peter and St. Paul had met together to hold mass. Then the monks, who owned the church where we went down, gave us these holy relics. 'Tis a little piece of such a sponge as the holy maids used to wipe up the blood of the martyrs withal, that it might not be lost; and a knuckle of a finger-joint of a holy man whose name God alone knows. Then did we four promise one another that we would every day call upon this holy one whose honour is unknown to men, and we took this nameless martyr to witness that we should never forget how quite unworthy we were to be rewarded of God and honoured of men, and ever remember that naught in the world is worthy to be desired save only His mercy." . . .

Kristin kissed the cross reverently and gave it to Orm, who did the like. Then Gunnulf said suddenly:

" I will give you this holy relic, kinsman."

Orm knelt on one knee and kissed his uncle's hand. Gunnulf hung the cross around the youth's neck.

" Would you not be fain to see these places, Orm? "

The boy's face lighted up in a smile:

" Yes — and I know now that some day I shall come thither."

" Have you never had a mind to be a priest? " asked Gunnulf.

" Yes," answered the boy. " When father has cursed these weak arms of mine. But I know not if he would like that I should be a priest. And then there is that you wot of," he said softly.

" For your birth a dispensation could be had, I trow," said the priest quietly. " Maybe, Orm, some day we might journey southward together, you and I — "

" Tell us more, uncle," prayed Orm softly.

" Aye, that will I." Gunnulf clasped the arms of the chair with his hands and looked into the fire.

" While I wandered there, seeing naught else but memorials of the blood-witnesses, and remembered the unbearable torments they had endured for Jesu name's sake, there came upon me a sore temptation. I thought of how the Lord had hung nailed to the Cross those six hours. But His witnesses had been tormented with unutterable tortures for many days — women saw their children tortured to death before their eyes, young tender maids had their flesh torn from their bones with iron combs, young boys were driven on the claws of wild beasts and the horns of mad oxen. . . . Then seemed it to me as though many of these had borne more than Christ Himself. . . .

"I brooded over this till I thought that my heart and my brain must break in sunder. But at last the light I had begged and prayed for came to me. And I understood that as these had suffered, so ought we all to have strength to suffer. Who would be so foolish that he would not willingly endure pains and torment, when this was the path that led to a faithful and steadfast bridegroom, who waiteth with arms stretched out and breast bloody and burning with love?

"For He loved mankind. And therefore did He die, as the bridegroom who hath gone forth to save his bride from the hands of robbers. And they bind him and torment him unto death, while he sees his dearest love sit feasting with his slayers, jesting with them and mocking his torments and his faithful love —"

Gunnulf Nikulaussön buried his face in his hands:

"Then did I understand that this mighty love upholdeth all things in the world — even the fires of hell. For if God would, He could take the soul by force — we should be strengthless motes in His hand. But He loves us as the bridegroom loves his bride, who will not force her, but if she yield not to him willingly, must suffer that she flee him and shun him. But I have thought, too, that mayhap no soul can yet be lost to all eternity. For every soul must desire this love, methinks, but it seems so dear a purchase to give up all other delights for its sake. But when the fire hath burnt away all stiff-necked and rebellious will, then at last shall the will to God, were it no greater in a man than a single nail in a whole house, remain in the soul unconsumed, as the iron nail is left in the ashes of a house burned down —"

"Gunnulf" — Kristin half rose — "I am afraid —"

Gunnulf looked up, with white face and flaming eyes:

"I too was afraid. For I understood that this torment of God's love can have no end so long as man and maid are born upon this earth and He must be fearful that He may lose their souls — so long as He daily and hourly giveth His body and His blood on a thousand altars — and there are men who scorn the offering. . . .

" And I was afraid to think of myself, that unclean had served at His altar, said mass with unclean lips and lifted Him with unclean hands — and methought I was even as the man who had brought his beloved to a house of shame and betrayed her — "

He caught Kristin in his arms as she sank down, and he and Orm bore the swooning woman over to the bed.

In a little she opened her eyes — sat upright and covered her face with her hands. She burst into a wild, wailing weeping:

" I cannot, I cannot — Gunnulf, when you speak, I see that I can never — "

Gunnulf took her hand; but she turned her face away from the man's wild pale visage:

" Kristin, never can you content you with any lesser love than the love that is between God and the soul —

" Kristin, look about you — see what the world is. You who have borne two children — have you never thought on this: that every child that is born is baptised in blood, and that every human being born into this world draws in with his first breath the scent of blood? Think you not that you, who are a mother, should fix all your intent on this: that your sons fall not back to that first baptismal pact with the world, but hold fast to the other pact they made with God when made clean by the waters of the font — ? "

She sobbed and sobbed.

" I am afraid of you," she said again. " Gunnulf, when you speak thus, I see well that never can I find my way onward to peace."

" God will find you," said the priest softly. " Be still, and fly not from Him who hath sought after you before you were conceived in your mother's womb."

He sat awhile there by the bedside. Then he asked quietly and calmly if he might wake Ingrid and ask the woman to come and help her to undress. Kristin shook her head.

Then he made the sign of the cross over her thrice, and, bidding Orm good-night, went into the closet where he slept.

Orm and Kristin drew off their clothes. The boy seemed sunk in fathomless thoughts. When Kristin had lain down, he came across to her. He looked at her grey-flecked face and asked if she would have him sit by her till she slept.

" Oh, aye — oh, no, Orm; you must be weary, you that are young. The night must be far spent — ."

Orm stood yet a little while.

" Seems it not strange to you? " he said of a sudden; " father and my Uncle Gunnulf — unlike as they are to each other — yet they are like, too, after a fashion — "

Kristin lay a little, thinking:

" Aye, maybe so — they are unlike other men."

Soon after, she fell asleep and Orm went over to the other bed. He stripped and crept in. There was a linen sheet below, and linen covers on the pillows. The boy stretched himself out at ease on the smooth cool couch. His heart beat, thrilled with the thought of these new adventures whereto his uncle's words had shown the way. Prayers, fasts, all the observances he had practised because he had been taught to — all grew new of a sudden — weapons in a goodly warfare that he longed for. Maybe he would be a monk — or a priest — if he could win dispensation for his birth in adultery.

Gunnulf's couch was a wooden bench with a sheet of skin spread over a little straw, and a single small pillow — so that he was forced to lie stretched straight out. The priest took off his frock, lay down in his underclothes, and drew the thin coverlid of wadmal over him. The little lighted wick, twined round an iron rod, he left burning.

His own words had left him crushed with unrest and fear. He was faint with yearning for that time gone by — would he never again find that bridal gladness of heart that had filled his whole being that spring in Rome?

It was when he had come back to Norway that strong disquietude took hold upon him.

There was so much to disquiet him. There were his riches. The great inheritance from his fathers — and the rich benefice. There was the path that he could see lying before him. His place in the Cathedral chapter — he knew that it was meant for him. If he forsook not all his possessions, to go into the cloister of the Preaching

Friars, take the vows, and bow himself under the rule — this was the life he desired — with but half a heart.

— And then when he was old enough and hardened to the fight — There were men in Norway's realm that lived and died in utter heathendom, or led astray by the false doctrines that the Russians put forth under the name of Christendom. The Lapps and the other half-wild folks that he could never cease to think on — was it not as though God had wakened in him this longing to fare forth to their land, bringing the Word and the Light — ?

— But he thrust the thought of this mission from him, on the plea that he must obey the Archbishop. Lord Eiliv counselled him against it. Lord Eiliv had harkened to him and spoken with him, showing him clearly that he spoke as to the son of his old friend, Sir Nikulaus of Husaby: "But you can never keep you within measure, you that come of the line of old Skogheim-Gaute's daughters, whether 'tis good or ill you have set your heart upon." The Lapp-folks' salvation he had much at heart himself, he said — but they had no need of a teacher that wrote and spoke Latin as well as his mother-tongue, and was learned in the Law no less than in Arithmetica and Algorismus. Sure it was that he had been given learning that he might use it. "And to my mind 'tis uncertain whether you have been granted the gift of speaking to the poor and simple peoples up north."

Ah, but in that sweet spring his learning had seemed to him no more to be held in reverence than the learning every little maid gets from her mother — to spin and brew and bake and milk — the teaching every child needs that it may do its work in the world.

Gunnulf stood up. On one end-wall of the closet hung a great crucifix, and in front of it was a great flat stone upon the floor.

He knelt down upon the stone and stretched his arms out sidewise. He had used his body to endure this posture, so that he could kneel thus by the hour, still as stone. With eyes fastened on the crucifix he awaited the comfort that came to him when he could lose himself wholly in contemplation of the Cross.

But the first thought that came into his mind now was this: had he the will to part with this crucifix? St. Franciscus and his brethren had crosses that they joined together themselves out of branches of trees. He should give away this fair Rood — to the church at Husaby he might give it. Peasants, children and women that came thither to mass — they might well be strengthened by feeding their eyes with such a visible picture of the Saviour's lovely mildness in His Passion. Simple souls like Kristin — For himself it should not be needful.

Night after night he had knelt with close-shut senses and limbs benumbed, till he saw the vision. The hill with the three crosses against the sky. Yonder cross in the midst, which was destined to bear the Lord of earth and heaven, trembled and shook, it bent like a tree before the storm, affrighted that it should bear that all too precious burden, the sacrifice for the sins of all the world. The Lord of the Tents of Storm held it in, as the knight curbs his charger, the Chief of the Castle of Heaven it bore to battle. Then was made manifest the wonder that was the key to deeper and ever deeper wonders. The blood that ran down the Cross for the remission of all sins and the boot of all sorrows, that was the visible miracle. By this first wonder the soul's eye could be opened to behold the yet darker mysteries — God that descended unto earth, and became the Son of a Virgin and Brother to mankind, that harried hell, and stormed with his booty of souls set free up to the blinding sea of light, wherefrom the world hath issued and whereby the world is upholden. And towards those bottomless and eternal deeps of light his thoughts were drawn up, and there they passed into the light and vanished, as a flight of birds passes away into the glory of the evening sky.

Gunnulf did not move until the church-bell rang for matins. All was still when he passed through the hall — they slept, Kristin and Orm.

Out in the pitch-dark yard the priest tarried a little. But none of his house-folk came to go with him into the church. He required not that they should go to worship more than twice in the day's round; but Ingrid, his foster-mother, well-nigh always bore him company to matins. This morning it seemed she, too, slept. Aye, she had been late up the night before —

All that day the three kinsfolk spoke but little together, and of naught but small matters. Gunnulf looked weary, but he talked jestingly of this and that. " Foolish were we yester-evening — we sat there as sorrowful as three fatherless children," he said once; and told of some of the many merry little haps that befell here in

Nidaros — with the pilgrims and such folk — which the priests jested over among themselves. An old man from Herjedal had had errands here for all the folks of his parish, and got the prayers all mingled together — things would have looked but ill in the parish, it came into his head after, if St. Olav had taken him at his word!

Late in the evening Erlend came in, dripping wet — he had sailed in to the city and it was blowing hard again. He was raging, and fell upon Orm at once with furious words. Gunnulf listened awhile in silence; then:

" When you speak so to Orm, Erlend, you are like our father — as he used to be when he spoke to you — "

Erlend went silent at once. Then he flung round:

" Well I wot, so witlessly did I never bear myself when I was a boy — make off from the manor, a sick woman and a whelp of a boy, in a snowstorm! Else 'tis not much to brag of, Orm's manfulness, but you see that at least he fears not his father! "

" You feared not your father either," said his brother, smiling.

Orm stood up before his father, saying naught and striving to seem careless.

" Aye, you can go," said Erlend. And then: " I am nigh sick of the whole affair at Husaby. But one thing I know — this summer shall Orm fare with me northward — then I trow we will lick this pet lamb of Kristin's into shape. — He is not a bungler, either," he went on eagerly to his brother. " He shoots with a sure aim — and a coward he is not — but ever is he cross-grained and mopish, and 'tis as though he had no marrow to his bones — "

" Nay, if you berate your son often as you did but now, 'tis no marvel if he mope," said the priest.

Erlend changed his tone, laughing as he said:

" For that matter, I had often to suffer worse things from father — and God knows that I moped not much for that. But let that be — now I am come hither, let us even be merry for Yule, since Yule it is. Where is Kristin? — What was it she had to speak of to you now, again? "

" I believe not that she had aught to speak of with me," said the priest. " She had set her heart on hearing mass here at Yule."

" She might well make shift with those she hears at home, methinks," said Erlend. " But 'tis pity of her — as things are going, all youth is being worn away from her." He struck one hand against

the other. " I see not how the Lord can think we have need of a
new son every year — "

Gunnulf looked up at his brother:

" What — ! Nay, I know not what our Lord may deem that you
two need. But what Kristin needs most, I trow, is that you be
kind to her now — "

" Aye, like enough she does," said Erlend in a low voice.

The next morning Erlend went to the day-mass with his wife.
They were bound for St. Gregory's Church — Erlend heard mass
there always when he was in the city. The two walked alone; and
down the street, where the snow lay swept up into drifts, heavy
and wet, Erlend led his wife by the hand fairly and courteously.
He had not said a word to her of her flight from home, and he
had been friendly to Orm after the first storm.

Kristin walked quiet and pale, with head a little bent; the long
black fur cloak with the silver clasps seemed to weigh down her
slight thin body.

" Would you that I should ride with you homeward — and let
Orm sail with the boat? " said the man, to say somewhat. " Maybe
you would scarce care to cross the fjord? "

" No — you know that I like not to go on boats — "

It was calm now, and the weather mild — every moment a load
of heavy, wet snow would fall from the trees. The skies hung low
and dark-grey above the white town. There was a greenish-grey
watery tinge on the snow, and the houses' timber walls and the
fences and tree-trunks showed black in the damp air. Never,
Kristin thought, had she seen the world look so cold and wan and
faded. . . .

3

Kristin sat with Gaute on her lap, gazing from the little hill north
of the manor. The evening was so fair. The lake lay below her
bright and still, mirroring the hills and the farms of By, and the
golden clouds in the sky. It had rained earlier in the day, and the
smell of leaves and earth rose strongly up. The grass on the meadows below must be knee-deep already, and the fields were hidden
with the spears of corn.

Sounds came from far to-night. Now the pipes and drums and fiddles struck up again, down on the green at Vinjar — up here the sounds came so sweetly to the ear.

The cuckoo would fall into long spells of silence, and then send forth its call once and again from far off in the southern woods. And in all the groves round about the manor the birds whistled and sang — but in scattered notes and softly, for the sun was still high.

The home cattle came tinkling and lowing out of the pasture above the courtyard gate.

" See, see — my Gaute will get his milk soon," she babbled to the child, lifting him up. The boy, as was his wont, laid his heavy head down on his mother's shoulder. Now and then he clung closer to her — and Kristin took it for a sign that he *did* take in somewhat of her petting and her prattle.

She walked down to the houses. Before the door of the hall, Naakkve and Björgulf were running about, and trying to coax back the cat, which had fled from them up on to the roof. But in a moment they set to work again with the broken dagger they owned in common, digging deeper the hole they had made in the earthen floor of the outer room.

Dagrun came into the hall with goat's milk in a wooden pail, and the mistress gave Gaute ladleful after ladleful of the warm drink. The boy grunted angrily when the serving-woman spoke to him, and struck out at her and hid himself against his mother's breast when the woman would have taken hold of him.

" Yet methinks he comes on better," said the byre-woman.

Kristin lifted the little face in her hand — it was yellow-white like tallow, and the eyes were always weary. Gaute had a great, heavy head and thin, strengthless limbs. He would be two years old a week after Lawrence Mass, but as yet he could not set foot to ground, and he had but five teeth and could not speak a word.

Sira Eiliv said 'twas not rickets; for neither the alb nor the altar-books had availed. High and low, wherever he came, the priest sought for some remedy for this sickness that was come upon Gaute. She knew he remembered the child in all his prayers. But to her he could but say that she must bow in patience before the will of God. And she must give him plenty of warm goat's milk to drink. . . .

Poor, poor little boy of hers! Kristin hugged and kissed him when the woman was gone. So fair, so fair he was! She thought she saw he favoured her father's kindred — his eyes were dark grey and his hair flaxen white, thick, and soft as silk.

Now he began to whimper again. Kristin got up and walked about the room with him. Little and thin as he was, he grew heavy after a while — but Gaute would be content nowhere but in his mother's arms. So she bore him up and down the murky hall, crooning to him as she walked.

Someone rode into the courtyard, and Ulf Haldorssön's voice echoed loudly from the house-walls. Kristin came out to the doorway of the outer room, with the child in her arms.

"You must unsaddle your own horse to-night, Ulf, I fear — they are at the dancing — all the men. Shame it is you should be troubled, but you must forgive it — "

Ulf muttered testily as he unsaddled his horse. Naakkve and Björgulf pressed about him the while, and begged for a ride on the horse up to the garden-close.

"Nay, you must bide here with Gaute, my Naakkve — play with your brother and let him not cry while I am away in the kitchen — "

The boy looked glum. But in a moment he was down on all-fours, butting and lowing at the little one, whom Kristin had set down on a cushion at the door. The mother bent down and stroked Naakkve's hair. He was so good to his little brothers.

When Kristin came back to the hall bearing the great platter on her arms, Ulf Haldorssön sat on the bench playing with the children. Gaute was happy with Ulf, if his mother were but out of sight — but now he whimpered at once and reached out after her. Kristin set down the platter and took Gaute in her arms.

Ulf blew the froth off the newly-drawn ale, drank, and began eating from the small dishes on the platter.

"Are they out, all your maids, to-night?"

Kristin said:

"There are both fiddles and drums, and pipes too — a troupe of gleemen — come over from Orkdal from the bridal there. You may well believe, when they heard of it — they are but young girls after all — "

"You let them gad and frisk about their fill, Kristin. A man might think you were afraid 'twould be hard to find a wet-nurse here this autumn — "

Without thinking, Kristin smoothed her kirtle down over her slender waist. She had flushed darkly red at the man's words. Ulf laughed short and harshly:

"But if you will go about ever dragging Gaute with you, 'twill go with you as it went last year, I trow. . . . Come hither to your foster-father, boy, and you shall eat out of one dish with me." . . .

Kristin made no answer. She set her three small sons in a row on the bench by the other wall, and fetched a bowl of milk-porridge, and, for herself, a little stool. There she sat and fed them, though Naakkve and Björgulf grumbled — they would have had spoons to eat with themselves. One was four years old now, and the other nigh three.

"Where is Erlend?" asked Ulf.

"Margret had a mind to go to the dancing, so he went with her."

"'Tis well at least he hath wit enough to watch his own maid," said Ulf.

Again the wife said nothing. She undressed the children and put them to bed, Gaute in the cradle and the two others in her own bed. Erlend had resigned himself to have them there, since she had grown well of her great sickness the year before.

When Ulf was done, he stretched himself out on the bench. Kristin dragged the block-chair over to the cradle, fetched a basket of woollen yarns, and began winding balls of wool for her weaving, while she gently and softly rocked the cradle with her foot.

"Will you not go to rest?" she asked once without turning her head. "You must be weary, Ulf?"

The man rose, put some fuel on the fire, and came across to his mistress. He sat down on the bench over against her. Kristin saw he was not so worn out with hard living as he was wont to be when he had been some days in Nidaros.

"You ask not even what the tidings are from the city, Kristin," he said, leaning forward, elbows on knees, and gazing on her.

Her heart began to beat with fear — she understood from the man's looks and bearing that there must again be tidings that were not good. But she answered with a calm and gentle smile:

"You must tell me, Ulf; have you heard aught?"

"Oh, aye — " But first he brought his wallet and took out from it the things he had fetched for her from the town. Kristin thanked him.

" I see you have heard news in the city? " she asked a little after.

Ulf looked at his young mistress — then he turned his eyes to the pale child, asleep in the cradle.

" Does he always sweat so much in the head? " he asked, low, touching the hair gently where it was dark with damp. " Kristin, when you were wed to Erlend — the letter that was drawn out concerning the settlement of your goods — stood it not so that you should deal yourself at your will with the lands of his extra-gift and your morning-gift? "

Kristin's heart beat harder, but she spoke calmly:

" Aye, and so it is, Ulf, that Erlend has ever asked my counsel and sought my consent in all dealings with these lands. Speak you of the parcels of farms in Verdalen that he has sold to Vigleik of Lyng? "

" Aye," said Ulf. " Now has he bought Hugrekken * from Vigleik, so he will keep up two ships now, it seems. . . . And what are you to have, Kristin? "

" Erlend's part of Skjervastad, half a hide † in Ulfkelstad, and what he owns of Aarhammar," said she. " You sure did not believe that Erlend had sold those lands without my will and without making good their worth to me? "

" Hm." Ulf sat silent a little. " Yet will your incomings be less, Kristin. Skjervastad — 'twas there Erlend got hay last winter and released the rent to the farmer for three years — "

" 'Twas not Erlend's fault that we got no dry hay last year — I know, Ulf, you did all you could — but with all the misery there was here last summer — "

" Of Aarhammar he sold more than half to the Sisters of Rein convent, that time when he made ready to flee the land with you " — Ulf laughed a little — " or pledged it — 'tis the same thing with Erlend. Free from the King's levy — the whole of that is on Audun's shoulders, who holds the farm that now is to be called yours! "

" Can he not rent the land that is come under the convent? " asked Kristin.

" The Sisters' tenant on the neighbour farm hath rented it," said Ulf. " 'Tis a hard and an unsure task for tenants to make ends meet when the farms are split up as Erlend is busy doing."

Kristin was silent. She knew well enough it was true.

---

* Hugrekken = *The Valiant*.   † See Note 11.

" 'Tis ever quick work with Erlend," spoke out Ulf again. " His goods wane as swiftly as his household waxes."

As the woman made no answer, he spoke again:

" You will soon have many children, Kristin Lavransdatter."

" Yet none that I can spare," she answered in a voice that shook a little.

" Be not so afraid for Gaute — he will grow strong, I warrant him," said Ulf, in a low voice.

" It must be as God will — but 'tis long waiting."

He heard the hidden suffering in the mother's voice — a strange look of helplessness seemed to come upon the dark, heavy man.

" It avails so little, Kristin — much have you brought to pass here at Husaby, but if Erlend is to take the sea again with two ships — I believe not overmuch in peace coming in the north, and your husband is so little crafty that he knows not how to turn to his profit what he has won in these two years. Ill years have they been — and all through them you have been a sick woman. Should things go on in this wise, 'twill break your courage at last, young wife that you are. I have helped you all I could on the manor here — but this other thing — Erlend's unwisdom — "

" Aye," she broke in, " that God knows you have — you have been the staunchest kinsman to us, friend Ulf, and never can I thank you enough or repay you — "

Ulf stood up, lit a candle at the hearth, set it on the taper-holder on the table, and stood there with his back turned to his mistress. Kristin had let her hands sink into her lap — now she began again winding wool and rocking the cradle.

" Can you not send word home to your folks," asked Ulf softly, " so that Lavrans might come up too this autumn when your mother comes to you? "

" I had not meant to trouble my mother this autumn. She begins to grow old — and it befalls so often that I must lie in the straw that I can scarce ask her to come to me every time — " She forced a smile.

" But do it this time," answered Ulf. " And pray your father to bear her company — so that you may ask his counsel in these matters — "

" In this matter I will not ask my father's counsel," she said quietly and firmly.

" But Gunnulf, then? " asked Ulf in a little. " Can you not speak with him? "

" 'Twould not be seemly to trouble him with such things now," said Kristin as before.

" Mean you because he has withdrawn him into a cloister? " Ulf laughed mockingly. " Never did I mark that monks knew less of guiding goods and gear than other folks.

" If so be you will not take counsel of any, Kristin, then must you speak yourself with Erlend," he said, when she made no answer. " Think on your sons, Kristin! "

Kristin sat long in silence.

" You that are so good to our children, Ulf," she said at last, " methinks 'twere liker you should wed and have your own folk to care for than that you should go on here — plaguing yourself with Erlend's — and my — troubles."

Ulf turned towards the woman. He stood with his hands grasping the table-edge behind him and looked at Kristin Lavransdatter. Still was she as straight and slim and fair as ever, as she sat there. Her dress was of dark home-dyed woollen stuff, but the linen coif that lay around her still, pale face was fine and soft. The belt from which hung her bunch of keys was set with little silver roses. On her breast glittered two chains bearing crosses; the great one with gilded links hung down well-nigh to her waist — 'twas it she had had of her father. Above lay the thin silver chain with the little cross that Orm had prayed them to give to his stepmother and say that she should wear it always.

As yet she had arisen from each child-bearing fair as ever — only a little stiller, with the weight on her young shoulders a little heavier. A little thinner in the cheeks, the eyes a little darker and more sad under the broad white forehead, the mouth a little less full and red. But 'twas like her comeliness would be worn away ere she was many years older, if things went on as they were going. . . .

" Think you not, Ulf, it were happier for you if you settled down on your own farm? " she went on again. " You have bought twenty marks' worth more of Skjoldvirkstad land, Erlend said — you own nigh half the farm now. And Isak has but the one child — Aase is both comely and kindly, and a notable woman — and she seems to like you — "

" Yet will I not have her, if I must marry her," the man said gruffly, with a harsh laugh. "And Aase Isaksdatter is too good for — " His voice changed. "I never knew other father than a foster-father, Kristin — and I trow 'tis my lot that I shall have no children either but foster-children."

"Nay, I will pray Mary Virgin that you may have better fortune, kinsman."

"I am not so young, either. Five-and-thirty winters, Kristin," he laughed. "There wants not much but that I might be your father — "

"Nay, but then must you have sinned full early," answered Kristin, striving to speak lightly and laughingly.

"Would you not go to bed now? " asked Ulf soon after.

"Yes, in a little — but *you* must be weary, Ulf — you should go to rest."

The man bade her good-night quietly and went out.

Kristin took the candle from the board, and looked in by its light at the two boys sleeping in the box-bed. There was no matter on Björgulf's eyelashes — God be thanked for that. There had been fair weather for a while past. As soon as the wind came a little keen, or the weather was so rough that the children must play within by the hearth-fire, his eyes grew sore. She stood long looking at the two. Then she bent over Gaute in the cradle.

They had been as fresh and healthy as little birds, all her three young sons — until the sickness came to the country-side last summer. Folk called it the scarlet fever — it carried off children from the homes all around the fjord, so that 'twas a piteous thing to see or hear tell of. She had been granted grace to keep all hers — all her own. . . .

For five days and nights had she sat by the southern bed, where they lay, all three, with red spots over all their skin, and sick eyes that shunned the light — the little bodies fiery-hot. She sat with her hand under the coverlid patting the soles of Björgulf's feet, and sang and sang, till her slender voice was sunken to a hoarse whisper:

> Shoe, shoe, guardsman's steed —
> How can we shoe him best at need?
> Iron shoes are fitting for the guardsman's steed.
>
> Shoe, shoe, Earlie's steed —
> How can we shoe him best at need?
> Silver shoes are fitting for the Earlie's steed.

Shoe, shoe, King's own steed —
How can we shoe him best at need?
Gold shoes are fitting for the King's own steed.

Björgulf was the least sick and the most restless. If she stopped
singing but a moment, he would cast the coverlid off him at once.
Gaute was only ten months old — he was so deathly sick, she
deemed he could not live. He lay at her breast, wrapped in rugs
and furs, and had no strength to suck. She held him in one arm
and patted Björgulf's foot-soles with the other hand.

From time to time, when it chanced that all three slept for a little
space, she would lay herself down on the front of the bed beside
them, fully clothed. Erlend came and went, looking helplessly at
his three sons. He tried to sing for them, but they cared naught for
their father's mellow voice — 'twas their mother they would have
sing, though she had no singing-voice.

The serving-women hovered round and would have had their
mistress spare herself; the men came and asked tidings; Orm tried
to make sport for his little brothers. Margret Erlend had sent away
to Österdal, by Kristin's counsel; but Orm was set upon staying —
besides, he was grown up now. Sira Eiliv sat by the children's bed
when he was not out visiting his sick. Much toil and sorrow
stripped the priest of all the fat he had laid on at Husaby — it went
hard with him to see so many fair young children die. And some
grown folks died too.

The sixth evening all the children were so much better that
Kristin promised her husband that to-night she would take her
clothes off and go to bed — Erlend proffered to watch along with
the maids and call her if there were need. But at the supper-board
she saw that Orm's face was a fiery red — and his eyes shining with
fever. He said 'twas nothing — but suddenly he started from the
table and out. When Erlend and Kristin followed, they found
him vomiting in the courtyard.

Erlend threw his arms about him:

" Orm — my son — are you sick — ? "

" My head is aching so," moaned the boy, and let it sink heavily
on his father's shoulder.

And so that night they sat watching Orm. For the most part he
lay muttering in brain-sickness — he would shriek aloud and fight
the air with his long arms — it seemed as though he had ugly visions. What he said they could not understand.

And in the morning Kristin broke down. It proved that she had been with child again; now she miscarried, and afterward she lay sunk in a drowse, as though half dead, and then fell into a high fever. Orm had lain in his grave more than two weeks before she knew of her stepson's death.

She was so weak then that she scarce had strength to feel sorrow. She was so bloodless and faint that naught could come home to her keenly — it seemed to her that it was well with her now, as she lay there but half alive. There had been a dreadful time, when the women hardly dared touch her or do what was needed for cleanliness — but it all seemed part of her fevered wanderings. Now it was good to lie and be tended. Round her bed hung so many sweet-scented wreaths of mountain flowers to keep the flies away — folk had sent them down from the sæters, and they smelt so sweet, most of all when there was rain in the air. Erlend brought their children in to her one day — she saw that they were wasted by the sickness, and that Gaute knew her not again, but even that did not hurt her yet. She only felt that Erlend seemed ever to be by her.

He went to mass every day, and he knelt long praying by Orm's grave. The churchyard was by the parish church at Vinjar, but some of the little children of the house had been given burial in the chapel of ease at Husaby — Erlend's two brothers and a little daughter of Munan Bishopssön. Kristin had often felt pity for these little ones, lying all alone under the stone flags. Now had Orm Erlendssön found his last resting-place amongst these children.

It was while the others still feared for Kristin's life that the companies of beggars, which made into Nidaros as Olav's Wake drew nigh, came through the parish. 'Twas mostly the same mumpers, men and women, that came thither each year — the pilgrims were always open-handed to them, for it was held that the intercession of the poor availed much. And they had grown used to come round through Skaun in these years of Kristin's rule at Husaby, for they knew that there they would be given lodging for the night, food in plenty, and alms before they passed on their way. This time the serving-folk would have turned them away, since the mistress lay sick. But when Erlend, who had been away in the north the last two summers, heard that his wife had been wont to deal so lovingly with the beggars, he bade that they should be given lodging and entertainment even as they had had them of her. And in the morning he went himself among the beggars, helped to pour their liquor and bear round food for them, and gave them the almspennies himself, while he meekly begged them for their prayers for his wife. Many of the beggars wept when they heard that the gentle young woman lay at death's door.

Sira Eiliv had told her all this when she grew better. It was not till nigh on Yule-tide that she was strong enough to take up her keys again herself.

Erlend had sent word to her parents as soon as she fell sick, but then they were gone south to the wedding at Skog. Later they came to Husaby; she was better then, but so weary she was not fit to talk much with them. She was best pleased to have none but Erlend by her bedside.

Weak and chilly and bloodless, she crept for shelter into his health and strength. The old fire in her blood was gone, so utterly gone that she could not call to mind any more what it was like to love in such wise; but with it was gone the unrest and bitterness of the last years. It seemed to her that she was happy now — even though grief for Orm lay heavy on them both, and though Erlend knew not how afraid she was for little Gaute, yet was she happy with him now. She had understood how sorely he had feared to lose her. . . .

'Twas a nice and a hard matter, then, to have to speak to him now — to touch on things that might break the peace and the content that were between them.

She stood without before the door of the hall in the shining summer night when the house-folk came back from the dancing. Margret hung on her father's arm. She was clad and adorned more fittingly for a bridal feast than for a dance on the church-green, where all kind of folk come together. But the stepmother had quite given over making or meddling in the maid's upbringing. Erlend must guide his own daughter as he would.

They were thirsty, Erlend and Margret, and Kristin went to fetch ale for them. The girl sat awhile prattling — she and her stepmother were good friends, now that Kristin no longer tried to teach her. Erlend laughed at all his daughter's chatter of the dancing. But at last Margret and her maid went up to their loft to go to rest.

The man went on wandering up and down the hall — stretched

himself and yawned, but said he was not weary. He ran his fingers through his long black hair:

" There was not time for it, when we came from the bath-house — because of this dancing — I trow you must set to and cut my hair, Kristin — I cannot go about in this wise in the holy-days — "

Kristin made answer that it was dark — but Erlend laughed and pointed up at the smoke-vent — 'twas daylight again already. So she lit the candle again, bade him sit down, and spread a cloth over his shoulders. While she clipped, he shifted about ticklishly, and laughed when the scissors came near his neck.

She gathered the shorn hair carefully together and burnt it in the hearth-fire, and shook the cloth, too, over the fire. Then she combed Erlend's hair down smooth from the crown, and snipped with the scissors here and there where the edge was not quite even.

Erlend caught her hands as she stood behind him, held them together round his throat, and looked up at her with smiling face thrown backward.

" You are tired," he said then, letting go her hands and rising with a little sigh.

Erlend sailed to Björgvin when midsummer was but just past. He complained much because this time again his wife was unfit to bear him company — she smiled wearily; howsoever things had been, she said, she had not been able to leave Gaute.

Thus it came that Kristin was alone at Husaby again this summer. At least it was well that this year she looked not that the child should come till Matthews Mass; * 'twas doubly hard for both herself and for the ladies who came to tend her when it came at the busy harvest season.

She wondered whether things would go on thus ever. Times were not now as they had been when she was a girl. The Danish war she had heard her father tell of, and she remembered when he was from home on the war against Duke Eirik. 'Twas from that he had brought back the great scars on his body. But, all the same, at home in the Dales they seemed, as it were, so far from war — thither it would come nevermore — so, she felt, did all men think. Most of her memories were of peace, of her father dwelling at home, guiding his possessions, caring and taking thought for all of them.

* 21st September.

Now all the time there was unrest — all men spoke of contention and warlike levies and the government of the realm. In Kristin's mind it all went together with the picture of the sea and the coast, as she had seen them that single time when first she came hither to the north. Along the coast they came sailing, men that had their heads full of counsels and plans and counter-plans and deliberations, spiritual lords and laymen. Among these did Erlend belong, by his high birth and his riches. But she felt that he stood but half within their circle.

She pondered much on why it was that he stood thus, half without. What were his fellows' real thoughts of him?

When he was but the man she loved, she had never asked such questions. She had seen, indeed, that he was sudden and vehement, unthinking and ever apt to bear him unwisely. But then she had found excuses for all — had never troubled to think what his humour might bring down upon them both. When once they two had got leave to wed, all would be changed — so she had comforted herself. Sometimes she dimly felt that 'twas not till the hour when she knew they two had given life to a child that she had begun to think — what manner of man was Erlend, he whom folk called light-minded and unwise, a man in whom none could trust. . . .

She had trusted in him. She remembered Brynhild's loft; she remembered how the bond between him and that other had been cut asunder in the end. She remembered his dealings, after she was his lawfully betrothed bride. But he had held fast to her in despite of all rebuffs and abasements; and she had seen that, now too, he would not lose her for all the gold on earth. . . .

She could not but think of Haftor of Godöy. Ever, when they had met, he had been dangling about her with toying gallantry; but she had never troubled her for this. She deemed it was but his fashion of jesting. She could scarce believe aught else even now; she had liked the comely gamesome young man — aye, she liked him still. But that anyone could deem such things to be but a jest — no, that she could not understand.

She had met Haftor Graut again at the royal banquets at Nidaros, and he hung about her there too, after his wont. One evening he got her to go with him into a loft-room, and she lay down with him on a made-up bed that was there. At home in the Dales she could never have thought of doing aught of the kind — there 'twas no custom at the feasts for men and women to steal aside, thus alone, two and two together. But here all were used to it, and it seemed not that any found it unseemly — 'twas said it was a fashion of the knights and ladies in foreign lands. When first they came in, Lady Elin, Sir Erling's wife, lay on the other bed with a Swedish knight; she could hear that they were talking of the King's ear-ache — The Swede looked pleased when Lady Elin made a motion to get up and go back to the hall.

When she understood that Haftor meant in sober sadness what he prayed her for as they lay there talking, she had been so amazed that she seemed unable to be either afraid or greatly angered. Were they not, both of them, wedded, and had not both children by their wedded spouses? She felt she never could have fully believed before that such things happened. Even after all she herself had done and gone through — no; this she must have believed could not befall. Laughing and gay and coaxing had Haftor been with her — she could not bring herself to say he had tried to lure her astray; for that he had not been earnest enough. And yet it seemed he would have had her do the deadliest sin. . . .

He stepped down from the bed the moment she bade him begone — he had grown meek enough, but he seemed more amazed than beshamed. And he asked in sheer unbelief — did she truly dream that married folk were never unfaithful — ? Sure, she must know that few men could swear they had kept no paramours. Women, maybe, were somewhat better, but truly —

"Believed you then, too, when you were a young maid, all the priests preach of sin and suchlike?" he asked. "But then I understand not, Kristin Lavransdatter, how it could come to pass that Erlend had his will with you."

He had looked up into her face — and her eyes must have spoken, though not for much gold would she have talked with Haftor of this. For 'twas in a high singing voice of wonderment that he said:

"The like of this I had deemed was but a thing they told of — in songs and ballads — "

She had told no one of this; not even Erlend. He liked Haftor well. And truly it was fearful that there could be any folk as light-minded as Haftor Graut — but 'twas as though she could not feel that it touched her at all. Nor had he ever tried to be too free with her since — he but sat and stared when they met, his sea-blue eyes wide with wonderment.

No, if Erlend were light-minded, at least it was not in that way. And, she thought, *was* he so unwise? She saw that folk startled at things he said, and afterward laid their heads together over them. There was often much right and reason in what Erlend Nikulaussön put forth. 'Twas but that he never saw what the other great folk never lost from sight — the cautious heedfulness with which they kept watch on each other. Trickery, Erlend called it, and laughed his reckless laugh, which nettled folks somewhat but disarmed them in the long run. They too, would laugh then, and slap him on the shoulder, saying he might be sharp-witted enough, but short-witted he was for sure.

Then would he undo the work of his own words with wanton and malapert jesting. And folk would suffer much of that from Erlend. Dimly his wife felt — and was humbled by the feeling — why all men bore with his unbridled tongue. Erlend would flinch and give way the moment he met a man who stood firmly by his own judgment — even if, to Erlend, that judgment seemed folly, he would yet give up his own, whatever the matter might be, but would cover his retreat with fleering talk about the man. And folk were well content to know that Erlend had this timorousness of mind — reckless as he was of his own welfare, hungry for adventure, desperately in love with every peril that could be met by force of arms. After all, they felt, they need not be too much disquieted by Erlend Nikulaussön.

The year before, when the winter was well-nigh gone, the High Steward had been in Nidaros, and he had brought the little King with him. Kristin had been in the city for the great banquet in the palace. Still and stately she had sat in her silken coif, bearing her red bridal dress with all her richest adornments, amidst the most high-born ladies of the court. With watchful eyes she had followed her husband's doings among the men, watched and listened and pondered — even as she watched and listened and pondered wherever she went with Erlend, or whenever she marked that folk spoke of him.

One thing and another she had understood. Sir Erling Vidkunssön was willing to stake all on upholding the rule of Norway northward toward the Icy Sea, on guarding and securing Haalogaland. But the Council and the Knighthood were against him, and were loath to agree to any undertaking great enough to serve this purpose. The Archbishop himself and the priesthood of the archdiocese were not unwilling to stand by him with money help — this she knew from Gunnulf — but else all churchmen throughout the land were set against him, even though 'twas a war against God's enemies, heretics and heathens. And the great laymen worked against the High Steward, here in Trondheim at least. They had grown used to paying small regard to the words of the law-books and the rights of the Crown, and it liked them but little that Sir Erling stood so sharply in these matters for the spirit of his kinsman, King Haakon of happy memory. But it was not on this account that Erlend would not let himself be used, as she now understood the High Steward had meant to use her husband. With Erlend it was but that the other's grave and stately bearing wearied him — and he avenged himself by scoffing a little at his powerful kinsman.

Kristin thought she understood Erlend's footing with Sir Erling now. One thing was that the knight had had a sort of kindness for Erlend from their youth up; and then he had doubtless thought that, could he win over the high-born and valiant master of Husaby, who had gained some skill too in the craft of war from his service with Count Jacob — who at least knew more of war than most of his fellows, that had done naught but sit at home — he might thereby serve both his own plans and Erlend's welfare. But it had not fallen out as he planned.

Two summers had Erlend kept the sea till late autumn, wallowing in the seas that wash the long northern coast, and hunting the robbers' barks with the four small ships that followed his banner. He had come in for fresh meat to a new Norse settlement far north in Tana, just as the Karelians were hard at work plundering it — and, with the handful of men he had with him ashore, he had caught eighteen of the robbers and hung them to the roof-tree of the half-burnt barn. He had cut to pieces a band of Russians that was flying to the hills, and had burnt some enemy ships amid the outer skerries and destroyed their crews. The fame of his swiftness and daring had spread wide in the north; his Trönder and men of Möre loved their leader for his hardihood's sake and for his will to share all toil and all hardness with his men. He made friends both among the small folk and among the young sons of the great manors north in Haalogaland, where before the people had well-nigh grown used to thinking they must guard their coasts unaided.

Yet could not Erlend be of service to the High Steward in his plans for a great northern crusade. True, the folk of Trondheim bragged of his deeds against the Russians — if the talk turned on them, they let no one forget he was of their country-side. Aye, 'twas proven clearly enough that there was plenty of the good old mettle in the young fellows round about the fjord here. But what Erlend of Husaby said and what he did were not things that counted with full-grown and prudent men.

She saw that Erlend was still reckoned as one of the young men — though he was a year older than the High Steward. She understood that it suited many folk well that such he should be held to be, so that his words and his deeds could be belittled as being but the deeds and counsels of a hot-headed young man. Thus was he liked, spoiled and bragged of — but not accounted as a man come to man's estate. And she saw how willing he seemed to fall in with this and be what his fellows would have him be.

He spoke up for the Russian war; he spoke of the Swedes who owned half our King, and yet would not reckon the Norse gentry and knights as nobles, the equals of their own. Or had the like ever been heard of in any land, he asked, as long as the world had stood, that anyone had craved war-levies from noblemen in other wise than that they should ride their own horses and bear their own shields to the field? — Kristin knew that this was much what her father had said at the Thing in Vaage some years back, and he had pressed it on Erlend when his son-in-law had been loath to part company with Munan Baardssön and his counsels. No, said Erlend now — and he named his father-in-law's powerful kinsmen in Sweden — he knew well enough what account these Swedish gentry made of us. If we show not what we can do, we shall soon be fit but to be reckoned as pensioners of the Swedes. . . .

Aye, folk would say, there was somewhat in all this. But then they would talk again of the High Steward. Sir Erling had his own pot to boil in the north there; the Karelians had burned Bjarkö over his steward's head one year, and harried his farmers. And then Erlend changed his note and grew merry over the knight: Erling Vidkunssön thought not on his own concerns, of that he was sure. He was so noble and fine and stately a knight — no more worshipful man could they have found to be the corner-stone of their affairs. By God's Cross, Erling was as worshipful and as venerable as the bravest golden capital letter in the Book of the

Laws. Folk laughed, and bore in mind not so much Erlend's praise of the High Steward's honour as that he had likened him to a gilded letter in a book.

No, they took not Erlend in earnest — not even now, when he was honoured after a fashion. But in those days when, young and headstrong and desperate, he had lived in whoredom with a woman, and would not put her away in despite of King's command and Church's ban — then they had taken him sadly enough, turning their backs on him in furious wrath over his godless and shameless life. Now was all this forgotten and forgiven — and Kristin understood that there was something of thankfulness for this in her husband's willingness to yield, and be what folk would have him to be — he had suffered bitterly, she knew, in the days when he lived an outcast from among his fellows here in his home.

There was but one thing — she must needs think of her father when he forgave some good-for-naught his rent or his debt — with the slightest shrug of his shoulders. 'Twas our Christian duty to bear with them that could not play a man's part. Was it thus that Erlend had gained forgiveness for his sins of youth — ?

But Erlend *had* paid for those deeds of his when he lived with Eline. He had answered for his sin till the day when he had met *her* and she had followed him, nothing loath, into new sins. Was it she, then, who — ?

No. She grew afraid now of her own thoughts.

And she tried to shut out from her mind all care for things wherein she could take no hand. She would only think of those matters in which she could do some good by her carefulness. All the rest she must leave in God's hand. God had helped her in all things wherein her own toil and pains could avail. The home-farm at Husaby had now been worked up again into a good farm as of yore — in despite of the bad years. Three healthy comely sons had He vouchsafed her to bear — every year had He granted her life anew when she must face death in child-bearing; He had let her arise in full health after each childbed. All her sweet little ones had she been given grace to keep last year when the sickness bore away so many fair little children in the country round. And Gaute — Gaute *would* grow strong, that she believed full surely.

Doubtless it must be as Erlend said — he must needs spend freely as he did and have all things costly about him. Else could he never play his part amongst his peers or win his way to such rights and

rewards under the King as were his due by birth. She must believe
that he understood such things better than she.

'Twas witless to think things could have been better with him
in any wise in those days when he lived as in bonds of sin with
that other — and with herself. Glimpse after glimpse came before
her eyes of his face as it was in those days, ravaged with sorrow,
drawn with passion. No, no, 'twas well as now it was. He was but
somewhat too careless and unthinking.

Erlend came home at Michaelmas-tide. He had hoped to find
Kristin in bed; but she was still up and about, and she came to meet
him a little way. She was piteously heavy-footed this time — but
she bore Gaute on her arm, as ever; the two bigger boys ran before her.

Erlend leapt from his horse and set the two boys up on it. Then
he took the little one from his wife and would have borne him.
Kristin's white, worn face lighted up when Gaute showed no fear
of his father — it must sure be that he knew him again. She asked
not aught of her husband's doings; she talked only of the four little teeth Gaute had gotten. He had been so sick when he cut them.

Then the boy burst out screaming — he had scratched his cheek
on his father's neck-brooch. He fought to go back to his mother
again, and she would take him, in despite of all that Erlend
could say.

It was not till the evening, when they sat in the hall and the
children slept, that Kristin asked her husband of his sojourn in
Björgvin — as though it were a thing she had but now remembered.

Erlend stole a glance at his wife. Poor love — she looked so
wretched. So first he brought forth odds and ends of news. Erling
had prayed him to greet her and give her this — 'twas a bronze
dagger, green and eaten up with copper rust. They had found it
in a stone-heap out at Giske — they said such things would be
good to lay in the cradle, if 'twere rickets that ailed Gaute.

Kristin wrapped the cloth about the dagger again, rose toil-
somely from her chair, and went across to the cradle. She put the
little bundle in amongst all the other things that already lay there
under the coverings — a flint axe found in the earth, some beaver-
grease, a little cross of mezereon, heirloom silver, a fire-steel, roots
of purples and finger-fern.

"Lie down now, my Kristin," he begged lovingly. He came over and drew off her shoes and hose — and he told his tidings the while.

Haakon Ogmundssön was come back, and peace with the Russians and Karelians was made and sealed. He himself would have to journey north again now, this autumn. For 'twas nowise sure that things would calm down so quickly, and there was need that Vargöy * should be held by a man who knew the land and people. Aye, he would have full power as the King's Governor there — the fortress needed strengthening so that the King's peace might be upheld in the lands within the new boundary marks.

Erlend looked in suspense up at his wife's face. She seemed a little affrighted — but she asked not many questions, and it was clear that she understood not much of the full meaning of his tidings. He saw how weary she was — so he spoke no more of these things, but stayed by her awhile, sitting on the bed's edge.

He knew himself what he had undertaken. Erlend laughed quietly to himself as he lingered over his undressing. 'Twould be no sitting with silver-belted belly, giving ale-feasts to friends and kinsmen, and trimming your nails fine and even, while you sent your sheriffs and lieutenants hither and thither on your errands — after the fashion of the King's Governors in the castles down here in the south. For the castle of Vargöy — 'twas a stronghold of another kidney.

Lapps, Russians, Karelians, and the mixed spawn of all the races — troll-pack, wizards, heathen hounds, the foul fiend's own pet lambs — had to be taught to pay their dues again to the Norse commissaries, and to leave in peace the Norse homes lying scattered, with as far between them as from here out to Möre maybe. Peace — maybe the land up there would be at peace some time — in his time 'twould be but the peace there is while the devil is at mass. And then there would be his own dare-devils to keep in check. As they would be towards spring, when they began to grow brain-sick with the dark and the storms and the cold and the hellish noise of the sea — and meal and butter and drink began to run low, and they fought about their womenfolk, and life on the island was more than flesh and blood could bear. He had seen somewhat of it when he was there with Gissur Galle as a young lad; ho, ho — 'twould be no bed of roses.

* The modern Vardö.

Ingolf Peit, the man there now, was a good man enough. But Erling was right. A man from among the knighthood must take things up there in hand — till this was done, none would understand that 'twas the Norse King's firm intent to uphold his rule over the land. Ho, ho — in that land would he be stuck like a needle in a blanket. The nearest Norse parish down at Malang, the devil knows how far.

Ingolf was a worthy fellow — when he had someone over him. He would give Ingolf the command of *Hugrekken*. *Margygren* was the finest ship of them all, he had proved that now. Erlend laughed softly and happily. He had said it to Kristin so often — that was a henchwoman she must needs suffer him to cleave to.

He was waked by the noise of a child crying in the dark. Over in the bed by the other wall he heard Kristin moving and speaking coaxingly in a low voice — it was Björgulf that was crying. Sometimes the boy would wake in the night and could not open his eyes for the matter on the lashes — and then the mother would wet them with her tongue. It had ever seemed to him ugly to look on.

Kristin lulled the child softly. The thin small tones of her voice irked him.

Erlend remembered what he had dreamed. He was walking somewhere on a rocky strand — it was ebb-tide, and he leapt from stone to stone. The sea lay pale and bright, licking at the tangle far outside — 'twas like a still, clouded summer night, no sun. Against the silvery light at the fjord-mouth he saw his ship lying at anchor, black and slender, rocking gently, gently on the swell. There was an unearthly sweet smell of sea and sea-weed. . . .

His heart within him grew sick with longing. Now, in the darkness of the night, lying here in the guest-bed with the long-drawn tones of the nurses' lullaby chafing at his ears — now he felt how great his longing was. Away from his home and the children that the house overflowed with, away from talk of husbandry and housefolk and tenants and young ones — and from heart-heaviness for her who was ever sick and ailing, and whom he must for ever pity. . . .

Erlend pressed his clenched hands over his heart. 'Twas as though it had ceased beating and did but lie shaking with fear in his breast. He longed to leave her! When he thought on what she was to go through, weak and strengthless as she now was —

it might come at any moment, he knew — 'twas as though he strangled with fear. Should he lose Kristin — he saw not how he could endure to live without her. But neither could he endure to live with her — not now; he must needs come away from it all, and take breath again — 'twas as though *his* life were at stake too.

Jesus, my Saviour — oh, what sort of man was he! Now, to-night, he saw it clearly — Kristin, his sweet, his dearest love — true, deep-hearted joy he had never known with her, save in those days when he was leading her astray in sin.

And he had believed so surely that the day when he won Kristin to have and to hold her before God and man — that day all evil would be wiped away from his life so wholly that he would forget it had ever been.

He must be such an one that he could not suffer aught that was truly good and pure near him. For Kristin — aye, since she was escaped from the sin and uncleanness he had led her into, she had been as an angel from God's heaven. Mild and trusty, gentle, diligent, worthy of honour. She had brought honour to Husaby once more. She was become again what she had been on yonder summer night when the pure young maiden soul nestled in under his cloak out there in the cloister garden and he had thought, as he felt the slender young body against his side — the devil himself could not find in his heart to hurt this child or cause her sorrow. . . .

The tears ran down over Erlend's face.

— Then belike it was true, what they had told him, the priests, that sin ate up a man's soul like rust — for no rest, no peace was his, here with his own sweet love — he but longed to be gone from her and all that was hers. . . .

He had wept himself into a half-slumber, when he marked that she was up, and walking about the room lulling and crooning to the child.

Erlend leapt out of bed, stumbling in the dark over some children's shoes on the floor, came to his wife, and took Gaute from her. The boy shrieked aloud and Kristin said plaintively:

" I had almost gotten him to sleep."

The father shook the screaming child, gave him some slaps behind — and as the boy shrieked still louder bade him hush in such a harsh voice that Gaute suddenly stopped in terror. No such thing had ever befallen him before in his life. . . .

" Now, for God's sake, use any wits that you have left, Kristin."

His vehemency seemed to strip him of all strength as he stood
there in the pitch-dark room, naked, shivering and half awake,
with a sobbing child in his arms. " An end of this there must be,
I tell you — what have you nursemaids for? — the young ones must
sleep with them. You cannot go on thus."

"Can you not suffer me to have my children with me in the
time that is left to me? " answered his wife in a low, wailing voice.

Erlend *would* not understand what she meant.

" In the time that is left, what you need is *rest*. Lay you down
now, Kristin," he begged, more mildly.

He took Gaute with him to his own bed — lulled the child a
little and groped in the darkness till he found his belt on the bed-
step. The small silver scales it was set with chinked and tinkled as
the boy played with it.

" The dagger is not in it? " asked Kristin fearfully from her bed;
and Gaute set up a fresh howl when he heard his mother's voice.
Erlend hushed him again and tinkled the belt — and at last the
child gave way and grew quiet.

Poor miserable little soul, maybe one should scarce wish he
might grow up — 'twas unsure if Gaute had all his wits.

Oh, no, oh, no — most blessed maid Mary — he meant it not —
he wished not that his own little son should lose his life. No, no
— Erlend took the child close within his arms and laid his face
down on the warm downy hair.

Their fair sons — But he grew so weary of hearing of them early
and late; of stumbling over them wherever he went at home here.
That three small young ones could be in all places at once on a
great manor like this passed his understanding. But he remembered
his burning wrath with Eline because she had troubled herself
little about their children. An unjust man he must surely be — for
he was vexed now because he never saw Kristin anywhere without
children hanging about her.

Never had he known, when he took his true-born sons in his
embrace, the like of what he had felt the first time they laid Orm
in his arms. Oh, Orm, Orm, my son — He had been so weary of
Eline even then — sickened with her self-will and her rages and
her ungovernable love. He had seen that she was too old for him.
And he had begun to understand what this madness was like to cost
him. But he had thought: give her up he could not — since she had
lost all for his sake. The boy's birth had given him, he thought,

a cause the more to bear with the mother. He had been so young when he became Orm's father that he had not fully understood what the child's standing would be — with a mother that was another's wedded wife.

Weeping came over him again, and he drew Gaute closer to him. Orm — none of his children had he loved as he loved that boy; he missed him so, and he repented so bitterly every hard and hasty word he had said to him. It could not be that Orm had known how his father loved him. It had all come from his bitterness and despair, as he came to see clearly that never could Orm be counted for his true-born son, never could he bear his father's arms. And from jealousy, too, as he saw his son draw closer to his stepmother than to him; and this, too, that Kristin's even, gentle kindness to the youth seemed to him like a reproach.

And then came the days he could not endure to remember. Orm lay in the loft-room in the dead-straw, and the women came and told him they thought not that Kristin could live through her sickness. They dug Orm's grave over in the chapel, and asked if Kristin were to lie there or were to be taken in to St. Gregory's and buried where his father and mother lay.

Oh, but — and at this he held his breath in fear. Behind him lay all his life, filled with memories he fled from, because he could not endure to think of them. Now, to-night, he saw it — He could forget, after a sort, in the daily fellowship with his kind. But he could not so guard himself that it rose not up in some hour such as this — and then 'twas as though an evil spell had robbed him of all courage.

Those days at Haugen — at most times he had well-nigh managed to forget them. He had not been at Haugen since yonder night he and Björn had driven away from it; and he had not seen Björn and Aashild since his wedding-day. It was Sir Björn he had been afraid to meet. And now — He thought of what Munan had told him — 'twas said they walked there; Haugen was so felly haunted that the houses stood empty; none would live there now, not if they were given the farm free.

Björn Gunnarssön had had a kind of hardihood that Erlend knew he could never attain to. He had been steady of hand when he stabbed his wife — right in the heart, Munan said.

'Twould be two years next winter since Björn and Lady Aashild died. No smoke had been seen from the houses at Haugen for a week; and at last some men plucked up heart and went thither. Sir Björn lay in the bed with his throat cut across; he held his wife's body in his arms. Before the bed, on the floor, lay his bloody dagger.

None had doubted how this had come to pass. . . . Yet did Munan Baardssön and his brother so order things that the two were buried in hallowed ground. — 'Twas put about that it might well have been robbers; though the chest with Björn and Aashild's goods was untouched. The bodies were untouched by rats or mice — the truth was such vermin were not to be found at Haugen — and folk took this for a sure sign of the lady's skill in witchcraft.

Munan Baardssön was fearfully shaken by his mother's end. He had set forth straightway on pilgrimage to St. James of Compostella.

Erlend remembered the morning after the night his own mother died. They lay at anchor inside Moldöy Sound, but the white fog was so thick that 'twas but in short moments now and then they caught a glimpse of the cliff-wall they lay close under. Yet did it give back a muffled echo of the hollow sounds as the boat rowed landwards with the priest. He stood in the fore-part and watched them row away from the ship. All things he came near were wet with the fog; the wet stood in beads on his hair and his clothes, and the stranger priest and his acolyte sat in the boat's bow crouched with updrawn shoulders over the sacred elements in their lap. They looked like hawks in rainy weather. The oar-strokes and the creaking of the rowlocks and the echoes from the cliff sounded on faintly long after the boat was blotted out in the fog.

Then he too had vowed a pilgrimage. He had had but *one* thought then — that he must see again his mother's sweet and lovely face as it had been of old — with the soft smooth skin of palest brown. Now she lay dead below there, with face ravaged by the fearful sores, that cracked and oozed small clear drops of moisture when she had tried to smile to him. . . .

Was it his fault that his father had met his return in such a fashion? Or that he had turned him then to one who was outcast like himself — ? And after that he had thrust all thought of pilgrimage from his mind, and had not troubled to think of his mother any more. Ill as things had gone with her on earth 'twas like that now she was come where there was peace — and but little peace had fallen to *his* lot after he had sought Eline again. . . .

Peace — but once in his life, it seemed now, had he known it — that night when he sat behind the stone wall out towards the woods by Hofvin, and held Kristin in his lap, sleeping her soft, secure, unbroken, childlike sleep. Not for long had he been able to refrain him from breaking that calm. And 'twas not peace that he had found with her since — that he found with her now. Though he saw that all others in his home found peace with his young wife.

And now his one longing was to be gone to strife again. He longed wildly for that outermost barren rock, for the sea thundering round the northern forelands, for the endless coast, and the mighty fjords where all manner of snares and pitfalls might await him, for the folks whose tongues he knew but by bits and scraps, for their sorceries and fickleness and slippery wiles, for war and the sea, and the song of his men's weapons and his own —

He fell asleep at last, but wakened again — what was it he had just been dreaming? Aye, black Lapp girls — something half forgotten that had befallen when he was in the north with Gissur — a wild night when they had all been crazed with drink.

And here lay he with his little sick son in his arms and dreamed such dreams. — He grew so frighted of himself that he dared not try to sleep any more. And he could not endure to lie awake. Aye, truly he must be an unhappy wretch. — Stiff with dread, he lay unmoving and felt the heart tolling in his breast, while he longed for the dawn to release him.

He talked Kristin over into keeping her bed the next day; for he felt he could not bear to see her go dragging herself about the house — in such wretchedness. He sat by her and played with her hand. She had had the comeliest arms — slim, but so round that the fine small bones in the slender joints were not seen. Now they stood out like knots on the gaunt arms whose skin on the underside was more blue than white.

Without, it blew, and rained till the water came streaming from the hill-sides. Once, well on in the day, as he came down from the armoury, he heard Gaute screaming somewhere in the courtyard. In the narrow passage between two houses he found his three small sons, sitting in the midst of the runnels splashing from the roofs. Naakkve held the little one tight, while Björgulf tried to force a living earthworm into his mouth — he had his hand quite full of writhing pink worms.

The boys stood with injured looks when their father seized and scolded them. 'Twas old Aan, they said, that had told them of it — Gaute would get his teeth without pain or trouble if they could but get him to take a bite or two of living earthworms.

All three were dripping wet from top to toe. Erlend roared out for the children's nurses — they came rushing, one from the wright's shop and one from the stable. Their master cursed them heartily, then thrust Gaute under his arm like a sucking-pig, and drove the others before him into the hall.

Soon after, the three were sitting dry and happy in their blue holy-day kirtles on the step before their mother's bed. Their father had drawn up a stool for himself, and he chattered and romped, and, laughing, hugged the young ones to him, to deaden in his own mind the memory of last night's fear. But the mother smiled happily to see Erlend playing with their children. Erlend kept a Lapland witch, he said; she was two hundred winters old, and dried up till she was no bigger than *that*. He kept her in a skin bag in the great chest that stood in his ship-house. Food? Aye — she got food — every Yule night the thigh of a Christian man — she got through a whole year on that. And if they were not good and quiet and ceased not plaguing their mother, that was so sick, they should go into the skin bag too. . . .

" Mother is to have our little sister — that is why she is sick," said Naakkve, proud of having the clue to the riddle. Erlend pulled the boy by the ears on to his knee:

" Aye — and when she is born, this sister of yours, I will have my old Lapp hag throw a spell over you three, and you shall turn into white bears and root about in the wild woods; but my daughter shall inherit all my goods and gear."

The children shrieked, and clambered up to their mother in her bed — Gaute understood not what was amiss, but he shrieked and crawled up to keep his brothers company. Kristin chid her husband — such jesting was too uncanny. But Naakkve tumbled out again — in a rapture of laughter and fear he rushed at his father, hung on to his belt, and snapped at Erlend's hands, with mingled shrieks and shouts of joy.

Erlend did not get the daughter he would so fain have had this time either. Kristin bore him two great and comely sons, but they had well-nigh cost her life.

Erlend had them baptised, one after Ivar Gjesling and the other after King Skule. Skule's name had not been kept up among their kindred — Lady Ragnrid had said that her father was an ill-omened man, and it was best therefore that his name be let drop. But Erlend swore that none of his sons bore a prouder name than this, his youngest.

The autumn was so far spent that Erlend must needs set forth for the north as soon as Kristin was through the worst of the danger. And he thought in his heart 'twas as well he should be gone before she came upon her feet again. Five sons in five years — 'twas enough for any man; and he was loath to have cause to dread that she might die in childbed while he was tied up there at Vargöy.

He saw that Kristin, too, thought somewhat of the kind. She murmured no longer that he was to leave her alone. She had taken each child as it came, as a precious gift of God, and the troubles it brought as things she must bear without repining. But this time it had gone so fearfully hard with her that Erlend saw 'twas as though all heart had been wrung out of her. She lay there, her face yellow as clay, and looked on the two small bundles of swaddling-clothes by her side, and her eyes were not so happy as when she had gazed first on the others.

Erlend went through the whole journey north in his thoughts as he sat beside her. A hard voyage 'twould be, belike, so late in autumn — and strange to come up there into the long night. But he yearned to be gone, unspeakably. This last terror for his wife had broken down all resistance in his soul — will-lessly he gave himself up to his longing to flee away from home.

4

ERLEND NIKULAUSSÖN held the post of Captain of the Vargöy stronghold and keeper of the Northern Marches for well-nigh two years. In all that time he came not further south than to Bjarköy, and there but once, when he and Sir Erling Vidkunssön had made tryst there. The second summer Erlend was in the north, Heming Alfssön died at last, and Erlend was made Warden * of Orkdöla County in his stead. Haftor Graut went north to take his place at Vargöy.

* See Note 12.

Erlend was a glad man when he sailed for the south, some days after Mary's Mass in autumn. It was the cure for his honour that he had wished for all these years — to be given the Wardenship his father once held. Not that this had been a goal he had ever wittingly worked to reach. But it had ever seemed to him that 'twas this he needed, so that he might come into the place where he rightfully belonged — both in his own and in his fellows' eyes. Now 'twas no matter if men still deemed him to be somewhat unlike the other, the home-keeping nobles — there was no disgrace in the unlikeness any more.

And he longed to be home. Things had been more peaceful in Finmarken than he had looked for. Even the first winter had worn on him — he sat there idle in the castle, and could do naught at that season towards the mending and bettering of the works. They had been put in good order seventeen years before, but now were quite fallen in ruin.

Then came the spring and summer, with life and bustle — meetings here and there in the fjords with the Norse and half-Norse tax-gatherers and the spokesmen from the tribes of the uplands. Erlend roved the seas and fjords with his two ships and amused himself royally. On the island the houses were mended, and the works strengthened. But the next year there was but little doing.

Haftor would see to it, doubtless, that the quiet did not last long. Erlend laughed. They had sailed together eastward well-nigh as far as Trianema, and there had Haftor taken a Russian Lapp woman and had brought her back with him. Erlend had talked to him gravely: he must remember, 'twas above all needful that the heathen should understand always that we were the masters — and to that end, seeing one had but a handful of men, one must bear one so as not to stir up trouble needlessly. No making or meddling should the Lapps fight and slay each other; that pleasure one must let them enjoy in peace. But be ever ready to pounce like a hawk on Russians and Kolbjags and whatever else the pack might call themselves. And leave the womenfolk in peace — for one thing, they were witches, every one — and, for another, there were enough to proffer themselves. — But the Godöy lad must steer his course as he would; he would learn in time. Haftor was joyful at getting free from his farms and his wife, and now Erlend was fain to come home to his. He had a right blissful longing now for Kristin and Husaby and his own country-side and all his children — for all things at his home where Kristin was.

In Lyngsfjord he heard tidings of a ship with some mon}
aboard; 'twas said they were Preaching Friars from Nidaros, wh
were journeying north, bent on planting the true faith amidst th
heathen and heretics of the marches.

Erlend felt sure within him that Gunnulf was of the compan
And, true enough, three nights later he sat alone with his broth
in an earthen hut on a little Norse farm that lay by the stran
where they had met.

Erlend was strangely moved. He had heard mass and take
the sacrament with his crew — the only time since he came here t
the north, save that once when he had been at Bjarköy. The churc
at Vargöy was without a priest; a deacon had been left in the for
and he had striven to keep count of the holy-days for them, bu
else had there been but scurvy provision for the souls of the Norse
men in these northern lands. They must even comfort themselve
with the thought that it was a crusade of a kind they were or
and 'twas like they would not be held to such strict account fo
their sins.

He sat speaking to Gunnulf of this, and his brother listened wit
a far-off, strange smile on his wide thin lips. It looked as if he eve
sucked in the under-lip a little, as a man may often do when he i
thinking hard of some matter, and is nigh to understanding, bu
has not yet come to full clearness in his thoughts.

The night was far spent already. All other folks on the farn
were sleeping up in the shed; the brothers knew that they alon
were waking. And they were both stirred by the strangeness o
their sitting here — they two alone.

The roaring of the sea and of the storm came to them lulled an
deadened by the turf-walls. Now and then a puff of wind would
force its way in, blowing up the embers in the fire-place, and flap
ping the flame of the train-oil lamp a little. There were no furnish
ings in the hut; the brothers sat on the low earthen bench that ra
round three sides of the room, and between them lay Gunnulf'
writing-board, with ink-horn, feather pen and a roll of parchment
Gunnulf had been writing down one thing and another his brothe
had told him of trysting-places and settled farms, of sailing-mark
and weather signs and words in the Lapp's tongues — just as th
things chanced to come into Erlend's mind. Gunnulf commande
the ship — she was named the *Sunniva*, for the Preaching Broth

ers had chosen St. Sunniva as guardian saint for their mission.

"Aye, if only you come not to the same end as the Seljemen," * said Erlend, and again Gunnulf smiled a little.

"You tell me I am restless, Gunnulf," Erlend went on. "What should a man call you, then? First you go wandering about in the south-lands all those years, and no sooner are you come home but you must needs turn your back on living and prebends and be off to preach to the devil and all his imps away north in Velli-aa. You know not their tongue and they understand not yours. Methinks you are yet more unstable than I."

"I have neither goods nor kin to answer for," said the monk. "I have loosed me now from all bonds; but you have bound you, brother."

"Oh, aye. He is the free man that owns naught."

Gunnulf answered:

"All things that a man owns hold him far more than he holds them."

"Hm. Nay, by God, 'tis not ever so. Grant that Kristin holds me — but I have no mind that my lands and my children should own me."

"Think not so, brother," said Gunnulf, low. "For then may it easily come to pass that you lose them."

"Nay, no mind have I to grow like to all those other goodmen — sticking up to their ears in the mud of their lands," said Erlend, laughing, and again his brother smiled a little.

"Fairer children than Ivar and Skule have I never seen," he spoke. "Methinks 'twas so you must have looked at their age — no marvel that our mother loved you so much."

Each brother rested a hand on the writing-board that lay between them. Even in the faint light of the train-oil lamp it could be seen how unlike these two men's hands were. The monk's, bare of rings and all adornments, white and sinewy, smaller and much more closely set than the other's, looked also much stronger — though Erlend's fist was as hard as horn in the palm, and the bluish-white scar of an arrow-wound furrowed the dark flesh from the wrist up under the sleeve. But the fingers of his narrow brown-tanned hand, dry and knotted at the joints like the twigs of trees, were covered with golden and jewelled rings.

* For St. Sunniva and the Seljemen, see *The Bridal Wreath* (*The Garland*), Note 8.

Erlend would fain have taken his brother's hand, but he wa.
ashamed — so he but drank, pulling a wry face over the bad
beer.

" She seemed to you to be well and hearty again, Kristin? " Erlend asked in a while.

" Aye, she blossomed like a rose when I was at Husaby in the
summer," said the monk, smiling a little. He waited awhile and
then said gravely: " One thing I would pray you, brother — to
think somewhat more of Kristin's and the children's welfare than
till now you have done. And be counselled by her and clinch the
bargains that she and Sira Eiliv have agreed for; they wait but for
your assent to close them."

" I like not much these plans of hers you speak of," said Erlend
haltingly. " — And now too, my standing will be other than it has
been — "

" Your lands will be of more worth when you bring your hold-
ings close together," answered the monk. " Methought Kristin's
counsels were wise when she told me of the matter."

" I warrant there is scarce a woman in Norway's land that is
freer than she to guide things as she will," said Erlend.

" In the end 'tis you that guide things," answered the monk.
" And you — you guide Kristin, too, as you will," he added in a
low voice.

Erlend laughed softly, low in his throat, stretched himself, and
yawned. Then of a sudden he said soberly:

" You have guided her, too, at times, my brother. And I marvel
if sometimes your counsels have not come nigh to parting our
friendship."

" Mean you the friendship that has been betwixt you and your
wife, or the friendship between us two brothers? " said the monk
slowly.

" Both," said Erlend, as if it was a thought that but now came
to him. " So holy there is sure no need for a lay-woman to be," he
said more lightly.

" I have counselled her as I deemed to be best. As *is* best," he
corrected himself.

Erlend looked at the monk in the Preaching Brothers' coarse
grey-white frock, with the black cowl thrown back, so that it
lay in thick folds round the neck and over the shoulders. The
crown of the head was shaven now so that there was but a nar-

row fringe of hair about the round, lean, pallid face — but the hair was thick and black as in Gunnulf's earliest youth.

"Aye, you are no brother of mine now, I trow, any more than you are brother to all mankind," said Erlend, and wondered at the deep bitterness in his own voice.

"So is it not — though so it should be."

"So help me God — almost I believe 'tis therefore you would go to dwell among the Lapps," said Erlend.

Gunnulf bent his head. There was a glow in his yellow-brown eyes.

"Therefore it is — in some measure," he said low and quickly.

They spread out the skins and rugs they had brought with them. It was too cold and raw in the hut for them to take off aught, so they bade each other good-night and lay down on the earthen bench, which, to escape the smoke that hung above, was but little raised above the floor.

Erlend lay thinking of the tidings that had come to him from home. 'Twas not much he had heard in these two years — two letters from his wife had come to his hands, but they had been old already when they reached him. Sira Eiliv had written them for her — she could print herself, fair and plain, but she was ever loath to write, since it seemed to her scarce seemly for an unlearned woman.

Doubtless she would be yet holier now they had a new shrine in their neighbour parish, and that sacred to a man whom she had herself known in his life — and now had Gaute found healing for his sickness there, and she herself won her full health again, after being sickly ever since the birth of the twins. Gunnulf had told him that the Preaching Brothers at Hamar had at last been forced to give back Edvin Rikardssön's body to his brethren at Oslo, and these were now having full record made of all things concerning Brother Edvin's life, and the miracles 'twas said he had wrought both in life and after he was dead. It was their intent to send this writing to the Pope, and try to have the monk beatified. Some peasants from Gaudall and Medaldal had gone south and borne witness to wonders that Brother Edvin had wrought in their parishes by his intercession, and by means of a crucifix that he had carved out, and that now was at Medalhus. They had vowed to build a little church on Vatsfjeld, where he had lived some summers as a hermit, and where was a healing spring that owed to him its virtue. So they were given a hand from his body to enshrine in the church.

Kristin had made offering of two silver cups and of the great clasp set with blue stones that had come to her from her mother's mother, Ulvhild Haavardsdatter, and had had Tiedeken Paus, the goldsmith in the city, make of them a silver hand to hold the bones of Brother Edvin's hand and fingers. And she had been at the Vatsfjeld with Sira Eiliv and her children and a great following, when the Archbishop hallowed the church at St. John's Mass tide the year after Erlend had gone northward.

After this Gaute had gained health swiftly, and had learnt to walk and talk — he was now like other children of his age. Erlend stretched himself — sure it was the greatest joy that could have befallen them that Gaute was grown whole and well. He would give some land to that church. Gaute was fair, Gunnulf said, and comely of face like his mother. Pity that he had not been a little maid — then should he have been called Magnhild. Aye — he was fain now to see all these fair sons of his too. . . .

Gunnulf Nikulaussön lay thinking of the spring day, three years back, when he had ridden up toward Husaby. On the road he met a man from the manor — the mistress was not at home, he said — she was with a sick woman.

He rode along a narrow grassy path between old stick-fences; there were young leaf-trees covering the steep clay banks, both above him, and down towards the river, that ran below in the bottom, loud with the spring freshets. He rode towards the sun, and the tender green leaves glanced like golden flames on the twigs, but farther in the wood the shade lay cool and deep already on the grassy sward.

He rode on till he caught a glimpse of the lake, lying below him and mirroring darkly the farther shore, with the heavens all blue and the picture of the great summer clouds ruffled and broken by the current ripples. Deep down below the bridle-path lay a little farm on the green, flower-sprinkled slopes. A group of white-coifed housewives stood out in the courtyard — but Kristin was not amongst them.

A little farther on he saw her horse; it was loose in the close along with some others. The path dipped down in front of him into a hollow filled with green shadow, and where it wound up over the next billow of the clay banks she was standing by the

ence under the leaves listening to the birds' song. He saw her
tender black-clad shape bent over the fence in towards the wood;
only the coif and an arm showed white. He reined in his horse
and rode on towards her at a foot-pace; but when he came near he
saw that 'twas the trunk of an old birch tree that stood there.

The next evening, when his serving-folk sailed him in to the city,
the priest himself was at the heim. He felt his heart firm and, as it
were, new-born in his breast. Nothing now could shake his purpose.

He knew then that what had held him back, had kept him in
the world, was the unquenchable longing he had borne within him
from his boyhood up — the longing to win the love of men. That
he might be beloved he had been generous, mild and mirthful with
small folk; he had let his light of learning shine, but with all mod-
esty and humility, among the priests in the city, so that they might
like him; he had been compliant with Lord Eiliv Kortin, since the
Archbishop had been a friend of his father's, and he knew how
Lord Eiliv liked those around him to behave. He had been kindly
and gentle with Orm, to win a little of the boy's love away from
his fitful father. And he had been stern and unsparing with Kristin,
because he knew that she had needed to meet with somewhat that
did not give way when she grasped at it for support; something
that led her not astray when she came forward, ready to follow.

But that evening he had understood — he had sought to win her
trust in himself far more than to strengthen her trust on God. . . .

Erlend had found the word to-night. Not my brother more than
all men's brother. That was the way he must go, before his brotherly love could profit *any*.

Two weeks later he had parted all his goods between his kin
and the Church, and taken on the habit of a professed Preaching
Brother. And last spring, when all souls were deeply shaken by
the fearful calamity that had fallen on the land — the lightning
had struck Christ's church in Nidaros and half consumed St. Olav's
house — Gunnulf had won the Archbishop's support for his old
plan. Along with Brother Olav Jonssön, who was a consecrated
priest like himself, and three younger monks, one from Nidaros
and two from the Preachers' Convent in Björgvin, he was now
journeying northward to bring the light of the Word to the unhappy heathen who lived and died in gross darkness within the
boundaries of a Christian land.

Christ, Thou Crucified One, now have I given from me all that could bind me. Myself have I given into Thy hands, if Thou wilt deign with my life to buy Satan's household free. Take me, in such wise that I feel I am Thy thrall, for so shall I also possess Thee. — And so should his heart, maybe, one day sing and shout in his breast as it had sung and exulted when he walked the green plains by Romaborg, from pilgrims' church to pilgrims' church — " I am my Beloved's and to Him is my desire — "

The brothers lay, each on his bench in the little hut, thinking and thinking until they slept. A live ember on the hearth between them glowed faintly. Their thoughts drew them farther and farther away one from the other. And the next day the one set forth for the north and the other southward.

Erlend had promised Haftor Graut to sail round by Godöy, and take Haftor's sister with him southward. She was wed to Thoroli Aasulfssön of Lensvik — he, too, was a kinsman of Erlend's, but far off.

The first morning, when *Margygren* stood out of Godöy Sound, her sail bellying against the background of blue mountains in the fine breeze, Erlend stood on the after-deck and Ulf Haldorssön was at the helm. Lady Sunniva came up on deck. She had thrown back the hood of her cloak, and the wind blew the linen of her coif backwards, uncovering her curly sun-bright yellow hair. She had the same sea-blue glittering eyes as her brother, and, like him, she was fair of face, but thickly freckled, both on her face and her small plump hands.

From the first evening he saw her at Godöy — their eyes had met, and then they had looked aside, a secret smile on each face — Erlend had been assured that she knew him — and he knew her. Sunniva Olavsdatter — he could take her with his bare hands; and she looked for him to do it.

Now, as he stood with her hand in his — he had helped her up — he chanced to look at Ulf's rough, dark face. Ulf knew it too, he could see. He was strangely abashed at the man's look. He remembered in a flash all this kinsman and henchman of his had been privy to in his life — every coil his folly had snared him in from earliest youth up. Ulf had no need to look so scornfully at him — he comforted himself — as though he had meant to be more free with the lady than right and honour would allow. He was old enough now, and wise enough from much burning of his fingers, to be let loose in Haalogaland without tangling him up in witless folly with the wife of another. He had a wife himself now — he had been true to Kristin from the first day he had seen her till now — one or two matters that had befallen away in the north, no reasonable man would bring into the account. Else had he not once looked at a woman — in such wise. He knew it himself — with a Norse woman — and their equal in birth to boot — no, he would never have an hour's peace of mind if he was false to Kristin in such wise. — But this voyage southward with her on board — it might well be perilous.

It was some help to him that they met with rough weather along the coast, so that he had somewhat else to do than to dally with the lady. At Dynöy they had to take shelter, and tarry there in harbour some days. And while they lay there a thing befell which made Lady Sunniva seem much less alluring.

Erlend, with Ulf and one or two other men, slept in the same shed where she and her women lay. One morning he was alone in there and the lady was not yet risen. She called him to her — said she had lost a finger-ring in the bed. He had to come and help her to search — she was creeping about on the bed. They turned towards each other now and then in their search, and each time they had that lurking smile in their eyes. — But when she took hold of him — Aye, *he* had maybe not borne him in over-seemly wise — time and place were against it — but she was so bold and shameless that now of a sudden he grew hard and cold. Red with shame, he looked away from her face of laughter and wantonness; freed himself with scant excuse, then went out and sent in the lady's serving-women to her.

No, devil take it, he was not so young a bird as to be caught with chaff. 'Twas one thing to beguile — quite another thing to be beguiled. But he could not but laugh — here stood he, and he had just fled away from a fair dame, like yonder Hebrew, Joseph! Aye, strange things befall both by sea and land.

Nay — Lady Sunniva — Ah, he could not but remember *one* — one whom he knew. She had gone to tryst with him in a house of call for ribald men-at-arms — and she had come shamefast and worshipful as a young maid of kingly birth might go to mass. In woods and barns had she met him — God forgive him, he had forgotten her birth and her honour; and she had forgotten them for his sake, but she had not been able to fling them from her. Her blood rose up and spoke in her, even when she thought not on it.

God bless thee, my Kristin — so help me God, my faith that I pledged thee in secret and before the altar, that will I keep or nevermore be called a man. So be it.

He landed Lady Sunniva soon after at Yrjar, where she had kinsfolk. The best of the matter was that she seemed not too angry either when they parted. He had had no need to hang his head and mope like a monk — they had had much frolic and dalliance on the way. At parting he gave the lady some costly pelts for a cloak, and she promised he should see her in the cloak. They would surely meet now and then. — Poor woman, her husband was sickly and no longer young.

But he was happy that he was coming home to his wife and had naught on his mind that he need hide from her; and he was proud of his well-proved steadfastness. And he was dizzy and mad with longing for Kristin — she was the sweetest and loveliest of roses and lilies after all — and she was his.

Kristin was at the landing-place to meet him when Erlend came in to Birgsi. Fishers had brought word to Vigg that *Margygren* had been seen out at Yrjar. She had her two eldest sons and Margret with her, and at home at Husaby all was making ready for a great banquet to friends and kinsmen for Erlend's welcome home.

She was grown so fair that Erlend caught his breath when he saw her. But 'twas true she was changed. The girlish look that had still come back to her after she had come through each child-bed — the tender, frail, nun-like look under the matron's coif — was gone. She was a young, blooming wife and mother. Her cheeks were round and freshly red between the white lappets of her coif; her bosom full and firm for chains and brooches to glitter on. Her thighs were rounder and fuller under the key-belt and the gilded case that held knife and scissors. Yes, yes — she had but grown more fair — she looked not now as though they could blow her away from him to heaven so lightly as before. Even the long narrow hands were grown fuller and more white.

They tarried at Vigg for the night, in the Abbot's house there. And it was a young, rosy and joyful Kristin, mild and beaming with happiness, that went with him this time to the feast at Husaby, when they rode homeward next day.

There were many grave matters she should have spoken of to her husband when he came home. There were a thousand things about their children; misgivings for Margret; and there were her plans for putting the estates on their feet again. But all was swallowed up in the whirl of festivity.

They passed around from one banquet to another, and she bore the Warden company on his progresses. Erlend kept now yet more men at Husaby, for messages and letters were ever passing betwixt him and his sheriffs and deputies. All the time Erlend was joyous and reckless as ever — how should he not be the very man for Warden, he asked, he that had run his head against well-nigh every rule in the law of the land and the Church's law? Hardly learned was well remembered! — The man was of a quick and ready wit, he had been well taught in boyhood, and this now stood him in stead. He used himself to read his own letters, and took an Icelander into service as scribe. Till now he had been wont to set his seal to whatever others read out to him, and was ever loath to look on a line of writing — Kristin had seen much of the fruits of this in these two years, in which she had made acquaintance with all the papers in his muniment-chests.

But now there came on Kristin a recklessness the like of which she had never known. She grew livelier and less still in her mien when she was out among strangers — for she felt herself very fair, and she was healthful and fresh for the first time since she had been wed. And at nights when Erlend and she lay in a strange bed in a loft on one of the great folks' manors or in the hall of a farm, they laughed and whispered and made sport of the folk they had met, and jested over tidings they had heard. Erlend's tongue was more devil-may-care than ever, and folk seemed to like him better than ever before.

She saw it in their own children — they were almost spellbound with delight when their father would now and again take notice of them. Naakkve and Björgulf did naught now but play with bows and spears and axes and such gear. And it might chance, now and then, that their father would stop in crossing the courtyard, look at their games, and put them right: "Not like that, my son — hold it in this wise" — he changed the grip of the little fist and placed the fingers as they should be. When this chanced, they were beside themselves with eagerness.

The two eldest sons were not to be parted. Björgulf was the

biggest and strongest of the children, as tall as Naakkve, who was three half-years older, and stouter than he. He had tight-curled raven-black hair; his little face was broad but comely; the eyes dark blue. One day Erlend asked their mother somewhat fearfully if she knew that Björgulf had not good sight in one eye — and that he had the slightest squint, too. Kristin said she believed not there was much amiss; 'twas like he would grow out of it. Things had so fallen out that she had always made least ado with this child — he had been born when she was worn out with nursing Naakkve, and Gaute had followed so close on his heels. He was the strongest of the children, and, it seemed, the quickest-witted, but he was most silent. Erlend was fondest of this son.

Though he did not make it clear to himself, he had a little grudge against Naakkve, because the boy had come at an untoward time, and because he had to be called after his grandfather. And Gaute was not as he had looked to find him. — The boy had a great head, as was but reason, since for two years 'twas the only part of him that had grown — now his body and limbs were making up their growth. His wits were good enongh, but he talked right slowly, for if he spoke fast he began to lisp or stammer, and then Margret mocked at him. Kristin was most fond of this boy — though Erlend could see that, in a manner, the eldest was still dearest to her — but Gaute had been so ailing, and he favoured her father somewhat, with his flaxen hair and dark-grey eyes — and he was ever at his mother's skirts. He was a little lonely, between the two elder boys, who held together always, and the twins, who were still so small that they were ever with their foster-mothers.

Kristin had less time now to care for her children, and she was forced to do more as other ladies did and let the serving-women mind them — but the two eldest ran about, for choice, among the men on the farm. She no longer brooded over them with the old overwrought tenderness — but she laughed and played with them more, when she had time to gather them about her.

At the New Year there came to Husaby a letter under Lavrans Björgulfsön's seal. It was written with his own hand and had been sent by the priest of Orkedal who had been south — so 'twas two months old. The weightiest news it brought was that he had betrothed Ramborg to Simon Andressön of Formo. The wedding was appointed for the spring, at the time of the Feast of Holy Cross.

Kristin was amazed beyond measure, but Erlend said he had deemed things might go thus — ever since he had heard that Simon Darre was left a widower, and had come to live on his manor in Sil after old Sir Andres Gudmundssön's death.

5

Simon Darre had taken it as a thing that was as it should be, when his father had agreed with Lavrans Björgulfsön on his match with Lavrans' daughter. In his kindred it had ever been the custom that all such matters were in the parents' hands. He had been glad when he saw that his bride was so fair and gracious. He had, indeed, never looked for aught else than that he should be good friends with the wife his father chose for him. Kristin and he suited each other well in age and birth and fortune — if Lavrans were of a somewhat higher kin, his father, on his side, was a knight and had been much about King Haakon, while the other had always lived retired on his estates. And Simon had never marked aught else than that wedded folk agreed well together when they were an equal match.

Then came that night in the loft at Finsbrekken — when evil tongues would have undone the innocent young child. From that hour he had known well enough that his betrothed was dearer to him than if he had but loved her as in duty bound. He thought not much on the matter — but he was glad; he saw that the maid was bashful and coy, but he thought not much on that, either. Then came the time in Oslo, when he was forced to think things over — and then the evening in Fluga's loft.

He had come against something here that he had not thought could hap in this world — amongst honourable folk of a good kindred and in these times. Blinded and stunned, he had flung himself free of his ties — though in bearing he had been cool and calm and steady in talking of the matter with his father and hers.

Thus had he departed from the customs of his house; and next he had done another thing unheard of in his kindred: without even taking counsel with his father, he had wooed the rich young widow at Mandvik. He was dazzled when he saw that Lady Halfrid liked him — she was much more rich and high-born than

Kristin, being son's daughter to Baron Tore Haakonssön of Tuns-berg, and widow of Sir Finn Aslaksson — and she was comely, and had so fine and noble a bearing that, likened with her, all the women he was used to seemed to him but as farmers' wives. In the devil's name, he would show them all that he could win the noblest wife; in riches and all else she bore the bell from this Trönder that Kristin had let herself be smirched by. And a widow — that, too, was well — plain and above-board — the devil might trust in maids any more, for him.

He had been made to learn 'twas not such a plain straightfor-ward thing to live in the world as he had deemed it when at home at Dyfrin. There his father had ruled all things, and his judgments were right. True, Simon had been with the body-guard and served as page for a time, and he had gained a little learning from his father's house-priest at home — it might chance now and again that he deemed his father's wisdom a little behind the time. He would venture to gainsay him too, now and then — but it was but as in jest, and it was taken as a jest — a quick-witted lad, Simon, laughed his father and mother, and so said his brothers and sisters, who would never gainsay Sir Andres. But all things were done as his father willed — Simon himself deemed this but reason.

In the years when he was wedded to Halfrid Erlingsdatter and dwelt at Mandvik, he learnt each day more thoroughly that life might be more cross-grained and crooked than Sir Andres Gud-mundssön had ever dreamt.

That he should not be able to be happy with such a wife as he had won — such a thought could never have come to him. Deep down in his mind lurked a rueful wonder when he looked at his wife as she moved about the house all day long — so comely was she, with her gentle eyes and the mouth that was so sweet when the lips were shut — no woman had he ever seen wear her robes and her adornments with so much grace. And in the black dark-ness of the night distaste for her wore all youth and freshness out of him — she was sickly, her breath unhealthful, her caresses tor-tured him. She was so good that it filled him with a desperate shame — but he could not overcome his misliking.

And then 'twas not long after they were wed before he saw that she could never bear him a living, healthful child. He saw that she sorrowed over it herself even more than he — it cut him to the heart when he thought of *her* fate in that matter. One thing and another he had heard — 'twas so with her because Sir Finn had struck and kicked her more than once while she was wed with him, so that she had miscarried. He had been mad with jealousy of his young fair lady. Her kinsmen would have taken her from him, but Halfrid deemed that it behoved a Christian wife to cleave to her wedded husband, were he good or evil.

But should he not have children of her, then must he ever feel, as now he did, that it was *her* lands they dwelt on, *her* riches that he dealt with and controlled. He dealt with them heedfully and wisely. But all through these years there grew up in his mind a longing for Formo, the manor that was Sir Andres' mother's heritage, which it had always been meant he should take over after his father. He came at last to deem that his home was away yonder north in Gudbrandsdal, almost more than in Romerike.

Folks still went on calling his wife Lady Halfrid, as in the time of her first husband, the knight. And this made Simon feel all the more as if he were but her steward at Mandvik.

It chanced one day that they sat alone in the hall, Simon and his wife. One of the serving-women had come into the hall on some errand. Halfrid looked after her as she left.

" I wonder — " said she. " I fear me Jorunn is with child this summer."

Simon sat with a bow in his lap, mending its lock. He changed the tap-bolt, gazed down into the spring-box, and said, without looking up:

" Aye. And the child is mine."

His wife was silent. When at last he looked up at her, she sat sewing, as intent on her work as he had been on his.

Simon was sick at heart. Sickened because he had so affronted his wife, and sickened at his folly in having to do with the girl, and vexed that he had taken the fatherhood on his shoulders. He was in no wise sure himself. Jorunn was a light piece of goods, he knew. In truth, he had never much liked her; she was ugly, but had a sharp tongue in her head, and was merry to talk with; and it had been she who sat up for him ever when he had come home late during the last winter. He had answered over-hastily, fearing that his wife might complain and blame him. 'Twas a clownish fear; he should have known Halfrid would never stoop to such complaints. But now 'twas done — go back from his own word he

would not. He must even put up with being held for the father of
his serving-woman's child, whether he were so or not.

Halfrid spoke not again of the matter till a year after; then, one
day, she asked if he knew that Jorunn was to be wed over at Borg.
Simon knew it well enough, for he had given her dowry himself.
Where was the child to be? asked his wife. With its mother's parents, where it was now, answered Simon. Then said she:

" Methinks it would be more seemly that your daughter should
grow up here in your manor."

" In your manor, mean you? " asked Simon.

A little tremor passed over the lady's face.

" You know well, my husband, that as long as we both live, you
are master here at Mandvik," said she.

Simon went and laid his hands on his wife's shoulders:

" If, indeed, Halfrid, you deem you can bear to see the child
here in our home, great thanks shall I owe you for your high-
heartedness."

He liked it not. He had seen the young one more than once —
'twas not a comely child, and he could not see that it favoured
him or any of his folks. Less than ever did he believe that he was
the father. And he had been sorely angered when he heard that
Jorunn had had the child christened Arngjerd, after his mother,
without leave asked of him. But he must let Halfrid have her way.

She fetched the child to Mandvik, found a foster-mother for it,
and saw to it herself that the little one lacked naught. If her eyes
chanced to fall upon the child, she often took it on her lap and
tended it kindly and lovingly. And by little and little, as Simon
saw more of it, he grew fond of the little maid — he had a great
love of children. Now, too, he thought he could see a likeness in
Arngjerd to his father. It was like that Jorunn had been wise
enough to be on her good behaviour after the master had gone too
far with her. — So it might well be that Arngjerd was his daughter,
and what he had done at Halfrid's asking was the best and most
honourable way.

When they had been five years wedded, Halfrid bore her husband a son, a full-formed man-child. She was transfigured with
joy, but after her delivery she fell so sick that it was soon plain
to all that she must die. Yet was she of good cheer, the last time
when for a while she was herself. " Now shall you live on here as
master, Simon, and hand on Mandvik and all our lands to your
children and mine," she said to her husband.

After this the fever mounted so high that she knew no more, and she had not the grief, while yet on earth, of hearing that her boy had died a day before his mother. And in the other home, Simon thought, 'twas most like she felt no sorrow for such things, but was glad that she had their Erling with her.

Simon remembered afterward that, the night the two bodies lay up in the loft-room, he had stood leaning over the fence of a field that lay down by the sea-shore. It was just before St. John's Mass, and the night was so bright that the full moon's light was well-nigh blotted out. The water lay there palely shining, and plashed and gurgled a little on the strand. Simon had hardly slept more than an hour at a time, ever since the night the boy had been born — it seemed to him now very long ago — and he was so weary that he could scarce feel grief.

He was seven-and-twenty years old at this time.

Well on in the summer, when the estate was settled, Simon made over Mandvik to Stig Haakonssön, Halfrid's uncle's son. He moved to Dyfrin and stayed there the winter.

Old Sir Andres was bedridden, with dropsy and many other ills and aches; he was nearing his end now, and he bemoaned him much — life had not been so plain and simple for him either in these latter days. Things had not gone so with his fair and likely children as he had wished and looked that they should. Simon sat by his father and tried hard to get back to the easy jesting note of old — but the old man bemoaned himself without cease; Helga Saksesdatter, whom Gyrd had wedded, was so fine that she knew not what follies she should hit upon next — Gyrd dared not belch in his own house without asking his wife's leave. And this Torgrim, ever and always in a pother about his belly — never should Torgrim have had daughter of his, had he known that the man was such a poor wretch he could neither live nor die. Astrid could have no joy of her youth or her wealth so long as her husband lived. And here was Sigrid, broken and grieving — smiles and song had quite gone from her, his good child. That she should have had that child — and Simon no children! Sir Andres wept, an old, unhappy, sick man. Gudmund had set himself against every match his father had spoken of for him, and he was so old and useless now he had let the lad run wild altogether. . . .

— But all the ill fortune had begun when Simon and that maid from the Dale set themselves up against their parents. And 'twas

Lavrans' blame — for, bold a man as he was among men, he was chicken-hearted with his womenkind. The girl had snivelled and screeched, no doubt — and straightway he gave in and sent for that gilded whore-monger from Trondheim that could not so much as wait till he had been given his bride in wedlock. But if Lavrans had but been master in his own house, he, Andres Darre, would soon have shown that he could put sense in the head of a beardless whelp of a son. Kristin Lavransdatter — *she* bore children a-plenty — a strapping son every eleventh month, he had heard. . . .

"Aye, but that comes dear, father," said Simon, laughing. "The heritage comes to be split up sadly." He took Arngjerd up and set her on his lap — she had just come trotting into the room.

"Aye, 'twill not be through *her* that your heritage will be split up too small — whoever else it be that shall divide it," said Sir Andres testily. He was fond of his grandchild in a fashion, but it angered him that Simon had a base-born child. "Have you thought upon any new match, Simon?"

"Nay, you must let Halfrid grow cold in her grave first, father," said Simon, stroking the child's pale hair. "I shall wed again in good time — but sure there is no such haste —"

He took his bow and his ski and set forth for the woods, where he could breathe more freely. With his dogs he tracked the elk on the snow-crust, and he shot the capercailzie drowsing in the tree-tops. At night he slept in the Dyfrin forest sæter, and felt that 'twas good to be alone.

There was a scraping of ski outside on the hard snow; his dogs flew up barking, and other dogs answered from without. Simon opened the door upon a night blue with moonlight, and his elder brother Gyrd came in, tall and slender and comely and quiet. He looked younger now than Simon, who had ever been somewhat stout, and had grown a deal heavier in his years at Mandvik.

The brothers sat with the food-wallet between them, eating and drinking, and gazing into the hearth-fire.

"You must have seen," said Gyrd, "that Torgrim means to set us all by the ears when father is gone — and he has gotten Gudmund on his side. And Helga. They would fain keep Sigrid out of her full sister's share —"

"I have seen it. Her full share she shall have — you and I, brother, can sure make that good in despite of them."

" The best, mayhap, would be that father should take order in this before he dies," said Gyrd.

" Nay, let father die in peace," said Simon. " You and I between us should be able to guard our sister and see that they strip her not because she has fallen into such mischance."

Thus it came about that on Sir Andres Darre's death his heirs parted in bitter unkindness. Gyrd was the only one to whom Simon said farewell when he set out from home — and he knew that the life Gyrd's wife was leading him in these days was a none too happy one. Sigrid he took with him to Formo — she was to manage his house and he to see to her lands and goods.

He rode into his manor on a grey-blue day of melting snows, when the alder thickets by the Laagen were brown with blossom. When he had alighted and was entering the hall, with Arngjerd on his arm, Sigrid Andresdatter asked:

" Why smiled you, Simon? "

" Smiled — ? "

He had been thinking how far unlike was this home-coming to what he had looked for once — when the day came when he should take up his abode here on the manor of his father's mother's kin. A sister dishonoured, and a bastard child, these were his belongings now.

The first summer he saw but little of the Jörundgaard folks — he took much pains to shun them.

But the Sunday after the second Mary's Mass in the autumn, it chanced that he stood by Lavrans Björgulfsön's side in the church, so that 'twas they two that had to give each other the kiss of peace when Sira Eirík had prayed that the peace of Holy Church might be increased in us. And when he felt the elder man's thin, dry lips against his cheek, and heard him murmur the prayer for peace upon him, he was strangely moved. He saw that Lavrans meant more by it than but to follow a usage of the Church.

He hastened out when the mass was over; but at the standing for the horses he came on Lavrans, who prayed him to come with him to Jörundgaard and dine. Simon answered that his daughter was sick and his sister sitting by her. Lavrans then prayed that God might heal the child, and shook hands for farewell.

One evening some days after, they had been hard at work at

Formo getting in the harvest, for the weather looked doubtful. The most of the corn was housed by the evening, when the first shower came down. Simon ran across the courtyard in pouring rain, while a stream of yellow sunlight from between the clouds shone on the hall-house and the mountain wall behind it — and there he was ware of a little maid standing at the door in sun and rain. She had his favourite dog with her — it broke loose and leaped upon the man, dragging after it a woman's woven belt tied to its collar.

He saw that the girl was the child of a good house — she was cloakless and bare-headed, but her wine-red frock was of city-bought cloth, broidered, and made fast on the breast with a silver-gilt brooch. A silk cord held back the ringleted hair, now dark with the wet, from her forehead. She had a lively little face with broad forehead and pointed chin and great shining eyes, and her cheeks were flaming red, as though she had been running hard.

Simon saw who the maid must be, and greeted her by name, Ramborg.

" How comes it that you do me so much honour as to come hither to us? "

'Twas the dog, she said, as she went with him into the house out of the rain. It had a trick of running off to Jörundgaard; now had she brought it back. Aye, she knew it was his dog; she had seen it running after him as he rode by.

Simon rebuked her a little for having come hither on foot quite alone; he said he would have horses saddled and take her home himself. But first, to be sure, she must have some food. Ramborg ran across at once to the bed where little Arngjerd lay ailing, and both the child and Sigrid were much pleased with the guest, for Ramborg was quick and lively. She was not like her sisters, Simon thought.

He rode with Ramborg as far as the by-road to the manor, and would then have turned about; but there he met Lavrans, who had just learned that the child was not with her playmates at Laugarbru, and was setting forth with his people to search — he was much alarmed. Simon was made to come in, and when he had once taken his seat up in the hall his shyness fell from him and he felt quickly at home again with Ragnfrid and Lavrans. They sat late over their drink, and as it was now set in foul weather, he was thankful to stay the night.

There were two beds in the hall. Ragnfrid made up one of them fairly for the guest, and now someone asked where Ramborg was to sleep — with her parents, or in another house.

"Nay, for I will be in my own bed," said the child. "Can I not sleep with you, Simon?" she begged.

Her father said their guest must not be plagued with children in his bed; but Ramborg went on clamouring that she *would* sleep along with Simon. At last Lavrans said sternly that she was too old to share a bed with a strange man.

"No, father, that am I not," she said stubbornly. "I am not too big, am I, Simon?"

"You are too little," said Simon, laughing. "Ask me in five years, Ramborg, and be sure I shall not say you nay. But I warrant that then you will have another sort of man, little Ramborg, than a fat and ugly old widower."

It seemed that Lavrans liked not the jest; he told the girl sharply to hold her tongue and go lie down in her parents' bed. But Ramborg cried out once more:

"Now have you asked for me, Simon Darre, and in my father's hearing."

"So have I, indeed," answered Simon, laughing. "But I fear me, Ramborg, he will answer no."

After this day the Jörundgaard folks and those of Formo were much together. Ramborg was over at the neighbour manor whenever a chance served; she played with Arngjerd as if the child had been her doll, ran about with Sigrid helping in the housekeeping, and would sit in Simon's lap when they were in the hall. He fell again into the habit of petting and romping with the maid, as he had been used to do in old days, when she and Ulvhild had been as little sisters to him.

Simon had dwelt two years in the Dale, when Geirmund Hersteinssön of Kruke made suit for Sigrid Andresdatter. The Kruke kindred were of old yeoman stock, but though one and another of the men had served the Kings in the body-guard, they had never won any name beyond their own country-side. Yet was it as good a match as Sigrid could look to make, and she herself was willing to be wed with Geirmund. So her brother closed the bargain, and Simon held his sister's wedding at his house.

One evening just before, while the hurry and bustle of making ready for the feast were at their worst, Simon said in jest that he knew not what would become of his house when Sigrid had left him. Then said Ramborg:

" You must do the best you can for two years, Simon. At fourteen years a maid is fit to wed, and then you can bring me home."

" Nay, *you* will I not have," said Simon, laughing. " I dare not undertake to bridle so wild a maid as you."

" 'Tis the stillest tarns that run the deepest, says my father! " Ramborg cried. " *I* am the wild kind, I. My sister, she was meek and mild. Have you forgotten Kristin now, Simon Andressön? "

Simon leapt up from the bench, lifted the maid up against his breast, and kissed her throat so hard that the skin was flecked with red. Aghast and amazed at himself, he loosed her, caught up Arngjerd, and threw her up and crushed her to him in the same way to hide his disorder. He went on romping with the two, the little and the half-grown maid, and chasing them about, while they fled from him up on tables and benches; at last he set them up on the cross-beam next the door, and ran out.

— Kristin's name was scarce ever named at Jörundgaard — in his hearing.

Ramborg Lavransdatter grew comely as she grew in years. The talk of the country-side grew busy making matches for her. At one time it was Eindride Haakonssön of the Valders Gjeslings. They were kin in the fourth degree, but Lavrans and Haakon were both so rich they could well afford to send letters to the Pope in Valland and get dispensation. The match would put an end to some of the old suits-at-law that had gone on ever since the old Gjeslings went out with Duke Skule, and King Haakon took the Vaage lands from them and gave them to Sigurd Eldjarn. Ivar Gjesling the Young had won back Sundbu by weddings and exchanges, but these matters had led to endless jars and dissensions. Lavrans laughed at it all himself; the part of the spoil he could claim in his wife's right was not worth the calfskin and wax he had used up in the suit — to say naught of the trouble and the journeys. But seeing he had been in the broil ever since he was a wedded man, he must hold out to the end. . . .

But Eindride Gjesling took another maid to wife, and the Jörundgaard folks seemed not overmuch cast down. They were at the bride-ale, and Ramborg told her friends proudly, when she came home, that four men had come forward to sound Lavrans about her, either for themselves or for kinsmen. Lavrans had answered that he would not make any bargain for his daughter's hand till she was old enough to say a word in the matter herself.

So things went on till the spring of the year when Ramborg was fourteen winters old. One evening that spring she was in the byre at Formo with Simon, looking at a calf that had been born. It was white with a brown patch, and the patch seemed to Ramborg to be the very shape of a church. Simon sat on the edge of the cornbin, while the girl leaned across his knees, and he pulled at her plaits:

" Then I wager 'tis a token that you will soon ride to church, a bride, Ramborg."

" Aye, you know well enough my father will not answer no the day you ask for me," she said. " I am so grown up now, I might well wed this year."

Simon was a little taken aback, but he tried to laugh:

" Are you there again with that foolish old jest? "

" You know well that 'tis no jest," said the girl, looking up at him with her great eyes. " I have known it long — that 'tis to you here, at Formo, I would most fain come. Why have you kissed me and set me in your lap many a time and often, if you would not have me? "

" Right fain would I be to have you, my Ramborg. But I had never thought that so fair and young a maid could be meant for me. I am seventeen years older than you — you have not thought, I trow, how you would like to have an old blear-eyed, big-bellied husband when you were a woman in your best years — "

" *These* are my best years," said she, beaming, " and not yet are you so old and tottering, Simon! "

" But ugly I am — soon would you be sick of kissing *me*."

" That have you no cause to believe," she answered, laughing as before, and held up her mouth to be kissed. But he did not kiss her.

" I will not profit by your simpleness, my sweet. Lavrans will take you with him to the south this summer. Should you not have changed your thoughts ere you come back, then will I thank God and Our Lady for better fortune than I had looked for — but bind you I will not, fair Ramborg."

He called his dogs, took his spear and bow, and went up on the hills that same evening. There was much snow in on the uplands

still; he struck off to his sæter and got him a pair of ski, then lay
out for a week by the tarn south of the Boar Fells and hunted reindeer. But the evening he set off down towards home he grew uneasy and fearful again. 'Twould be like Ramborg if she had spoken
of it to her father in spite of all. When he came over the hill-
crest by the Jörundgaard sæter, he saw smoke and sparks going
up from the roof. He thought maybe 'twas Lavrans himself that
was there, and he went up to the huts.

He thought he could see from the other's bearing that he had
guessed right. But they sat there talking of the bad summer last
year and of when it would likely be best to move up the cattle this
year, of the hunting, and of Lavrans' new hawk, which sat on the
floor, flapping its wings over the pluck of the birds that were roasting on a spit over the fire. Lavrans had come up but to see to his
horse-shelter in Ilmandsdal — some folks from Alvdal that had
come by it that day had told him it was fallen down. So passed
the most of the evening. At last Simon spoke up:

"I know not if — has Ramborg said aught to you of a matter
she and I spoke of one night?"

Lavrans said slowly:

"Methinks it had been well you had spoken to me first, Simon
— you might have known what answer you would have had of
me. Aye, aye — I understand how it may have chanced that you
named it first to the maid — and it shall make no odds. I am glad
that things are so that I can bestow the child in a good man's
hands."

After this there was not much more to be said, thought Simon.
Strange enough, all the same — here sat he who had never dreamed
of making too free with an honest maid or a wife, and he was
bound in honour to wed one whom he would liefer not have had.
But he made one trial:

"Yet neither is it so, Lavrans, that I have gone wooing your
daughter behind your back — I thought I was so old that she would
not take it for more than brotherly kindness from old days that I
spoke so much with her. And if you deem I am too old for her, I
should not marvel at it, nor let it part the friendship betwixt us."

"Few men have I met whom I would rather have in a son's stead
than you, Simon," said Lavrans. "And I would fain give Ramborg
away myself. You know who will be her guardian when I am
gone." It was the first time aught had been said between these two

of Erlend Nikulaussön. " In many ways my son-in-law is a better man than I took him to be, when first I knew him. But I know not if he is the man to deal wisely with the giving of a young maid in marriage. And I mark well that Ramborg herself is willing."

" So thinks she now," said Simon. " But she is scarce out of her childhood. Therefore have I no wish to press the matter on you now, if you deem it should stand over yet awhile."

" And I," said Lavrans, frowning a little, " have no wish to force my daughter upon you — believe not that."

" *You* must believe," said Simon quickly, " there is no maid in Norway's land that I would rather have than Ramborg. So it is, Lavrans, that I deemed it all too great good fortune for me if I should get me so fair and young and good a bride, rich, and come on both sides of the highest kin. And you for father-in-law," he said a little sheepishly.

A slight laugh came from Lavrans:

" Oh, you know well what I think of you. And I know you will so deal with my child and her heritage that we never shall have cause to repent this bargain, her mother and I — "

" That will I, God and all holy men helping me," said Simon.

On that they shook hands. Simon remembered the first time he had clasped hands with Lavrans on such a bargain; and his heart grew little and sore in his breast.

But Ramborg *was* a better match than he could have looked for. There were only the two daughters to divide between them what Lavrans left. And he would be as a son to the man whom, of all men he knew, he had ever honoured and loved the most. And Ramborg was young and fresh and sweet. . . .

And surely by this time he should be a grown man with a grown man's wit. Had he been waiting here thinking that he might wed as a widow her whom he could not win as a maid — after yon other had enjoyed her youth — and a dozen of stepsons of that breed — nay, then he would be rightly served if his brothers had him adjudged incapable and set him aside from managing his own affairs. Erlend would live to be as old as the hills — such fellows as he always did. . . .

Aye, so now they were to be brothers-in-law. They had not seen each other since that night in yonder house at Oslo. Well, it must be yet less joyful for the other to remember than for him.

He would be a good husband to Ramborg, without falsehood

or guile. Though it might almost be said the child had beguiled *him* into a snare —

"You are laughing?" asked Lavrans.

"Did I laugh? 'Twas but a thought that came into my head."

"You must tell me what it was, Simon — so that I may have a laugh too."

Simon Andressön fastened his little, sharp eyes on the other.

"I was thinking of — women. I marvel if any woman regards men's faith and men's laws as we do amongst ourselves — when she or hers can gain by setting them at naught. Halfrid, my first wife — aye, this have I never told to any Christian soul before you, Lavrans Björgulfsön, and to none other will I ever tell it — she was so good and holy and upright a woman that methinks her like has scarce ever lived — I have told you how she took the matter of Arngjerd's birth. But that time when we saw how things were with Sigrid — aye — she would have had me hide away my sister and that *she* should feign to be with child, and should pass off Sigrid's child for hers. For thus had we had an heir, and the child had been well provided, and Sigrid could dwell with us and need not be parted from it. I verily believe she understood not it would have been treachery against her own kinsmen — "

Lavrans said, after a pause:

"Then you could have kept Mandvik, Simon — "

"Aye." Simon Darre laughed harshly. "And mayhap with as good a right as many another man to the land he calls the heritage of his fathers. Since we have naught to trust to in such matters but the honour of women."

Lavrans slipped the hood over his falcon's head, and lifted the bird upon his wrist.

"This is strange talk for a man thinking of marriage," he said low. There was something like distaste in his voice.

"Of *your* daughters I trow none thinks such things," answered Simon.

Lavrans looked down at the falcon and scratched its feathers with a stick.

"Not of Kristin either?" he asked yet lower.

"No," said Simon firmly. "She behaved not well towards me, but never did I find that she dealt in falsehood. She told me plainly and honestly that she had met a man whom she loved more than me."

" When you gave her up so willingly," asked the father in a low voice, " was it not because you had heard some — some rumours — about her? "

" No," said Simon as before. " I had never heard rumours about Kristin."

It was fixed that the betrothal-ale should be drunk that same summer, and the wedding be held after Easter the next year, when Ramborg would be full fifteen years old.

Kristin had not seen her home since the day she had ridden away from it as a bride — 'twas now eight winters since. Now she came back with a great company — her husband, Margret, five sons, nurse-girls, handmaids, men and pack-horses with baggage. Lavrans rode out to join them, and met them at Dovre. Kristin no longer wept so lightly as in her youth, but when she saw her father come riding to meet her, her eyes filled with tears. She stopped her horse, slipped down from the saddle, and ran to meet him, and when they met she took his hand and kissed it humbly. Lavrans leapt from his horse at once, and lifted his daughter up in his arms. Then he shook hands with Erlend, who had also alighted, and now came to meet his father-in-law with a reverent greeting.

The next day Simon came over to Jörundgaard to greet his new kinsfolk. Gyrd Darre and Geirmund of Kruke were with him, but their wives they had left at Formo. Simon had chosen to hold his wedding at home, so the women there were in a great bustle.

As to the manner of the meeting — Simon and Erlend greeted each other freely and without constraint. Simon was master of himself, and Erlend was so gay and cheerful that Simon thought he must have forgotten where they had last seen each other. Then Simon gave Kristin his hand. They were less sure of themselves, and their eyes met but for an instant.

Kristin thought to herself that he had fallen off greatly. In youth he had been comely enough, although even then too thick-set and short-necked. His steel-grey eyes had looked little under the full eyelids; his mouth had been too small, and the dimples in his round boyish face too large. But he had had a fresh-hued visage, and a broad milk-white forehead beneath goodly light-brown curly hair. The curly hair he had still, as thick and nut-brown as

before, but his face was now an even red-brown all over, wrinkled
under the eyes, and with heavy cheeks and a double chin. His
body, too, was grown heavy — and he had something of a paunch.
He looked not now like a man who would care to lie at night on
the edge of a bed for the sake of whispering with his betrothed
maid. Kristin felt pity for her young sister; she was so fresh and
gracious and so childishly joyful that she was to be wed. The very
first day she had shown Kristin the chests filled with her bridal gear
and Simon's betrothal-gifts — and she had told how she had heard
from Sigrid Andresdatter of a gilded casket that stood in the bridal-
loft at Formo; there were twelve costly linen coifs in it, and they
were to be a gift to her from her husband the first morning. Poor
little soul, how could she understand what marriage was? 'Twas
pity that she knew so little of this young sister — Ramborg had been
at Husaby twice, but there she had ever been sullen and unfriendly
— she could not get to like Erlend, nor yet Margret, who was of her
own age.

Simon thought that he had looked — perhaps hoped — that Kristin should seem somewhat worn, seeing she had had so many children. But she bloomed with youth and health, and she bore her
as proudly straight as ever, and walked as graciously, though it
might be she trod the earth now a little more firmly than of old.
She was the comeliest mother, with her five fair little sons around
her.

She was clad in a dress of home-made rusty-brown woollen with
dark-blue birds woven into it — he remembered standing about
and leaning up against her loom while she sat weaving on the stuff.

There was a little trouble when they came to sit down to table
in the upper hall. Skule and Ivar began shrieking, for they were
bent on sitting between their mother and their foster-mother as
they were used to do. Lavrans thought it not seemly that Ramborg
should sit below her sister's serving-woman and small children —
so he bade his younger daughter sit in the high-seat beside him,
since she was so soon to be parted from her home.

The little lads from Husaby were restless, and seemed not to
know much of behaviour at the board. The meal had not gone far,
when the little fair-haired boy slid down under the table and came
up by the wall-bench beside Simon's knee.

" May I look at that strange sheath you have there in your belt,

kinsman Simon? " he said; he spoke slowly and gravely. It was the
great silver-mounted sheath to hold a spoon and two knives he had
caught sight of.

"You may so, kinsman. What is your name, cousin? "

" Gaute Erlendssön is my name, cousin."

He put down the piece of bacon he was holding on the lap of
Simon's festal doublet of silver-grey Flemish cloth, drew the
knife from the sheath, and looked closely at it. Then he took the
knife Simon was eating with, and the spoon, and put them all in
their places, so that he could see how it looked when all the things
were in the sheath. He was exceeding grave and exceeding greasy
on fingers and face. Simon smiled as he looked at the little visage,
so comely and so intent.

Soon after, the two eldest also made their way across to the
men's bench; and the twins slipped down under the table and began crawling about there under folk's feet — then out and away
to the dogs by the fire-place. There was little chance for the
grown-up folk to eat in peace. The children's mother and father
spoke to them, indeed, and bade them sit down prettily and be
quiet; but the children paid no heed; and the parents, on their
side, laughed at them the whole time and seemed to think their
ill behaviour no great matter — not even when Lavrans, somewhat
sharply, bade one of the serving-men take the dogs down into the
room below, so that folks might be able to hear themselves speak
in the upper hall.

Ramborg left the hall with her betrothed and went with him
through the spring night a little way up between the fences. Gyrd
and Geirmund had ridden on ahead, and Simon stopped to say
good-night. He had his foot in the stirrup already — when he
turned again, took her in his arms, and crushed the slender child
to him so tightly that she moaned softly and happily.

" God bless you, my Ramborg — so fine and fair as you are —
all too fine and fair for me," he murmured into her tangled curls.

Ramborg stood looking after him as he rode off in the misty
moonlight. She rubbed her upper arm — he had grasped it so hard
that it hurt her. Dizzy with joy, she thought: in three days more
she would be wed to him.

Lavrans stood with Kristin before the children's bed, and
watched her tucking the small bodies into their places. The eldest

were big boys already, with thin bodies and slender bony limbs; but the two little ones were plump and rosy, with creases in their flesh and dimples at the joints. A fair sight they seemed to him, lying there red and warm, their thick-growing hair damp with sweat, breathing evenly in their sleep. They were healthy, comely children — but never had he seen young ones so ill brought up as these grandsons of his. 'Twas well, indeed, that Simon's sister and brother's wife had not been there that night. But maybe 'twas not for him to talk about breaking in children — Lavrans sighed a little, and made the sign of the cross above the small heads.

So Simon Andressön drank the bride-ale with Ramborg Lavransdatter, and the wedding was in all ways fair and sumptuous. Bride and bridegroom looked joyous, and many deemed that Ramborg was lovelier on her day of honour than her sister had been — not dazzling fair, like Kristin, but far gentler and more glad; all could see in the clear innocent eyes of this bride that she bore the golden crown of the house of Gjesling with full honour this day.

And glad and proud she sat in the arm-chair before her bride-bed with hair bound up when the guests next morning came up to greet the young folk. With laughter and free jesting they looked on while Simon laid the housewife's head-dress over his young wife's head. Shouts of greeting and the clashing of arms made the rafters ring, as Ramborg rose and took her husband's hand, upright and red-cheeked under the white coif.

It was not so often that two children of great houses of the one parish were wedded — when the kindred was gone through in all its branches, the kinship would most often be found too near. So all accounted this wedding a rare and joyous festival.

6

ONE of the first things Kristin had marked at her old home was that all the old heads of men, that had stood where the verge-boards crossed at the house-gables, were gone now. Instead there had been set up spires with carven birds and foliage-work, and the new storehouse had a gilded weather-vane. The old posts of the high seat in the hearth-room house, too, had been changed for new. The old ones had been carved in the likeness of two men; ugly enough — but 'twas thought they had been there ever since the house was built, and the custom had been to smear them with fat and bathe them with ale at festivals. On the new posts her father had carved out two men with helms and shields marked with the Cross. 'Twas not St. Olav himself, said he, for it seemed to him unmeet that a sinful man should have images of the holy ones in his house, except to pray before them — but they might, he thought, be two warriors of Olav's guard. All the old carvings Lavrans had himself cut up and burnt — the serving-men dared not touch them. It was with some doubt he still let them bear out food to the great stone at Jörund's grave-mound on holy eves — but yet he deemed 'twere sin and shame to deny to the tenant of the mound what he had been used to be given ever since folk had dwelt upon the place. He had died long before Christendom had come to Norway, so it was not his fault that he was a heathen.

Folks liked these new-fangled doings of Lavrans' but little. 'Twas well enough for him, who could afford to buy himself protection in other quarters. What he got seemed, indeed, to have all the virtue needed, for he had the same good fortune in husbandry as before. But there were those who asked whether yonder folk would not avenge themselves when there came a master to the manor who was less pious and not so open-handed towards the Church and all her belongings. And for small folk 'twas cheaper to give the old ones what they were used to have, rather than make foes of them and trust wholly to the priests.

Besides, it was none too sure, folk deemed, how 'twould go with the friendship between Jörundgaard and the parsonage when Sira Eirik should pass away. The priest was grown old and weakly now, so that he had need of a chaplain to help him. He had first spoken to the Bishop of his daughter's son Bentein Jonssön — but Lavrans, too, spoke to the Bishop, who was a friend of his of old. Folks deemed this misjudged. Truly it might well be that the young priest had been too forward with Kristin Lavransdatter that evening and maybe frighted the girl — but none could know that she might not herself have given some cause for the fellow's boldness. It had come out plainly enough since that she was none so coy as she had seemed. But the truth was, Lavrans had ever put too much faith in that daughter of his, adoring her almost as if she had been a sacred thing.

Afterwards there had been coldness for a time between Sira Eirik and Lavrans. But then came this Sira Solmund as chaplain, and he straightway fell at loggerheads with his parish priest over some lands, whether they belonged to the glebe or were Sira Eirik's own. Lavrans knew more than all other men in the parish of all sales of land and the like from the earliest days, and it was on his witness that the case was adjudged. Since then he and Sira Solmund had not been friends; but Sira Eirik and Audun, the old deacon, now lived at Jörundgaard, one might say; for they went thither daily and sat with Lavrans, bemoaned the wrongs and vexations they had to suffer at the hands of the new priest, and were waited on as they had been two bishops.

Kristin had already heard somewhat of all this from Borgar Trondssön of Sundbu; he had wedded a wife from the Trond-heim country, and had been a guest at Husaby more than once. Trond Gjesling was dead some years ago; none deemed him much loss, for he had been a cankered shoot of the old tree, churlish, cross-grained and sickly. Lavrans was the only one who had put up with Trond; he pitied his brother-in-law, and yet more Gudrid, his wife. Now they were gone, all their four sons lived together on the manor; they were comely, bold and likely men, so folk deemed it a good exchange. There was close friendship between them and their uncle at Jörundgaard — he rode over to Sundbu a couple of times each year and went a-hunting with them in the West Hills. But Borgar had told Kristin 'twas beyond all reason, the way Lavrans and Ragnfrid tormented themselves now with penances and godliness. " He swills down water as hard as ever on fast-days; but he communes not with the ale-cup, your father, with the good old heartiness that he used," said Borgar. None could understand the man — 'twas not to be believed that Lavrans had any secret sin to atone for; so far as folks knew, he must sure have lived as Christianly as any son of Adam, saving the holy saints.

Deep down in Kristin's heart there stirred a dim surmise why her father strove thus to come near and ever nearer to his God. But she dared not think it clearly out.

She would not own to herself that she saw how changed her father was. 'Twas not that he was so greatly aged; he had kept his shapely form and his upright and gracious bearing. He was grey-ing fast, but folk marked it not much, because his hair had always been so light in hue. And yet — her remembrance was ever haunted by the picture of the young, fair-shining man — the fresh round-ing of the cheeks in the long narrow face, the clear red of the skin under the sunburn, the red full mouth with deep-cut corners. Now was the well-rounded muscular body shrunk into naught but bone and sinew, the face brown and sharp, as though carven in wood, the cheeks were flat and lean, the mouth had a knot of muscle at each corner. Aye, but then he was no young man any more — though neither, after all, was he so old.

Quiet, sedate and thoughtful he had always been, and she knew that from childhood up he had followed the commands of Christ with a rare zeal, had loved masses and prayers in the Roman tongue, and ever sought the church as the place where he found his best solace. But all had felt that a full, gentle tide of courage and joy in life flowed through the quiet man's soul. Now 'twas as though something had ebbed away from him.

She had not seen him drunken more than a single time since she came home — it was one evening of the wedding-feast at Formo. He had staggered somewhat then and been thick of speech, but he had not been out of the way merry. She remembered him as he had been in her childhood at the great ale-drinkings in festival seasons and at banquets — laughing his great laughter and slapping his thighs at each jest; offering to fight and wrestle with any man there who had a name for strength; trying horses; leaping about in the dance, and the first to laugh when his feet failed him; strewing around gifts and overflowing with goodwill and loving-kindness toward all mankind. She understood that her father had need of these great outbursts of revelry, in the midst of his stead-fast labours, his strenuous fastings and his quiet home life with his own folks, who saw in him their best friend and surest stay.

She felt, too, that if her husband never had this need to drink himself drunken, 'twas because he kept so little check on himself even if he were never so sober, but ever followed his own devices without much pondering over right and wrong or what folk ac-counted seemly and wise behaviour. Erlend was the most sober man as to strong drink that she had known — he drank to quench his thirst and for the sake of good-fellowship, without caring much about the matter.

But now Lavrans Björgulfsön had lost his good old heartiness over the ale-cup. No longer had he that within him which needed to be given vent in revelry. It had never come into his mind to drown his cares with hard drinking, and it came not now into his mind — to him it had ever seemed that a man should take his joy to the drinking-feast.

With his sorrows he had gone elsewhere. There was a picture which always hung dim and half-remembered in his daughter's mind — her father on that night when the church was burned. He stood beneath the crucifix that he had saved from the flames, bearing the cross and staying himself by it. Without thinking it clearly out, Kristin felt in her heart that it was in part fear for her and her children's future with the man she had chosen, and the feeling of his own helplessness in this matter, that had changed Lavrans.

This knowledge gnawed secretly at her heart. And, as it was, she had come to Jörundgaard weary of the restless winter they had spent, and of her own weakness in making no stand against Erlend's heedlessness. She knew that he was, and would ever be, a spendthrift; that he had no wit in guiding goods and gear — they dwindled under his hands slowly but ceaselessly. One thing and another she had got him to set in order as she and Sira Eiliv had counselled — but she could not evermore be speaking to him of such things; and it was tempting, too, now to give herself up to gladness with him. She was so weary of striving and struggling with all things both without her and in her own soul. And yet was she such an one that careless pleasure, too, made her careworn and fearful.

Here at home she had looked to find again the peace she had felt in her childhood under her father's safe-keeping.

But no — she felt so unsafe. Erlend had good incomings from his Wardenship, but he was living now with yet more pomp, with a greater household and the following of a great chief. And he had begun to keep her quite outside all things in his life that touched not their most private life together. She understood that he would not have her heedful eyes watching his doings. With men he would talk willingly enough of all he had seen and gone through in the north — but to her he never named it. And there were other things. He had met Lady Ingebjörg, the King's mother, and Sir Knut Porse more than once in these years; it had never so chanced at these times that she could be with him. Sir Knut was now a Duke in Denmark, and King Haakon's daughter had bound her to him in wedlock. The marriage had waked bitter wrath in many Norsemen's minds; and steps — Kristin understood not what they were — had been taken against the lady. But the Bishop of Björgvin had sent certain chests to Husaby; they were now on board *Margygren*, and the ship lay out at Ness. Erlend had been given letters and was to sail for Denmark later in the summer. He pressed her to go with him — but she set herself against it. She knew that Erlend moved among these great folk as their equal and dear kinsman, and she feared what might come of it; 'twas unsafe with so rash a man as Erlend. But she could not pluck up heart to go with him — never could she get him to hearken to counsel there, and she was loath to adventure herself in company with folks among whom she, a plain housewife, could scarce hold her own. And then there was the terror of the sea — sea-sickness to her was a thing worse than the hardest childbed.

Thus, as she went about in her old home, her heart was tremulous and ill at ease.

One day she had gone with her father down to Skjenne. And she had seen again the precious rarity which the folk of that manor had in their keeping. 'Twas a spur of the purest gold, huge and in shape old-fashioned, with strange chasings. Like every child in the country-side, she knew where it had come from.

'Twas in the first times after St. Olav had christened the Dale that Audhild the Fair of Skjenne was spirited away into the mountain-side. They dragged the church-bell up on to the mountain and rang for the maid — and the third evening she came walking over the pastures, so decked out with gold that she shone like a star. Then the rope broke, the bell rolled down the scree, and Audhild must turn back again into the hillside.

But many years after there came one night twelve warriors to the priest — he was the first priest that ever was in Sil. They had golden helms and silver corselets, and they rode on dark-brown stallions. 'Twas Audhild's sons by the Mountain-king, and they prayed that their mother might be given burial as a Christian woman and a grave in hallowed earth. She had striven to hold fast her faith and to keep the Church's holy days in the mountain, and she had prayed so sorely for this grace. But the priest denied it to her — folk said because of this he himself had found no rest in his grave, but in autumn nights he could be heard walking in the grove north of the church, weeping and bemoaning his harshness. The same night Audhild's sons had appeared at Skjenne, bearing their mother's greeting to her old parents. And in the morning they found the golden spur in the courtyard. And 'twas clear that yonder folk still accounted the men of Skjenne as kin, for they had ever rare good fortune in the mountains.

Lavrans said to his daughter, as they rode homeward in the summer night:

"These Audhildssons said over the Christian prayers they had learnt of their mother. God's name and Jesu name they could not name; but they said the Lord's Prayer, and the Credo in this wise: I believe on yonder Almighty One, I believe on the only-begotten Son, I believe on the most mighty Spirit. And then they said: Hail thou Lady that art the blessed one among women — and blessed is the fruit of thy womb, the Comfort of all the world — "

Kristin looked timidly up in her father's lean weather-beaten face. In the light summer night it looked so ravaged with sorrows and broodings as never before she had seen it.

"This you had never told me before," she said in a low voice.

"Had I not? Oh, no; I may have deemed it might give you heavier thoughts than your years gave you strength to bear. Sira Eirik says it is written in the books of St. Paul the Apostle: not Manhome alone groaneth in travail — "

One day Kristin sat sewing on the topmost step of the stair to the upper hall, when Simon came riding into the courtyard and stopped just below her, but saw her not. Her parents both came out to him. No, Simon would not alight; Ramborg had but bidden him ask, as he was passing by here — the sheep that had been her pet lamb, they would scarce have sent it to the hills; she would fain have it with her now.

Kristin heard her father smite his hand to his head. Aye, Ramborg's sheep — He gave an angry laugh. An ill thing, this — he had hoped she had forgotten it. For he had given his two eldest grandsons a little hatchet each; and the first thing they had used them for was to slaughter Ramborg's sheep.

Simon laughed a little:

"Aye, the Husaby boys — a rascal crew they are — ! "

Kristin ran down the stairway, loosing her silver scissors from its belt-chain:

"Give Ramborg this in amends for my sons' killing her sheep

— I know she has wanted this ever since she was small. None shall say that my sons — " She had spoken hotly, and now she fell suddenly silent. She had seen her father's and mother's faces — they looked on her gravely and wonderingly.

Simon made no motion to take the scissors; he seemed somewhat abashed. Then he caught sight of Björgulf and, riding across to him, leaned over and lifted the boy to the saddle-bow in front of him: " So — you're a Viking harrying our coasts? Well, now are you my prisoner, and to-morrow your parents can come over to me and we will bargain about your ransom — "

Therewith he waved laughingly to the others and rode off, with the boy struggling and laughing in his arms. Simon had come to be right good friends with Erlend's sons; Kristin remembered that he had ever had a way with children; her little sisters had loved him. It vexed her strangely that he should be so fond of children and have such a turn for playing with them, when her husband was ever so loath to hearken to children's talk.

The day after, though, when they were at Formo, she could see well that Simon's wife had given him small thanks for bringing this guest home with him.

"No one could look that Ramborg should greatly care for children now," said Ragnfrid. "She is scarce out of childhood yet, herself. She will change, I warrant, as she grows older."

"Doubtless she will." Simon and his mother-in-law exchanged a glance and the slightest of smiles. Ah, thought Kristin — aye, 'twas nigh on two months from the wedding now. . . .

In the trouble and unease of mind that Kristin now suffered, she was apt to vent her disquiet on Erlend. He took this sojourn on the manor of his wife's father contentedly and happily, like a man with conscience at ease. He was good friends with Ragnfrid, and made no secret of his hearty love for his wife's father. Lavrans, too, seemed fond of his son-in-law. But so sore and watchful was Kristin now grown that she felt that in Lavrans' kindness for Erlend there was much of that pitying tenderness that Lavrans had always had for every living thing that seemed to him in some measure unfit to stand on its own feet. His love for his other daughter's husband was not of this kind — Simon could meet him as a friend and comrade.

Simon and Erlend, too, were good friends when they met, but

they sought not each other's company. Kristin still felt a secret shrinking from Simon Darre — both by reason of what he knew of her, and still more because she knew that from that day at Oslo he had come off with honour and Erlend with shame. She raged at the thought that even this Erlend should be able to forget. Thus she was not ever good-humoured with her husband. And if Erlend chanced to be in the mood to bear her testiness good-humouredly and with meekness, it vexed her that he took her words so little to heart. Another day it might chance that his temper was short, and then he would grow hot, and she would answer him coldly and bitterly.

One evening they sat in the hearth-room house at Jörundgaard. Lavrans still felt most at home in this house, most of all in rainy weather when the air was heavy, as to-day, for in the great hall the roof was flat, and the smoke from the fire-place was a plague; but in the hearth-room the smoke rose up and hung under the roof-tree even when they had to shut the vent-hole against the weather.

Kristin sat by the hearth, sewing; she was moody and dull. Over against her, Margret was half asleep over her seam, and yawned now and then; the children were romping noisily in the room. Ragnfrid was at Formo, and the most of the serving-folk were gone out. Lavrans sat in his high-seat, and Erlend at the upper end of the outer bench; they had the chess-board between them, and moved the pieces in silence and after much pondering. Once when Ivar and Skule seemed set on pulling a puppy into two pieces betwixt them, Lavrans rose and took the shrieking little beast from them; he said nothing, but sat down again to the game holding the puppy in his lap.

Kristin went over to them and stood with a hand on her husband's shoulder, watching the game. Erlend had much less skill as a chess-player than his father-in-law, and most often lost when they played in the evenings; but he took such things with careless good-humour. This evening he played yet worse than was his wont. Kristin chid him for it once or twice — not too mildly and sweetly. Then Lavrans said at last, somewhat testily:

"How should Erlend keep his thoughts on the game while you stand thus disturbing him? What would you here, Kristin? You have never had any skill of these games."

"No; I trow you folks think I have no understanding of aught — "

"Of one thing I see you have no understanding," said her father sharply, "and that is how it beseems a wife to speak to her husband. Better were it you should go and keep your young ones in bounds — the din they make is worse than the Wild Hunt."

Kristin went and set up her children in a row on the bench and sat down beside them.

"Be still now, my sons," she said. "Your grandfather likes not that you should romp and play in here."

Lavrans looked at his daughter, but said no word. Soon after, the foster-mothers came in, and Kristin, the maids and Margret went out with the children to put them to bed. Erlend said, when he was alone with his father-in-law:

"I could have wished, father-in-law, that you had not chidden Kristin as you did. If it comfort her to pick at me when she is in ill humour, why — it boots not to speak to her, and she will not suffer any to say a word about her children —"

"And you," asked Lavrans, "mean you to suffer your sons to grow up so uncorrected? Where are they got to, the maids that should keep the children by them and see to them — ? "

"To your serving-men's quarters, I warrant," said Erlend, laughing and stretching himself. "But I dare not say a word to Kristin about her serving-maids — she grows wroth in earnest then, and casts it in my teeth that she and I have scarce been a pattern for others."

The day after, as Kristin went plucking strawberries along a meadow south of the manor, her father called to her from the smithy-door, and bade her come to him.

Kristin went, somewhat against the grain. 'Twas Naakkve again, likely — this morning he had left a gate open and the home cattle had gotten into the barley-field.

Her father took a red-hot iron from the forge and laid it on the anvil. The daughter sat and waited, and for long there was no sound but the strokes of the hammer, as they beat the sparking iron into a pot-hook, and the answering clang of the anvil. At last Kristin asked what he would with her.

The iron was cold now. Lavrans put from him tongs and sledge-hammer and came to her. With the soot on his face and hair, his clothes and hands black, and the great leathern apron in front of him, he looked sterner than was his wont.

" I called you to me, my daughter, to say to you this: Here in my house you must show your wedded husband such reverence as beseems a wife. I will not hear my daughter speak to her master as you answered and spoke to Erlend yesterday."

" 'Tis somewhat new, father, that you should deem Erlend to be a man to whom folks should show reverence."

" He is *your* man," said Lavrans. " I put not force upon you either to bring about your match with him. That you should bear in mind."

" You two are such warm friends," answered Kristin. " Had you known him then as you know him now, doubtless you would have been fain to put force on me."

Her father looked down at her, gravely and sadly:

" Now do you speak over-hastily, Kristin, and say that which you know is untrue. I tried not to put force upon you, even when you were bent on throwing off your lawful betrothed husband, though you know that I loved Simon heartily — "

" No — but since Simon too would have none of *me* — "

" Nay. He was too high-minded to stand stiffly on his rights, seeing you were unwilling. But I know not if in his heart 'twould have gone so much against him had I done as Andres Darre would have had me — paid no heed to the wilfulness of you two young folks. And I could well-nigh doubt whether Sir Andres was not right — now when I see that you cannot live in seemly wise with the husband you set all at naught to win — "

Kristin laughed aloud, an ugly laugh:

" Simon! Never would you have forced Simon to take for wife the woman whom he had found with another man in such a house — "

Lavrans caught his breath. " House? " he gasped out.

" Aye — a house such as you men call a bordel. She that owned it — she had been Munan's paramour — she warned me herself that I should not go thither. I said I went to meet my kinsman — I knew not that he was *her* kinsman — " She laughed again, a wild, cruel laugh.

" Be silent! " said the father.

He stood still a moment. A shiver passed over his face — a smile that seemed to blanch it. There came to her the thought of a wooded hillside — how it whitens when a storm-gust turns over all its leaves in a wave of palely glittering light:

" He learns much that questions not — "

Kristin huddled down where she sat on the bench, leaning on one elbow, and hiding her eyes with the other hand. For the first time in her life she was in fear of her father — in deadly fear.

He turned him from her, went and took up the sledge, and put it in its place amongst the other hammers. Then he gathered together files and other small tools, and set himself to placing them in order on the cross-beam between the walls. He stood with his back to her; his hands shook violently.

"Have you never thought, Kristin — that Erlend kept silence about this?" He stood before her, looking down into her white frighted face. "I gave him no for an answer, curtly enough, when he came to me at Tunsberg with his rich kinsmen and made suit for you — I knew not then that I should have been but too thankful that he was willing to restore my daughter's honour. — Many men would have let me know it then. . . .

"*He* came again and made suit for you in full honour. Not all men would have been so steadfast in striving to win to wife one who was already — was already — what you then were."

"*That* I trow no man had dared to tell to you — "

"'Tis not of cold steel that Erlend has ever been afraid — " Lavrans' face had grown unspeakably weary; his voice had gone hollow and dead. But soon he spoke again quietly and firmly:

"Ill as all this has been, Kristin — methinks 'tis worst of all that you should tell it, now he is your husband and the father of your sons —

"If it be as you say, you knew the worst of him before you braved all things that you might wed him. And he was willing to buy you at as great a price as though you had been an honest maid. Much freedom to rule your life and manage your affairs has he given you — therefore should you make amends for your sin by managing with understanding, and making up for what Erlend lacks in prudence — so much do you owe to God and your children.

"I have said myself — and others have said the same — that Erlend seemed not to be fit for aught else than to beguile women. You are answerable in part for such things being said — to that you have now yourself borne witness. Since then, he has shown that after all he *was* fit for somewhat else — your husband has won himself a good name for a bold and swift leader in war. 'Tis no small gain for your sons that their father has won fame for boldness and skill in arms. That he was — unwise — *you* should have known best of all of us. Best may you make amends for your shame by honouring and helping the husband yourself have chosen — "

Kristin had bent forward over her lap, her head in her hands. Now she looked up, wildly and despairingly:

" Cruel was it of me to tell you this. Oh — Simon begged me — 'twas the only thing he begged of me — that I should spare you the knowledge of the worst — "

" Simon bade you spare me — ? " She heard the suffering in his voice. And she knew this, too, was cruel of her, to tell him that a stranger had seen she needed to be bidden spare her father.

Then Lavrans sat down by her, took one of her hands between both of his, and laid them on his knee.

" Cruel it was, my Kristin," he said gently and sadly. " Kind are you to all, my child, my treasure, but — I have seen it before this too — you can be cruel to them you love too dear. For Jesu sake, Kristin, spare me from the need of going in such fear for you — fear that this wild heart of yours will yet bring more sorrow over you and yours. You tug and strain like a young horse when 'tis first tied up to the stake, wherever you are tied by your heart-strings."

Sobbing, she sank against him, and her father drew her into his arms and held her close and firmly. They sat thus a long while, but Lavrans said no more. At last he lifted up her head.

" Now you are all black," he said with a little smile. " There is a cloth in yonder corner — but 'tis like it would but make you blacker. You must go home and make you clean again — anyone can see you have been sitting in the smith's lap — "

He pushed her gently out of the door, closed it behind her, and stood still a space. Then he staggered the few steps across to the bench, sank down on it and sat with head thrown back against the log wall and upturned, distorted face. With all his force he pressed one hand against his heart.

Well that it never lasted long. The breathlessness, the black dizziness, the pain shooting out through the limbs from the heart that struggled and shook, gave one or two heavy thuds, and then stood quivering still again. The blood hammering in the neck-veins.

'Twould pass in a little while. It passed always when he had sat still a little. But it came again, more and more often.

Erlend had trysted his ship's crew to meet at Veöy * on the eve of St. James' Mass, but he tarried at Jörundgaard a little longer to go with Simon and hunt down a big bear that had been harrying the sæter cattle. When he came home from the hunt, he found word awaiting him that his men had fought with the townsmen and he must hasten thither to bail them out. Lavrans had an errand in those parts, so he rode along with his son-in-law.

It was nigh the end of the Olav's Mass feast when they came out to the island. Erling Vidkunssön's ship lay there, and at evensong in Peter's Church they met the High Steward. He came with them to the monastery where Lavrans had taken lodging, ate supper with them there, and sent his men down to the ship to fetch some rarely good French wine he had gotten at Nidaros.

But the talk went but haltingly over the wine. Erlend sat wrapped in his own thoughts, his eyes bright and eager, as ever when a new venture was before him, but unheedful of the others' speech. Lavrans but sipped the wine, and Sir Erling was quiet and said little.

" You look weary, kinsman," said Erlend to him.

Aye, they had had heavy weather crossing Husastadviken the night before; he had been up —

" And you must ride hard if you would be at Tunsberg by Lawrence Mass day. And much rest or solace you will scarce find there either. Is Master Paal with the King now — ? "

" Aye. Do you touch at Tunsberg on your way? "

" To ask if the King would have me bear his loving and duteous greetings to his mother? " Erlend laughed. " Of if Bishop Aulfinn would send word by me to the Lady — ? "

" Many wonder that you should be journeying to Denmark, now that the chief men of the kingdom are gathering to the meeting at Tunsberg," said Sir Erling.

" Aye, is it not strange that folk must ever be wondering at me? Surely 'tis no marvel if I have a mind to see a little of such manners and breeding as I have not seen since I was last in Denmark — to ride in a tourney once again — and since our kinswoman has bidden us to come. You know well that none other of her kindred in this land will avow her now, save only Munan and I."

" Munan — " Erling frowned, and then laughed. " Is there so much life left in the old boar, I had well-nigh asked, that he can

* See Note 13.

still move his brawn about? — So Duke Knut is to hold a tourney.
Doubtless, then, Munan is to ride in the jousting?"

"Aye — 'tis pity of you, Erling, that you cannot bear us company and see that sight." Erling, too, laughed. "I mark well that
you fear Lady Ingebjörg has bidden us to this christening-ale so
that we may brew the ale for another feast and bid her to it. Nay,
you should know best that I am too heavy-handed and too light
at heart to be of use in hatching plots. And you have drawn every
tooth in Munan's head —"

"Oh, no, we are not so fearful either of plots from that quarter.
Methinks it must be clear as day to Ingebjörg Haakonsdatter now
that she made forfeit of all rights in her own land when she wedded with the Porse. 'Twill be a hard matter for her to get a foot
inside our doors, now she has laid her hand in that man's whose
least finger we will never suffer in our affairs."

"Aye, 'twas wisely done of you, indeed, to part the boy from
his mother," said Erlend darkly. "He is but a child yet — and already have we Norsemen cause to hold our heads high when we
think of the King we have sworn fealty to —"

"Be still!" said Erling Vidkunssön, low and vehemently. "It —
for sure it is untrue —"

Erlend said:

"'Tis whispered in every manor and in every cabin in our north
country that Christ's Church burned because our King is unworthy to sit in St. Olav's seat —"

"In God's name, Erlend — I say 'tis unsure whether it be true.
And if it were, a child, like King Magnus, we must sure believe is
without sin in God's eyes — he can redeem himself — Say you
that *we* have parted him from his mother? I say, God punish that
mother who betrays her son as Ingebjörg betrayed hers — and put
not your trust in such an one, Erlend — bear in mind that they are
faithless folk you journey now to meet!"

"Methinks they have kept faith with each other fairly enough.
— But, as for you, you talk as if letters from Heaven dropped every
day into your lap — 'tis that, maybe, makes you so bold to fight
with the Lords of the Church."

"Nay, let us have an end of this, Erlend. Talk of things you have
wit to understand, boy, and else be silent." — Sir Erling had risen,
and he and Erlend stood face to face, red with anger.

"Oh, take heed of your tongue, Erlend," he went on in a little.

" Think twice before you speak, where you are going. And think, and think again twenty times, before you do aught — "

" If 'tis so that *you* do, you who rule the roost here, then I marvel not that all things move but haitingly. But you need not be afraid," he yawned. " I — shall do naught, I trow. But 'tis grown a rare land to live in now, this of ours — "

"Aye — you are setting forth early to-morrow. And my father-in-law is weary — "

The two others sat on in silence, after he had bidden them good-night. — Erlend was sleeping aboard his ship. — Erling Vidkunssön sat turning his goblet between his fingers.

" You are coughing? " he said, that he might say somewhat.

" Old men grow full of rheum so easily. We have many plagues, you see, my lord, that you young folk know naught of," said Lavrans smiling.

Again they were silent, till Erling Vidkunssön said, as though half to himself:

" Aye — so think all men — that this land is ill guided. Six years ago at Oslo I deemed I had seen clearly that there was a firm intent to uphold the kingly power — among the men of the houses to whom that duty falls by birth. I — built upon that."

" I believe you saw rightly, my lord. But you said yourself — we are used to rally round our King — and now our King is a child — and half the time in a foreign land — "

" Aye. There be times when I think — nothing is so ill but it is in some ways good. In the old times, when our Kings bore them like wild stallions — there was store of brave foals to rear; our folk needed but to choose the one that was the best fighter — "

Lavrans laughed a little: " Oh, aye — "

" We talked together three years ago, Lavrans Lagmandssön, when you came back from pilgrimage to Skövde and had seen your kinsfolk in Gautland — "

" I remember, my lord, you did me the honour to seek me out."

" Nay, nay, Lavrans, no need for so much *kurteisi*." He struck out a little impatiently with his hand. " 'Tis even as I said then," he went on gloomily. " None now can bring together the nobles of this land. *They* push to the front that are most fain to fill their bellies — there is yet some meat left in the trough. But they that might aspire to win might and riches by such service as was held in honour in our fathers' days, they come not forth! "

"So would it seem. True it is that honour follows the banner of the chief."

"Then men must deem, I trow, that with my banner there follows little honour," said Erling dryly. "You, too, have held aloof from all that might have made you a name, Lavrans Lagmandssön."

"So have I done ever since I have been a wedded man, my lord. I was wedded early — my wife was sickly, her health could not bear much going about in company. And it seems as if our stock doth not thrive here in Norway. My sons died early, and only one of my brother's sons lived to a man's age."

They sat again in silence awhile.

"Such men as Erlend," said the High Steward low — "they are the most dangerous. They that have thoughts that go a little farther than their own concerns — but not far enough. Aye, is he not like an idle child, this Erlend — ?" He shoved his wine-cup round about on the table in his vexation. "He is no dullard! And he has birth and valour. But never doth he trouble to hear so much of any matter as to understand it through and through. — And should he ever care to hear a man out, he had forgot the beginning, like enough, before one got to the end — "

Lavrans looked across at the other. Sir Erling had aged much since last he had seen him. He looked worn and weary — seemed not to fill his seat so fully as before. He had fine, clear-cut features, but they were a little too small, and his hue was, as it were, a little faded — had been so always. Lavrans felt that this man — though he was an upright, knightly man, prudent, and willing to serve faithfully and unflinchingly — yet, however measured, was somewhat too small to be the first man in the realm. Had he been a head taller, 'twas like he would more easily have found full following.

Lavrans said low:

"Sir Knut, too, be sure, is wise enough to see this — if they are hatching aught down there — that in any secret counsels he would find Erlend of small use — "

"You like this son-in-law of yours in a fashion, Lavrans," said the other, almost testily. "Though, truth to tell, cause to love him you have not — "

Lavrans sat drawing with his finger on the table in some spilled wine. Sir Erling marked how loosely the rings sat on his fingers now.

"Have *you* cause?" Lavrans looked up with his faint smile. "And yet I trow that you like him too."

"Oh, aye. God knows —

"But you may make your oath, Lavrans, many things are running in Sir Knut's head now — he is father of a son that is King Haakon's grandson."

"Aye, but even Erlend must sure understand that that child's father has all too broad a back for the little lordling ever to be able to get around it. And the mother has our whole country against her because of this marriage."

A little while after, Erling Vidkunssön stood up and buckled on his sword; Lavrans had courteously taken his guest's cloak from the hook where it hung, and stood with it in his hands — then of a sudden he swayed and would have fallen to the ground, had not Sir Erling caught him in his arms. With much pains and labour he managed to bear the other, a big, tall man, over to the bed. A stroke it was not — but Lavrans lay there, his lips blue and white, with slack, strengthless limbs. Sir Erling ran across the yard and waked up the hospice-father.

Lavrans seemed much abashed when he came to himself. Aye, it was a weakness that took hold on him now and then — 'twas from an elk-hunt he had been on two winters back — he had lost his way in a snowstorm. Maybe something like this was ever needed to teach a man his youth is gone from him — he smiled in excuse.

Sir Erling tarried till the monk had bled the sick man, though Lavrans prayed him not to trouble himself, seeing that he was to set forth at daybreak. . . .

The moon shone bright, riding high above the hills of the mainland, and the water lay black in their shadow, but out on the fjord the light floated in flakes of silver. No smoke from any vent-hole — the grass on the house-roofs glittered with dew in the moonlight. Not a human soul in the one short street of the little town, as Sir Erling walked swiftly the short space, but a few steps, to the King's mansion, where he slept. He looked strangely slim and small in the moonlight — with the black cloak gathered closely about him — shivering a little. A pair of sleepy serving-men, who had sat up for him, came tumbling out into the courtyard with a lanthorn. The High Steward took the lanthorn and sent the men to bed — he shivered a little again as he climbed the staircase to the store-house-loft, where he was to sleep.

7

A LITTLE after Bartholomew Mass, Kristin set out on her homeward journey, with her great company of children and serving-folk, and all their baggage. Lavrans rode with her to Hjerdkinn.

They walked up and down the courtyard in talk, he and his daughter, the morning he was to set forth down the Dale again. The hill country round them lay in sparkling sunshine — the mosses were red already, and the knolls yellow as gold with the birch copses; out on the upland wastes, tarns glittered and grew dark again, as the shadows of the great shining fair-weather clouds floated across them. They kept rolling up unceasingly, and sank down over the distant clefts and glens, amidst all the grey-stone peaks, and blue mountains with combs of new snow, and old snow-fields, that lay around as far as the eye could reach. The little grey-green patches of corn belonging to the rest-house stood out strangely against the autumn hues of this shining mountain world.

The wind blew fresh and sharp — Lavrans drew up the hood of Kristin's cloak, which had blown back upon her shoulders, and smoothed with his fingers the strip of linen coif that showed beneath it.

" Methinks you have grown pale and thin-cheeked in my house," said he. " Have we not taken good care of you at home, Kristin? "

" That you have. 'Tis not that — "

" Truly, too, this is a toilsome journey for you, with all these children," said her father.

" Oh, aye. Though 'tis not because of these five that my cheeks are pale — " A smile flitted over her face, and when her father looked at her questioningly, in alarm, she nodded and smiled a little again. The father looked away from her, but in a little while he asked:

" Since this is so, then maybe 'twill not be so soon that you can come home to us in the Dale again? "

" At least I hope 'twill not be eight years this time," she said in the same tone. Then she caught a glimpse of the man's face: " Father! Oh — father! "

" Hush, hush, my daughter — " Unwittingly he caught her by

the upper arm and stopped her as she would have flung herself upon him. " Nay, Kristin — "

He took her hand firmly in his, and began walking again beside her. They had come away from the houses; they were following now a little path in among the yellow birch thickets — they marked not where they were going. Lavrans jumped over a little rill that crossed the path, turned towards his daughter, and gave her his hand over.

She saw, even in this little movement, he was no longer springy and nimble as of old. She had seen before without marking it — he no longer leapt into the saddle as lightly as he had done; he ran no longer up a loft-stairway; he lifted not a heavy thing easily as he was wont to do. He bore his body more stiffly and carefully — as if he had a slumbering pain within him and went softly so as not to wake it. The blood could be seen beating in his neck-veins when he came in from riding. Sometimes she had seen what seemed swellings or pouches under his eyes — and she remembered that one morning when she came into the hall he lay half dressed in the bed with his naked legs over the bed-foot, and her mother was crouched in front of him, chafing his ankle-joints.

" Should you sorrow for every man that old age strikes down, child, much will be your mourning," he said, evenly and quietly. " You have great sons yourself now, Kristin; sure it cannot come on you unlooked for that you see your father will soon be an old fellow. When we parted in old days while I was yet young — we could not know any more then than we know now, whether 'twas to be our lot to meet again on this earth. I may yet live long — 'twill be as God wills, Kristin."

" Are you sick, father? " she asked, tonelessly.

" Some ailments come with the years," answered her father, lightly.

" You are not old, father. You are but two and fifty years — "

" My father never was so old. Come and sit here by me."

There was a low grass-grown shelf under a rocky wall that leaned over the beck. Lavrans unclasped his cloak, folded it together, and, sitting on it, drew her down beside him. In front of them the beck clucked and rippled over the little stones in its bed, swaying a branch of willow that lay in the water. The father sat with his eyes fixed on the blue and white mountains far off behind the warm-hued autumn uplands.

" You are cold, father," said Kristin; " take my cloak — " She unfastened it; and he drew the skirt of it round his shoulders, so that they both sat in its shelter. Under it he put one arm about her waist.

" You know it well, my Kristin: unwise is he that mourns a man's going hence — let Christ have thee, rather than I — 'tis like you have heard the saying. I trust firmly in God's mercy. 'Tis not so long, the time for which friends are parted. Maybe 'twill seem so to you sometimes, while yet you are young; but you have your children and your husband. When you come to my years you will deem 'tis no time since you saw us who are gone away, and you will wonder, when you reckon up the winters that have passed, that they are so many. . . . To me it seems now 'tis not long since I myself was a boy — and yet is it many years since you were the little light-haired maid that ran about after me, wherever I might stand or go — you followed your father so lovingly — God reward you, my Kristin, for the joy I had of you — "

" Aye — if He reward me as I rewarded you — " She sank on her knees before him, caught his wrists, and kissed the palms of his hands as she hid her weeping face in them. " Oh, father, my dear father — no sooner was I a grown maid than I paid you for your love with the bitterest sorrow — "

" Nay, nay, child; weep not so." He drew his hands loose, and lifted her up beside him, and they sat as before.

" Much joy have I had of you, in these years too, Kristin. Fair and hopeful children have I seen growing up by your knee, a notable and understanding woman are you grown — and I have seen that more and more you have used yourself to seek help where it may best be had, when you were in any trouble. Kristin, my most precious gold, weep not so sorely. You may hurt him you bear under your belt," he whispered. " Nay, sorrow not so."

But he could not check her weeping. Then he lifted his daughter up into his lap and sat her on his knee; now he had her even as when she was a little one — her arms around his neck and her face pressed to his shoulder.

" There is a thing I have never told to any mother's child but to my priest — now will I tell it you. In the days when I was growing up — at home at Skog, and when first I was with the body-guard — I had a mind to take the vows, as soon as I were old enough. Nay, I made no promise, not even in my own heart. There was much that drew me the other way, too. — But when I lay out fishing in the Botn Fjord and heard the bells ring from the cloister on Hovedö — it seemed that drew me most of all. — Then, when I was sixteen years old, father had made for me that habergeon of mine of Spanish steel plates soldered with silver — Rikard the Englishman at Oslo welded it together; and I got my sword too — the one I use always, and my horse-armour. 'Twas not so peaceful in the land then as in your young years — there was war with the Danes — and I knew I was like soon to have the chance to use my fair weapons. And I could not lay them from me. — I comforted me with the thought that my father would mislike it if his eldest son turned monk, and that I should not cross my parents.

"But 'twas I myself that made choice of the world, and I have striven to think when the world went against me: unmanful would it be to murmur at the lot I had chosen myself. For I have seen it more and more with each year I have lived — no worthier work can there be for a human soul that has found grace to conceive somewhat of God's loving-kindness, than to serve Him and watch and pray for those men whose sight is still darkened by the shadow of the things of this world. Yet must I needs say, my Kristin — hard would it be for me to give up for God's sake the life I have lived on my farms and lands, with cares for earthly things and with worldly cheer — with your mother by my side, and with you my children. Therefore must a man suffer in patience, when he has begotten offspring of his body, that it scorch his heart if he lose them or the world go badly with them. God, who gave them souls, owned them, and not I — "

Kristin's body was still shaken with weeping; and her father began rocking her in his arms like a little child.

"Many things there are that I understood not when I was young. Father held Aasmund dear too, but not so as he loved me. 'Twas for my mother's sake, you see — her he never forgot, though he took Inga because 'twas his father's will. Now would I wish that I could have met my stepmother again in this earthly home and prayed her to forgive that I set no store by her kindness — "

"But you have said often, father, that your stepmother did you neither good nor evil," said Kristin, through her weeping.

"Aye, God help me — 'twas my lack of understanding. Now does it seem a great thing to me that she hated me not, and never gave me an angry word. How would you like it, Kristin, if so it were that you saw a stepson put before your own son, at all times and in all things? "

Kristin was grown somewhat quieter. She lay now with her face turned outwards looking towards the mountain range. A great grey-blue pile of cloud was passing over the sun, darkening the air — some yellow beams stabbed through it, and a sharp glitter was thrown up from the water of the beck.

Then her tears broke out anew:

" Oh, no — father, my father — should I nevermore see you in life — "

" God guard you, Kristin, my child, so that we may find each other again on yonder day, all we who were friends in life — and every human soul. — Christ and Mary Virgin and St. Olav and St. Thomas will keep you all your days." He took her face between his hands and kissed her on the mouth. " God be gracious to you — God give you light in this world's light and in that great light hereafter — "

Some hours later, when Lavrans Björgulfsön rode off from Hjerdkinn, his daughter went with him some way, walking by his horse's side. Lavrans' man had gotten a long way ahead, but he still kept on at a foot's pace. It was grievous to look on her despairing face, all marred by weeping. So had she sat in the guest-shed too, all the time, while he ate and talked to the children, jested with them, and took them in his lap, one by one.

Lavrans said softly:

" Grieve no more for what you have to repent toward *me*, Kristin. But remember it, when your children grow big, and you may deem that they bear them not towards you or towards their father as you might think was right. And remember then, too, what I said to you of my youth. Faithful is your love to them, I know it well; but you are hardest where you love most, and I have marked that in these boys of yours dwells self-will enow," he said with a little smile.

At last Lavrans bade her turn and go back: " I would not have you go alone any farther from the houses." They were come into a hollow between little hills with birch trees round their foot and stone screes higher up their sides.

Kristin pressed herself against her father's foot in its stirrup. She groped with her fingers over his clothes and his hand and the saddle and the horse's neck and quarters, rocked her head from side to side, and wept with such a deep lamentable sobbing that her father thought his heart must break to see her plunged in such great sorrow.

He sprang from his horse and took his daughter in his arms, holding her in his embrace for the last time. Again and again he made the sign of the cross over her and commended her to the keeping of God and the holy saints. At last he said that now she must let him go.

So they parted. But when he was gone a little way, Kristin saw that her father slackened his horse's pace, and she knew that he was weeping as he rode away from her.

She ran into the birch-wood, hastened through it, and began climbing up over the golden lichen-covered stones of the scree on the nearest knoll. But the stones were big, and hard to climb over, and the little hill was higher than she had thought. At last she was at the top, but by that time he was gone from sight among the low hills. She laid her down in the moss and bear-berry heath that grew on the top of the knoll, and there lay long weeping, with her face hidden in her arms.

Lavrans Björgulfsön came home to Jörundgaard of an evening late. A cheering little warmth passed over him when he saw folks were still up in the hearth-room house — there was a faint flicker of firelight behind the tiny pane of glass in the pent-house wall. He had always felt that in this house was most of home.

Ragnfrid sat alone in the room with a great seam of work before her on the table — a tallow candle on a brass holder stood by her. She rose to her feet at once, bade him good-evening, put more wood on the hearth-fire, and went herself to fetch food and drink. No — she had sent the maids to bed long ago — they had had a hard day; but now, at any rate, they had barley-bread ready baked to last till Yule. Paal and Gunstein had gone to the hills to gather moss. Speaking of moss — would Lavrans have his winter clothes made from the litmus-dyed web of cloth or from the heather-green? Orm of Moar had been there that morning asking to buy some leather rope. She had taken out the ropes that hung next the door in the shed, and said he could have them as a gift. Aye — his daughter was going on a little better now — the wound on her leg was healing up well. . . .

Lavrans answered or nodded, as he and his man ate and drank. But the master was soon done eating. He stood up, dried his knife on the back of his thigh, and took up a bobbin that lay by Ragnfrid's place. The thread was wound on a pin that was carven into a bird at each end — one of these had had a piece of its tail broken off. Lavrans rounded off the break, and carved a little on it, making the bird dock-tailed. At one time, long ago, he had made a great many such bobbin-pins for his wife.

" Must you mend these yourself? " he asked, looking at her work. It was a pair of his leather hose; Ragnfrid was sewing patches on the inside of the thighs, where they had been worn by the saddle. " 'Tis stiff work for your fingers, Ragnfrid."

" Oh — " His wife laid the pieces of leather edge on edge and bored holes in them with her awl.

The servant bade good-night and went out. Man and wife were alone. He stood by the hearth warming himself, with one foot on the hearth-rim and a hand on the pole of the smoke-vent. Ragnfrid looked across at him. And she grew aware that the little ring with the rubies — his mother's betrothal-ring — was gone from his hand. He saw that she had marked it.

" Aye — I gave it to Kristin," said he. " It has ever been meant for her — methought 'twas as well she should have it now."

At times thereafter one of them would say to the other — maybe 'twas time they went to bed. But he stood up where he was, and she sat on at her work. They spoke some words about Kristin's journey; about work that was towards on the farm, about Ramborg and Simon. Then they said somewhat again about its being, perhaps, well to go to rest — but neither of them moved.

Then Lavrans took the gold ring with the blue and white stone from off his right hand, and went across with it to his wife. Shyly and awkwardly he took her hand and slipped the ring on to it — he had to change it once or twice before he found the finger it fitted. It came to rest on the middle finger, above her wedding-ring.

" I would have you take this now," he said, low, without looking at her.

Ragnfrid sat still as a stone — her cheeks blood-red.

" Why do you this? " she whispered at last. " Think you I grudge our daughter her ring? "

Lavrans shook his head and smiled a little:

" Oh, methinks you know why I do it."

"You said before, this ring you would take with you to the grave," she said in the same whisper. "None was to bear it after you were gone —"

"Therefore must you never take it from off your hand, Ragnfrid — promise me that. I would not have any bear it after you —"

"Why do you this?" she asked again, holding her breath.

The man looked down into her face.

"Last spring 'twas four and thirty years since we were wedded to each other. I was not yet a full-grown man — and all through my manhood you were at my side, both when sorrow came and when things went well with me. God help us — all too little did I understand how heavy was the burden you bore, while we lived together. But methinks now that it ever seemed good to me that you were there. . . .

"I know not whether 'tis so that you have deemed I held Kristin dearer than you. True it is that she was my greatest joy and that she brought me my worst sorrow. — But you were mother to them all. It seems now to me that the worst of all will be to leave you, when I go hence. . . .

"Therefore must you never give my ring to any — not to either of our daughters even — but say that they must leave it on your hand.

"Maybe you deem, wife, you have had more sorrow with me than joy — and in a way things went wrong between us; but yet methinks through all we have been faithful friends. And I have thought that hereafter we shall find each other again in such wise that the wrong will not part us any more, but the love that was between us God will build up again, better than before —"

The wife lifted her pale, furrowed face — her great sunken eyes burned as she looked up at her husband. He held her hand still; she looked at it as it lay in his, lifted a little. The three rings gleamed, one above the other — lowest down the betrothal-ring, then the wedding-ring, and above it this one.

It came over her so strangely. She remembered when he had put the first on her hand — by the hearth in the hall of her Sundbu home, their fathers standing by them. He was white and red, round-cheeked, scarce out of his boyhood — a little bashful as he stepped forward from Sir Björgulf's side.

The other he had set on her finger before the church-door at Gerdarud, in God's triune name, under the priest's hand.

She felt it — with this last ring he had wedded her again. When, in a little while, she sat over his lifeless body, he willed she should know that with this ring he had espoused to her the strong and living force that had dwelt in that dust and ashes.

She felt as though her heart was cloven in her breast, and bled and bled, wildly as in youth — for sorrow for the warm and living love she still secretly bemoaned that she had missed, for fearful joy in this pale, shining love that drew her with it towards the uttermost bounds of the earthly life. Through the pitchy darkness that was coming she saw the glimmer of another, milder sun, she smelt the scent of the herbs in the garden at the world's end. . . .

Lavrans laid his wife's hand back in her lap, and sat down on the bench, a little way from her, with his back to the board, and one arm upon it. He looked not at her, but gazed into the hearth-fire.

When she spoke again, her voice was calm and quiet:

"I had not thought, my husband, that I had been so dear to you."

"Aye, but you were; " he spoke as evenly as she.

They sat silent awhile. Ragnfrid moved her sewing from her lap to the bench beside her. In a while she asked in a low voice:

"The thing I told you that night — have you forgotten it? "

"Such things a man cannot forget in this earthly home. And so it is, I have felt myself, that things grew not better between us after I had come to know it. Though God knows, Ragnfrid, I strove hard that you might never mark I thought so much of it — "

"I knew not that you thought so much of it."

He turned sharply towards his wife and looked at her. Then said Ragnfrid:

" 'Twas my fault that things grew worse between us, Lavrans. Methought that since you could be to me in all ways as you were before — after that night — then must you have cared about me even less than I had believed. Had you grown to be a hard husband to me — had you struck me, if only once and when you were drunken — then could I have better borne my sorrow and my remorse. But that you took it so lightly — ! "

"Did you deem that I took it lightly? "

The faint tremble in his voice made her wild with longing. She longed to plunge herself within him, to sound the unquiet depths from which his voice came forth strained and labouring. She flamed up:

"Aye, had you taken me in your arms one single time, not for that I was your Christian wedded wife that they had laid at your side, but that I was the wife you had longed for and fought to win — never then could you have been to me as though those words had been unspoken."

Lavrans thought a space:

"No. It — may be I could not. No."

"Had you joyed in the betrothed that was given you, as Simon joyed in our Kristin — "

Lavrans made no answer. In a little he said softly, as though against his will and in fear:

"Why named you — *Simon?* "

"Nay, it could not come to my mind to liken you with the other," answered the wife, herself somewhat confused and fearful, but trying to smile: "You and he are too unlike."

Lavrans rose to his feet and walked a few steps, restlessly — then he said yet lower:

"God will not forsake Simon."

"Seemed it never to you," asked his wife, "as though God had forsaken *you?* "

"No."

"What were your thoughts on that night we sat there in the barn — when you learned in *one* hour that we whom you had held dearest and loved most faithfully, we had both been false to you as we could be — "

"I thought not much, I trow," said the man.

"And since," his wife went on, "when you thought upon it always — as you say you did — "

Lavrans turned away from her. She saw a flush spread over his sun-burned neck.

"I thought on all the time I had been false to Christ," he said very low.

Ragnfrid rose — she stood still a moment before she ventured to go to her husband and lay her hands on his shoulders. When he put his arms around her, she bowed her forehead against his breast; he felt that she was weeping. He drew her close in to him and pressed his face down on her head.

"Now, Ragnfrid, we will go to rest," he said in a little.

Together they went over to the crucifix, bowed before it, and crossed themselves. Lavrans said over the evening prayers; he spoke, low and clearly, in the Church's tongue, and his wife spoke the words after him.

They took off their clothes. Ragnfrid lay down on the inner side of the bed — the pillows were made up now much lower than of old, because her husband in these latter days had been often troubled with dizziness. Lavrans bolted and barred the room-door, scraped ashes over the fire on the hearth, blew out the light, and lay down beside her. They lay in the darkness, their arms touching. In a little the fingers of their hands twined together.

Ragnfrid Ivarsdatter thought — 'twas like a new bridal night, and a strange bridal night. Happiness and unhappiness flowed together and lifted her up on waves so mighty that she felt within her now the first loosening of the roots of her soul — now had death's hand given her, too, a wrench — the first time.

"Speak to me, Lavrans," she prayed him softly. "I am so weary — "

The man whispered:

"*Venite ad me, omnes qui laboratis et onerati estis. Ego reficiam vos,** hath the Lord said."

He passed an arm around her shoulders and drew her in to his side. They lay a little, cheek against cheek. Then she said softly:

"Now have I prayed God's Mother to make for me this prayer, that I may not outlive you, my husband, many days."

His lips and eyelashes touched her cheek in the darkness as lightly as the touch of butterflies' wings.

"My Ragnfrid, my Ragnfrid — "

8

KRISTIN stayed at home at Husaby this autumn and winter and would go nowhither — she gave for a reason that she was ailing. But she was only tired. So tired she had never been before in her life — tired of being merry and tired of sorrowing, and tired, most of all, of brooding.

It would be better when this new child had come, she thought — she longed much for it; it was as though it was to be the saving of her. If it were a son, and her father died before its birth, it

* Matthew xi. 28.

should bear his name. And she thought how she would love this child, and nurse it at her own breast — it was so long since she had nursed a child that she could weep with longing when she thought that now she should soon have a suckling in her arms again.

She gathered her sons about her knee again as she had been used to do in early days, and strove to make their upbringing somewhat more orderly and mannerly. She felt that in this she was obeying her father's wish, and this brought some peace into her soul. Sira Eiliv had begun now to teach Naakkve and Björgulf their letters and the Latin tongue, and Kristin often sat over in the priest's house when the children were there at their book. But as scholars they showed not much thirst for knowledge, and all the children were wild and unruly, save Gaute alone, so that he still was his mother's poppet, as Erlend called it.

Erlend came back from Denmark about All Saints' tide, in high feather. He had been entertained with the greatest honour by the Duke and his kinswoman Lady Ingebjörg; they had thanked him right heartily for his gifts of silver and furs; he had ridden in the jousts, and chased the hart and the hind; and when they parted, Sir Knut had bestowed on him a coal-black Spanish stallion, while the Lady had sent loving greetings and two silver-grey greyhounds to his wife. Kristin deemed that these outlandish hounds looked faithless and treacherous, and she was afraid they might do her children hurt. And the folk all through the countryside talked much of the Castilian steed. 'Twas true, Erlend looked well on the long-legged, light-built horse; but such beasts suited not this northern land, and God only knew how the stallion would get about on the hill-paths. Howbeit, Erlend bought up now, wherever he went about in his charge, the bravest black mares, till he had made him a stud that was fair to look on at the least. In other days Erlend Nikulaussön had used to give his riding-horses fine outlandish names: Belkolor and Bayard and suchlike; but this horse, he said, was so rare a beast that he needed no such adornment — plain Soten * should be his name.

Erlend chafed much that his wife would not go about with him anywhither. Sick he could not mark that she was — she neither swooned away nor vomited this time — no sign was to be seen upon her yet — and most like her paleness and weariness were

* Soten = Soot.

from evermore sitting indoors brooding and pondering over his misdeeds. Yule-tide came round — and hot quarrels arose between them. And now Erlend no longer came afterward to beg forgiveness for his hot temper, as he had ever used to do before. Till now he had thought always, when there was strife between them, that 'twas he was at fault. Kristin was good; she was ever in the right; and if he wearied and was ill at ease in his home, it was but that his nature was such that he grew weary of what was good and right when he had too much of it. But last summer he had marked more than once that his father-in-law held with him, and seemed to deem that Kristin was lacking in wifely gentleness and forbearance. And then it came into his thought that she took things to heart in a petty way and was hardly brought to forgive him small misdeeds that had not been so ill meant on his part. Always had he prayed her for forgiveness when he had had time to think — and she had said that she forgave, but afterward he had been made to see that 'twas hidden away, but not forgotten.

So he was much from home, and now he often took his daughter Margret with him. The maid's upbringing had ever been one of the things that set them at odds. Kristin had never said aught of it, but Erlend knew well what she — and others — thought. He had dealt with Margret in all ways as she had been his true-born child, and folk made her welcome as though she were such when she went about with her father and stepmother. At Ramborg's wedding she had been one of the bridesmaids, and had borne a golden garland on her flowing hair. Many of the women liked this but ill, but Lavrans had talked them round, and Simon, too, had said that none must say aught against it to Erlend or speak of it to the maid herself — 'twas not the fair child's fault that she was so luckless in her birth. But Kristin saw that Erlend had planned to wed Margret to an esquire bearing arms, and that he believed, with the standing he now had, he would be able to bring this about, although the maid was begotten in adultery, and 'twould be a hard matter to win for her a safe, firm footing amongst good folk. It might, perchance, have been done if folk had felt any right faith that Erlend had it in him to keep up and increase the might and riches in his house. But though Erlend was liked and honoured after a fashion, 'twas as though no one had full faith that the fair fortunes of Husaby would endure. Thus Kristin feared he would be hard put to it to bring his plans for Margret to a good end. And

hough she liked not Margret overmuch, yet she pitied the maid,
nd dreaded the day when, maybe, her pride must be broken — if
he must be content with a much humbler match than her father
ad taught her to look for, and quite another way of life than the
ne he had nurtured her in.

Thus things were, when just after Candlemas three men from
'ormo came to Husaby; they had come across the hills on ski in
aste, bringing Erlend letters from Simon Andressön. Simon wrote
hat their father-in-law had now fallen so sick that 'twas not to be
ooked for that he could live long; and that Lavrans had bade him
ray that Erlend would come to Sil if 'twere possible for him; he
vas fain to have speech with his two sons-in-law of how all things
hould be ordered when he was gone.

Erlend went about casting stolen glances at his wife. She was
ar gone with child now, pale and thin-faced — and she looked
o sorrowful — every moment the tears would be welling up. He
egan to repent his behaviour to her in the winter — her father's
ickness had not come on her unlooked for, and if so it was that
he had had to bear about this secret sorrow, he could better for-
ive her unreasonable ways.

Alone he could have made the journey to Sil and back swiftly
nough, going on ski across the mountains. But if he took his wife
vith him, 'twould be a slow and toilsome business. And then he
vould need to tarry till after the wapinschaws * in Lent, and set
rysts there with his sheriffs; and there were some meetings, too,
hat he must attend himself. Before they could set forth, 'twould
e perilously near the time she looked to be delivered — and Kris-
in, too, who could nowise endure the sea even when she was well!
sut he was loath to think of her not seeing her father before he
ied. In the evening, when they had lain down, he asked her if
he dared make the journey.

It seemed to him he was well repaid when she threw herself
veeping in his arms, full of thankfulness, and of penitence for her
nfriendliness towards him in the winter. Erlend grew soft and
ender, as he ever was when he had brought grief to a woman
nd had to see her sorrow it out before his eyes; and he bore well
nough afterward with Kristin's fantasies. He had said from the
rst, the children he would not have with them. But the mother
vould have it that Naakkve was so great a boy now, 'twould be

* Wapinschaw = Arms-muster.

well for him to see his grandfather's going hence. Erlend said
No. Then she was sure that Ivar and Skule were too small to b
left behind in the serving-women's charge. No, said their father
And then Lavrans had been so fond of Gaute. No, said Erlend -
'twas hard enough as it was — things being as they were with her -
for Ragnfrid to have a childbirth in the house, while her husban
lay on his sick-bed — and for themselves on the journey home
ward with a new-born babe. Either must she give the child ou
to nurse on one of Lavrans' farms, or she must tarry at Jörund
gaard till 'twas summer — but then he must come home befor
her. He had to put all this to her, over and over again; but he strov
to speak calmly and reasonably.

Then he bethought him that he should take from Nidaros on
thing and another that his mother-in-law might need for th
grave-ale — wine and wax, wheat flour and millet and the like
But at length they were ready to set forth, and they came t
Jörundgaard the day before Gertrude's Mass.

But Kristin found 'twas far otherwise than she had though
to be at home at this time.

She should have rejoiced with all her heart that it had bee
given her to see her father once again. And when she remembere
his joy at her coming and how he had thanked Erlend for it, sh
was indeed glad. But she felt that she was shut out now from s
much that passed, and this hurt her.

It was but a short month before her time; and Lavrans utterl
forbade that she should have the least hand in nursing or tendin
him; they would not let her watch by him at night in turn wit
the others, nor would her mother suffer her to move a finge
towards helping in all the press of work. She sat by her father al
day, but 'twas seldom that they were alone at any time. Almos
daily there came guests to the house — friends come to see Lav
rans Björgulfsön once again in life. These visits pleased her father
though they made him exceeding weary. He talked heartily an
cheerfully with all, men and women, rich and poor, young an
old — thanked them for their friendship, asked their prayers fo
his soul — and God grant that we may meet on the day of bliss
At night, when only his own folk were with him, Kristin la
above in the upper hall, staring into the dark, and could not slee
for thinking on her father's going and on her own heart's foll
and wickedness.

Lavrans' end was swiftly drawing nigh. He had kept himself
up and about till Ramborg had borne her child, and there was no
more need for Ragnfrid to be so much at Formo; he had had himself driven down there one day and seen his daughter and grand-
daughter; Ulvhild the little maid had been called. But after that
he took to bed, and it was not likely he would ever rise again.

He lay in the great room under the upper hall. They had made
a kind of bed for him there on the bench of the high seat, for he
could not endure to have his head pillowed high — when it was
so, he grew dizzy at once and had swooning-fits and heart-spasms.
They dared not let him blood any more; they had had to do it so
often all through the autumn and winter that now he was quite
drained of blood; and he could eat and drink but little.

Her father's fine and comely features were sharp now, and the
brownness was faded from his face that had weathered before to
so fresh a hue; it was yellow now as bone, and the lips and corners
of the eyes pale and bloodless. The thick hair, flaxen but powdered
with white, lay unclipped, withered and strengthless over the blue-
patterned pillow-cover, but what changed him most was the coarse
grey stubble growing now on the lower face and on the long wide
throat, where the sinews stood out like strong cords. Lavrans had
always been so nice in shaving himself before each holy day. His
body was wasted till it was little more than a skeleton. But he said
that he was easy so long as he lay stretched out and moved but
little. And he was cheerful and glad at all times.

They slaughtered and brewed and baked for the grave-ale; had
out bed-gear for all the beds and went through it with care — all
that could be got out of hand now was done, so that all might be
still and quiet when the last struggle came. It cheered Lavrans
greatly to hear of all that was making ready — his last feast would
not be the least of all the festivals that had been held at Jörundgaard; in honour and worship would he depart from the govern-
ance of his lands and his people. One day he had a mind to see
the two cows that were to follow in his funeral train, as gifts for
Sira Eirik and Sira Solmund; and they were led into the hall. They
had been given double feed all the winter, and they were, in sooth,
as fine and fat as sæter cattle at Olav's Mass, though it was now
the midst of the spring dearth. He was the one that laughed most
when one of them dropped somewhat on the hall-floor. — But he
was fearful that his wife would be altogether worn out. Kristin
had thought she herself was a notable housewife — she had the

name of one at home in Skaun; but it seemed to her now that beside her mother she was naught. None could understand how Ragnfrid was able to compass all she did — and yet she seemed never to be long away from her husband; and she took her share of watching every night.

"Never trouble about me, husband," she said, laying her hand in his. "When you are dead, you know that I shall rest altogether from all such cares."

Lavrans Björgulfsön had bought him some years back a resting-place in the church of the Preaching Friars at Hamar, and Ragnfrid Ivarsdatter was set on going thither with his corpse and dwelling there near by it; she was to be a commoner in a hospice the monks owned in the town. But first the coffin was to be taken into the Olav's Church here at home, with great gifts to the Church and the priests; his stallion was to be led after with his armour and weapons, and these were to be redeemed by Erlend for five-and-forty marks of silver. One of his and Kristin's sons would most like be given these things — for choice the child she was soon to bear, if 'twere a son — perhaps he might some day be Lavrans of Jörundgaard, said the sick man with a smile. On the way down through Gudbrandsdal, too, the body was to be taken into certain churches over-night — and these were all remembered in Lavrans' testament with money-gifts and wax tapers.

Kristin felt sick, but it was with sorrow and disquiet of soul. For she could not hide from herself — it hurt her the more, the longer she was at home. Such was her heart that it hurt her to see that, now her father was drawing nigh to death, 'twas his wife that was nearest to him of all.

Ever had she heard her parents' life together held up as a pattern of seemly and worthy wedlock in unity, troth and loving-kindness. But she had felt, though without thinking upon it, that none the less there was somewhat that stood between them — an uncertain shadow, but it dulled the life in their house, though they lived together in peace and kindness. Now was there no shadow any more between her parents. They talked evenly and quietly together, mostly of the little things of every day; but Kristin felt that there was something new in their eyes and in the tone of their voices. She saw that her father missed his wife always when she was not by his side. When he had himself talked her over into going to seek a little rest, he would lie as if waiting somewhat restlessly; and when she came in, 'twas as though peace and gladness came with her to the sick man. One day she heard them speaking of their dead children; yet did they look happily. When Sira Eirik came over and read to Lavrans, Ragnfrid sat ever beside them, and then he would often take his wife's hand, and lie playing with her fingers and turning the rings on them.

She knew that her father loved her not less than before. But she had not seen clearly before now that he loved her mother. And she understood how unlike must be the man's love for his wife, who had lived with him a long life in evil days and good, to his love for the child who had but shared his joys and taken to herself his inmost heart's tenderness. And she wept and prayed God and St. Olav for help — for she remembered that tearful and tender farewell last autumn on the hills, but it *could* not be true that she wished now that farewell had been the last!

On the day that begins the summer half-year * Kristin bore her sixth son, and already, the fifth day after, she was up and had gone across to the hall to sit with her father. Lavrans misliked this — it had never been the use in his house for a lying-in woman to come into the open air before the day she went to be churched. At least, he said, she must never cross the courtyard except when the sun was in the heavens. Ragnfrid was listening when he spoke of this.

"I was thinking but now, husband," she said, "that from us, your womenkind, you have never had great obedience, but we have most often done as we ourselves would."

"Knew you not that before?" asked her husband, laughing. "'Tis not your brother Trond's fault, then — mind you not that he would rail at me always for an old woman because I let you women have the upper hand?"

Sira Eirik came over daily to the dying man. The old parish priest's sight was nearly gone, but the story of the creation in the Norse tongue, and the evangels and psalter in Latin, he read as plainly and flowingly as ever, for he knew the books so well. But Lavrans had gotten a great book some years before down at Saastad, and he was most fain to be read to from it — but Sira Eirik could not manage to read in it, by reason of his bad eyes. So her father prayed Kristin to try if she could read it. And when she

* Summer day = 14th April.

was grown a little used to the book, she found, sure enough, that she could read from it fairly and well, and it was a great joy to her that now there was somewhat that she could do for her father.

In this book were such things as debates between Fear and Courage, between Faith and Doubt, Body and Soul. There were likewise some sagas of holy men, and more than one account of men who, while yet alive, had been rapt away in the spirit and had seen the pains of the place of torment, the tribulations of purgatory fire, and the bliss of the heavenly kingdom. Lavrans spoke much now of purgatory fire, which he looked soon to enter; but he was quite without fear. He hoped for great solacement from his friends' and the priests' intercessions, and trusted firmly that St. Olav and St. Thomas would give him strength in this his last trial, as he had so often felt that they had strengthened him in this life. He had ever heard that he that was firm in the faith would never for a single moment lose from before his eyes the bliss to which the soul was going through the scorching fires. Kristin deemed that her father thought with gladness of what was coming, as of a trial of his manhood. She remembered dimly from her childhood that time when the King's sworn men from the Dale set out for the war against Duke Eirik — it seemed to her that now her father looked forward to his death as he had looked forward then to adventures and battles.

One day she said to him she deemed he had had so many trials in this life that 'twas like he would come off lightly from those of the life to come. Lavrans answered: it seemed not so to him now; he had been a rich man; he had been born of a noble house; friends had he had and good advancement in the world. " My heaviest sorrows were that I never saw my mother's face, and that I lost my children — but soon these will be sorrows no longer. And so it is with other things that have weighed on me while I lived — they are no longer sorrows."

Her mother was often with them while Kristin read; strangers, too; and Erlend now was glad to sit and listen. All these folks had delight of the reading, but she herself was shaken and made hopeless by it — she thought on her own heart that knew so well what good and right were, and yet was ever intent on unrighteousness. And she feared for her little child — scarce dared sleep at night for fear it might die a heathen. She had two women ever to sit up and watch, and yet was she afraid to fall asleep herself

Her other children had all been baptised before they were three
days old; but they had put off this one's christening, since it was
a big, strong child, and they would fain name it after Lavrans —
and in the Dale here folk held stiffly to the custom that children
must not be named after living men.

One day when she sat by her father and had the child in her lap,
he prayed her to unwrap its swaddling-clothes; for as yet he had
seen no more than the little lad's face. She did so and laid the boy
in her father's arm. Lavrans stroked the little rounded breast and
took one of the small tight-clenched hands in his:

"Strange it is, kinsman, that you are to bear my breastplate —
now would you fill no more room in it than a worm in a hollow
nut, and this hand has a great way to grow before it can grasp my
sword-hilt round. When a man sees such things as this little knave,
he well-nigh comes to understand that God's will with us was not
that we should bear arms. But not much greater shall you be, you
little one, before you long to take them up. 'Tis but the fewest
men born of women that bear so great love towards God that they
will forswear the bearing of arms. I had not such love."

He lay a little, looking at the babe.

"You bear your children under a loving heart, my Kristin —
the boy is great and fat, but you are pale and thin as a wand, and
so, your mother says, it was with them all when you were delivered of them. Ramborg's daughter was little and thin," he said,
laughing, "but Ramborg blooms like a rose."

"Yet seems it to me strange that she would not suckle her child
herself," said Kristin.

"Simon would not have it either — he says he will not repay
her for the gift by letting her wear herself away. Bear in mind,
Ramborg was not full sixteen years — she had scarce worn out her
own childish footgear when she had this daughter — and never had
she felt an hour's sickness before — 'twas no marvel that her patience was short. You were a grown woman when you were wedded, my Kristin."

Of a sudden Kristin fell into a wild weeping — she scarce knew
herself what she wept for so. But it was so true — she had loved her
children from the first hour that she knew she bore them in her
womb; she had loved them while they plagued her with unrest,
weighed her down and made her uncomely. She had loved their
little faces from the first moment she saw them, and had loved

them every hour as they grew and changed. But none had right
loved them with her, and joyed with her in them — 'twas not E
lend's way — he was fond of them enough; but Naakkve he deeme
had come too early, and as each of the others came, he had ev
thought him one too many. She dimly remembered what she ha
thought of the fruit of sin the first winter she was at Husaby
she knew that she had been forced to taste its bitterness, thoug
in other wise than she had feared. Something had gone awry be
tween her and Erlend in those first days, and 'twas like it coul
never be made straight again.

"What is it now, Kristin?" asked her father quietly, in a whil
She could not tell him all this. So she said, as soon as she coul
speak for weeping:

"Should not I sorrow, father, when you lie here — ? "

At length, when Lavrans pressed her, she spoke of her fear fo
the unchristened child. On this he gave order straightway that th
child should be brought to church the next holy-day — he said h
believed not that this would slay him before God's good time.

"Besides, I have lain here long enough now," he said, laughin
"Sad work there is over our coming and our going, Kristin — i
sickness are we born and in sickness do we die, he that dies not o
a sudden. To me when I was young the best death seemed to b
slain on the battle-field. But a sinful man may well have need of th
sick-bed — though now I cannot feel that my soul is like to grov
stronger through my lying on here — "

So the boy was christened the next Sunday, and was given hi
mother's father's name. Kristin and Erlend were much blame
for this in the country-side, though Lavrans Björgulfsön said t
all who came to see him that 'twas done at his desire: he woul
not have a heathen in his house when death came to the door.

Lavrans began now to grow fearful lest his death should fa'
in the midst of the spring sowing, thereby putting to great hard
ship the many folk who would be fain to honour his funeral b'
following in its train. But one morning, fourteen days after th
christening, Erlend came to Kristin in the old weaving-hous
where she had lain since the boy's birth. It was well on in th
morning, past the dinner-time; but she was still abed, for the bo
had been restless. Erlend was much moved; he said to her, quietl
and lovingly, that she must get up now and come to her father
Lavrans had had some fearful heart-spasms at daybreak, and sinc

d lain long swooning. Sira Eirik was with him now and had just
ard his confession.

It was the fifth day after Halvard's Mass. Rain was falling gently
d steadily. When Kristin came out into the courtyard, there
me to her on the soft breath of air from the south the smell of
lds new-ploughed and dressed. The country-side lay brown un-
r the spring rain, the air was blue between the high mountains,
d the mists drifted along halfway up the hill-sides. A tinkling of
tle bells came from the thickets along the brimming grey river —
e flocks of goats had been let loose, and were nibbling at the
ossoming twigs. 'Twas the weather that had ever rejoiced her
ther's heart, the end of winter and cold for folk and for cattle,
e beasts all set free from narrow dark byres and scanty forage.

She saw at once in her father's face that now death was very
ar. About his nostrils the skin was snow-white, his lips and the
rcles round his great eyes were bluish, the hair had fallen apart,
d lay in damp strands over the broad dewy forehead. But he was
his full senses now, and spoke clearly, though slowly and in a
eak voice.

The house-folk went forward to his bed, one by one, and Lav-
ns took each of them by the hand, thanked them for their service,
de them farewell, and prayed them to forgive him if he had
er wronged them in any wise; he prayed them, too, to think of
m with a prayer for his soul. Then he said farewell to his kindred.
e bade his daughters bend down so that he might kiss them, and
called down the blessing of God and of all the saints upon them.
oth wept bitterly, and young Ramborg threw herself into her
ster's arms; then, with arms twined round each other, Lavrans'
vo daughters went to their place at their father's bed-foot, the
ounger one still weeping on Kristin's breast.

Erlend's face quivered, and tears ran down over his cheeks when
e lifted Lavrans' hand and kissed it, while he prayed his wife's
ther in a low voice to forgive him all his sins against him at all
nes. Lavrans said he did so with all his heart, and he prayed that
od might be with him all his days. There was a strange pale light
er Erlend's comely face when he came softly round and stood
his wife's side, hand in hand with her.

Simon Darre wept not, but he knelt down when he took his
ther-in-law's hand to kiss, and he stayed kneeling a little while
olding it fast. " Warm and good is your hand, son-in-law," said

Lavrans with a faint smile. Ramborg turned her to her husba
when he came to her side, and Simon threw his arm about h
slender girlish shoulders.

Last of all, Lavrans bade farewell to his wife. They whisper
some words to each other that none could hear, and exchang
a kiss in the sight of all, as was fitting and seemly, since death w
in the room. After this, Ragnfrid kneeled down in front of h
husband's couch, with her face turned towards his; she was wh
and calm and still.

Sira Eirik tarried on after he had anointed the dying man wi
the sacred oil and given him the viaticum. He sat by the bed-hea
saying over prayers; Ragnfrid was sitting now on the bed's edg
Some hours went by. Lavrans lay with half-shut eyes. Now a
again he moved his head restlessly on the pillow, groped a lit
with his hands on the cover-lid, and breathed heavily and moa
ingly once or twice. They deemed that he had lost power
speech, but there were no death-throes.

It grew dusk early, and the priest lit a candle. The folk sat sti
looking at the dying man and listening to the dripping and tric
ling of the rain without the house. Then an unrest seemed to cor
upon the sick man, his body shook, a blue shade came upon h
face, and he seemed to struggle for breath. Sira Eirik passed h
arm behind his shoulders and lifted him up to a sitting postu
while he stayed his head on his own breast and held the cross
before his face.

Lavrans opened his eyes, fixed them on the crucifix in t
priest's hand, and spoke softly, but so clearly that most in t
room heard the words:

"*Exsurrexi, et adhuc sum tecum.*" *

Once more some tremors passed over the body, and his han
groped on the coverlid. Sira Eirik went on holding him close for
little while. Then he warely laid his friend's body back on t
pillows, kissed the forehead and smoothed the hair about it, befo
he pressed the eyelids and nostrils shut, then rose to his feet ar
began to pray.

Kristin was given leave to take her turn in watching the body
night. They had laid out Lavrans on straw in the upper hall; f

* Psalm cxxxix. 13.

there was most room there, and they looked to have a great gathering of folk for the wake.

Her father seemed to her unspeakably beautiful as he lay there in the tapers' light with his pale-golden visage bared. They had turned down the napkin from his face so that it might not be soiled by the hands of the many folk that came to see the corpse. Sira Eirik and the parish priest from Kvam chanted over him — the Kvam priest had come up in the evening to bid Lavrans a last farewell, but had been too late.

But already next day the guests began to come riding to the manor, and now it behoved Kristin, for seemliness' sake, to betake her to bed again, since she had not yet been to church. Now it was her turn to have her bed decked out with silken coverings and the finest cushions the house could furnish. The Gjesling cradle was brought back from Formo on loan; Lavrans the younger was laid in it, and every day people came in and out to see her and the child.

Her father's body kept fresh and sweet, she heard — it was but grown somewhat more yellow. And none had seen before so many candles brought to set about a dead man's bier.

On the fifth day began the grave-ale — and 'twas stately beyond measure in every wise — there were more than a hundred strange horses on the manor and at Laugarbru, and, besides, some guests had to lie at Formo. On the seventh day the heirs divided the lands and goods in all friendliness and concord — Lavrans had taken order for all things himself before he died, and all followed his wishes faithfully.

The next day the body, which lay now in the Olav's church, was to be brought forth to begin the journey to Hamar.

The evening before — rather 'twas far on in the night — Ragnrid came into the hearth-room house, where her daughter lay with her child. The mistress of the house was exceeding weary, but her face was clear and calm. She bade the serving-women go out:

" Every house on the place is full, but I trow you will find a corner somewhere; I have a mind to watch over my daughter myself, on this my last night in my home."

She took the child from Kristin's arms, bore it across to the hearth, and made it ready for the night.

" Strange must it be for you, mother, to flit away from this place where you have lived with my father all these years," said Kristin. " I scarce understand how you can bear it."

" Much less could I bear it, methinks," said Ragnfrid, rocking little Lavrans in her lap, " to live here and not see your father going about among the houses.

" You have never heard how it came about that we flitted hither to the Dale and made our home here," she began again in a while. " The time word came that they looked my father, Ivar, should soon breathe his last, I was unfit to take the road; Lavrans had to journey north alone. I mind well 'twas such fair weather the evening he set forth — already in those days he had come to like riding late, in the cool; so he was to ride to Oslo that night; 'twas just before midsummer. I went with him to where the road from the manor cuts the church road — mind you? there are some great bare rocks there and barren soil round about — the worst lands on all Skog, they ever feel the drought first — but that year the corn grew well and fairly on those fields, and we spoke of it. Lavrans walked, leading his horse; and I had you by the hand — you were four winters old —

" When we came to where the roads joined, I told you to run home to the houses. You were loath to go, but then your father said that you should see if you could find five white stones and set them in a cross in the beck below the spring — 'twas to guard him from the trolls of the Mjörsa Wood when he sailed by there. Then you set off running — "

" Is that a thing that folks there tell? " asked Kristin.

" I have never heard it, either before or since. Your father must have made it up, methinks, there and then. Mind you not, he made up so many tales when he played with you? "

" Yes, I remember."

" I went with him through the wood, all the way to the dwarf-stone. Then he bade me turn back, and he, too, went back with me to the cross-roads again — he laughed and said I might have known he would not let me walk alone through the wood, and when the sun was gone down, too. As we stood there at the cross-roads, I put my arms round his neck; I was so cast down because I could not come back home — I never could thrive rightly at Skog, and I longed ever to be back north in the Dale. Lavrans comforted me and at last he said: ' When I come back, if I find you with my son in your arms, then you may ask me for what you will, and if 'tis

in the power of man to give it, you shall not have asked in vain.'
I answered: then would I pray that we might flit up hither and
dwell on the lands of my heritage. Your father liked this but little, and he said: 'Could you not have found a greater thing to
pray for?'—he laughed a little, and I thought: he will never do
this—and it seemed to me, too, but reason that he should not.
Afterward you know how things went with me—Sigurd, your
youngest brother, lived not an hour—Halvdan christened him
and he died straightway after. . . .

"Your father came home one morning early—he had heard at
Oslo, the night before, how things stood at home, and had ridden
straight on without tarrying. I was still in bed; I was so sorrowful
I had not the heart to rise—it seemed to me I would liefest never
have risen again. God forgive me, when they brought you in to
me, I turned my face to the wall, and would not look on you, my
little child. But then said Lavrans, as he sat on my bedside, with
his cloak and sword still on him, that now must we try whether
things would go better for us if we lived here at Jörundgaard—
and 'twas thus we came to make our flitting from Skog. But since
it was so, you may think that I have no mind to dwell here, now
Lavrans is gone."

Ragnfrid came over with the child and laid it to its mother's
breast. She took the silk coverlid that had been spread over Kristin's bed in the day-time, folded it up, and laid it aside. Then she
stood a while looking at her daughter, and touched the thick
yellow-brown plait that lay between her white breasts:

"Your father asked me so often if your hair were as thick and
fair as ever. 'Twas a great joy to him that you lost not your loveliness through bearing so many children. He rejoiced much over
you in these last years, that you had grown to be so notable a
woman and still stood fresh and fair with all your fair little sons
about you."

Kristin gulped down her tears once or twice.

"To me, mother, he would often speak of how you had been
the best of wives—he said I should tell you—" She stopped
abashed, and Ragnfrid laughed softly.

"Lavrans might have known that he needed not to have any
bear me word of his loving-kindness towards me." She stroked the
child's head and her daughter's hand, which was round the little
one. "But maybe he would have—It is not so, my Kristin, that

on any day I have envied you your father's love. 'Twas but right and reason that you have loved him more than me. You were so sweet and lovely a little maid — I was not grateful enough that God had let me keep you. But I ever thought more on what I had lost than on what I possessed."

Ragnfrid sat down on the bedside:

"They had other ways at Skog than our ways at home here. I cannot call to mind that my father ever kissed me — he kissed my mother when she was laid in the dead-straw. Mother kissed Gudrun at mass, for she stood nearest her, and then sister kissed me — but else we never used to kiss. . . .

"At Skog there was a custom that when we came from church after having taken the sacrament, and we alighted from our horses in the courtyard, Sir Björgulf kissed his sons and me on the cheek, and we kissed his hand. Afterward all married pairs kissed each other, and then we shook hands with all the serving-folk that had been at the service, and wished each other all good of the sacred food. And it was much their use, Lavrans' and Aasmund's, to kiss their father's hand when he made them gifts and at suchlike times. When he or Inga came in, the sons rose always to their feet and stood till they were bidden to sit down. At first these all seemed to me foolish, outlandish ways. . . .

"Afterward, in the years I lived with your father, when we lost our sons, and through all those years when we suffered such great fear and sorrow for our Ulvhild — it was well for me then that Lavrans had been nurtured so — to follow gentler and more loving ways."

In a while Kristin said, low:

"Father never saw Sigurd, then?"

"No," said Ragnfrid in the same low tones. "I saw him not either while he lived."

Kristin lay silent awhile; then she said:

"None the less, mother, so it seems to me, you have yet had much good in your life — "

Tears began to drip down over Ragnfrid Ivarsdatter's white face:

"Aye, God help me. To me, too, it seems so now."

Soon after, she took the babe, which was sleeping now, from its mother's breast, and laid it in the cradle. She fastened up Kristin's shift with its little brooch, stroked her daughter's cheek, and bade her sleep now. Kristin lifted a hand.

"Mother —" she said beseechingly.

Ragnfrid bent down, drew her daughter close in her arms, and kissed her many times. She had not done this before in all the years since Ulvhild died.

Next day 'twas the fairest spring weather, as Kristin stood behind the corner of the hall-house and looked over at the hill-sides beyond the river. The smell of growth was everywhere, and the song of becks set free; there was a tinge of green on all the woods and meadows. Where the road ran along the mountain-side above Laugarbru, a patch of winter rye shone out fresh and bright — Jon had burnt the undergrowth there last year and sowed rye in the burned plot.

She would see the funeral train best when it passed by there. . . .

And there it was, moving slowly along, below the hill-side scree, and above the fresh new rye-field.

She could make out all the priests riding ahead of all; there were acolytes, too, in the first troop, bearing crosses and tapers. She could not see the flames in the bright daylight, but she saw the tapers themselves as slender white streaks. Then came two horses bearing between them her father's coffin on a litter; and then she could pick out Erlend on his black horse, her mother, Simon and Ramborg, and many of her kinsfolk and friends in the long funeral train.

For a while she could clearly hear the priests' chant above the roar of the Laagen, but then the sound of the hymn died away, lost in the noise of the river and the humming of the becks on the hill-sides. Kristin stood still, gazing, long after the last pack-horse with baggage was lost from sight in the wayside woods.

THE MISTRESS OF HUSABY

PART THREE

ERLEND NIKULAUSSÖN

ERLEND NIKULAUSSÖN

I

RAGNFRID IVARSDATTER lived not full two years after her husband's death; she died early in the winter of 1332. It is far from Hamar to Skaun, so that they heard not aught of her death at Husaby till she had lain in her grave more than a month. But at Whitsuntide the next year Simon Andressön came to them; there was one thing and another to be talked over between the kinsfolk concerning Ragnfrid's inheritance. Kristin Lavransdatter owned Jörundgaard now, and it was settled that Simon should hold the charge of her lands and goods, and draw her farmers to account; he had managed his mother-in-law's estates in the Dale while she had dwelled at Hamar.

Just at this time Erlend had much trouble and vexation over certain cases that had come up in his Wardenship. The autumn before, Huntjov, the farmer of Forbregd in Updal, had slain a neighbour of his for calling his wife a troll-woman. The parish folk brought the slayer bound to the Warden, and Erlend had him shut up in a loft. But when the cold grew fierce in the winter-time, he let the man go about loose among his followers. Huntjov had been with Erlend in *Margygren* in the north, and had done manful service there. So when Erlend sent in letters touching Huntjov's case, praying that he be given grace * to abide at home till his case was judged, he set the man in the fairest light; and, as Ulf Haldorssön went surety that Huntjov would present him in due time at the Orkedal Thing, Erlend let the man go home for the Yule holy-days. But from home he and his wife set out to visit the rest-house keeper in Drivdal — he was a kinsman of theirs — and on that journey they disappeared. Erlend believed that they had lost their lives in the great storm that had raged about that time; but many folk said they had run away — the Warden's people might whistle for them now. And then new matters were brought up

* See Note 14.

against the runaways — that Huntjov had killed a man some years before away in the hills and buried his body in a scree — a man that he thought had slashed his mare on the rump. And it came out clearly that the wife had dealt in witchcraft.

Next the Updal priest and the Archbishop's commissary set to work to search and sift all these rumours of witchcraft. And this led to sorry things coming out about the way folks held by their Christian faith in many parts of the Orkdöla County. 'Twas most in the outlying parishes, like Rennabu and Updalsskog; but the case of one old man from Budvik, too, was brought before the Archbishop's Court at Nidaros. And in this Erlend showed so little zeal that there was much talk of it. It was the old carl Aan, who had lived down by the lake below Husaby, and must wellnigh be reckoned as one of Erlend's house-folk. He had dealt in runes and spells, and there was talk of some images in his hut, which folk said he had used to sacrifice to. But naught of this kind was found after his death. Erlend himself and Ulf Haldorssön had been with him, 'twas known, when he died — and doubtless they had made away with both one thing and another before the priest came, people said. Aye, and when folk came to think of it, had not Erlend's own mother's sister been charged with witchcraft, whoredom and husband-murder? — though Lady Aashild Gautesdatter was too crafty and slippery, and no doubt besides had had too many mighty friends, for aught to be proved against her. And at the same time people called to mind that Erlend in his youth had lived in sadly unchristian fashion, and had set at naught the ban of the Church.

The end of all this was that the Archbishop summoned Erlend Nikulaussön to come and confer with him at Nidaros. Simon went with his brother-in-law into the city; he was to fetch his sister's son from Ranheim, for it was meant that the boy should go back with him to the Dale, and be with his mother for a while.

It was but a week from the time set for the Frostathing, and the city was full of people. When the brothers-in-law came to the Archbishop's palace and were shown into the hall of audience, a number of Crossed Friars were there, and some laymen of standing — among them, the Lagmand of the Frostathing, Harald Nikulaussön; Olav Hermanssön, Lagmand of Nidaros; Sir Guttorm Helgessön, Warden of Jemtland; and also Arne Gjavvaldssön, who at once came up to Simon Darre and greeted him heartily. Arne drew Simon apart with him into a window-nook and they sat down there.

Simon was somewhat ill at ease. He had not met the other since he had been at Ranheim ten years before, and, though the Ranheim folk had then welcomed him most fairly, his visit there on such an errand had left a sore spot in his mind.

Whilst Arne was bragging of young Gjavvald, Simon sat watching his brother-in-law. Erlend stood talking with the Treasurer,* whose name was Sir Baard Peterssön, but who was not of kin to the Hestnæs house. One could not have said that Erlend's bearing lacked due courtesy; yet he was exceeding free and unabashed as he stood there talking with the old nobleman — swaying a little back and forth, with his hands laid together behind his back. As was mostly his use, he was clad in dark colours, but most richly: violet *kothardi* sitting close to his body and slashed up the sides, black tippet, with hood thrown back to show the grey silk lining, silver-mounted belt, and long red boots that were laced tight round the calves and set off the man's slender, shapely legs and feet.

In the sharp light from the glass windows of the hall, 'twas plain enough to see that the hair at Erlend Nikulaussön's temples was not a little sprinkled with grey. Round his mouth and beneath the eyes the fine sunburned skin was scratched, as it were, with fine wrinkles, and cross-furrows had appeared in the long, fairly arched neck. Yet he seemed full young amongst the others there — though he was in no wise the youngest man in the room. 'Twas that he was slender and lithe as ever, bore his body in the same supple, somewhat careless fashion as in his youth, and walked no less lightly and springily, as now, after the Treasurer had left him, he began to stroll up and down the room, still with his hands clasped behind him. All the other men were seated; they talked a little among themselves in low, dry voices. Erlend's light step and the jingle of his small silver spurs were too clearly heard.

At length one of the younger men testily bade him sit down, " and be a little quieter, man! "

Erlend stopped short and knit his brows, then turned to the man who had spoken.

" Where were you drinking yestereven, kinsman Jon, that your head is so sore to-day? " he said with a laugh, sitting down. When Harald Lagmand came across to him, he rose, indeed, and stood till

* See Note 15.

the other had sat down, but then he dropped down by the Lagmand's side, crossed one leg over the other, and sat with his hands clasped over his knee, while Harald was speaking.

Erlend had told Simon frankly of all the trouble he had fallen into by reason of the manslayer and the witch-woman having slipped through his fingers. But no man could have seemed more care-free than Erlend, as he sat talking the matter over with the Lagmand.

Now the Archbishop entered. He was led to his high seat by two men, who propped him up with pillows. Simon had never before seen Lord Eiliv Kortin. He looked old and feeble, and seemed to be cold, though he was clad in a fur cloak and wore a fur-lined cap. When their turn came, Erlend led his brother-in-law up to him, and Simon knelt on one knee while he kissed Lord Eiliv's ring. Erlend, too, kissed the ring reverently.

He bore him most seemly and reverently, too, when at last he stood forth before the Archbishop, after the churchman had spoken a good while with the others on divers matters. But he answered somewhat lightly the questions one of the Canons put to him, and his mien was that of a man confident in his innocence.

Yes, he had heard the common talk of witchcraft for many years. But, so long as no one had come to him for guidance, surely he could in no wise be bound to search out the truth of all the talk that went on among the womenfolk in a parish. Surely 'twas the priest's affair to make inquiry, if there were grounds for making out a case against any.

Then he was asked of the old man who had dwelt at Husaby, and who folks said was a wizard.

Erlend smiled a little; yes, Aan had bragged of it himself, but no proof of his mystery had Erlend ever seen. From his childhood up he had heard Aan talk of some women he called Hæn and Skögul and Snotra, but he had never taken all this to be aught else but toys and nursery-tales. " My brother Gunnulf and our priest, Sira Eiliv, cross-questioned him once or twice, I know, but I trow they cannot have found aught against him, since they did nothing. The man came to the church each mass-day, and knew his Christian prayers." Great faith in Aan's sorceries he had never had, and since he had seen somewhat in the north of Lapp magic and spells, he had seen full well that the magic Aan dealt in was but foolery.

Then the priest asked if 'twas true that Erlend himself had once

been given a thing by Aan — something that was to bring him fortune in *amor?*

Aye, answered Erlend quickly and clearly, with a smile. 'Twas
when he was about fifteen, he thought — eight-and-twenty years
ago or so. A skin pouch with a little white stone in it, and some
dried-up things — bits of some beast, he believed. But he had not
had much faith in such things in those days either — he had given
it away the next year, the first year he was at the palace. It was in
a bath-house up in the town — in a rash, jesting moment he had
shown the charm to some other young lads — and afterwards one
of the gentlemen of the guard had come to him wanting to buy it.
Erlend had given it him in barter for a razor of fine steel.

It was asked who this gentleman might be.

At first Erlend would not come out with it. But the Archbishop
himself bade him speak. Then Erlend looked up with a gleam of
mischief in his blue eyes. " 'Twas Sir Ivar Ogmundssön."

There came a somewhat strained look into the men's faces.
Strange snorting sounds came from old Sir Guttorm Helgessön.
Lord Eiliv himself had some ado not to smile. Then Erlend, growing venturesome, went on, with eyes cast down and biting his
under lip a little:

" My Lord, I trust you will not trouble the good knight with
this ancient matter. As I have said to you, I believe not much in the
thing myself, and I have never marked that it made any odds to
either of us, my giving him this treasure — "

Sir Guttorm doubled up in a roar, and the other men had to
give in, one after the other, and laugh aloud. The Archbishop tittered a little, coughing and shaking his head. It was well known
that Sir Ivar's will had ever been better than his fortune in certain
matters.

In a while, however, one of the Crossed Friars grew sober again
and reminded the company they were come together to speak
of grave matters. Erlend asked a little sharply if a charge had been
laid against him from any quarter, and if he were on his trial — he
had not supposed aught else than that he had been sent for to a
friendly conference. The talk then went on as before, but some
disorder was caused by Guttorm Helgessön bursting out every
now and then into little snickers of laughter.

The day after, when the brothers-in-law rode home from Ranheim, Simon brought up the matter of this meeting. It seemed to

Simon that Erlend took the thing over-lightly — he thought he had marked clearly that more than one of the great folk there would be fain to do him an ill turn if they could.

Erlend said he knew well enough they would, if they had the power. For here in the north most men leaned to the Chancellor's party — not the Archbishop, though: in him Erlend had a trusty friend. But Erlend's dealings in all things were conformable to the law — he took counsel in all cases with his clerk, Klöng Aressön, who was most skilful in such matters. Erlend spoke gravely now, but he smiled slightly as he said that he deemed none had looked that he should be as well skilled in the matters of his charge as he was — neither his dear friends in this country-side nor the lords of the Council. For the rest, he was not sure that he cared to keep the Wardenship if 'twas to be on other terms than those he had while Erling Vidkunssön was at the helm. His affairs were now in such a posture — the more so since his wife's parents' death — that he had no need to bargain for the favour of the men that had come to power when the King was declared of age.

Aye, that rotten boy they might just as well call of age now as later; 'twas unlike he would grow more of a man by keeping. One would come to know all the sooner what he was planning — he or the Swedish lords that pulled the strings. Folk would soon own that Erling had been clear-sighted after all. It would cost us dear if King Magnus tried to bring Skaane under the Swedish crown, and 'twould mean war with the Danes the moment *one* man, be he Danish or German, came to power in Denmark. And the peace in the north that was to last ten years — half the time was gone by now, and 'twas unsure whether the Russians would hold to the pact even for the five years left. Erlend had little faith in them, nor had Erling either, for that matter. Aye, Chancellor Paal was doubtless a learned man, long-headed too, in many ways, perhaps. But these gentry of the Council who had taken him for their leader — Soten here had more wit than the whole of them put together. Well, now they had got quit of Erling — for the time. And for the time, Erlend, too, had just as lief step aside. But Erling and his friends would doubtless rather that Erlend kept a hold on his powers and fortunes in the north here — so he had not made up his mind.

" Methinks you have learned now to sing Sir Erling's tune," Simon Darre could not help saying.

Erlend answered: aye, it was so. He had dwelt in Sir Erling's

house last summer, when he was at Björgvin, and he had learned
to understand the man better now. So it was that Sir Erling wished
above all things to uphold the King's peace in the land. But he
wished, too, that Norway's realm should have the lion's peace —
that none should have leave to break a tooth or clip a claw of their
kinsman King Haakon's lion — and that it should not be turned,
either, into a trained hunting-dog for the people of another land.
For the rest, Erling had it much at heart now to bring to an end
the old quarrels between Norsemen and Lady Ingebjörg. Now that
she had been left a widow by Sir Knut, one could not but wish
that she should get some power over her son again. True it was
that she bore such exceeding great love to the children she had
borne to Knut Porse that it seemed she had in some measure forgotten her eldest son, but doubtless all this would be changed when
she came to meet with him again.

Simon deemed that all this sounded as though Erlend were
well-informed of what was afoot. But he wondered at Erling Vidkunssön — did the fallen High Steward believe that Erlend Nikulaussön had the wit to form a judgment in such things, or was it
that Erling was catching now at any straw within reach? Like
enough, the Knight of Giske was loath to loose his grasp on power.
None could ever have said of him that he used it for his own
profit, but then, with his riches and his standing, he had no need to
do so. And all said that as the years of his Stewardship went on he
had grown more and more self-willed and wise in his own con-
ceit, and as the other lords of the Council began more and more
to withstand him, he had at last grown so masterful that he would
scarce deign to listen to a word from any man.

It was like Erlend that he had now, so to speak, gotten aboard
Erling Vidkunssön's ship with both feet — just as it had met with
head winds and it seemed most unsure whether his throwing himself with all his heart on his rich kinsman's side would profit
either Sir Erling or Erlend himself. Yet Simon could not but confess to himself that, rashly as Erlend talked both of people and of
affairs, there seemed to be a kernel of good sense in what he said.

But that night he was in a wild and reckless mood. He was dwelling now in Sir Nikulaus' mansion, which his brother had given to
Erlend when he took the cowl. Kristin was with him, with three of
their children, the two eldest and the youngest, and his daughter
Margret.

Late in the evening many folk looked in on them, amongst them some of the men who had been at the meeting at the Archbishop's the morning before. As they sat drinking at the board after supper, Erlend overflowed with noise and laughter. He had taken an apple from a dish upon the table, and he cut scrolls and scratches on it with his knife — and then rolled it across the board into the lap of Lady Sunniva Olavsdatter, who sat over against him.

The lady who sat by Sunniva's side wanted to see the apple, and snatched at it; the other would not give it up, and the two women pushed and struggled with each other, with laughter and little shrieks. But Erlend shouted out that Lady Eyvor should have an apple all to herself. Before long he had thrown apples to all the women in the company, and there were love-runes carved on them all, he said.

" You'll be ruined, lad, should you redeem all these pledges! " cried out a man.

" Then will I let them go unredeemed — 'tis not the first time I have had to," Erlend answered back; and again there was much laughter.

But Klöng, the Icelander, had looked at one of the apples and he cried out that these were not runes, but only meaningless scrolls. He would show them, he said, how runes should rightly be cut. But Erlend cried out he must do no such thing:

" For then 'tis like they would bid me lay you by the heels, Klöng — and I cannot get on without you."

In the midst of all this turmoil, Erlend and Kristin's youngest son had come toddling into the hall. Lavrans Erlendssön was a little over two years old now, and was as comely a child as one could see, fair and fat, with silky-fine yellow curly hair. And so all the women on the outer bench were at once set on getting hold of the child — they passed him from lap to lap, and caressed him, not too gently, for they were now all heated and in wild mirth. Kristin, who sat with her husband in the high-seat against the wall, begged to have the child brought round to her, and the little one whimpered and tried to come at her, but 'twas of no avail.

Of a sudden, Erlend leapt across the table and took the child, which was shrieking now, because Lady Sunniva and Lady Eyvor were dragging at him and struggling over him. The father took the boy up in his arms, coaxing him, and as the little one still went on crying, he began hushing and lulling him, walking up and down with him out in the hall in the half-darkness. It seemed now as though Erlend had quite forgotten his guests. The child's little bright head lay on its father's shoulder under the man's black hair, and now and then Erlend would caress, with lips half opened, the little hand that rested on his breast in front. So he walked up and down till the maid came in that should have looked to the child and put him to bed long before.

Some of the guests called out now that Erlend should sing for them to dance to — he had such a fine strong voice. At first he was unwilling, but then he went over to where his young daughter sat on the women's bench. He put his arm around Margret and drew her out on to the floor.

"You must come along, then, my Margret, and dance with your father."

A young man came forward and took the maid's hand — "Margret has promised to dance with me to-night" — but Erlend lifted his daughter in his arms and set her down on his other side:

"Dance you with your wife, Haakon — never did I dance with others when I was as newly wed as you are."

"Ingebjörg says she cannot dance to-night — and I have promised Haakon to dance with him, father," said Margret.

Simon Darre had no mind to dance. He stood awhile with an old lady, looking on — now and then his glance rested a moment on Kristin. While her serving-maids were clearing the board and wiping it dry and bearing in more drink and dishes of walnuts, she stood up at the end of the table. After, she sat down by the fire-place and talked with a priest who was among the guests. In a while Simon sat down beside the two.

When they had danced one or two dances, Erlend came over to his wife.

"Come and dance with us, Kristin," he said beseechingly, holding out his hand.

"I am tired," she said, looking up for an instant.

"Do you ask her, Simon — she cannot deny you a dance."

Simon half rose from his seat and reached out his hand, but Kristin shook her head: "Ask me not, Simon — I am so weary —"

Erlend stood there a little; he looked as though he were sorely vexed at this. Then he went back to Lady Sunniva and took her hand in the chain of dancers, while he called out that now Margret should sing for them.

"Who is he that is dancing next your stepdaughter?" asked

Simon. He thought in his mind that he liked the man's looks but
little — though he was a fine manful-looking young fellow with
a fresh brown skin, good teeth and shining eyes — but the eyes
were set close in to the bridge of the nose, and, though he had a
big strong mouth and chin, his forehead and upper head were
narrow. Kristin said 'twas Haakon Eindridessön of Gimsar, grandson of Tore Eindridessön, the Warden of Gauldöla County.
Haakon had but just been wedded to the comely little woman
that sat there in Olav Lagmand's lap — Olav was her godfather.
Simon had marked this woman, for she somewhat favoured his
first wife, though she was not so fair. As he found out now that
there was a distant kinship, too, he went over and greeted Ingebjörg and sat down and talked with her.

The ring of dancers broke up in a while. The elders betook them
to the drinking-board; but the young folks went on singing and
disporting themselves out in the hall. Erlend came over to the
fire-place along with some of the older men, but he still held Lady
Sunniva's hand and led her with him, as if without thinking. The
men sat down near the fire; there was no seat for the lady, but she
stood before Erlend, eating walnuts, which he cracked for her
with his fingers.

" An uncourteous man you are, Erlend, for sure," she said, suddenly. " There you sit, and I have to stand in front of you."

" Nay, do you sit too," said Erlend, laughing, and pulled her
down into his lap. She struggled, laughing, and called out to the
mistress of the house, asking if she saw how her husband was be-
having to her.

" 'Tis but the kindness of Erlend's heart," answered Kristin,
laughing. " Never does my cat rub herself against his legs but he
must needs take her up and lay her in his lap."

Erlend and the lady sat on as before, making no sign, but both
had grown very red. He held one arm loosely about her, as if he
hardly marked that she sat there, whilst he and the other men
talked of the feud between Erling Vidkunssön and Chancellor
Paal, which was so much in folks' thoughts just then.

" What are you thinking on now, Kristin? " Simon asked in a
while — she was sitting quite still and straight, with her hands
folded in her lap. She answered:

" I was thinking now of Margret."

Later in the night, when Erlend and Simon had an errand out

in the courtyard, they frighted away from each other a couple
that was standing behind the house-corner. The night was clear
as day, and Simon knew them for Haakon of Gimsar and Margret
Erlendsdatter. Erlend looked after them — he was sober enough —
and Simon saw that he misliked this; but he said, as though in excuse, that those two had known each other from childhood and
were for ever teasing and jesting with each other. Simon thought
that even if there were no other harm, 'twas pity of the young
wife, Ingebjörg.

But the day after, when young Haakon came to the house on
some errand and asked after Margit, Erlend flamed out at him:

"My daughter is not *Margit* to you. And if so be you left your
talk unfinished yesterday, you had best keep awhile what you
have to say to her — "

Haakon shrugged his shoulders and, when he left, begged them
to greet *Margareta* from him.

The Husaby folk stayed in Nidaros till the Thing was over, but
Simon felt none too happy or at home among them. Erlend was apt
to fall into fretful moods when in his town-house, because Gunnulf had given the hospital, which lay on the other side of the
orchard, the right to use some of the houses that opened from the
orchard, and also some rights in the garden. Erlend had set his
mind on buying out these rights; he liked not to see the sick folk in
the garden and in the courtyard — many of them, indeed, were an
ill-favoured sight — and he was fearful lest his children might take
some sickness. But he could not come to agreement with the monks
who managed the hospital.

Then there was Margret Erlendsdatter. Simon understood that
there was much talk about her, and that Kristin was disquieted
by it; but the girl's father seemed not to care — it seemed that he
felt sure he could guard his own maid and that there was naught
to dread. Yet he named one day to Simon that he thought Klöng
Aressön had a mind to wed his daughter, and he knew not rightly
what to do in the matter. He had naught else against the Icelander
than that he was the son of a priest — he was loath it should be said
of Margret's children that there was a stain on both their parents'
birth. Else was Klöng a man that all liked, cheerful, keen-witted
and most learned. His father, Sira Are, had brought him up and
taught him himself; he had meant his son to be a priest, and 'twas

said he had even taken steps to get a dispensation for him, but Klöng had drawn back and would not take the frock. It seemed as though Erlend was minded to let the matter rest awhile — if no better match offered, he could always give the maid to Klöng Aressön.

Yet was it known that Erlend had already had such a good offer for his daughter that folk had had much to say of his pride and folly in letting the bargain slip. It was from a grandson of Baron Sigvat of Leirhole — Sigmund Finssön was the man's name; he was not rich, for Finn Sigvatssön had had eleven children who all lived; and he could not be called young — he was about Erlend's age — but he was a man in good esteem and of a good understanding. And with the lands that Erlend had given his daughter when he wedded Kristin Lavransdatter, and with all the jewellery and costly gifts he had given the child from time to time, and with the dowry he had agreed with Sigmund to give with her, Margret would have been more than well-to-do. Erlend, indeed, had been glad enough to find such a suitor for his base-born daughter. But when he came home to his daughter with the bridegroom, the maid took a whimsy that she would not have him because Sigmund had some warts on the edge of one of his eyelids, and she said this gave her such a loathing of him. Erlend gave in to the girl; and when Sigmund grew angry and talked of breach of troth, Erlend, too, grew hot, and said that the other must surely understand that all betrothal-pacts were made on condition that the maid was willing — his daughter should not be forced into her bride-bed. Kristin thought with her husband in so far as that he should not force the girl, but 'twas known that she had deemed Erlend should have spoken in sober sadness to his daughter and made her understand that Sigmund Finssön was so good a match as, seeing how things stood with her birth, she could not hope to find a better. But Erlend had been wroth with his wife for venturing to speak thus, though she said it to him only. These things Simon had heard at Ranheim. The folk there foretold that all this must needs end badly; 'twas true Erlend was a man of weight now, and the maid was a passing fair maid, but yet 'twas impossible it could be for her good that her father had spoiled her all these years and fed the flames of her pride and self-will.

After the Frosta Thing, Erlend went home to Husaby with his wife and children, and with them went Simon Darre.

Now, when the eldest sons were big enough to ride abroad with Erlend, he had begun to take more heed of the boys. Simon marked that Kristin was not wholly glad of this — she deemed that 'twas not only good they got by going amongst their father's men. And it was about the children that unfriendly words most often passed between this wedded pair — even if they did not quarrel outright, they often came more nigh to it than Simon deemed fitting. And it seemed to him that Kristin was the most at fault. Erlend was quick-tempered and hasty, but she often spoke as though from a deep-hidden grudge. So it was one day when she made some complaint about Naakkve. Erlend answered that he would speak strictly to the boy, but, on his wife's saying something more, he broke out testily, saying he could not well thrash a big boy like him, because of the house-folk.

"No, 'tis too late now; had you done it while he was younger, he might have hearkened to you now. But in those days you never so much as looked his way."

"Oh, but I did. Though it was but reason surely that I should let him go about with you when he was little — and 'tis no work for a man, I trow, to beat little breechless brats."

"You thought not so last week," said Kristin, scornfully and bitterly.

Erlend made no answer, but rose to his feet and went out. And to Simon this seemed an ill speech of Erlend's wife. She was recalling a thing that had befallen the week before; as Erlend and Simon came riding into the courtyard, little Lavrans had come running towards them with a wooden sword, and as he ran by his father's horse, he struck it, in mischievous play, on the leg with his sword. The horse reared — and next moment the boy had fallen to the ground beneath its feet. Erlend jerked back and flung the horse to one side, then leapt down, throwing the rein to Simon; his face was white with fear when he lifted the boy up in his arms. But when he saw that the child was quite unhurt, he laid him over his left arm, took the wooden sword, and thrashed him with it on the bare bottom — the boy had not been breeched yet. In his flurry he knew not how hard he struck, and Lavrans was still going about black and blue. But since then Erlend had tried all the time to make friends again with the boy — while the little man sulked, held to his mother's skirts, and threatened and slapped at his father. And when Lavrans had been put to rest in the evening in his parents' bed, where he slept (for he was still

nursed by his mother at night), Erlend sat over on the bedside
the whole evening, looking down on the sleeping child and touching him. He said himself, to Simon, that this boy was the one of
his sons that he loved best.

When Erlend set forth for the summer meetings in his charge,
Simon took the road for home. He galloped south through Gauldal, so that the sparks flew from the stones under his horse's hoofs.
Once, when they rode a little slower up a steep hill, his men asked,
laughing, whether they were to ride three days' march in two.
Simon laughed back, and said he had more than a mind they
should — " for now am I fain to be back at Formo."

He ever longed to be back when he had been away from his
manor awhile — he was a home-loving man, and rejoiced always
when he turned his horse into the homeward road. But it seemed
to him that so much as this time he had never before yearned to
get back to the Dale, and his manor, and his little daughters —
aye, and now he longed for Ramborg too. It seemed to him that
he had no good reason for this great eagerness, but the life at
Husaby had so weighed upon his mood that he deemed he knew
now from himself how the cattle feel when a storm is gathering.

2

ALL the summer through, Kristin thought of little else than what
Simon had told her of her mother's death.

Ragnfrid Ivarsdatter had died all alone — none had been near
when she drew her last breath, saving a serving-woman, who slept.
'Twas not much comfort, what Simon said — that, though death
came so suddenly, she was yet well prepared. It seemed like a special providence of God that, a few days before, she had felt in her
such a hunger for her Redeemer's Body that she had confessed
and taken the sacrament from the priest in the cloister who was
her director. 'Twas certain she had made a good death — Simon
had seen her body, and said it had seemed to him a marvellous
sight. In death she had been so fair; she was, one knew, a woman
nigh threescore years of age, and for many years her face had
been much wrinkled and furrowed; but this was changed alto-

gether: her face was grown young and smooth, so that she looked like naught else but a young woman fallen asleep. Now had she been laid to rest by her husband's side; thither, too, had they brought Ulvhild Lavransdatter's bones a short time after her father's death. Over the graves was laid a great stone slab, divided in two by a fairly carven cross, and on a winding scroll was written a long Latin verse that the Prior of the cloister had made; but Simon could not remember it rightly, for he knew but little of that tongue.

Ragnfrid had had a house to herself in the yard up in the town where the commoners of the cloister lived — a single room and above it a fair loft-room. There she dwelt alone with a poor peasant woman who had been taken in by the friars for small payment, in return for her helping one or other of the richer women-commoners. But for the last half-year at least it had rather been Ragnfrid who helped the other, for the widow — Torgunna was her name — had been ailing, and Ragnfrid tended her with great kindness and care.

The last evening of her life she had been at evensong in the cloister-church, and went afterwards into the kitchen of the commoners' yard. There she cooked a good bowl of soup with strengthening herbs in it, and said to the other women who were there that she would give this to Torgunna, and she hoped the woman would be well enough in the morning to come with her to matins. This was the last time any saw the Jörundgaard widow alive. They came not to matins — neither she nor the peasant woman — nor yet to prime. When some of the monks in the choir marked that Ragnfrid was not in the church for the day-mass either, they began to wonder — she had never before missed three services in a day. They sent word up to the town to ask if Lavrans Björgulfsön's widow were sick. When the folk came into the loft, they found the bowl of soup standing untouched on the board; in the bed Torgunna was sleeping sweetly by the wall, but Ragnfrid Ivarsdatter lay on the outside of the bed with her hands crossed on her breast, dead, and well-nigh cold already. Simon and Ramborg had come down to her burial, and it was a most fair one.

Now that the household at Husaby was grown so great and Kristin had six sons, she could no longer take a hand herself in all parts of the housekeeping. She was obliged to have a housekeeper

under her, and so it came about that most of the time the mistress
of the house sat in the hall sewing; there was ever someone wanting clothes — Erlend, Margret or the boys.

The last she had seen of her mother was riding after her husband's bier — that bright spring day when she had stood in the
meadow at Jörundgaard and seen her father's funeral train pass
the green patch of winter rye beneath the scree.

Kristin's needle flew and flew, and she thought on her parents
and their home at Jörundgaard. Now, when all was memory, she
seemed to herself to grow ware of much that she had not seen
when she lived in the midst of it, and took as things of course her
father's tender guardianship and her silent, sad-faced mother's
quiet, constant work and care. She thought on her own children
— they were dearer to her than her own heart's blood; they were
not out of her mind one hour of her waking life. Yet was there
much in her mind that she pondered over more — she loved her
children without brooding on the matter. She had never thought
aught else, when she was at home, but that her parents' whole
life and all their doings and strivings were for herself and her
sisters. Now she seemed to see that betwixt those two, who in
their youth had been brought together by their fathers, well-nigh
unasked, there had run strong swift currents both of sorrow and
of joy — yet *she* knew naught of it save that they had passed now,
hand in hand, out of her life. Now she understood that this man's
and woman's lives had held much beside their love for their children — and yet that love had been strong and wide and unfathom-
ably deep, while the love she gave them back had been weak and
thoughtless and self-seeking, even when, in her childhood, those
two had been her whole world. She seemed to see herself standing
far, far away — so small, so small beyond that great stretch of
time and distance; she stood in the beam of sunlight that streamed
down through the smoke-vent in the old hearth-room house at
home, the winter-house of her childhood. Her parents stood a
little back, in the shadow — they bulked as great as they had
seemed to her sight when she was small, and they smiled to her —
the smile that she knew now comes to one's face when a little
child comes and thrusts aside heavy and troublous thoughts.

" I thought, Kristin, when you had borne a child yourself, you
would surely understand better."

She remembered when her mother had said these words. Sorrowfully she thought — it was not true, she feared, even now, that she understood her mother. But she began to understand how much there was she did not understand.

This autumn Archbishop Eiliv died. And about the same time King Magnus changed the terms of service of many of the Wardens, but not Erlend Nikulaussön's. When Erlend was in Björgvin the last summer of the King's nonage, he had been given letters granting him the fourth part of all grace-payments,* fines and forfeitures in his Wardenship — the thing had made much talk, that he should have been given such a grant towards the close of a Regency. Since Erlend now owned much land in the country, and most often lived on his own farms when he moved round his Wardenship, and as he let his farmers redeem their land-dues, his incomings were large. True, this meant that the incomings from land-dues in kind were small; and he kept a great and costly train — besides his own manor-folk he had never fewer than twelve men-at-arms with him at Husaby; these were bravely mounted and exceeding well armed; and when he moved about his charge, his men lived like lords.

There was some talk of this one day when Lagmand Harald and Tore the old Warden of Gauldöla County were at Husaby. Erlend made answer that many of these men had been with him when he kept the marches in the north; "and there we shared alike in such cheer as was to be had — dried fish and sour small beer. Now the men I give food and clothes to know that I grudge them not white bread and strong ale; and if now and then, in a rage, I bid them to go to hell, they understand well enough that I mean not they should set forth before I lead the way myself."

Ulf Haldorssön, who was the headman of Erlend's guard now, said afterwards to his mistress that 'twas even so. Erlend's men loved him, and he had them wholly in his hand.

"You know yourself, Kristin, none should take much account of what Erlend says; 'tis what he does one must judge him by."

Another matter that made much talk was that, besides his house-carls, Erlend had men all about the country-side — and not in Orkdöla County only — that he had sworn to his service on his sword-hilt. Some time back he had received royal letters about this matter, but he had answered that these men had made up his

* See Note 14.

ship's crew, and that he had taken oath from them the first spring
when he was to sail for the north. Upon this it was enjoined upon
him that he should loose these men from their oath at the next
Thing he held to publish the judgments and decrees of the Lagthing, and that, to that end, he should summon thither the men
from outside the county, bearing himself the costs of their journeys. And in truth he had sent for some of his old sailors from
Möre to the Orkedal Thing; but no one heard aught of his having
loosed them, or any other man who had ever been his follower,
from their oaths. Howbeit the matter was not again opened; and
so, as the autumn passed, the talk about it died down.

Late in the autumn Erlend journeyed south, and stayed over
Yule-tide at King Magnus' Court, which was at Oslo that year.
He was vexed that he could not bring his wife to go with him;
but Kristin shrank from the toilsome winter journey, and stayed
on at home at Husaby.

Erlend came back three weeks after Yule, bringing fair gifts to
his wife and all the children. Kristin had given her a silver bell to
ring for her maids; but to Margret he gave a clasp of pure gold,
for she had naught of the sort before, though she had many ornaments of every kind of silver and silver gilt. But while the women
were putting away these costly gifts in their jewel-chests, something in Margret's chest caught on her sleeve and hung from it.
The girl covered it up swiftly with her hand, saying to her stepmother:

" 'Twas my mother left me this, so father would not that I
should show it to you."

Kristin had flushed much redder than the maid. Her heart beat
hard with fear, but it seemed to her that she *must* speak a word to
the young girl to warn her.

In a little she said in a low, faltering voice:

" 'Tis like the gold buckle that Lady Helga of Gimsar used to
wear at festivals."

" Aye — many gold things are alike," answered the girl, shortly.

Kristin locked her chest and stood still with her hands resting
on it, so that Margret might not see how they shook.

" My Margret," she said softly and gently — she had to stop —
but she gathered all her strength and went on:

" My Margret, bitterly have I repented — never could I joy
fully in any gladness, though my father forgave me with all his

heart for all that I had sinned against him — you know that I sinned against my parents for your father's sake. But the longer I live and the more I come to understand, the heavier it grows for me to remember that I repaid their goodness towards me by bringing them sorrow. My Margret, your father has been good to you all the days of your life —"

"You need not be afraid, mother," answered the girl. "I am not your own daughter; you need not be afraid that I shall ever wear out your dirty shift or stand in your shoes —"

Kristin turned a face flaming with wrath on her stepdaughter. Then she clutched the cross she wore about her neck tightly in her hand, and forced back the words that were on her lips.

She went to Sira Eiliv with this the same evening after Vespers, and she looked in vain in the priest's face for a sign — had the worst befallen already, and did he know it? She remembered her own wildered youth, and she remembered Sira Eirik's visage that betrayed nothing, while he lived day by day with her and her trusting parents, with her sinful secret locked in his bosom — and herself hard and dumb under his harsh threats and warnings. And she remembered the time after she had been lawfully betrothed to Erlend, when she herself showed her mother the gifts he had given her at Oslo. The mother's mien had been immovable in its calmness while she took things in her hand, one by one, looked at them, praised them, and laid them away.

She was in deadly, hopeless fear, and kept as wary a watch as she could on Margret. Erlend marked that there was something amiss with his wife, and one evening, when they had gone to rest, he asked if it was that she was with child again.

Kristin lay silent for a little before she answered that she believed it was so. And when her husband, on this, took her lovingly in his arms and asked no more, she could not bring herself to say that 'twas somewhat else that was weighing on her. But when Erlend whispered to her that this time she must do her devoir and give him a daughter, she had no power to answer, but lay there stiff with dread, thinking that Erlend might come to know all too soon what kind of joy a man has of his daughters.

Some nights after this the folk at Husaby had gone to bed somewhat in drink and heavy with much eating, for it was in the last days before the Fast began — and thus all slept heavily. But well on in the night little Lavrans woke in his parents' bed and, still half asleep, began to whimper and cry for his mother's breast. But the time had now come for him to be weaned. Erlend woke up, grunted angrily, but took the boy and gave him milk from a cup that stood on the bed-step, and laid him down then at his other side.

Kristin had sunk again in deep drowsiness, when, of a sudden, she felt Erlend sit upright in the bed. Half awake, she asked what it was — he bade her hush, in a voice she did not know. Without a sound he slipped out of the bed; she marked that he was putting on some pieces of clothing, but when she raised herself on her elbow, he pressed her down again on the cushions with one hand while he leant in above her and took his sword, that hung above the bed-head.

He moved as silently as a lynx; but she felt that he had gone off to the ladder that led up to Margret's bower above the outer room.

For a moment she lay palsied with dread; then she sat up, found her shift and skirt, and groped in the dark for her shoes on the floor by the bed.

At the same moment a woman's shriek rang out from the loft-room — it must have been heard over the whole manor. Erlend's voice shouted a word or two — then she heard the ring of clashing swords and the trampling of feet up above — then the noise of a weapon falling on the floor, and a shriek of terror from Margret.

Kristin knelt crouching by the hearth — raked away the hot ashes with her bare hands and blew on the embers. When she had gotten the fir-root torch alight and held it up in her shaking hands, she saw Erlend high up in the darkness — he leapt down without heeding the ladder, bearing his naked sword in his hands, and ran out of the outer door.

From every side, in the darkness, the boys' heads peeped out. She went to the northern bed, where the three eldest slept, bade them lie down, and shut the bed-door. Ivar and Skule, who sat up on the bench where their beds had been made, blinking in fear and bewilderment at the light, she made creep into her own bed and shut them, too, in. Then she lighted a candle and went out into the courtyard.

It was raining — for one moment, while the light of her candle was mirrored in the wet-shining ice-crust, she saw a crowd of folk outside the door of the nearest house — the servants' quarter where Erlend's house-carls slept. Then her light was blown out — for a moment 'twas pitch-black night — but then Ulf Haldorssön came from the servants' quarter, bearing a lantern.

He bent down over a dark body that lay in a huddled heap on the wet lumpy ice. Kristin knelt down and felt the man's body with her hands — 'twas young Haakon of Gimsar — and he was swooning or dead. Straightway her hands were covered with blood. Helped by Ulf, she turned and straightened out the body. The blood was gushing from the right arm, from which the hand had been cut off.

Unawares she cast a glance upward to where the shutter of the window-hole of Margret's bower was clapping in the wind. She could not see any face up there — but 'twas exceeding dark.

While she knelt in the puddles pressing Haakon's wrist with all her might to stop the gush of blood, she was dimly aware of Erlend's men standing around, half clad. Then she saw Erlend's grey, writhen face — with the skirt of his mantle he was wiping his bloody sword — he was naked beneath and his feet were bare.

" One of you, find me a band," she said, " and you, Björn, go up and wake Sira Eiliv — we must bear him up to the priest's house."

She took the leather strap that someone reached her and wound it tight around the stump of the arm. Of a sudden Erlend said, in a wild, hard voice:

"Let none touch him! Let the man lie where himself has laid him — "

" You know well, husband," said Kristin calmly, though her heart was beating till 'twas like to choke her, "that that cannot be."

Erlend thrust the sword-point hard against the ground.

" Aye — your flesh and blood it is not — that have I been made to feel each day in all these years."

Kristin rose and spoke softly, close in to him:

" Yet would I be fain for her sake that this should be hid — if hid it can be. You men " — she turned to the men that stood about — " are true enough to your master, I trow, not to speak of this till he has told you all of how this strife between Haakon and him came about? "

All the men answered, yes. One ventured forward — they had been wakened, he said, by hearing a woman shriek as though one

were ravishing her — then straightway someone had leapt down
on the roof of their house, but he must have slipped on the ice-
crust, for they heard something sliding down and then a heavy
fall in the courtyard. But Kristin bade the man be silent. Now
came Sira Eiliv running.

When Erlend turned and went in, his wife ran after him, trying
to thrust past him. When he made for the loft-ladder, she got
before him and caught him around the arms.

" Erlend — what would you do with the child? " she gasped out
into his grey, wild face.

He made no answer — he tried to fling her aside, but she held
fast to him.

" Stay, Erlend, stay — your child! You know not — the man was
fully clad," she cried despairingly.

He gave a loud hoarse cry before answering — and she grew
deathly white with horror — his words were so gross and his voice
so changed by his wild agony.

Again she wrestled dumbly with the raging man that growled
and gnashed his teeth together. At last she caught his eyes in the
half-light:

" Erlend — let me go to her first. I have not forgotten the day
when I was no better than Margret — "

Then he loosed her and, staggering back against the closet-wall,
stood there quivering like a dying beast. Kristin went and lit a
candle, then came back and went past him up to Margret in her
bower.

The first thing the light fell on was a sword that lay on the
floor not far from the bed, and, close by, a man's severed hand.
Kristin tore off her head-dress, which, hardly knowing it, she
had flung loosely round her flowing hair before she went out to
the men. Now she threw it over those things lying on the floor.

Margret sat huddled together on the pillows of the bed-head
gazing at Kristin's light with great wide-open eyes. She held the
bed-clothes up about her, but her naked shoulders shone white
through the golden locks of her hair. There was much blood all
about the room.

The strain of Kristin's spirit burst in a vehement fit of weeping
— 'twas so miserable a sight to see the fair child amidst all this
horror. Then Margret shrieked aloud:

" Mother — what will father do with me? "

Kristin could not help it — in the midst of her deep pity for the girl, her heart seemed to grow small and hard in her breast. Margret asked not what her father had done with Haakon. In a flash it came before her — Erlend lying on the ground, her father standing over him with a bloody sword, and she herself — But Margret had not moved from the spot. She could not hinder the old scornful dislike for Eline's daughter from coming up in her again, as Margret clung to her, shaking, well-nigh crazy with fear, and she sat down on the bed's edge and strove to quiet the child a little.

So they sat when Erlend came up through the trap-door. He was fully clad now. Margret shrieked again, and hid in her stepmother's arms — Kristin looked up at her husband for a moment — he was calm now, but pale and strange of face. For the first time he looked as old as he was.

But when he said quietly: "You must go down, Kristin — I would speak with my daughter alone," she obeyed. She laid the girl down in the bed carefully, covered her up to the chin with the clothes, and then went down the ladder.

As Erlend had done, she dressed herself fully — 'twas certain none at Husaby would sleep any more that night — and set herself to quiet the frightened children and serving-women.

The next morning, in a driving snowstorm, Margret's maid went weeping off the place with all her worldly goods in a sack on her back. Her master had driven her out with the direst words, and threats that she should be flayed alive because she had sold her mistress thus.

Then he put the rest of the serving-folk to the question — had not the maids suspected mischief when Ingeleiv in the autumn and winter had begun sleeping with them, instead of in Margret's bower? And how came it that the dogs had been locked inside their house? But they denied all, as 'twas like they would.

Last of all, he took his wife to task, they two alone. Heart-sick and weary, Kristin listened to him and strove to turn aside his injustice with soft answers. She denied not that she had been fearful, and she refrained her from saying that she had not spoken to him of her fear, because she had never reaped aught but unthankfulness from him when she had tried to counsel either him or Margret for the maid's good. But she swore by God and Mary Virgin that she had never known, nor could have thought, such a thing as that this man came to Margret in the loft at night.

" You! " said Erlend scornfully. " You say yourself you mind the time when you were no better than Margret — and the Lord God in heaven knows that you have let me mark, every day of the years we have lived together, that you remembered the wrong I did you — though your will was as good as mine, and your father and not I caused much of the trouble by denying to let you wed me — *I* was willing enough from the first hour to make amends for the sin. When you saw the Gimsar gold " — he gripped her hand tightly and held it up so that the two rings she had had of him at Gerdarud glittered in the light — " knew you not what it meant? You have worn every day in these years the rings I gave you when you gave me your honour — "

Kristin was ready to sink down with weariness and sorrow; she answered in a low voice:

" I marvel, Erlend, if you still remember the time you over-came my honour — "

He buried his head in his arms, and flung himself down on the bench, tossing and writhing. Kristin sat down a little way off — she wished she could help her husband. She understood that this calamity fell yet more hardly upon him because he himself had sinned against others in the same sort as now he had been sinned against. And he, who had never been willing to look his fault in the face in any trouble he himself had caused, could never bear to take the blame for this — and there was none else but she on whom he could fasten it. But she was not so much angered as sorrowful, and fearful of what now might come to pass.

Now and again she was above with Margret. The girl lay white and unmoving, staring before her. She had not yet asked what had befallen Haakon — Kristin knew not whether 'twas that she dared not, or that she was quite dulled by her own misery.

Well on in the afternoon Kristin saw Erlend and Klöng the Icelander going together through the thick-falling snow to the armoury. But a short time passed, and Erlend came back alone. Kristin looked up a moment as he came into the light and passed her by — afterward she did not dare to turn her eyes toward the corner of the hall where he hid himself away. She had seen that he was quite broken.

Soon after, when she had an errand over at the storehouse, Ivar

and Skule came running and told their mother that Klöng the Icelander was going away that evening — the boys were sad about
it, for the clerk was a good friend of theirs. He was packing his
things now, and was to go down to Birgsi to-night —

She had guessed already what must have befallen. Erlend had
offered his daughter to the clerk, and he had refused to have a
fallen maid. But what that parley must have meant to Erlend —
she grew dizzy and sick and could not bear to think the thought
out.

The day after, word came from the priest's house. Haakon Eindridessön prayed that he might have speech with Erlend. Erlend
sent back in answer that he had naught more to say to Haakon.
Sira Eiliv said to Kristin that if Haakon lived he would be crippled
wholly — besides that he had lost his right hand, he had hurt his
back and hips badly in falling from the roof of the servants' house.
But he was set on coming home, even as he was, and the priest had
promised to get him a sleigh. He repented his sin now with all
his heart — he said that Margret's father had been within his rights,
however the law might stand; but he was most fain that all should
do their best to hush up the matter, so that his misdeed and Margret's shame should be hidden as much as might be. In the afternoon he was borne out to the sleigh, which Sira Eiliv had borrowed from Repstad, and the priest himself rode with him to
Gauldal.

Thus the next day, which was Ash Wednesday, the Husaby
folk had to go down to Vinjar to the parish church. But at the
time of vespers Kristin had the acolyte let her into the chapel at
home.

She could feel the ashes still on her forehead when she knelt
down by her stepson's grave and said over the paternosters for
his soul.

Not much but bones would be left of the boy now, down under
his stone. Bones and the hair, and some shreds of the clothes they
had been laid in. She had seen the bones of her little sister when
they took her up that they might bring her to her father at
Hamar. Dust and ashes — she thought of her father's comely
visage, of her mother with the great eyes in the furrowed face,
and the form that still kept so strangely young and slim and light,
though her face grew old so early. There they lay under a stone,

falling in sunder, as houses fall to ruin when the folks that lived there are gone. Pictures flitted and faded — the burned ruins of the church at home; a farm in Silsaadal that they used to ride by when they went to Vaage — the houses stood empty and were falling in pieces, the folk that tilled the lands dared not go nigh after the sun was down. She thought upon her beloved dead — their looks and their voices and smiles and ways and bearing — now that they themselves were gone away to yonder other country, to think on their shapes was sore; 'twas like remembering one's home when one knew that it stood desolate, and the rotting timbers were sinking into the soil.

She sat on the wall-bench in the empty church, and the smell of cold stale incense held her thoughts fast bound to pictures of death and the decay of all earthly things. And she was powerless to lift up her soul to see a glimpse of the land where her beloved were, whither all goodness and love and truth at last were taken away and there treasured up. Every day when she prayed for the peace of their souls, it seemed to herself strange and unmeet that she should pray for them whose souls already on this earth had possessed a peace far deeper than she had ever known since she grew to be a woman. Sira Eiliv, indeed, said that prayer for the dead was good always — good for oneself, even if those others were already inheritors of God's peace.

But it helped not her. It seemed to her that when her weary body at last was rotting under a tombstone, her restless spirit would still be doomed to wander about somewhere near by, as an unhappy ghost wanders lamenting round the tumble-down houses of a ruined farm. For in her soul sin still had its being, as the root-tissue of the weeds is inwoven in the soil. It flowered and flamed and scented the air no longer, but 'twas still there in the soil, bleached, but strong and full of life. In despite of all the tenderness that welled up in her heart when she saw her husband's despair, she had not will or strength to stifle the voice in her that cried out, in bitterness and anger: Can you speak thus to *me*? Have you forgotten the time when I gave you my troth and my honour? Have you forgotten the time when I was your dearest love? And yet she knew that as long as this voice questioned thus within her, so long would she speak to him as though *she* had forgotten.

She flung herself in her thoughts before St. Olav's shrine;

caught at the mouldering bones of Brother Edvin's hand far off in the church at Vatsfjeld; clenched her hands about the reliquaries with the shreds of a dead woman's shroud, and the splinters of the bones of an unknown blood-witness — caught for a safeguard at the small remains that through death and nothingness had kept a little of the virtue of the departed soul — like the magic power that clings about the rust-eaten swords dug up from ancient warriors' barrows.

The day after, Erlend rode into the city, taking with him only Ulf and one other man. All through the fast-time he came not home to Husaby, but Ulf came to fetch his body-guard and took them to meet him at the mid-fast Thing in Orkedal.

In talk with Kristin alone, Ulf told her that Erlend had agreed with Tiedeken Paus, the German goldsmith at Nidaros, that Margret should wed Tiedeken's son Gerlak as soon as Easter was past.

Erlend came home at Easter. He was quiet and calm now, but Kristin thought she could see that he would not be able to shake this off as he had shaken off so much else — whether 'twas because he was no longer so young, or because nothing before had ever humbled him so deeply. Margret seemed quite heedless how her father was ordering things for her.

But one evening when man and wife were alone, Erlend said:

" Had she been my true-born child — or her mother an unwed woman — never would I have given her to a stranger while things are so with her; I could have sheltered and guarded both her and hers. This is an ugly way out, but, seeing what her birth is, a wedded husband can best safeguard her."

While Kristin was making all ready for her step-daughter's going, Erlend said one day, curtly:

" Belike you are scarce well enough to go with us to the city? "

" If you wish it, you know that I will go," said Kristin.

" Why should I wish it? Since before you have never stood in a mother's stead to her, there is no need you should do so now — and a joyous wedding 'twill scarce be. Lady Gunna of Raasvold and her son's wife have promised to come for our kinship's sake."

So Kristin stayed at Husaby, while at Nidaros Erlend gave his daughter to Gerlak Tiedekenssön.

3

THAT summer, just before St. John's Mass, Gunnulf Nikulaussön came back to his cloister. Erlend was in the city then for the Frosta Thing; he sent word to his wife asking her if she deemed she was able to come in thither to meet her brother-in-law. Kristin was none too well, but yet she came. When she met Erlend, he told her that his brother's health seemed to him quite broken down. They had made but little speed with their undertaking in the north, the Friars of Munkefjord. The church they had built they could never get consecrated, for the Archbishop could not journey so far north in these unquiet times; they had had to say mass the whole time at their travelling-altar. At length they came to lack both bread and wine and candles and oil for the services; and when Brother Gunnulf and Brother Aslak set sail for Vargöy to fetch these things, the Lapps had cast a spell on them, so that they capsized and had to sit for three days and nights on a rocky islet — after this they both fell sick, and Brother Aslak died some time after. They had suffered much from scurvy in the Long Fast, for they lacked both meal and herbs to eat with the dry fish. Therefore had Bishop Haakon of Björgvin and Master Arne (who were at the head of the Cathedral Chapter at Nidaros while the new Archbishop, Sir Paal, was gone to the Curia to be consecrated) ordered the monks who yet lived to come back home, and that the priests of Vargöy should tend the flock at Munkefjord till further order.

But though she was thus not unprepared, yet was Kristin dismayed when she saw Gunnulf Nikulaussön once more. She went with Erlend to the cloister the next day, and they were led into the parlour. The monk came in — his form was bent and crooked, the ring of hair was grown quite grey, under the sunken eyes the skin was wrinkled and dark-brown, but on the smooth white skin of the face were lead-coloured spots, and his hand showed like patches when he drew it out of the sleeve of his gown and held it out towards her. He smiled — and she saw that many of his teeth were gone.

They sat down and talked awhile, but it was as though Gunnulf had forgotten how to speak. He said as much himself before the others left him.

"But you, Erlend, are still the same — you seem not to have grown older," he said with a little smile.

Kristin knew well enough that she herself looked wretchedly just now. And Erlend was a comely sight, as he stood there tall and slender and dark and richly clad. And yet Kristin thought that he, too, had changed much — 'twas strange that Gunnulf saw it not — he had used to be so sharp-sighted.

One day of late summer Kristin was in the clothes-loft, and Lady Gunna of Raasvold was with her — she had come to Husaby to help Kristin, now her lying-in was at hand. Standing there, they heard Naakkve and Björgulf singing out in the courtyard, while they sharpened their knives, a coarse ribald song that they were bawling at the top of their voices.

Their mother was beside herself with anger — she went down to the boys and chid them with the harshest words. And then she said she must know whom they learnt such things from — most like 'twas in the servants' house, but which of the men was it that taught children such things? The boys would not answer. Then Skule came out from under the loft-stairway, and said mother had best be still, for they had learnt the song from hearing father sing it.

Lady Gunna spoke up then; had they so little fear of God that they could sing such things — and now, when they could not know, any night when they lay down to rest, that they might not be motherless before cock-crow? Kristin said no more, but went quietly into the house.

After, when she had lain down for a little on her bed, Naakkve came in and went over to her. He took his mother's hand, but said nothing, and then he began to cry quite quietly. She spoke to him then mildly and jestingly, telling him not to weep or wail; she had won through this trouble six times, and surely she would win through the seventh time too. But the boy wept more and more. At last she had to let him creep in between her and the wall, and there he lay weeping with his arms around her neck and his head against her breast; but she could not make him say for what he sorrowed so, though he lay there by her until the serving-woman bore in the supper.

Naakkve was now in his twelfth year; he was a great boy for his age, and was most fain to bear himself grown-up and manly; but he had a soft heart, and the mother could see sometimes that he was still most childlike. He was old enough to have been able to understand his half-sister's mischance; the mother wondered if he understood, too, how much since then his father was changed.

Erlend had always been a man who could say the worst of things when he was enraged — but before this he had never given hard words to any save in wrath; and he had been quick to make all good when he himself was cool again. But now he could say hard and ugly things in cold blood. He had been a terrible man for cursing and swearing; yet had he, in some measure, left off this evil habit, because he saw it hurt his wife and gave offence to Sira Eiliv, for whom he had grown, little by little, to feel much respect. But never had he been foul-mouthed or unseemly in his talk — in that matter he had been much more modest than many a man who had led a purer life. Sorely as it hurt Kristin to hear such words on her young sons' boyish lips, most of all in the state she was in, and to hear that they had learnt them of their father, there was yet another thing which left the bitterest taste of all in her mouth: she saw that Erlend was still childish enough to deem he could brave out the shame of his daughter's fall by taking impure and unseemly words on his lips.

Fru Gunna had told her that Margret had had a still-born son a while before Olav's Mass. The lady had come to know, she said too, that Margret was already not so ill-content — she agreed well with Gerlak and he was kind to her. Erlend went to see his daughter when he was in the city, and Gerlak made a great to-do of his wife's father, though Erlend was none too forward to own the other as kinsman. Erlend himself had not named his daughter's name since she left Husaby.

Kristin bore yet another son; and he was christened Munan after Erlend's father's father. In all the time she lay in the little hall, Naakkve came daily in to his mother with berries and nuts he had plucked in the woods, or wreaths of healing herbs that he had plaited. Erlend came home when the new son was three weeks old; he sat much with his wife, and strove to be kind and loving — and this time he made no complaint because the new-born child was not a little maid, or because it was weakly and throve but ill. But Kristin made not much answer to his kind words; she was quiet and sadly brooding — and this time her strength came back to her exceeding slowly.

All through the winter Kristin was ailing, and the child seemed little like to live and thrive. Thus its mother had little thought to spare for aught else than the poor little being, and she heard with but half an ear all the talk of the great tidings that were stirring this winter. King Magnus had fallen into the greatest straits for money by reason of his endeavours to win the lordship over Skaane, and he had called for succours from Norway. Some of the lords of the Council were willing to stand by him in this matter. But when his messengers came to Tunsberg, the Treasurer had gone away, and Stig Haakonssön, who was Governor in Tunsberghus, shut the gates of the castle against the King's men, and made ready to hold the place by force of arms. He had but few folk with him, but Erling Vidkunssön, who was his uncle by marriage, and was then at his manor in Aker, sent forty of his men-at-arms to strengthen the fortress, while he himself sailed westwards. Much about the same time the King's cousins, Jon and Sigurd Haftorssön, rose against the King, on account of a judgment that had been passed against some of their men. Erlend laughed at this, and said the Haftorssöns had shown themselves raw and foolish. There was great discontent now with King Magnus throughout the land. The nobles demanded that a High Steward should be put at the head of the affairs of the realm and the great seal placed in the hands of a Norseman, since the King, for the sake of his affairs in Skaane, seemed minded to spend most of his time in Sweden. The townsmen and the clergy in the cities had been frighted by the rumours of the King's borrowings from the German cities. The haughtiness of the Germans and their flouting of the laws and customs of the land were already greater than could be borne, and now 'twas said that the King had promised them yet greater rights and franchises in Norwegian cities, so that things would become quite unbearable for the Norse traders, who were already hard put to it. Among the commons the rumours concerning King Magnus' secret sin were still widespread, and many of the parish priests and of the wandering monks were at one in this, if in nothing else, that they believed this was the cause why the Olav's Church in Trondheim had burned down. And so the farmers, too, sought in this the reasons for the many mischances that in these last years had visited now one and now another country-side — plagues among the cattle, blight in the corn, causing sickness and disease to man and beast, and bad harvests of corn and hay. So Erlend said if only the Haftorssöns had had wit enough to hold still awhile yet and win themselves a name for open-handedness and chieftainly dealings, for sure folk would soon have called to mind that they were King Haakon's grandsons too.

These disorders quieted down, but their upshot was that the King made Ivar Ogmundssön High Steward in Norway. Erling Vidkunssön, Stig Haakonssön, the Haftorssöns and all their following were threatened with attainder of high treason. On this they yielded, came in, and made their peace with the King. There was a powerful man of the Uplands named Ulf Saksessön, who had joined in the Haftorssöns' rising; and he did not go with the others to make his peace, but came to Nidaros after Yule. He was much with Erlend in the city, and from him the folk north of Dovre had accounts of all these affairs, in the light he saw them in. Kristin greatly mistrusted this man; she knew him not, but she knew his sister, Helga Saksesdatter, who was wed with Gyrd Darre of Dyfrin. She was fair, but exceeding proud and haughty, and Simon liked her not, though Ramborg agreed well with her. Soon after the Fast was begun, letters came to the Wardens ordering that Ulf Saksessön be proclaimed an outlaw at the Things, but by that time he had left the land, having sailed in the depth of winter.

That spring Erlend and Kristin were at their town-house for Easter, and they had their youngest child, Munan, with them, for there was a sister at Bakke Cloister who was so skilled in leechcraft that all the sick children who were put in her hands got well, if so be it were not the will of God that they should die.

One day just after the holy-day, Kristin came home from the cloister with the little one. The serving-man and the maid who had been with her came with her into the hall. Erlend was alone there, lying on one of the benches. After the man was gone out and the woman had laid by their cloaks — Kristin had sat down by the fire with the child, and the maid was warming some oil they had gotten from the nun — Erlend began asking, from where he lay, what Sister Ragnhild had said of the child. Kristin gave short answers, as she sat unwrapping the child's swaddling-clothes; and at last she made no answer at all.

" Are things so ill with the child, Kristin, that you have no mind to speak of it? " he asked with a little impatience in his voice.

" You have asked this before, Erlend," answered his wife coldly,
" and I have told you all there is to tell many times. But since you
care not enough for the boy to remember it from one day to
another — "

" It has chanced to me, too, Kristin," said Erlend, rising and
coming over to her, " that I have had to answer you two and three
times about things you yourself had asked of me, because you
cared not to remember what I said."

" They were not things of such import as the children's health,
I trow," she said in the same tone.

" They were not trifles, either — this last winter; I, at least, had
them much at heart."

" 'Tis not true, Erlend. 'Tis many a long day since you talked to
me of the things you have most at heart."

" Go out, Signe," said Erlend to the maid. He had flushed to the
forehead — now he turned to his wife. " I understand what you
would speak of. Of that matter I would not speak to you in your
serving-maid's hearing — even if you are such good friends with
her that you count it for nothing she should be by when you
pick a quarrel with your husband, and tell me I speak untrue — "

" 'Tis the last thing a man sees, the beam in his own eye," said
Kristin shortly.

" I understand not well what you mean. Never have I spoken
ungently to you in strangers' hearing, or forgot to show you all
honour and worship before our serving-folk."

Kristin burst into a strange, heart-sick, unsteady laugh.

" You are good at forgetting, Erlend! Through all these years
has Ulf Haldorssön lived with us. Mind you when you sent him
and Haftor to bring me to you in the sleeping-loft of Brynhild's
house at Oslo? "

Erlend sank down on the bench, gazing at his wife, with parted
lips. But she went on:

" Not much has befallen at Husaby — or elsewhere — of unseemly or dishonourable that you have taken thought to hide
from your serving-folk — whether 'twere yourself or your wife
it put to shame — "

Erlend sat still, looking at her in dismay.

" Mind you the first winter we were wed? I was with child of
Naakkve, things were so that 'twas hard enough for me to win

obedience and honour from my household. Mind you how you helped and stayed me? Mind you when your foster-father came to be our guest with strange ladies and maids and men, and our own folk sat at the board with us — mind you that Munan dragged off from me every rag I might have hid me with, and you sat mute and dared not stop his mouth — ? "

" Jesus! Have you stored this up against me for fifteen years! " He looked up at her — his eyes, in that glance, seemed strangely light-blue, and his voice was weak and helpless. " Yet, my Kristin — methinks 'tis worse than this that we two should say unfriendly and bitter words to each other — "

" Aye," said Kristin, " worse indeed did it cut into my heart that time at our Yule-tide feast when you chid and rated me because I had thrown my cloak over Margret — and ladies from three counties were standing by and listening — "

Erlend made no answer.

" And now you blame me because things went with Margret as they did — when each time I tried to correct her with a word she would run to you, and you would bid me, in unfriendly words, to let the maid be — for she was yours and not mine — "

" Blamed you — I have not! " answered Erlend in a laboured voice, striving hard to speak calmly. " Had one of our children been a daughter, it had mayhap been easier for you to understand how such things as this that befell my daughter — how they pierce a father to the marrow — "

" I deemed I had shown you last year that I understood," said his wife in a low voice. " I needed but to think of my own father — "

" For all that," said Erlend, speaking quietly as before, " this was a worse thing. I was an unwed man.. This man — was — wedded. I was not bound — I was not so bound," he corrected himself, " that I could never be set free — "

" And yet you did not free yourself," said Kristin. " Mind you how it came to pass that you were set free — ? "

Erlend sprang up and struck her in the face. Afterward he stood gazing, aghast — a red mark came out on her white cheek. But she sat stiff and silent, with hard eyes. The child had begun to cry with fear — she rocked it a little in her lap and hushed it.

" 'Twas — 'twas cruelly spoken, Kristin," said the man, in a shaken voice.

"Last time you struck me," she said softly, "I bore your child beneath my heart. Now have you struck me whilst I sat with your son upon my lap — "

"Aye, these children — we are never without them — " he cried impatiently.

They fell silent. Erlend began walking swiftly up and down the hall. She bore the child into the closet and laid it on the bed; when she came out through the closet-door, he stopped in front of her:

"I — I should not have struck you, my Kristin. I wish with my heart I had not done it — I shall repent it, I trow, for as long as I repented the last time. But you — you have taunted me because you deem I forget too lightly. But you forget naught — no single wrong that I ever did you. Yet I have tried — I have tried to be a good husband to you; but that, I trow, you deem not worth remembrance. You — you are fair, Kristin — " He looked after her as she went past him.

Aye, the housewife's still and stately bearing was as beautiful as had been the young maid's supple loveliness; her bosom and hips were grown broader, but she was taller, too; she held herself upright, and the neck bore up the little round head proudly and graciously as ever. The pale, close-shut face with its great dark-grey eyes stirred and kindled him even as the round, rosy child-face had stirred and kindled his restless soul by its mysterious calm. He went over and took her hand:

"For me, Kristin, you are and ever will be the fairest of all women, and the dearest — "

She let him hold her hand, but gave not back the pressure of his. Then he flung it from him, as his bitterness overcame him again.

"Forgotten, say you I have? I trow 'tis not ever the worst of sins — to forget. I have never set up to be a pious man; but I remember what I learned of Sira Jon when a child, and God's ministers have reminded me of it since. 'Tis sin to brood and call back to mind the sins we have confessed to the priest and done penance for before God, and been granted His forgiveness for through the priest's hand and mouth. And 'tis not from holiness, Kristin, that you are ever tearing open these old sins of ours, but 'tis to have a weapon against me each time I go against you in aught — "

He walked away from her, and then came back.

" Greedy to rule — God knows that I love you, Kristin — yet do I see that you are greedy to rule, and never have you forgiven me that I did you wrong and tempted you to wrong. Much have I borne from you, Kristin, but I will no longer bear never to be left in peace for these old mischances, nor to have you speak to me as though I were your thrall — "

Kristin was shaking with passion as she answered:

" Never have I spoken to you as though you were a thrall. Have you *once* heard me speak harshly or angrily to any human being that could be counted as lesser than I — if it were the worst and most worthless of our servant-folk? I know myself free before God from the sin of having offended His poor in word or deed. But you should be my *master;* you should I obey and honour, bow myself before and stay myself on, next to God — according to God's law, Erlend. And if so be I have lost patience, and have spoken to you in such wise as it befits not a wife to speak to her husband — I trow it has been because you have many a time made it hard for me to bow my simplicity before your better under-standing, to honour and obey my husband and lord so much as I fain would have done — and maybe I looked that you — maybe I deemed I might spur you on to show that you were a man, and I but a poor simple woman —

" But take comfort, Erlend. I shall not offend you with my words any more, for after this day never shall I forget to speak to you as gently as though, in truth, you were born of thralls — "

Erlend's face flushed darkly red — he lifted his clenched fist — then turned sharp about on his heel, seized his cloak and sword from the bench by the door, and rushed out.

Without there was sunshine and a sharp wind — it was cold, but the bright sparkles that besprinkled him from house-eaves and from wind-swept trees were drops of water thawed out and frozen again in the air. The snow on the house-tops shone like silver, and behind the dark-green tree-clad hills around the town the mountains glittered cold blue and shining white in the bitter, bright, wintry spring day.

Erlend passed through streets and lanes — swiftly, at haphazard. He was boiling inwardly — *she* had been wrong, 'twas as clear as day she had been wrong from the first, and he had been right; and he had played the fool and struck her and made him seem less

right — but the wrong *was* with her. What he should do with
himself now, he knew not. He had no mind to go to any acquaintance' house, and home he would not go.

There was some hurry and bustle in the city. A big trader from
Iceland — the first of the year — had come in to the wharves in
the morning. Erlend wandered westward through the lanes, came
out by St. Martin's Church, and went down toward the water-
side alleys. Though 'twas early in the afternoon, already there
was noise and yelling in the ale-houses and from the taverns. In
his youth he had been able to go into such houses himself, with
his friends and fellows. But now all the folks would stare the eyes
out of their heads, and talk themselves hoarse afterwards, if the
Warden of Orkdöla County, with his great house in the city,
with ale and mead and wine at home to his heart's desire, should
come into an ale-house and ask for a drink of their bad small beer.
Yet truly this was what he had a mind to do — to sit and drink
with small farmers in town for the day and serving-men and sea-
men. There was no to-do when those fellows caught their woman
a buffet on the ear; and after that all was well again — hell and
furies! how should a man rule a woman when he cannot thrash
her soundly, by reason of her birth and his own honour? — at
bandying words the devil himself could be no match for them.
Troll she was — and so fair, too — if only he could beat her till she
grew good again. . . .

The bells began ringing from all the city churches to call folks
together to Vespers — the spring wind mingled all the notes together in the unquiet air above his head. 'Twas like she was going
to Christ's Church now, the holy troll — to bemoan her to God
and Mary Virgin and holy Olav that her husband had hit her
a buffet on the ear. Erlend sent up towards his wife's guardian
saints a greeting of sinful thoughts, while the bells clashed and
clanged and resounded. He made his way towards St. Gregory's
Church.

His father and mother's graves were before St. Anne's altar in
the northern aisle. Whilst he said over his prayers, he caught
sight of Lady Sunniva Olavsdatter and her maid coming in at the
church-door. When he had done praying, he went across and
greeted her.

It had been the way of these two, ever since he had come to

know the lady, that whenever they met they fell to somewhat free toying and jesting. And this evening as they sat on the wall-bench waiting for evensong to begin, he was so forward that she had more times than one to remind him that they were in church and that folk kept coming by them.

" Aye, aye," said Erlend, " but you are so fair to-night, Sunniva! 'Tis so good to jest with a lady that has such gentle eyes — "

" Little do you deserve, Erlend Nikulaussön, that I should look at you with gentle eyes," said she, laughing.

" Then will I come and jest with you when 'tis dark," said Erlend, laughing too. " When evensong is over, I will go home with you — "

Then the priests came into the choir, and Erlend went across to the southern aisle to take his place among the men.

When the service was at an end, he went out at the great door. He saw Lady Sunniva and her maid a little way down the street, and thought he had best not go with her, but go home straight-way. At that moment a band of Icelanders from the trader came up the street; they staggered along, holding on to each other, and seemed as they would block the two women's passage. Erlend ran after the lady. As soon as the sailors saw a gentleman with a sword at his belt come toward them, they swerved aside and made room for the women to pass.

" I trow I had best go home with you, after all," said Erlend. " The city is none too quiet to-night."

" Can you believe it, Erlend? — old a woman as I am, maybe I like it not ill that some men think I am yet so fair, 'tis worth while blocking my way — "

There was but one answer that a courteous man could make to this.

He came home to his own house the next morning in the grey of dawn, and stood a little outside the locked door of the hall, frozen, dead-weary, heart-sore and sickened. Rouse the house-hold with his knocking; go in and creep into bed beside Kristin lying with the child at her breast — no! He had on him the key of the eastern storehouse loft; there were some goods stored there that he was answerable for. He let himself in, pulled off his boots, and got together some webs of wadmal and some empty sacks and spread them on straw in the bedstead. He wrapped his cloak about him, crept under the sacks, and, tired out and harassed as he was, was able at last to forget everything in sleep.

Kristin was pale and weary with waking when she sat down to the morning meal with her house-folk. One of the men told her that he had prayed the master to come to breakfast — he was sleeping up in the east storehouse loft, he said — but Erlend had bidden him go to the devil.

Erlend had a tryst out at Elgesæter after the day-mass; he had to witness some dealings in land. But he managed to slip away from the feast that followed in the refectory, and from Arne Gjavvaldssön, who, like himself, could not stay and drink with the Brothers, but was set on having Erlend go with him to Ranheim.

Afterwards he repented that he had parted company with the others — dismay came over him as he went back alone to the town — now must he needs think over what he had done. For a moment he had a mind to go straightway to St. Gregory's Church — he had leave to confess to one of the priests there, when he was in Nidaros. But if he did this again, after he had confessed, the sin would be much greater. 'Twere better to wait awhile —

She must think now, Sunniva, that he was a chicken she had caught with her bare hands. But devil take him if he had ever thought a woman had been able to teach him so much that was new — here was he going about yawning still from the adventure. He had flattered himself he was not unskilled in *ars amoris*, or whatever the learned men called it. Had he been young and green, like enough he had been proud of himself and deemed it fine and brave. But he liked not the woman — the mad creature — he was sick of her; he was sick of *all* women save his wife — and he was sick of her too! By the Cross itself — he had been so wedded to her that he had grown most holy himself — for he had believed in her holiness — but 'twas a fair reward he had had from his holy wife for his faithfulness and love — troll that she was! He remembered her scorching venomous words of the day before — so she deemed he bore himself as though he were born of thralls! — And the other, Sunniva, she thought, doubtless, he was naught but a raw weakling, since he had let himself be taken by surprise and had shown some dismay at her way of love-making. He would show her now that he was no more of a holy man than she was a woman. He had promised her to come down to Thorolf's town-house that night, and he might e'en as well go; the sin was sinned: why not enjoy any disport it might bring with it? "

Since he had broken his troth to Kristin already — and she herself had brought it about, by her hateful and unjust ways towards him —

He went home, and wandered about the stables and outhouses seeking for somewhat to find fault with; he had words with the priest's serving-maid from the hospital because she had brought malt into his drying-house, though he knew well that his housefolk would have no use for the house this time while they were in the town. He wished he had had his boys here — they would have been some company — he wished he could set forth back to Husaby at once. But he must needs wait in the city for letters from the south — 'twas too venturesome to have such things come to hand at one's home in the country.

The mistress of the house came not in to supper — she was lying down on the bed in the closet, said Signe, her maid, looking at her master reproachfully. Erlend answered harshly that he had not asked after her mistress. When the house-folk had left the hall, he went into the closet. It was pitch-dark in there. Erlend bent over the bed.

" Are you weeping? " he asked very low, her breath came so strangely. But she answered in a thick, husky voice that she was not weeping.

" Are you weary? Aye — I will go to rest too, now," he said in the same low voice.

Kristin's voice quivered as she said:

" Then I had liefer, Erlend, that you should go and lie to-night where you lay last night."

Erlend made no answer. He went out and fetched the candle from the hall into the closet, and opened his chest of clothing. He was well clad enough already to go wherever he listed, for he still bore the violet *kothardi* he had worn at Elgesæter in the morning. But now he changed his clothes slowly and deliberately — put on a red silk shirt and a mouse-grey knee-long velvet coat with little silver bells on the sleeve-points, brushed his hair, and washed his hands. Time and again he looked over towards his wife — she lay silent and motionless. Then he went out without bidding good night. Next day he came home openly at the breakfast-hour.

So things went on for a week. Then Erlend came home one evening from Hangrar where he had been on an errand and learnt that Kristin had ridden off that morning home to Husaby.

It had grown clear to him already that never had any man had less joy from a sin than he from these dealings of his with Sunniva Olavsdatter. In his heart he was so deadly weary of the crazy creature — sick of her even while he caressed and toyed with her. 'Twas a mad and reckless thing, too — like enough it was all over the town and the country-side by now, that he had his nightly resort in Thorolf's house — and to smirch his name for Sunniva's sake! Now and then he had thought, too, that the thing might raise some trouble — the woman had a husband such as he was, old and sickly — 'twas pity of Thorolf that he should be wed to such a wild and witless woman — most like *he* was not the first that had made free with the husband's honour. And Haftor — he had clean forgotten, when he had to do with Sunniva, that she was Haftor's sister — he remembered it only when it was too late. All was as bad as it could be — and now he could see that Kristin knew it.

She surely could not take it in her head to bring suit against him before the Archbishop — crave leave to depart from him. She had Jörundgaard to take refuge in — but it was impossible to travel thither over the mountains at this time of year, quite impossible if she would take the small children with her — and Kristin would not leave *them*. No — he thought, to comfort himself — and she could not go by sea either, with Munan and Lavrans, so early in the spring. Oh, but 'twould be unlike Kristin to crave the Archbishop's help against him — though she had good reason for it — but he would keep away from her bed of his own accord — till she saw that he repented from his heart. Kristin could never wish to have this thing publicly brought to question. But he knew in his heart that 'twas long since he had rightly known what his wife could or could not do.

He lay at night in his own bed, letting his thoughts go hither and thither. It dawned upon him that he had behaved yet more witlessly than he had understood at first, to let himself be tangled in this wretched adventure, now, when he was in the thick of the greatest plans of State.

He cursed himself that he was still such a fool about his wife that she had been able to drive him to this. He cursed both Kristin and Sunniva. In the devil's name, sure he was no fonder on women than other men — rather he had had to do with fewer of them than most others that he knew of. But 'twas as though the foul fiend himself had the ordering of things for him — he could not come near a woman without finding himself up to the neck in a bog. . . .

There should be an end of it now. God be thanked and praised that he had other things on hand. Soon, soon, for sure, would he have Lady Ingebjörg's letters. Aye, in that matter, too, he had to reckon with women's whims; belike that was God's punishment for the sins of his youth. Erlend laughed to himself in the dark. The lady must see that things were as they had so clearly set them forth to her. The question was whether it should be one of her sons or the sons of her base-born sister that the Norsemen set up against King Magnus. And she loved her children by Knut Porse as she had never loved her other children.

Soon, soon, 'twould be the sharp wind and the salt sea breakers that should fill his embrace. God in heaven! it would be good to be drenched by the waves once again and have the wind blow freshness to his very marrow — be quit of all womankind for a long, delicious time.

Sunniva — she might think what she would. Thither he would go no more. And Kristin might fare to Jörundgaard if she would, for him. 'Twould mayhap be best and safest for her and the children if they were well out of the way in Gudbrandsdal this summer. Afterward there was no fear but he could make friends with her again. . . .

Next morning he rode up into Skaun. Say what he would, he could not rest till he had made sure what his wife meant to do.

She met him with gentle, cold courtesy when he reached Husaby late in the day. She spoke not a word to him of her own accord, nor any unfriendly word; and she said naught against it when, in the evening, as if feeling his way, he came over and lay down in their bed. When they had lain awhile, he tried, falteringly, to lay a hand on her shoulder.

Kristin's voice shook, but Erlend could not tell whether it were in sorrow or from anger, as she whispered:

" So base a man I trow you are not, Erlend, that you would make this worse for me than need be. I cannot strive with you, with our children sleeping around us. And since I have seven sons by you, I would be loath that our house-folk should see that I know I am a wronged wife — "

Erlend lay long and silent before he ventured to answer:

" Aye. God have mercy on me, Kristin, I have wronged you. I had not — had not done it if I could have taken more lightly the cruel words you said to me that day at Nidaros. It is not so that I am come home to beg you for forgiveness; for I know well that that would be a great thing to ask you now — "

" I see that Munan Baardssön spoke true," answered his wife; " the day will never come when you will stand up and take the blame on yourself for what you have done amiss. 'Twere best you turned you to God and sought to make your peace with Him — you have less need to ask my forgiveness than His — "

" Aye, so much I can see," said Erlend bitterly. After this they spoke no more. And the next morning he rode back to Nidaros.

He had been in the city some days when Lady Sunniva's woman came to him one evening in St. Gregory's Church. It seemed to Erlend that after all it were well he should speak with the lady one last time; and he bade the girl keep watch that night — he would come by the same way as before.

He had had to creep and clamber about like a poultry-thief to come up into the loft where they had their meetings. It made him sick with shame now to think he had been such a fool — a man of his age and his place. But at first he had deemed it sport to play such youthful pranks.

The lady was in bed when he came in.

" Come you at long last and so late? " she laughed, and yawned. " Quick now, love, and come to bed; and we can talk afterward about where you have been so long — "

Erlend knew not rightly what to do, or how to tell her what he had at heart. Without thinking, he began to loose the fastenings of his dress.

" Foolhardy is it, this that we have done, Sunniva — I trow it were not well that I should stay here to-night. Thorolf must be looked for home ere long? " he said.

" Are you frighted at my husband? " asked Sunniva teasingly. "You saw yourself Thorolf never so much as pricked up an ear when we toyed and jested before his very eyes. Should he hear that you have been coming about the house, I warrant I make him believe that it is but the old foolery. He trusts me all too well—"

" Aye, it seems indeed that he trusts you all too well," laughed Erlend, burying his fingers in the bright hair on her firm white shoulders.

" Say you so? " She caught him round the wrist. " Yet you trust your wife too. And *I* was yet modest and shamefast when Baard wedded me—"

" *My* wife we will leave outside of this matter," said Erlend sharply, letting go his hold.

" Why so—? Think you 'tis more unseemly that we should speak of Kristin Lavransdatter than of Sir Thorolf, my husband? "

Erlend set his teeth hard and made no answer.

" Methinks you are one of those men, Erlend," said Sunniva mockingly, " that think you are so winning and fair that it can scarce be reckoned a fault in a woman that her virtue was as frail as glass against you—she may be staunch as steel against all others."

" Of you I have never thought so," answered Erlend coarsely.

Sunniva's eyes gleamed:

" What would you with me, then, Erlend—since you were so happily wedded? "

" I have said, you shall not name my wife—"

" Your wife or my husband—"

" 'Twas ever you that began to speak of Thorolf; and 'twas you that scoffed at him worst," said Erlend bitterly. " And if you had not flouted him in words—'twas plain enough how dear you held his honour, when you took another man to you in your husband's place. *She*—is not brought low by my misdoing."

" Is this what you would say to me—that you love Kristin, though you like me well enough to play with me—"

" I know not how well I like you—you showed that you liked me—"

" And Kristin sets not your love at its true worth? " she scoffed. " I have seen well enough how gently she is used to look on you, Erlend."

" Hold your tongue, now! " shouted the man. " Maybe she knew what I deserved! " he said harshly and savagely. " You and I may well be each other's like—"

" Is it so," asked Sunniva threateningly, " that I was to be but a whip for you to lash your wife with? "

Erlend stood breathing hard:

" Call it so, if you will. But you laid yourself ready to my hand."

" Beware," said Sunniva, " that that whip smite not yourself — "

She sat up in the bed and waited. But Erlend offered not to gain-say her or to seek to make up the quarrel. He re-dressed fully and left her without a word.

He was not greatly pleased with himself, or with the fashion in which he had parted from Sunniva. There was small honour in it for him. But it could not be helped — and at least he was quit of her now.

4

THIS spring and summer not much was seen of the master at Husaby. At such times as he was at the manor, he and his wife met each other with courtesy and friendliness. Erlend in no way tried to break down the wall she now built up between them, though he would often look after her searchingly. For the rest, he seemed to have much to think on outside his home. Touching the management of the estate he never asked a single word.

It was this matter of the estates his wife brought forward when, just after the spring Holy Cross day, he would have had her go with him to Raumsdal. He had business in the Uplands — would she not take the children with her, stay awhile at Jörundgaard, and see her kinsfolk and friends in the Dale? But Kristin would on no account agree to this.

He was in Nidaros at the time of the Lagthing, and afterward out in Orkedal; then he came home to Husaby, but at once busied himself making ready for a journey to Björgvin. *Margygren* was lying out at Nidarholm, and he but waited for Haftor Graut, who was to sail along with him.

Three days before Margaret's Mass * they began the hay-harvest at Husaby. It was the fairest weather, and when the hay-makers went back to the meadows after the midday rest, Olav, the foreman, got leave for the children to go with them.

Kristin was in the clothing storehouse that was in the second story of the armoury building. The house was so built that an outer stairway led up to this room, which had a balcony before it;

* 10th June.

the third story — the armoury itself — stood out above the balcony, and it could be reached only by a loose ladder from the clothing loft leading to a trap-door on the floor. The trap-door was open, for Erlend was up in the armoury.

Kristin bore out the fur cloak that Erlend was to take with him for the sea-voyage, and shook it out in the balcony. Then she was ware of the noise of a great company of horsemen, and at the same moment she saw folks come riding out of the woods on the Gauldal road. The next moment Erlend stood by her side.

" Was it so, did you say, Kristin, that the fire in the kitchen was put out this morning? "

" Aye — Gudrid upset the broth-cauldron. We must borrow a light from Sira Eiliv — "

Erlend looked across at the priest's house.

" No; he must not be mixed in this. Gaute," he called softly to the boy, who was loitering under the balcony, lifting one rake after another, unwilling to set out to the haymaking. " Come up hither, up the stairs — no farther, or they might see you."

Kristin gazed at her husband. Like this she had never seen him before — the strained, alert calm in his voice, in his face, as he spied out southward along the road — in the whole of his tall supple form as he ran into the loft and came back at once with a flat packet, sewn up in linen cloth. He gave it to the boy:

" Hide this in your breast — and mark well what I say to you. You must save these letters — more is at stake than you can understand, my Gaute. Put your rake over your shoulder and go quietly down across the fields till you come to the alder-thickets. Keep well among the bushes till you get down to the wood — you know all the paths there, I know — and creep through the thickest brush all the way across to Skjoldvirkstad. When you get there, make sure first that all is quiet on the farm. Should you see signs of aught amiss or of strangers about, then hide you. But should you be sure all is safe, go down to the farm and give this to Ulf, if he be at home. But if you cannot give the letters into his hands while you are sure that none is near, burn them the moment you can come by the wherewithal to do it. But be sure that both writing and seals are altogether burnt up, and that they come not into any man's hands but Ulf's. God help us, my son — these be great matters to put in the hands of a boy of ten winters — the lives and welfare of many good men — understand you that much is at stake, Gaute? "

"Aye, father. I have understood all that you have said to me."
Gaute looked up from the stairway, his little fair face full of earnestness.

"Say to Isak, if Ulf is not at home, that he must ride straight out
to Havne and on all night — and tell them he wots of, that a head
wind has sprung up, and I fear me evil spells have spoiled my journey. Do you understand?"

"Aye, father. I mind well all you have said to me."

"Go, then. God keep you, my son."

Erlend ran up into the armoury, and would have closed the
trap-door, but Kristin was already half-way through the opening.
He waited till she was up, then shut the trap, ran over to a chest,
and took out some written parchments. He tore the seals off and
trampled them to pieces on the floor, tore the parchments into
rags and wrapped them together round the key of the chest and
dropped the little bundle from the window-hole into the midst of
the nettles that grew high behind the storehouse. With his hands
on the window-frame, he stood gazing after the little boy walking
along the edge of the cornfield down towards the meadow, where
the mowers were moving forward in a line, plying their scythes
and rakes. When Gaute disappeared into the little copse between
the corn-field and the meadow, he closed the shutter. The noise
of hoofs came loudly now and from near by.

Erlend turned towards his wife:

"Can you have what I threw out but now made away with? —
send Skule, he has his wits about him — tell him to fling it down
into the pit behind the byre. Like enough they will keep an eye on
you, and mayhap on the big boys too. But they will scarce search
you —" He put the fragments of the seals down inside the bosom
of her dress. "None could make them out, methinks; but yet —"

"Are you in peril, Erlend?" she asked quietly. When he had
looked into her face, he drew her outspread arms around him. For
a moment he pressed her to him:

"I know not, Kristin. We shall see soon, I trow. Tore Eindridessön rides at the head of the men, and Sir Baard is with them, if I
saw aright. I can scarce deem that Tore comes hither for any
good —"

The horsemen were in the courtyard now. Erlend stood still a
moment. Then he kissed his wife vehemently, opened the trap-
door, and ran down. When Kristin came out into the balcony,

she saw Erlend in the courtyard helping the Treasurer, who was an old man and a heavy, to dismount from his horse. There were thirty men-at-arms, at least, with Sir Baard and the Warden of Gauldöla County. As Kristin crossed the yard, she heard the Warden say:

"I bring you greetings from your cousins, Erlend. Borgar and Guttorm Trondssöns are the King's honoured guests at Veöy, and I trow Haftor Toressön will have paid a friendly visit by this time to Ivar and the young lad at their home at Sundbu. Sir Baard took the Graut into keeping in the city yestermorn."

"And now I see you are come hither to bid me to this same meeting of the guardsmen," said Erlend, smiling.

"So it is, Erlend."

"And doubtless you would search my manor here too? Oh, I have done my part in such affairs so often that I ought to know the way 'tis done."

"Such great affairs as a high treason cause you have scarce had in your hands," said Tore.

"No, not before now," said Erlend. "And it looks as though I were playing with the black men, Tore, and you had mated me — is it not so, kinsman?"

"We must find forth the letters you have had from Lady Inge-björg Haakonsdatter," said Tore Eindridessön.

"They are in the chest covered with red leather up in the armoury — but there is not much in them save such greetings as dear kinsfolk use to send to each other — and they are all old. Stein here can take you up."

The stranger horsemen had dismounted now, and the house-folk were coming crowding into the courtyard.

"There was more in the one we took from Borgar Trondssön," said Tore. Erlend whistled softly.

"We had best go into the hall," he said; "it begins to grow crowded here."

Kristin followed the men into the hall. At a sign from Tore two of the stranger men-at-arms came with them.

"You must give up your sword, Erlend," said Tore of Gimsar, when they stood within, "for a sign that you are our prisoner."

Erlend smote his thighs to show that he wore no other weapon than the dagger in his belt. But Tore said again:

"You must reach us your sword for a token —"

" Aye, aye, if all is to be done to such a nicety — " said Erlend, laughing a little. He went over and took his sword from its peg, and holding the scabbard, held out the hilt to Tore Eindridessön with a little bow.

The old man of Gimsar loosened the fastenings, drew the blade right out, and ran his fingers along its groove.

" Was it this sword, Erlend, that you — ? "

Erlend's blue eyes glittered like steel, his mouth grew narrow and straight-lipped:

" Aye. 'Twas with this sword I chastised your grandson when I found him with my daughter."

Tore stood holding the sword; he looked down at it and spoke threateningly:

" You that should uphold the law, Erlend — you must sure have known that that time you went a little farther than the law would follow you — "

Erlend threw back his head, flushing, and said hotly:

" There is a law, Tore, that cannot be set aside by Kings or Thingmen — his women's honour a man may guard with the sword — "

" Well for you, Erlend Nikulaussön, that no man has put that law to use against you," answered Tore of Gimsar malignantly. " Else had you need of as many lives as a cat — "

Erlend said with stinging slowness of speech:

" Think you not this matter is so grave that 'tis untimely to mix up with it old stories from my youth? "

" I know not if Thorolf of Lensvik deems those matters are so old."

Erlend flamed up and would have answered; but Tore shouted:

" You should try first, Erlend, whether your mistresses have skill to read writing, before you run about to nightly trysts with secret letters in your waist-band! Ask you of Baard there who it was that warned us that you were hatching traitorous counsels against your King that you have sworn troth to, and hold your place in fee from — "

Unwittingly Erlend raised a hand to his breast — he glanced for a moment at his wife, and his face flushed darkly. Then Kristin ran forward and threw her arms about his neck. Erlend looked down into her face — he saw naught in it but love:

" Erlend — husband."

The Treasurer had scarce spoken a word hitherto. Now he went over to the pair and said softly:

"Dear lady — mayhap it would be best that you take the children and your serving-women with you into the women's house, and stay there as long as we are on the manor."

Erlend loosed his wife, with a last pressure of his arm about her shoulders.

"It is best so, my own Kristin — do you as Sir Baard counsels."

Kristin lifted herself on tiptoe and offered him her mouth to kiss. Then she went out into the courtyard. And out of the confused throng of folks she gathered together her children and serving-women, and carried them with her into the little hall — other women's house there was not at Husaby.

For some hours they sat there, and the mistress' calm and steadfastness kept the frightened little company's terror somewhat in check. Then Erlend came in, disarmed and clad as for a journey. Two stranger men-at-arms took post down by the door.

He took his eldest sons by the hand, and then lifted the little ones in his arms, while he asked where Gaute was — "but you must greet him from me, Naakkve. He is run off to the woods with his bow, I warrant, as his wont is. Tell him he can have my English long-bow after all — I denied it him when he asked for it on Sunday."

Kristin crushed him to her without a word.

"When will you come back, Erlend dearest?" she whispered pleadingly.

"That must be as God will, my wife."

She drew back from him, struggling that she might not break down. He was never used to speak to her but by her christened name, and these last words of his shook her to the very heart. It was as if only now she understood to the full what it was that had befallen.

At the sunset hour Kristin sat up on the hill north of the houses.

She had never seen the sky so red and golden before. Above the hill right over against her lay a great cloud; it was shaped like a bird's wing, it glowed within like iron in the forge, it shone clear as amber. Little golden wisps like feathers loosed themselves from it and floated out into the sky. And deep below on the lake in the valley-bottom the sky was mirrored with the cloud and the hill-side above it — it seemed as though it were from down there in the depths that the burning glow streamed up to tinge all that lay before her.

The grass in the meadows was seeding, and its silken spikes shone darkling red in the red light from the sky; the barley was in ear, and caught the radiance on its young silky-bright beards. The turf house-roofs of the manor were thick with sorrel and buttercups, and the sunlight lay in broad rays across them; the blackish shingles of the church-roof glowed darkly, and the light stones of the walls were softly gilded.

The sun broke forth beneath the cloud, rested on the mountain-crest and sent his light out over range behind range of wooded hills. The evening was so clear — the light showed up to sight little clearings among the pine-covered hill-sides; she could see sæters and little farms in among the woods that she had never before known one could see from Husaby. Great hill masses, deep violet in hue, rose in the south, in toward Dovre, where else there were wont to be clouds or haze.

The least of the bells in the chapel below began to ring, and the church-bell at Vinjar answered. Kristin sat bowed over her folded hands till the last of the three triple strokes died away on the air.

Now the sun was below the mountain-top, the golden radiance grew paler and the red more rosy and soft. After the bells had fallen silent, the soughing of the woods seemed to grow again and spread abroad; the noise of the little beck that ran through the leaf-woods down in the valley sounded louder on the ear. From the close near by came the well-known clinking from the bells of the home cattle; a flying beetle hummed half-way round about her, and was gone.

She sent a last sigh after her prayers — a prayer for forgiveness because her thoughts had been elsewhere while she prayed.

The great goodly manor lay below her on the hill-side, like a jewel on the hill's broad bosom. She looked out over all the lands that she had owned along with her husband. Thoughts of this estate, cares for it, had filled her mind to the brim. She had worked and striven — never till to-night had she known herself how she had striven to set this manor on its feet and keep it safe — nor all she had found strength to do and how much she had compassed.

She had taken it as her lot, to be borne patiently and unflinchingly, that all this rested on her shoulders. Even so she had striven to be patient and to hold her head high under the burden her life laid on her, each time she knew she had again a child to bear under her heart — again and again. With each son added to the flock, she had felt more strongly the duty of upholding the welfare and safety of the house — she saw to-night, too, that her power to overlook the whole, her watchfulness, had grown with each new child she had to watch and strive for. Never had she seen so clearly as this evening what fate had craved of her and what it had granted her, in giving her these seven sons. Over again and over again had joy in them quickened the beating of her heart, fear for them pierced it — they were her children, these great lads with their lean angular boys' bodies, as they had been when they were so small and plump they could scarce hurt themselves when they tumbled in their journeys between the bench and her knee. They were hers, even as they had been when, as she would lift one of them from the cradle up to her breast for milk, she had to hold up its head, because it nodded on the slender neck as a bluebell nods on its stalk. Wherever they might wander out in the world, whithersoever they might fare, forgetful of their mother, she felt as though for her their life must still be an action of her life, they must still be as one with herself as they had been when she alone in all the world knew of the new life which lay hidden within and drank of her blood and made her cheeks pale. Over again and over again had she proved the sickening sweating terror when she felt: now her time was come again, now again was she to be dragged under in the breakers of travail — till she was borne up again with a new child in her arms; how much richer and stronger and braver with each child, never till to-night had she understood.

And yet she saw to-night that she was still the Kristin of Jörund-gaard, who had never learned to endure an ungentle word, because she had been shielded all her days by so strong and tender a love. In Erlend's hands she was still the same. . . .

Aye. Aye. Aye. 'Twas true that she had gone on storing up, year in, year out, the memory of every wound he had dealt her — though she had known always that he had wounded her, not from ill will as a grown man wounds another, but as a child strikes his playfellow in their play. She had tended the memory of each time when he had offended her, as one tends a festering sore. And every abasement he had brought upon himself by following his own every whim struck her like a whip-stroke on the flesh and left a

unning weal. 'Twas not so that she willingly and of purpose stored
up grudges against her husband; she knew that towards others she
was not petty-minded, but when he was concerned she grew so
straightway. When Erlend was in question, she could forget nothing, and every least scratch on her soul went on smarting and
bleeding and swelling and throbbing, when 'twas he that had
dealt it her.

Towards him she never grew wiser, never stronger. She might
strive to seem, in her life with him too, capable and brave and
strong and pious, but 'twas not true that she was so. Ever, ever
had longing gnawed within her — the longing to be again his
Kristin of the woods of Gerdarud.

In those days she had been willing to do all that she knew was
evil and sinful rather than lose him. To bind Erlend to her, she
had given him all that was hers: her love and her body, her honour
and her part in the salvation of her Lord. And she had given him
what she could find to give that was not hers: her father's honour
and his trust in his child; all that wise and prudent grown men had
built up to safeguard a little maid in her nonage she had overturned;
against their plans for the welfare and advancement of their race,
against their hopes that their work would bear fruit when they
themselves lay under the mould, she had set her love. Much more
than her own life had she staked in the game, wherein the sole
prize was Erlend Nikulaussön's love.

And she had won. She had known, from the time when he kissed
her for the first time in the garden by Hofvin, even till to-day
when he kissed her in the little hall before he was led away a prisoner from his home — Erlend loved her as his own life. And if he
had not guided her life well, yet had she known well-nigh from the
first hour she met him how he had guided his own. If he had not
ever dealt well by her, yet had he dealt better by her than with
himself.

Jesus, how she had won him! She confessed to herself this evening — she herself had driven him to breach of his marriage-vows
by her coldness and by her venomous words. She confessed to
herself now — even in these years when she had looked on, time
and again, at his unseemly dalliance with this woman Sunniva, and
had been angered by it, she had felt in the midst of her wrath a
haughty and defiant joy — none knew of any open stain on Sunniva
Olavsdatter's honour, yet Erlend talked and jested with her as a

serving-man might with an ale-house wench. And of her he ha
known that she could lie and betray those that trusted her best, tha
she willingly let herself be lured to the most shameful places — ye
had he trusted her, yet had he honoured her so far as in him lay
Easy as it was for him to forget all fear of sin, easy as it had beer
for him to break his promise made to God at the altar, yet had h
sorrowed over his sins against her, and had struggled for year
that he might be able to keep his promises to her.

She had chosen him herself. She had chosen him in a frenzy o
love, and she had chosen anew each day of those hard years a
home at Jörundgaard — chosen his wild reckless passion befor
her father's love that would not suffer the wind to blow ungently
upon her. She had thrown away the lot her father had shaped for
her, when he would have given her to the arms of a man who
would surely have led her by the safest ways, and would have
stooped down, to boot, to take away each little stone that she
might have dashed her foot against. She had chosen to follow the
other, who she knew was straying in perilous paths. Monks and
priests had pointed the way of repentance and atonement to lead
her home to peace — she had chosen turmoil rather than let slip
her darling sin.

So there was but one way for her — not to murmur or cry out,
whatever should befall her at this man's side. Dizzily far behind
her it seemed now, the time when she had left her father. But she
saw his beloved face, remembered his words that day in the smithy
when she dealt his heart the last stab, remembered their talk together, up in the mountains in the hour when she saw that the
door of death stood ajar waiting for him. Unworthy is it to murmur at the lot one has chosen for oneself. — Holy Olav, help me
that now I may not show me altogether unworthy of my father's
love!

Erlend, Erlend — When she met him in her youth, life had become for her a swift river rushing over rocks and rapids. In these
years at Husaby, life had spread out, lying wide and ample like a
lake, mirroring all that surrounded her. She remembered, at home,
when the Laagen overflowed in spring-time, and lay grey and
mighty in the valley-bottom, bearing on its bosom the driftage
that came floating, while the tops of the growing leaf-trees in its
course swayed on the waters. Out in its midst showed little dark

threatening eddies, where the current ran swift and wild and perilous under the shining surface. Now she knew that even so had her
love for Erlend run like a swift and perilous current beneath the
surface of her life through all these years. Now 'twas bearing forward — she knew not to what.

Erlend, beloved — !

Once more Kristin breathed an Ave out into the evening glow.
Hail Mary, full of grace! I dare pray thee but for one mercy, that
see I now: Save Erlend, save my husband's life — !

She looked down at Husaby and thought of her sons. Now when
the manor lay there in the evening light like a dream vision that
might melt away — now that fear for her children's doubtful fate
shook her heart, it came to her mind: Never had she thanked God
fully for the rich fruits her toil had borne in these years; and never
had she thanked Him as she ought that seven times He had granted
her a son.

Out of the dome of the evening heaven, from all the country-side
beneath her eyes, came the murmured words of the mass that she
had heard thousands of times, in her father's voice that had set
forth the words for her when she was a little child at his knee:
Thus sings Sira Eirik in the *Præfatio*, when he turns him to the
altar, and thus it says in the Norse tongue:

It is truly meet and just, right and available to salvation, that we
should always, and in all places, give thanks to Thee, O holy Lord,
Father Almighty, eternal God.

When she lifted up her face from her hands, she saw Gaute
coming up the hill. Kristin sat still and waited till the boy stood
before her, then she stretched out her hand and took his. There
was grassy sward a good way round the stone where she was sitting, with no place where any might hide.

" How did you do your father's errand, my son? " she asked
softly.

" As he bade me, mother. I came to the farm so that none saw
me. Ulf was not at home, so I burned what father had given me on
the hearth-fire in the hall. I took it out of the cloth." He hesitated
a little. " Mother — there were nine seals to it — "

" My Gaute." The mother moved her hands up till they rested
on the boy's shoulders, and looked into his face. " Your father has
had to lay great matters in your hands. If you deem that you can-

not but speak of them to someone, then tell your mother what is weighing on you. But best of all would it like me if you could altogether be silent, my son."

The light-hued face under the smooth flaxen hair, the great eyes, the full, firm red mouth — how like he was to her father now! Gaute nodded. Then he laid an arm on his mother's shoulder.

Sweetly and sorrowfully it came on Kristin that now she could lean her head against the boy's spare little breast; he was so tall now that when he stood and she sat, her head reached to just above his heart. For the first time it was she that leaned against her child.

Gaute said:

" Isak was alone at home. I showed him not what I was bearing, but said only that I had somewhat I must burn. So he made up a big fire on the hearth before he went out to saddle his horse."

His mother nodded. Then he let go of her, turned towards her, and said, with childish awe and wonder in his voice:

" Mother, know you what they say? They say that father — would have been *King* — "

" It sounds not over-likely, boy — " she answered with a smile.

" But he is of kingly birth, my mother," said the boy earnestly and proudly. " And methinks father would be fitter to be a King than most men."

" Hush." She took his hand again. " My Gaute — you must understand, now that father has shown such trust in you — you and we all must say nor think nothing, but must watch our tongues well till we have learnt somewhat, so that we can judge whether and how we should speak. I ride to Nidaros to-morrow, and if I come to speech with your father alone at any time, I shall surely tell him that you have done his errand well — "

" Take me with you, mother! " begged the boy vehemently.

" We must not let any think, Gaute, that you are aught else than a thoughtless child. You must try, little son, to play about here at home and be as joyful as you can — so will you serve your father best."

Naakkve and Björgulf came slowly up the hill. They came up to their mother and stood there, their young faces strained with feeling. Kristin saw they were still so far children that they took refuge with their mother in this disquietude — and yet were come so far towards manhood that they would fain have comforted her and heartened her, if they could but find the way. She held out a hand to each of the boys. But not much was said between them.

Soon after, they all went down, Kristin with a hand on a shoulder of each of her two eldest sons.

" Why are you looking so at me, Naakkve? " But the boy grew red, turned away his head, and made no answer.

He had never before thought about his mother's looks. It was many a long day since he had begun to compare his father with other men — his father was the most comely of them all, and the most like a chieftain. His mother was the mother that had new children, who, as they grew from out the hands of the women, joined the little troop of brothers, to share its life in fellowship, its friendship and its strife; mother had open hands through which flowed all that they needed; mother knew what to do for well-nigh all ills; mother was like the fire on the hearth, she bore the life of the home as the lands round about Husaby bore the crops year by year; life and warmth streamed from her as from the cattle in the byre or the horses in the stalls. The boy had never thought of likening her to other women. . . .

This evening he saw all at once: she was a proud and fair lady. With the broad, white forehead under the linen coif, the steel-grey eyes' straight gaze under the calmly arched brows; with the heavy bosom and the long, shapely limbs. She bore her tall body straight as a lance. But he could not speak of this; he walked on flushed and silent with her hand upon his neck.

Gaute walked behind Björgulf and held by his mother's belt. The elder brother began grumbling because Gaute was treading on his heels — the two set to pushing and scuffling a little. The mother stopped the quarrel and bade them be quiet, and, so doing, her grave face softened into a smile. After all they were but children, her sons.

Kristin lay awake at night — Munan was sleeping at her breast, and Lavrans between her and the wall.

She tried to come to some judgment of her husband's case. She could not believe the peril could be so great. Erling Vidkunssön and the King's cousins at Sudrheim had been charged with disloyalty and treason; yet were they back at their homes now as safe and as rich as ever, though they stood not so high as before in the King's favour.

'Twas like that Erlend had engaged in some unlawful courses to serve Lady Ingebjörg. In all these years he had kept up the friendship with his noble kinswoman; she knew that he had given her some sort of unlawful aid that had to be kept secret, five winters ago when he was her guest in Denmark. Now that Erling Vidkunssön had taken up the lady's cause, and would have put her in possession of the estates she owned in Norway, it might well be that Erling had counselled her to go to Erlend, or that she had turned to her father's kinsman of her own accord, after Erling had made his peace with the King. And that Erlend had dealt foolhardily with the matter. . . .

But she could not well understand how her kinsfolk at Sundbu could be mixed up in this.

Yet 'twas impossible that the end of the matter could be aught else than that Erlend came to full atonement with the King, if all his offence was to have been too zealous in the King's mother's service.

High treason. She had heard of Audun Hestakorn's downfall — and his death on the gallows at Nordnes — it was in her father's youth that it befell. But frightful misdeeds had been charged against Sir Audun. No; she would not think on such things. 'Twas so little likely that Erlend's cause should have a worse outcome than — than Erling Vidkunssön's and the Haftorssöns', for example.

— Nikulaus Erlendssön of Husaby. Ah, now it seemed so to her too — Husaby was the fairest manor in Norway's land.

She would go to Sir Baard and find out all that could be known. The Treasurer had always been her friend. Olav Lagmand too — in former days. But Erlend had taken it in such bad part when the Lagmand's decree went against him in that suit about the townhouse. And Olav had taken so much to heart the mischance that had befallen his god-daughter's husband.

Near kinsfolk they had none, neither Erlend nor she — widespread as their kindred was. Munan Baardssön scarce counted any more. He stood condemned for unlawful dealings when he held the Wardenship of Ringerike; he sought too eagerly to get his many children on in the world — four he had had in wedlock and five outside it. And 'twas said he had fallen away much since Lady Katrin's death. Inge of Ryfylke; Julitta and her husband; Ragnrid, who was married in Sweden, knew but little of Erlend — these were the other children left by Lady Aashild. Between the Hestnes folk and Erlend there had been no friendship since Sir Baard Peterssön died; Tormod of Raasvold was in his second childhood; his and Lady Gunna's children were dead, and their grandchildren still in their nonage.

She herself had no other kin on her father's side in Norway than Ketil Aasmundssön of Skog, and Sigurd Kyrning, who was wedded to Aasmund's eldest daughter. The other daughter was a widow, and the third a nun. The men of Sundbu seemed to be all four mixed in the case.

The sick monk in the Preachers' Cloister was Erlend's only near kinsman. And the man who stood nearest to her in the world was Simon Darre, since he was wed with her only sister.

Munan awoke, whimpering. Kristin turned in her bed and laid the child to her breast on the other side. She could not take him with her to Nidaros, uncertain as all things were. Maybe this would be the last time this little one would drink from his own mother's breast. Maybe this would be the last time in this world that she should lie thus, holding a little child close to her, so blissfully, so blessedly. If Erlend's life were forfeit — ! Blessed Mary, Mother of God, had she on any day or in any hour murmured by reason of the children God had granted her — ? Would this be the last kiss she should ever have from such a little milky mouth as this — ?

5

KRISTIN went to the palace the next evening as soon as she was come into the city. Where in all this great mansion have they put Erlend? she thought, as she looked round at the many stone houses. It seemed to her she thought more of how Erlend might be faring than of what she might have to learn. But she was told, on asking, that the Treasurer had left the town.

Her eyes smarted after the long boat-journey in the glittering sunlight, and her breasts, overfilled with milk, troubled her. When the serving-folk who lay in the room were gone to sleep, she got up and walked the floor all through the night.

Next day she sent Haldor, her own man, to the palace. — He came home, terrified and unhappy — Ulf Haldorssön, his father's brother, had been taken prisoner on the fjord, trying to come over to the cloister at Holm. The Treasurer was not yet come back.

This tidings put Kristin, too, in the greatest fear. Ulf had not dwelt at Husaby this last year, but had been working as one of the Warden's sheriffs, for the most part at Skjoldvirkstad, of which he now owned the greatest part. What kind of cause could this be, in which so many men were entangled? She could no longer keep at bay the worst fears, sick and worn with waking as she was now.

On the morning of the third day Sir Baard was still not come home. And a message that Kristin had tried to send to her husband did not reach him. She thought of seeking out Gunnulf in the cloister, but felt she could not. She walked and walked up and down the hall at home, with half-shut burning eyes. Sometimes 'twas as though she were walking half in her sleep; but as soon as she lay down, the fear and the pains came over her again so strongly that she was forced to rise again, broad awake, and walk, so as to endure them.

Just after nones Gunnulf Nikulaussön came in to her. Kristin went swiftly to meet the monk.

"Have you seen Erlend — Gunnulf, what is it they charge against him — ?"

"There are heavy tidings, Kristin. No, they will not let any come near Erlend — least of all us cloister-folk. They believe that Abbot Olav has been privy to his plans. 'Tis true he borrowed money there, but the Brothers all swear that they knew naught of what he meant to do with it, when they put the Convent's seal to the deed. And the Abbot will give no account of his doings — "

"Aye. But what is it? — Is it the Duchess that has lured Erlend on to this — ?"

Gunnulf answered:

"It seems rather as though they had to press her hard before she would join in their plans. The letter that — someone — has seen a draft of, which Erlend and his friends sent her last spring, they can scarce lay hands on, I trow, except they can force the lady to give it up to them. And they have found no draft. But by the answering letter and Sir Aage Laurissen's letter, which they took from Borgar Trondssön at Veöy, it seems sure enough that she has had such a writing from Erlend and the men who had bound them to stand by him in this plot. It seems to be clear that she was long afraid to send Prince Haakon to Norway — but that they urged upon her that, whatever the outcome of the matter might be, 'twas not possible that King Magnus should harm the child, his own brother. Should Haakon Knutssön not win the crown of Norway, he would not be much worse off than before — but these men were willing to venture their lives and all their goods to set him upon the throne."

For a long time Kristin sat quite still.

" I understand. These are greater matters than those that were between Sir Erling or the Haftorssöns and the King? "

" Aye," said Gunnulf in a low voice. " 'Twas to be given out that Haftor Graut and Erlend sailed for Björgvin. But it was Kalundborg they were bound for, and they were to bring Prince Haakon back with them to Norway, while King Magnus was yet abroad about his wooing — "

A little after, the monk said, still low:

" 'Tis more than — 'tis well-nigh a hundred years now since any Norwegian noble has dared the like of this; tried to overthrow him who was King by inheritance, and set up a rival King — "

Kristin sat gazing before her. Gunnulf could not see her face.

" Aye," she said in a while, thoughtfully. " The last men who ventured on that game were your forbears and Erlend's — and that time, too, my dead and gone kinsmen of the Gjesling house stood by King Skule."

She met Gunnulf's questioning look, and burst out, hotly and vehemently:

" I am but a simple woman, Gunnulf — little heed did I pay when my husband spoke with other men of such things — and unwilling was I to listen when he would have spoken with me of them — God help me, such weighty matters were beyond my understanding. But, simple woman as I am, unskilled in aught but my household work and the nurture of my children — even I know that right and justice had too far to travel before any man's cause could win through to the King and back again whence it sprung; and I have understood, too, that the common folk of this land have less prosperity and harder times now than when I was a child and King Haakon of blessed memory was our overlord. My husband " — she breathed quickly and tremulously once or twice — " my husband, I see it now, had taken up a cause so great that none of the other chiefs of this land dared set a hand to it — "

" That had he." The monk clenched his hands tightly together;

his voice sank to a whisper. " So great a cause that many will deem it an ill thing that he should himself have brought about its downfall — and in such wise — "

Kristin cried out and started up. The sudden violent motion made the pain in her breast and arms so sharp that her whole body was bathed in sweat. Wildly and feverishly she turned on the monk and cried loudly:

" 'Twas not Erlend did it — it was doomed so to be — it was his evil chance — "

She flung herself forward on her knees, with her hands pressed against the bench, and lifted her flushed, despairing visage towards the monk:

" You and I, Gunnulf — you, his brother, and I, his wife for thirteen years — we should not throw blame on Erlend, now he is a poor prisoner, in peril of his life maybe — "

Gunnulf's face quivered. He looked down at the kneeling woman.

" God requite it to you, Kristin, that you can take this matter so." Again he wrung his wasted hands together. " God — God grant Erlend life, and the power to repay you for your faithfulness. God turn away this evil from you and from your children, Kristin — "

" Speak not so! " She drew herself upright on her knees and looked up into the man's face. " No good has come of it, Gunnulf, when you have stepped in, in Erlend's affairs and mine. None has judged him so hardly as you — his brother and God's servant! "

" Never has it been my will to judge Erlend more harshly than — than I must." His white face had grown yet whiter. " None upon earth have I held so dear as my brother. It may well be therefore that it wrung my soul as it had been my own sin that I must myself atone for, when Erlend offended against you. And then there is Husaby — 'twas for Erlend alone to carry onward the race that is mine as well as his. The greatest part of my heritage I gave into his hands. Your sons are the men that are nearest to me in blood — "

" Erlend has *not* offended against me! I was no better than he! Why speak you so to me, Gunnulf? — you have never been my confessor. Sira Eirik did not blame my husband to me — he corrected *me* for my sins when I laid bare my troubles to him. He was a better priest than you — and he it is that God has set over me, that I should hearken to him — and he has never said that I suffered wrong. I will hearken to him! "

Gunnulf had risen when she stood up. He muttered, his face pale and troubled:

" You speak the truth. 'Tis Sira Eirik you must hearten to — "

He turned to go, but she caught his hand impetuously:

" Nay, go not from me so! I remember, Gunnulf — I remember when I was your guest here in this house — 'twas yours then; and you were good to me. I mind the first time I met you — I was plunged in fear and pain — I remember you spoke to me in Erlend's excuse — you could not know — You prayed and prayed for my life and my child's life. I know that you wished us well, you held Erlend dear —

" Oh, speak not hardly of Erlend, Gunnulf — which of us is clean before God? My father grew to be fond of him; our children love their father. Remember, he found me weak and easy to lure astray, and he set me in a good and honourable place. Oh, aye, 'tis fair at Husaby — the last evening before I left home it was so fair, the sunset that evening was so beautiful. We have lived many a good day there together, Erlend and I. — However it may go, however it may go, yet is he my husband, my husband whom I love — "

" Kristin — trust not to the sunset glow and to the — love — you remember now that you fear for his life.

" — I remember a thing when I was young — a subdeacon only. Gudbjörg, that was after wedded with Alf of Uvaasen, was a servant at Siheim then; she was charged with stealing a golden ring. It came out that she was guiltless; but the shame and fear had so shaken her soul that the enemy won power over her; she went down to the lake and would have thrown herself in. And she often bore witness for us afterwards that, as she went in, the world seemed to her so red and golden and fair, and the water shone bright and felt warm and comforting, but when she stood in it to her middle she was moved to name Jesu name and cross herself — and then did the whole world grow grey, and the waters cold, and she saw whither she had been bound — "

" Then will I not name it," Kristin spoke softly — she stood stiffly upright — " if I could believe that then I would be tempted to forsake my lord in his need. But methinks 'twould not be Christ's name, but rather the enemy's, that could do the like — "

" I meant not that; I meant — God strengthen you, Kristin, to bear your husband's faults with a loving spirit — "

" You see that I do so," said the wife in the same tone.

Gunnulf turned from her, white and trembling. He passed his hand over his face:

" I will go home. I can more easily — at home I can more easily gather my thoughts — that I may do all that lies in my power for Erlend and you. God — God and all holy men preserve my brother's life and freedom. Oh, Kristin — never believe that my brother is not dear to me — "

But after he was gone, Kristin deemed that all things were grown worse. She would not have the serving-folk in with her, but walked and walked, wringing her hands and moaning softly. The evening had grown late, when there came a noise of people riding into the courtyard. A moment after, the door was opened, and a tall, stout man in a riding-cloak, first dimly seen in the twilight, came quickly towards her with jingling spurs and trailing sword. When she knew him for Simon Andressön, she burst out into loud sobbing and ran towards him with outstretched arms, but she cried out in pain when he drew her to him.

Simon loosed his hold. She stood with her hands on his shoulders and her forehead leaned upon his breast, sobbing helplessly. He put his arm lightly around her:

" In God's name, Kristin! " — It seemed as though there was rescue in the very tones of his dry, warm voice, in the living smell of man that came from him — mixed of sweat, dust of the high-road, horses and leather garments. " In God's name — 'tis all too soon to lose hope and courage yet. — There must be some way out, be sure — "

In a little she had grown calm enough to beg him for pardon. She was quite sick and wretched, she said, for she had had to take her youngest child from the breast so suddenly.

Simon learned how she had fared these three days and nights. He called her serving-maid and asked angrily if there was not a single woman in the house that had wit enough to know what ailed their mistress. But the woman was a raw young maid, and the bailiff of Erlend's town-house was a widower with two unmarried daughters. Simon sent a man out into the town to fetch a leech-woman, and bade Kristin go to bed. When she had grown a little easier, he would come in and speak with her.

While they waited for the leech-woman, he and his man were served with food in the hall; and over his meal he talked with her as she undressed in the closet. Yes, he had ridden north as soon as he had heard what had befallen at Sundbu — he had come hither, and Ramborg gone thither to be with Ivar's and Borgar's wives. Ivar they had taken to Mjös Castle, but Haavard they had left at large, yet had he been made to promise not to leave the parish. 'Twas said that Borgar and Guttorm had been lucky enough to get clear away — Jon of Laugarbru had ridden out to Raumsdal for tidings, and was to send word hither. Simon had been at Husaby at midday, but had not tarried long. All was well with the boys, but Naakkve and Björgulf had begged and begged him to take them with him.

Kristin had got back her courage and calm when, late in the evening, Simon sat by her on the bed's edge. She lay, in the grateful weariness that comes after racking pains are gone, and looked at her brother-in-law's heavy sunburned face and small strong eyes. It stayed and comforted her that he had come. Simon grew most grave, indeed, when he heard more fully how the matter stood, but yet he spoke hearteningly.

Kristin lay looking at the elkskin belt round his bulky waist. The great flat buckle of copper thinly coated with silver, without other adornment than a pierced A and M, betokening Ave Maria; the long dagger with the silver-gilt mountings and great rock-crystals set in the hilt; the poor little table-knife with the handle of cracked horn mended with brass bands — all this she had known ever since she was a child as part of her father's everyday gear. She remembered when Simon had got these things — just before her father died, he had been minded to give Simon his gilded best belt, and silver to make plates enough to lengthen it to fit his son-in-law. But Simon begged he might be given this one — and when Lavrans said he was cheating himself, Simon would have it that the dagger, at least, was a costly piece. " Aye, and then the knife," said Ragnfrid with a little smile; and then the men laughed and said: " Aye, the knife, to be sure." For about this knife her father and mother had had so much debate. It was a daily and hourly vexation to Ragnfrid to see such an ugly, paltry thing at her husband's belt. But Lavrans swore she should never gain her end and part him from it. " Never have I drawn it against you, Ragnfrid; and 'tis as fine a knife as any in Norway's land to cut butter with — when 'tis hot enough."

She begged Simon to let her see the knife, and lay awhile with it in her hands.

"I could wish that I owned this knife," she said softly and beseechingly.

"Aye — that I can well believe — glad am I that I own it — I would not sell it for twenty marks." He caught her wrists laughingly, and took the knife back from her. Simon's small plump hands were always so good to touch, so warm and dry.

A little after, he bade her good-night, took the candle, and went into the hall. She heard him kneel before the crucifix in there, stand up again, throw off his boots on the floor, then in a little lie heavily down on the bed by the north wall. Then Kristin sank into a fathomless, sweet sleep.

She did not wake till far on in the next day. Simon Andressön had gone out long before, and the house-folk had orders to pray her from him that she stay quietly at home in the house.

It was well-nigh the time of nones before he came back; but he said at once:

"I bear you greetings from Erlend, Kristin — I came to speech with him."

He saw how young her face grew, how soft and anxiously tender. So he took her hand in his while he told his story. It was not much that he and Erlend had been able to say to each other, for the man that had brought Simon to the prisoner had stayed by them all the time. Olav Lagmand had got Simon leave for this visit, for the sake of the kinship that had been between them while Halfrid lived. — Erlend sent loving greeting to her and the children; he had asked much about them all, but most of all about Gaute. Simon thought that in some days Kristin might get leave to see her husband. Erlend had seemed calm and in good heart.

"Had I gone out with you to-day, I might have seen him too," said the wife softly.

Simon said no; he had got in because he came alone. "In many a wise, Kristin, it may be easier for you to make way when a man goes ahead of you."

Erlend was kept in a room in the East Tower, out towards the river — one of the gentlefolks' rooms, though a small one. Ulf, they said, was in the dungeon. Haftor in another cell.

Warily feeling his way, to make sure how much she could bear,

Simon told her what he had heard in the town. When he saw that she already understood the case to the full, he hid not from her that he, too, thought it a perilous matter. But all those he had talked to said that 'twas not possible Erlend could have dared to plan such an undertaking, and to carry it forward as far as he had done, except he was sure that he had a great part of the knights and the nobles at his back. And since the malcontent great folk were so strong in numbers, it was not like that the King would dare to deal too hardly with their leader; but rather that he must let Erlend make his peace with him in some fashion.

Kristin asked in a low voice:

" Where does Erling Vidkunssön stand in this matter? "

" *That* I can see many a man would give something to know," said Simon.

Though he said it not to Kristin, and had not said it to the men with whom he had talked of this, it seemed to him little likely that Erlend should have at his back any powerful band of men who had bound themselves to risk life and goods in such a perilous affair — had it been so, they would scarce have chosen him their chief, for that Erlend was rash and unstable all his fellows must know well. It was true that he was kinsman to Lady Ingebjörg and the young pretender; he had enjoyed much power and esteem in these latter years, he was not quite so unpractised in war as were most men of an age with him — was known as one that his men liked and followed — and though he had so often borne him witlessly, yet could he, when he would, speak well and to the point, so that it might well be thought that he had now at long last learnt prudence from his mischances. Simon thought 'twas most like there were some who had known of Erlend's undertaking and had pushed him forward; but he could scarce believe that they had bound them so strongly that they could not draw back now and leave Erlend to bear the brunt alone.

Simon deemed he had seen that Erlend himself looked for naught else, and that his mind seemed made up to having to pay dearly for his desperate venture. " When kine lie mired, 'tis for the owners to hang on to their tails," he said, laughing a little. But, to be sure, Erlend had not been able to say much, with a third man listening.

Simon marvelled that this meeting with his brother-in-law had moved him so much. But the narrow little turret-chamber, where

Erlend had prayed him to take a seat on the bed — it went from
wall to wall and filled half the room — Erlend's straight, slender
form, as he stood by the little slit in the wall whence the light came
— Erlend quite unafraid, clear-eyed, untroubled by either fear or
hope — he was a fresh, cool, manful fellow, now all the clogging
cobwebs of love-dalliance and foolery with women had been
blown from off him. True, it was women and the commerce of
love that had brought him hither, with all his daring plans that
were ended ere yet he had brought them out into the light. But on
that Erlend seemed not to think. He stood there like a man who
had dared a desperate throw, had lost it, and knew how to suffer
defeat well and manfully.

And his wondering and joyous thankfulness when he saw his
brother-in-law sat well on him. Simon had said, when he saw it:

" Mind you not, kinsman, that night we watched together by
our father-in-law? We gave one another our hands, and Lavrans
laid his hand on ours — and we promised him and each other that
we would stand together like brothers all our days."

" Aye." Erlend's face lit up with a smile. " Aye, and I trow Lavrans thought not that you would ever need *my* help."

" Nay," said Simon, unmoved, " 'tis most like he deemed you, as
you were placed, might well prove a stay to me, and not that you
were like to need help from me."

Erlend smiled again:

" Lavrans was a wise man, Simon. And, strange as it may sound
— I know that he liked me well."

Simon thought, aye, strange it was, God knew — yet even he
himself — despite of all he knew of Erlend, and of all the other had
done to him — even he could not help now feeling somewhat of a
brother's tenderness towards Kristin's husband. Then Erlend asked
of her.

Simon told him of how he had found her, sick and full of fear
for her husband. Olav Hermanssön had promised to do his best to
have her let in to see him, as soon as Sir Baard came home.

" Not before she is well! " said Erlend quickly. A strange flush,
like a young girl's, passed over his brown unshaven face. " 'Tis the
one thing I dread, Simon — that I should not have strength to bear
it well when I see her."

But in a little he said, as calmly as before:

" I know that you will stand by her faithfully, if she should be left a widow this year. Penniless they will not be, she and the children, having her heritage from Lavrans. And she will have you near by, should she dwell at Jörundgaard."

The day after the Nativity of Mary,* the High Steward, Sir Ivar Ogmundssön, came to Nidaros. Twelve of the King's sworn liegemen from north of Dovre were named now as a Court to try Erlend Nikulaussön's cause. Sir Finn Ogmundssön, the High Steward's brother, had been chosen so set forth the charge against him.

Some time before this, in the summer, Haftor Olavssön of Godöy had slain himself with the little knife that each prisoner had been allowed to keep to cut his food with. Folk said that prison had so told on Haftor that he had not been in his right mind. Erlend said to Simon, when he heard of it, that now he need have no fear of Haftor's tongue. But yet he was much moved.

As time went on, it happened now and then that the guards would make themselves an errand without when Simon or Kristin was with Erlend. Both of these two saw — and spoke of it to each other — that Erlend's first and last thought was to come through this business without the names of those with him in the plot being discovered. To Simon one day he said so straight out. He had promised all who had joined in his counsels that he would hold the rope so that if it came to the worst, the blow should fall on his hands only, "and never yet have I betrayed any that put their trust in me." Simon looked at the man — Erlend's eyes were blue and clear; 'twas plain that he said this of himself in all good faith.

Nor had the King's agents yet been able to track down any other who had taken part in Erlend's treason, save the brothers Greip and Torvard Toressöns of Möre; and these would not confess that they had known the intent of Erlend's plan to be aught else than that he and other men had moved the Duchess to let Prince Haakon Knutssön be brought up in Norway. Afterwards it was meant that the chiefs should make prayer to King Magnus that 'twould be for the good of both his kingdoms if he gave his half-brother the name of King in Norway.

Borgar and Guttorm Trondssön had been lucky enough to escape from the palace at Veöy — none could say how, but folk guessed that Borgar had got help from some woman — he was a comely youth and something of a light liver. Ivar was still in prison

* 8th September.

in Mjös Castle; young Haavard his brothers seemed to have kept outside their counsels.

While the meeting of King's-men sat in the castle, the Archbishop held a concilium in his palace. Simon was a man with many friends and acquaintances; he could thus tell Kristin what was going forward. All deemed it likely that Erlend would be outlawed and banished and his lands and goods be forfeit to the King. Erlend, too, said 'twas like it would be so; he was in good heart — he meant to seek refuge in Denmark. As things stood in that land, the road to advancement was ever open to a man of mettle and skill in arms, and Lady Ingebjörg would surely welcome his wife as her kinswoman and keep her with her in all seemly honour. Simon would have to take the children, save the two eldest sons, whom Erlend was minded to have with him in Denmark.

Kristin had not been outside the city for a day in all this time, and had not seen her children, save Naakkve and Björgulf; they had come riding into the courtyard one evening alone. Their mother kept them with her for some days; but then she sent them to Raasvold, where Lady Gunna had taken the little ones to be with her.

Erlend wished it should be so. And Kristin was afraid of the thoughts that might arise in her if she were to see her sons about her, listen to their questions, and try to make things clear to them. She strove to thrust away from her all thoughts of her wedded years at Husaby. So rich had been those years that they seemed to her now to have been one great calm — even as there seems a sort of calm on a billowy sea when one stands high enough above it on a great cliff. The waves that chase each other seem everlasting and unchanging — even so had life billowed through her soul in those spacious years.

Now was it with her again as in her youth, when she had pitted her will to win Erlend against all things and all men. Now again was her life but a waiting from hour to hour, between the hours when she saw her husband, sat by his side on the bed in the turret-chamber of the castle, talked with him calmly and evenly — till by some chance they would be left alone for a moment, and would fall into each other's arms, with endless passionate kisses and wild embraces.

At other times she sat in Christ's Church, hours at a time. She kneeled, gazing up at St. Olav's golden shrine behind the grated lattice of the choir. Lord, I am his wife. Lord, I held fast to him when I was his in sin and unrighteousness. Through God's mercy were we two, all unworthy, joined together in holy wedlock. Seared with the brands of sin, weighed down with sin's burden, we came together to the threshold of God's house, and together received the body of our Redeemer from the priest's hands. Should I now murmur if God puts my faithfulness to the proof? Should I think of aught else than that I am his wife and he is my husband as long as we both live — ?

The Thursday before Michaelmas, the meeting of the King's-men's court was held and judgment given on Erlend Nikulaussön of Husaby. He was found guilty of having plotted to despoil King Magnus of land and lieges by treachery, to raise revolt against the King within the land, and to lead into Norway forces hired from without. After having made search into all such cases in former times, the judges decreed that Erlend Nikulaussön had forfeited his life and all his goods into King Magnus' hands.

Arne Gjavvaldssön came down to Simon Darre and Kristin Lavransdatter in the Nikulaus town-house. He had been at the meeting.

Erlend had not tried to deny what he had done. Clearly and firmly he had acknowledged his purpose, by these measures to force King Magnus to give his young half-brother, Prince Haakon Knutssön Porse, the kingship of Norway. Arne had deemed that Erlend spoke exceeding well. He had pointed to the great hardships and troubles suffered by the people of the land, by reason that the King, in these later years, had scarce set foot on Norwegian soil, and had ever shown unwillingness to appoint Stadtholders who could do justice and wield the kingly powers. By reason of the King's undertakings in Skaane, and of the wastefulness and the unwisdom in money matters that were shown by the men he most hearkened to, the folk suffered oppression and impoverishment, and could never feel safe from new demands for help and new-fangled taxes. Since the Norwegian knights and esquires bearing arms had far fewer rights and liberties than the Swedish knighthood, it was hard for them to contend with the Swedes on equal terms, and it was but reason and nature that a man like Sir Magnus Eirikssön, young and unskilled in affairs, should hearken more to his Swedish lords and love them more, since they had greater riches and therefore more power to support him with well-armed and well-trained warriors.

He and his confederate friends had deemed they had such sure knowledge of the minds of the greatest part of the folk, both nobles, peasants and townsmen, in the north and west of Norway, that they had doubted not at all they would find full following there, if they could bring forward a Prince as nearly akin to their dear lord, King Haakon of blessed memory, as he they had now. He had looked that then the folk of the land would agree together that we should move King Magnus to let his brother mount the throne here; while Prince Haakon should swear to maintain peace and brotherhood with King Magnus, to guard the realm of Norway in accordance with the ancient boundaries, to uphold the rights of God's Church, the laws and customs of the land as handed down from of old, and the rights and liberties of both country folk and townsmen; and to put a stop to foreigners' forcing their way into the kingdom. This plan it had been his and his friends' intent to put before King Magnus in friendly wise. Yet had it ever from of old been the right of the Norwegian farmers and chieftains to set aside a King who tried to rule unlawfully.

Of Ulf Saksesön's doings in England and Scotland, he said that Ulf's intent was but to win favour there for Prince Haakon, if so be God would grant that he became our lord. With him in this undertaking there had been no Norseman, saving Haftor Olavssön of Godöy (to whose soul God be merciful), his kinsmen Trond Gjesling's three sons of Sundbu, and Greip and Torvard Toressöns of the Hatteberg kindred.

Erlend's words had moved his hearers strongly, said Arne Gjavvaldssön. But at the end, when he spoke of the support they had looked for from the Church's men, he had recalled those old rumours of the time when King Magnus was not yet grown up, and that, Arne deemed, had been unwise. The Archbishop's officer had taken him sharply to task — Archbishop Paal Baardssön, as they knew, both while he was Chancellor and since, bore great love towards King Magnus, by reason of the King's godly turn of mind; and folk were fain now to forget that such rumours had ever been spread about their King; besides, he was even now about to wed a lady, the Count's daughter of Namur — had there ever been any truth in the matter, it must be deemed that now Magnus Eirikssön had altogether turned him from all such things.

— Arne Gjavvaldssön had shown Simon Andressön the greatest friendliness while Simon had been in Nidaros. It was Arne, too, who now reminded Simon that it must be open to Erlend to appeal from this judgment, as unlawfully come to. According to the words of the law, the charge against Erlend should have been brought forward by one of his peers; but Sir Finn of Hestbö was a knight, and Erlend but an esquire. It might well be, thought Arne, that a new court would find that a harder punishment than outlawry could not be awarded Erlend.

As for what Erlend had set forth, concerning the kind of kingly rule he deemed this land would best be served with, it had sounded fair and fine, truly. And all men knew where the man was to be found who would have been glad enough to take the helm and steer this course while the new King was in his nonage — Arne scratched the grey stubble on his chin, and glanced across at Simon.

"None has heard from him, or of him, this summer?" asked Simon in a low voice.

"No. He says, I did hear, that he is out of favour with the King and stands outside all such matters. 'Tis many a long day since he has been content to sit so long at home and listen to Lady Elin's talk. His daughters are as fair and as dull as their mother, folks say."

Erlend had heard the doom of the court with steadfast calm, and he had saluted the members of the court as mannerly, freely and fairly when he was led out as when he had come in. He was calm and cheerful when Kristin and Simon were granted speech with him next day. Arne Gjavvaldssön was with them, and Erlend said that he would follow Arne's counsel.

"Never could I bring Kristin here to come with me to Denmark in former days," he said, putting an arm about his wife's waist. "And I had ever such a mind to go forth into the world with her."

A kind of quiver passed over his face, and of a sudden he kissed her pale cheek vehemently, heedless of the two lookers-on.

Simon Andressön rode out to Husaby to take order for the moving of Kristin's goods to Jörundgaard. He counselled her to send the children, too, to Gudbrandsdal, at the same time. Kristin said:

"My sons shall not depart from their father's house till they are driven out."

"I would not wait for that, if I were in your place," said Simon. "They are so young, they can scarce rightly understand this mat-

ter. 'Twere better you let them leave Husaby believing that they
are going but to visit their mother's sister, and to see to their
mother's heritage in the Dale."

Erlend held with Simon in this. But the upshot was that only
Ivar and Skule went south with their aunt's husband. Kristin could
not send the two little ones so far away from her. When Lavrans
and Munan were brought to her in the town-house, and she saw
that her youngest son knew her not again, she quite broke down.
Simon had not seen her shed a tear since the first evening he came
to Nidaros; but now she wept and wept over Munan as he sprawled
and struggled, close pressed in his mother's arms, striving to come
to his foster-mother; and she wept over young Lavrans, who crept
up into her lap and caught her round the neck, weeping because
she wept. So she kept the two with her, and Gaute too — he was
unwilling to go with Simon, and it seemed to her unwise to let
this child, who was bearing a load all too heavy for his years, out
of her sight.

Sira Eiliv had brought the children to the city. He had prayed
the Archbishop to let him leave his church awhile and visit his
brother at Tautra; and this was readily granted to Erlend Nikulaussön's house priest. And since it seemed to him that Kristin
could scarce take care of so many children while staying alone in
the city, he proffered to take Naakkve and Björgulf out with him
to the cloister.

The last night before the priest and the boys were to set forth —
Simon had left already with the twins — Kristin made confession
to the holy and pure-hearted man who had been her spiritual father
all these years. They sat together many hours, and Sira Eiliv was
instant with her to be humble and obedient towards God, and patient, faithful and loving towards her wedded husband. She knelt
by the bench where he sat; then Sira Eiliv rose up and knelt by her
side, still bearing the red stole, the token of the yoke of Christ's
love, and prayed long and fervently without words. But she knew
that he prayed for the father and mother and the children and all
the household, whose souls' health he had so faithfully striven to
further all these years.

The day after, she stood on the shore at Bratören and watched
the lay brothers from Tautra setting sail on the boat that was to
bear away the priest and her two eldest sons. On the way home
she went into the Minorites' Church, and tarried there till she

deemed she was strong enough to venture back to her own house. And in the evening, when the two little ones were gone to sleep, she sat with her spinning and told Gaute stories till it was bedtime for him too.

6

ERLEND was held prisoner in the castle till nigh upon Clement's Mass.* Then there came word and letters ordering that he should be taken south under safe-conduct,† to be brought before King Magnus. The King purposed to hold the Yule-tide feast at Baagahus ‡ that year.

Kristin was thrown into deadly fear. With unspeakable struggles she had used herself to keep calm, with Erlend a prisoner under doom of death. Now was he to be taken far away to a doubtful fate; folk said all manner of things about the King, and in the band of men who were about him Erlend had no friends. Ivar Ogmundssön, who now was Governor of the castle at Baagahus, had spoken of Erlend's treason in the harshest words. And 'twas said he had been set against Erlend the more by being told of some malapert speech of Erlend's about him in former days.

But Erlend was glad of the tidings. Kristin saw, indeed, that he took not the parting now at hand lightly. But this long imprisonment had begun to wear so upon him that he grasped eagerly at the thought of the long sea journey, and seemed careless well-nigh of all else.

In three days all was ready, and Erlend set sail in Sir Finn's ship. — Simon had promised to come back to Nidaros before Advent, when he had cast about him a little and ordered his affairs at home; but if before that there were any new tidings, he had prayed Kristin to send him word, and he would come at once. Now it came to her that she would journey south to him, and from thence would she go on to where the King was, and would fall at his feet and pray for mercy for her husband — gladly would she offer all her possessions to redeem his life.

Erlend had sold or pledged his mansion in Nidaros to divers people; the Nidarholm cloister owned the hall-house now, but

---

* 23rd November.   † See Note 16.   ‡ See Note 17.

Abbot Olav had written lovingly to Kristin, praying her to use it as long as she had need. She was there alone with one serving-maid, Ulf Haldorssön (who had been set free, since they had not enough proof against him), and his nephew Haldor, Kristin's own man.

She took counsel with Ulf, and at first he showed himself somewhat doubtful — he deemed it would be too hard a journey for her across the Dovrefjeld; much snow had fallen in the hills already. But when he saw the woman's anguish of soul, he turned round and counselled that she should go. Lady Gunna took the two little children out to Raasvold; but Gaute would not be parted from his mother, and she felt, too, that she dared not well let the boy stay north of Dovre and out of her sight.

They met such hard weather when they came south on to the high mountains, that by Ulf's counsel they borrowed ski at Drivstuen and left their horses behind there, lest they should be forced to pass the next night in the open. Kristin had not had ski on her feet since she was a little maid, and it was hard for her to make headway on them, though the men upheld and helped her to the utmost. They could come no farther that day than midway in the hills between Drivstuen and Hjerdkinn; and when it grew dark, they had to seek shelter in a birch-wood and dig themselves down into the snow. At Toftar they were able to hire horses again; here they plunged into mists, and when they came a little down into the Dale, they found rainy weather. When, some hours after dark had fallen, they rode into the Formo courtyard, the wind howled about the house-corners, the river roared, and a rushing, soughing sound came from the hill-side woods. The courtyard was like a swamp, and deadened the sound of the horses' hoofs — in the Saturday evening holiday from work there was no sign of life on the great manor, and neither the folk nor the dogs seemed to be ware of their coming.

Ulf thundered on the door of the hall-house with his spear; a serving-man came and opened. A moment after, Simon himself stood in the outer-room door, broad and dark against the light behind, with a child on his arm; he drove the barking dogs behind him. He gave a cry when he saw his wife's sister, set down the child, and drew her and Gaute in, taking off their soaking outer garments himself.

It was goodly and warm in the hall, but the air was very thick, for it was a fire-place room with flat ceiling under the upper hall.

And 'twas full of folk, and children and dogs seemed swarming out of every corner. Then Kristin made out her two little sons' faces, red, warm and joyous, in behind the table where a candle stood burning. They came forward now and greeted their mother and brother a little shyly. Kristin saw that she had broken in here into the midst of these good folks' comfort and cheer. For the rest, the whole room was in a litter, and at each step she took she trod on crunching nutshells — they were scattered all over the floor.

Simon sent the serving-men and women out on divers errands, and the most part of the dogs and children followed them, as well as the grown folks — these were neighbours with their following. — While he questioned and listened to her, he fastened up his shirt and coat, which had stood open, showing his naked, hairy chest. The children had made him in this plight, he said in excuse. He was indeed in sad disarray: his belt was twisted awry, his hands and clothes dirty, his face sooty, and his hair full of dust and straw.

Soon after came two serving-women and brought Kristin and Gaute over to Ramborg's ladies' hall. A fire had been lit there, and busy serving-maids lighted candles, made up the bed, and helped her and the boy into dry clothes, while others set the board with meat and drink. A half-grown maid with silk-bound plaits brought Kristin a foaming mug of ale. The girl was Simon's eldest daughter, Arngjerd.

Then he himself came in; he had made himself trim and was more as Kristin was used to see him — well and richly clad. He led his little daughter by the hand, and Ivar and Skule came with him.

Kristin asked after her sister, and Simon said Ramborg had gone with the ladies from Sundbu down to Ringheim; Jostein had come to fetch his daughter Helga, and he had wished to take Dagny and Ramborg with him too; he was a cheerful kindly old man, and he had promised to take the best care of the three young wives. So maybe Ramborg would stay there through the winter. She looked to have another child at St. Matthew's Mass or thereabout — and then Simon had thought that 'twas like he might have to be away from home this winter; so she would be better off with her young kinswomen. Oh, no — for the housekeeping here at Formo, it made no odds whether she were at home or away, laughed Simon — for he had never craved of a young child like Ramborg that she should wear herself out with the drudgery of a great household.

On hearing Kristin's plans, Simon said at once that he would go with her south. He had so many kinsfolk there, and so many old friends of his father's and his own, that he hoped he could be of more service to her there than in Trondheim. Whether it would be wise for her to seek the King herself, he could better judge when they came thither. He would be ready for the road in three or four days.

They went together to mass the next day, being Sunday, and afterward went to see Sira Eirik at Romungaard. The priest was old now; he welcomed Kristin lovingly, and seemed most sorrowful at her mischance. Then they went round by Jörundgaard.

The houses were the same, and in the rooms were the same beds and benches and tables. This was now her own manor, and it seemed most like that 'twas here her sons would grow up, and that here she herself would one day lay her down and close her eyes for ever. But never had she felt so clearly as in this hour that it was on her father and mother all the life of this home had rested. Whatever hidden troubles they might have had to struggle with, warmth and help, peace and safety had flowed out from them to all that lived about them.

Restless and heavy of heart as she was, it wearied her a little when Simon talked of his own affairs, his estates and the children. She saw herself that there was no reason in it; he was ready to help her with all his might; she saw that 'twas most good of him to be willing to leave his home at Yule-tide, and to be parted from his wife at a time like this — he surely was thinking much on whether he would soon have a son now — for he had only the one child by Ramborg as yet, though they would soon have been wedded six years. She could not look that he should take her mischance and Erlend's so much to heart as quite to forget all joy in his own happy lot; but it was strange to go about with him here, and see him so joyful and warm and secure in his own home.

Unwittingly Kristin had thought that Ulvhild Simonsdatter would be like her own little sister, whom she had been named after — would be fair-haired and slender and clear-skinned. But Simon's little daughter was round and fat, with cheeks like apples and a mouth like a red berry, quick grey eyes like her father's in his youth, and with his goodly brown curling hair. Simon loved the bonny, lively child much, and was proud of her quick-witted prattle.

" Though yet this little girl is so ugly and loathly and ill-favoured," he said, putting his hands on each side of her chest and twirling her while he lifted her into the air, " I deem 'tis a change-ling that the trolls up in the fell here have brought for her mother and me and put into the cradle, such a grim and grum little thing is it "; then he set her down suddenly, and hastily made the sign of the cross over her three times, as though frighted by his own rash words.

His base-born daughter, Arngjerd, was not fair, but she looked good and understanding, and her father took her about with him as often as 'twas possible. He was full of praises of her handiness. — Kristin was made to look into Arngjerd's chest, and see all the things she had spun and woven and sewed already for her dowry.

" The day I lay the hand of this daughter of mine in a good true-hearted bridegroom's hand," said Simon, looking long after the girl, " will be one of the gladdest days I have known."

To save the cost and to get the journey over quickly, Kristin would not take with her any maid, nor any man other than Ulf Haldorssön. Fourteen days before Yule, then, she and he set forth from Formo, in company with Simon and his two stout young serving-men.

When they came to Oslo, Simon soon learnt that the King would not come to Norway — he was to hold the Yule-tide feast at Stockholm, it seemed. Erlend was in the castle at Akersnes; the Governor of the castle was away, so that in the meantime 'twas not possible for any of them to see the prisoner. But the Under-Treasurer, Olav Kyrning, promised to let Erlend know they were in the city. Olav showed much friendliness toward Simon and Kristin, for his brother was wedded to Ramborg Aasmundsdatter of Skog, so that he counted him a far-off kinsman of Lavrans' daughters.

Ketil of Skog came into the city and bade them out to Skog to drink Yule-tide with him; but Kristin would not keep the holy-days with feasting while things stood thus with Erlend. And Simon would not go alone, though she prayed him much to do so. Simon and Ketil knew somewhat of each other, but Kristin had seen her uncle's son but once since he was grown up.

Kristin and Simon took lodging in the same mansion where she had once been his parents' guest when they two were betrothed; but they dwelt in another house. There were two beds in the room; she slept in one, and Simon and Ulf in the other; the men lay in the stable.

On Christmas Eve, Kristin wished to go to the midnight mass in Nonneseter church — she said it was because the sisters sang so sweetly. So they all five went together. The night was clear starlight, mild and fair, and it had snowed a little in the evening, so that 'twas somewhat light. When the bells began ringing from the churches, folk streamed out of all the houses, and Simon had to lead Kristin by the hand. Now and then he stole a glance at her. She was grown greatly thinner this last autumn, but it was as though her tall, straight form had got back somewhat of the young maid's supple and tranquil grace. Over her pale face there was come again the look she had had in youth of calm and gentleness covering a deep and hidden, listening expectancy. She had taken on a strange ghostly likeness to the young Kristin of that Yule-tide long ago. — Simon pressed her hand, and knew not that he had done so till he felt an answering pressure. He looked up — she smiled and nodded, and he understood that she had taken his hand-clasp as a warning to her to be brave — and now she was striving to show him that indeed she was brave.

Toward the end of the holy-days, Sir Munan came to her — he had only now heard she was in the city, he said. He greeted her heartily, likewise Simon Andressön and Ulf, whom he spoke to at every second word as " kinsman " and " dear friend." It might be hard for them to gain sight of Erlend, he said; he was most strictly guarded — *he* had not been able to win in to see his cousin. But Ulf said, with a laugh, when the knight was gone, that he deemed not Munan had pressed so exceeding hard to gain entrance — he was in such deadly fear of being tangled in the affair that he could scarcely bear to hear it named. Munan had grown exceeding old, exceeding bald, and wasted in flesh; the skin hung loose on his bulky frame. He dwelt out at Skogheim, and had with him one of his base-born daughters who was a widow. The father would gladly have been quit of her, for none of his other children, neither those born in wedlock nor the others, would come near him so long as this half-sister ruled his house; she was an overbearing, greedy and shrewish woman. But Munan dared not bid her begone.

At length, some time on in the new year, Olav Kyrning got leave for Erlend's wife and Simon to see him. And now again it fell to

Simon's lot to bear the sorrowful wife company at these heart-breaking meetings. Much stricter watch was kept here than at Nidaros to see that Erlend spoke with none, except the Governor's folk were by.

Erlend was calm as before, but Simon saw that this waiting was beginning to wear upon the man. He made no complaint at any time, and said that he suffered no ill-usage and that all was done for him that could be done; but he owned that he was much plagued with the cold — there was no fire-place in the cell. And 'twas not in his power to indulge himself overmuch in cleanliness — though, he laughed, had he not had the lice to fight with, like enough the time would have seemed yet longer out here.

Kristin, too, was calm — so calm that Simon waited in breathless fear for the day when she should break down altogether.

King Magnus made his royal progress in Sweden, and there seemed no likelihood that he would cross the boundary soon, or that any change in Erlend's state was at hand.

On the day of Gregory's Mass,* Kristin and Ulf Haldorssön had been at church at Nonneseter. When, on their way back, they had crossed the bridge over the Nonnebeck, she took not the way down towards her lodging, which lay near the Bishop's palace, but turned eastward towards the open place by Clement's Church, and into the narrow lanes between the church and the river.

The day was grey and thick — there had been soft weather for a time — and their footgear and the skirts of their cloaks quickly grew wet and heavy with the yellow clay of the riverside. They came out on the open lands towards the high bank of the river. Once their eyes met. Ulf laughed noiselessly, and his mouth twisted into a sort of grimace, but his eyes were sorrowful; Kristin smiled — a strange, sick smile.

Soon after they stood at the edge of the high ground; there had once been a landslip in the clay bank here, and Fluga's house lay right under it, so close up against the dirty yellow slope, where a few black stunted weeds were growing, that the stench of the pigsty, which they looked down on, came rankly up to them — two fat sows were snuffling about in the black mud. The river-bank was but a narrow strip here; the muddy grey river-current, with the jostling ice-flakes on it, came right up to the tumble-down houses with their bleached grey shingle roofs.

* 13th February.

Whilst they stood there, a man and a woman came up to the fencing of the sty and looked at the pigs — the man leaned over and began scratching one of the sows with the shaft-end of the silver-mounted light axe he was using as a staff. It was Munan Baardssön himself, and the woman was Brynhild. He looked up and was ware of them — he stood gaping up at them, and Kristin called out a cheerful greeting.

Sir Munan fell a-laughing loudly.

"Come down and have a drink of warm ale to keep out this filthy weather," he called up.

As they went down to the gate of the houses, Ulf told Kristin that Brynhild Jonsdatter kept neither lodging-house nor ale-tap any more. She had been in trouble many times, and at last had been threatened with flogging, but Munan had got her out and gone surety for her that she would altogether cease her unlawful traffickings. Her sons, too, had now got so far on in the world that for their sake their mother was forced to think of bettering her ill repute. After his wife's death, Munan Baardssön had taken up with her again, and he was often to be found in her house.

He met them at the gate.

"Here we are — kinsfolk, all four of us, in a fashion," he snickered — he was a little in drink, but not much. "You are a good woman, Kristin Lavransdatter, pious but not proud. — Brynhild, too, is an honourable, worshipful woman now — and I was not yet a wedded man when I got the two sons I have by her — and they are much the best of all my children. — I have told you as much every day in all these years, Brynhild. Inge and Gudleik are dearest to me of all my children — "

Brynhild was comely still, but her skin was a pale yellow, and looked as if it must feel clammy, Kristin thought, as when one has stood all day over the fat-cauldrons. But her house was well kept, the food and drink that she put on the board were of the best, and the vessels fair and clean.

"Aye, I look in here when I have an errand in Oslo," said Munan. "You understand, the mother is fain to hear tidings of her sons. Inge writes to me from time to time, for he is a learned man, Inge; a Bishop's commissary must be so, you know — and I got him well wedded too, with Tora Bjarnesdatter of Grjote; think you many men have got such a wife for their bastard? So we sit here and talk about this, and Brynhild bears in the meat and ale to me, just as she used in days gone by, when she bore the keys of my house at Skogheim. 'Tis heavy work sitting out there now thinking of my wife that is gone. — So I ride in hither to find a little comfort — when it chances that Brynhild is in such mood that she grudges me not a little friendliness and comfort."

Ulf Haldorssön sat with his chin resting on his hand, looking at the lady of Husaby. Kristin sat and listened and answered quietly and gently and mannerly — as calm and courtly as if she had been a guest at one of the great folk's manors at home in Trondheim.

"Aye, you, Kristin Lavransdatter, you won a wife's name and came to honour," said Brynhild Fluga, "though you came willingly enough to meet Erlend in my loft. I have been called slut and loose woman all my days — my stepmother sold me into his hands, there — I bit and scratched, and left the marks of every one of my nails on his face before he had his will of me — "

"Must you speak of this ever?" grumbled Munan. "Be sure — I have told it you so often too — I had let you go in peace had you borne you like a human creature and bidden me spare you — but you flew at my face like a wildcat before I was well inside the door — "

Ulf Haldorssön laughed softly to himself.

"And I dealt well by you evermore thereafter," said Munan. "You had but to point to a thing and I gave it you — and our children — aye, for sure they are far better off and safer this day than Kristin's poor sons — God guard the poor young lads, so as Erlend has guided things for his children! Methinks that should mean more than the name of wife to a mother's heart — and you know that I wished often your birth had been such that I could have wedded you lawfully — no woman have I liked as well as you — though you were but seldom kind or good to me — and the wife I did get, God reward her — ! I have set up an altar for my Katrin and myself out in our church at home, Kristin — I have thanked God and Our Lady every day for my wedded life — no man has had a better — " He whimpered and sniffed.

Soon after, Ulf Haldorssön said that they must go. He and Kristin exchanged not a word on the way back. But outside the door she reached out her hand to the man:

"Ulf — my kinsman and my friend."

"If it could help aught," he said in a low voice, "I would gladly go to the gallows in Erlend's stead — for his sake and for yours!"

That evening, a little before bedtime, Kristin sat alone in the hall with Simon. Of a sudden she began telling him where she had been that day. She told of the meeting at Brynhild Fluga's.

Simon sat on a stool not far from her. Leaning forward a little, with his arms resting on his thighs, and hands hanging down, he sat looking up at her with a strange, searching look in his small, sharp eyes. He spoke not a word, and not a muscle moved in his big, heavy face.

Then she let fall that she had told all to her father, and what he had said to her.

Simon sat as before, immovable. But in a while he said calmly:

" 'Twas the one thing I ever prayed of you, in all the years we have known each other — if I mind aright — that you would not — but if you could not keep silence to spare Lavrans, why — "

Kristin's whole body trembled:

" Aye! But — oh, Erlend, Erlend, Erlend — "

At the wild cry the man leaped up — Kristin had thrown herself forward, with her head between her arms, and was rocking her body from side to side, still calling on Erlend, between quivering, moaning sobs that seemed to tear their way out of her body.

" Kristin — in Jesu name! "

When he seized her upper arm and tried to stay her sobbing, she flung herself on him with all the weight of her body, and caught him round the neck, while through her weeping she went on calling her husband's name.

" Kristin — be still — " He held her tight in his arms and saw that she marked it not — she was weeping so that she could not stand upright. Then he lifted her up in his arms — crushed her to him a moment, and then bore her over and laid her on the bed.

" Be still," he prayed her again, in a choking, almost a threatening voice — he laid his hands over her face, and she caught his wrists and arms and clung close to him.

" Simon — Simon — oh! he must be saved — "

" I do what I can, Kristin — but now you *shall* be still." He turned sharply, walked over to the door and out into the yard. He shouted, till the echoes rang back from the house-walls, for the maid whom Kristin had hired in Oslo. The girl came running, and Simon bade her go in to her mistress. In a moment she came out again — her mistress would be alone, she said affrightedly to Simon, who still stood on the same spot.

He nodded and walked over to the stables; and stayed there till Gunnar, his man, and Ulf Haldorssön came to give the beasts their evening feed. Simon talked with them awhile, and then went with Ulf back again to the hall.

Kristin saw not much of her brother-in-law the next day. But after nones, as she sat sewing on a garment she meant to take out to her husband, he came running in, said naught to her and looked not at her, but flung open the lid of his travelling-chest, filled his silver goblet with wine, and rushed out again. Kristin stood up and went after him. Before the door of the hall stood a strange man, still holding his horse — Simon drew a gold ring from his finger, dropped it into the goblet, and drank to the newcomer.

Kristin guessed what this must be, and cried out joyfully:

" You have a son, Simon! "

" Aye." He slapped the messenger on the shoulder, as the man, thanking him, put up the goblet and the ring safely inside his belt. Then Simon caught his wife's sister round the waist and whirled her round and round. He looked so glad that Kristin could not but put her two hands on his shoulders — and then he kissed her full on the mouth and laughed aloud.

" Then 'twill still be the Darre stock that will hold Formo when you are gone, Simon," she said joyfully.

" Aye, so will it be — if God will. — No, to-night I would go alone," he said, when Kristin asked if they should go together to evensong.

That night he said to Kristin that he had heard Sir Erling Vidkunssön was now at his manor of Aker near Tunsberg. And that morning he had hired him passage in a ship going down the fjord — he was minded to speak with Sir Erling of Erlend's case.

Kristin said not much in answer. They had barely touched on it before — had kept them from going much into the question — whether Sir Erling had been privy to Erlend's plans or not. Simon said now it would be well that he should ask Erling Vidkunssön's counsel as to Kristin's plan that Simon should go with her to Lavrans' powerful kinsfolk in Sweden to claim kinship and crave their help.

Then Kristin spoke her thought:

" But, now you have had these great tidings, brother-in-law, me-thinks that it were but reason you should put off this journey to

Aker — and first ride up to Ringheim and see to Ramborg and your son."

He was forced to turn away, so overcome was he. He had waited so for this — whether Kristin would make any sign that she understood how he longed to see his son. But when he had mastered himself somewhat, he said, with some shyness in his voice:

"I have been thinking, Kristin — mayhap God will vouchsafe that the boy thrive and prosper the better if I can be patient and hold in check my longing to see him till I have managed to help you and Erlend a little forward in this matter."

The day after, he went out and bought rich and costly gifts for his wife and the boy — and for all the women, too, who had been with Ramborg when she bore the child. Kristin took out a fair silver spoon she had had from her mother's heritage — it was to be for Andres Simonssön — but to her sister she sent the heavy silver-gilt chain that Lavrans had given her in her childhood along with the reliquary cross. The cross she fastened now to the chain Erlend had given her as a betrothal-gift. The next day at midday Simon sailed.

In the evening the ship lay to under an island in the fjord. Simon stayed on board; he lay in a sleeping-bag of hide with some pieces of wadmal over him, looking up at the starry skies, where the constellations seemed to climb and dive again as the boat pitched on the sleepily gliding swell. The water splashed and the ice-flakes scraped and thumped softly against the vessel's sides. 'Twas almost comforting to feel the cold creeping farther and farther through his body. It deadened —

Yet now he was sure: so ill as things had been with him they could never be again. Now that he had a son. It was not that he thought he could be fonder of the boy than he was of his daughters. It was somewhat else. For all the heart's gladness that his little maids could give him, when they sought their father with their games and laughter and prattle — sweet as it was to hold them in his lap and feel their soft hair against his chin — yet in this wise a man could never take his place in the succession of the men of his house, if his lands and goods and the memory of his doings in the world must pass with a daughter's hand over into a strange kindred. But now, when he might hope, if God would but grant that this little son should grow to manhood, that a Formo son should come after father — Andres Gudmundssön, Simon Andressön, Andres Simonssön — now it must surely follow of itself that he must stand before Andres as his father had stood before himself, an honest man in his secret thoughts no less than in his open acts.

— Sometimes things had been so that he understood not how he could bear it any longer. Had he seen but *one* token that she understood aught! But she was to him as though they had been brother and sister by blood — careful for his well-being, kind and loving and gentle — And he knew not how long this would last — how long they should live together in this wise in one house. Did the thought never come to her that he could not forget — that even though he was wedded with her sister, he could never quite forget that they two had been meant once to live together in wedlock?

But now he had this son. He had ever been ashamed to add in his own words ought of his wishes or his thanks when he said over his prayers. But he deemed that Christ and Mary Virgin knew well what it had meant that he had said double number of Paternosters and Aves each day in these last days. And he would keep on with this so long as he was from home. And in other wise, too, he would show his thankfulness in fitting and open-handed fashion. And thus maybe he would win help on this present journey too.

Though, indeed, he deemed himself there was little reason to look for much from this visit. Sir Erling was quite estranged now from the King. And however powerful and secure the former Regent of the realm might be, and however little he needed to fear the young King, who was much more ticklishly placed than was he — the richest and most high-born man in Norway — yet it could not be looked for that he should be willing to anger King Magnus yet more against himself by pleading Erlend Nikulaussön's cause, and bringing suspicion on himself of having been privy to Erlend's treason. Even if he had had a part in it — aye, even if he had been at the bottom of the whole plan, ready to step in and have himself placed at the head of affairs the moment a minor King was once more upon the throne — he would scarce feel himself bound to venture aught to help the man who had brought the whole plan to ruin for the sake of a shameful love-adventure. 'Twas as though Simon half forgot it when he was with Erlend and Kristin — for they, too, seemed scarce to remember it any more. But so it was that Erlend had himself wrought the mischief — 'twas his doing that naught else had come of the whole undertaking than ruin for

himself — and for the good men who had been betrayed by his
wantonness and folly.

But he must try all shifts to help her and her husband. And now
he began to hope; for mayhap God and Mary Virgin, or some of
the saints whom he had used to honour with offerings and alms-
givings, would vouchsafe their aid in this as well.

He came to Aker somewhat late the next evening. A steward
met him, and sent off men, some with the horses, some with Simon's
man to the serving-men's house; while Simon himself went to the
loft-room where the knight was sitting drinking. Sir Erling himself
came out into the balcony straightway, and stood there while
Simon mounted the stair; then he greeted his guest courteously
enough, and led him into the hall, where was Stig Haakonssön of
Mandvik with Erling's only son, Bjarne Erlingssön, a quite young
man.

He was welcomed fairly enough — the serving-folk took from
him his outer garments and bore in meat and drink. But he guessed
that the men guessed — at least Sir Erling and Stig — what he was
come for, and he felt that they were holding back. So when Stig
began saying how rarely he was to be seen in this part of the country now — how seldom he darkened the doors of his former kinsfolk — and asked if he had ever been further south than Dyfrin
since Halfrid died — Simon answered: No, not before this winter.
But now he had been in Oslo some months with his wife's sister,
Kristin Lavransdatter, who was wed with Erlend Nikulaussön.

On this there was a short silence. Then Sir Erling asked courteously after Kristin and Simon's wife and his brothers and sisters;
and Simon asked after Lady Elin and Erling's daughters, and how
things were with Stig, and how his old neighbours at Mandvik
were, and what were the tidings from there.

Stig Haakonssön was a stoutly made, dark-haired man, some
years older than Simon, son of Halfrid Erlingsdatter's half-
brother, Sir Haakon Toressön, and brother's son of Erling Vidkunssön's lady, Elin Toresdatter. He had lost the Wardenship of
Skidu and the Governorship of the Tunsberg castles two winters
back, when he fell out with the King; but still was well enough off
with his Mandvik estates. But he was a widower and childless.
Simon knew him well, and had been good friends with him, as
with all his first wife's kin — even if the friendship had not been

over-hot. He knew exceeding well what they had all thought of Halfrid's second marriage — Sir Andres Gudmundssön's younger son was doubtless a man of substance and of good birth, but an even match for Halfrid Erlingsdatter he was not — besides that he was ten years younger; they could not understand why she had set her heart on this young man — but they must e'en let her do as she would, since she had suffered such unbearable misery with her first husband.

Erling Vidkunssön Simon had met but few times before; and then it had ever been in Lady Elin's company; and at such times no sound ever came from him — none needed say more than yes or no where she was in presence. Sir Erling had aged not a little since that time — he was grown somewhat stouter, but his form was still comely and noble, for he bore himself exceeding fairly, and it suited him well that his pale, reddish-yellow hair was now turned a shining silver-grey.

The young Bjarne Erlingssön Simon had not seen before. He had been brought up near Björgvin in the house of a cleric, a friend of Erling's — 'twas said among the kindred that this was because his father would not have him live out at Giske in the midst of a pack of foolish women. Erling himself was there no more than he was forced to be, and he dared not take the boy with him on his constant journeys, for Bjarne had been weakly and ailing as a growing lad, and Erling had lost two other sons in their childhood.

The boy looked exceeding comely as he sat with the light behind him, showing his side-face. Black, tightly curling hair rolled forward over his forehead, his great eyes seemed black, his nose was large and strongly curved, the mouth full and firm and fine and the chin well formed. Withal he was tall, slender and broad-shouldered. But when Simon had to sit down to the table to eat, the serving-man moved the candle, and now he saw that the skin of Bjarne's neck was quite eaten up with the scars of scrofula — they stretched on both sides right up under the ears and forward beneath the chin, dead, dull-white patches and bluish-red stripes and swollen knots. And then Bjarne had a trick of time and again pulling up the hood of the round fur-edged velvet cape that he wore even here in the room — pulling it up half-way over his head. When, soon after, it grew too hot for him, he would turn it down, and then draw it up again — he seemed not to know that he did it.

Simon felt his hands grow quite restless at length with but looking on at this — though he tried to keep from looking.

Sir Erling scarcely took his eyes from his son — but he, too, seemed not to know that he was gazing so intently at the boy. Erling Vidkunssön's face was set and unchanging and his pale-blue eyes showed his feeling but little — but beneath the somewhat vague and watery glance there seemed to lie the cares and thought and love of endless years.

So the three elder men exchanged mannerly, sluggish talk, while Simon ate, and the youth sat fiddle-faddling with his hood. Afterwards all four sat drinking for a fitting space of time, and then Sir Erling asked if Simon were not weary with his journey, and Stig asked if he would be pleased to sleep with him. Simon was glad to be able to put off speaking of his errand. This first evening at Aker had left him not a little cast down.

The next day, when he broached the matter, Sir Erling's answer was much what Simon had looked for. He said that King Magnus had never hearkened to him willingly, and he had seen, from the time Magnus Eiriksson was old enough to have a will of his own, that his will had been that Erling Vidkunssön should have naught to say in his affairs when once he was of age. And since the quarrel between him and his friends on the one side, and the King on the other, had been made up, he had heard, and tried to hear, naught of the King or the King's friends. If he pleaded Erlend's cause with King Magnus, it would scarce avail the man much. He knew well enough that many in this land believed that he had been in some wise at the bottom of Erlend's undertaking. But, whether Simon believed him or not, neither he nor his friends had known aught of what was hatching. Had this matter come to light in another fashion, or had these venturesome young dare-devils risked their throw and failed, then would he have stepped in and striven to make their peace. But as things had gone, he deemed not that any could justly crave of him that he should come forward and thereby strengthen all men's suspicion that he had played a double game.

But he counselled Simon to have recourse to the Haftorssöns. They were the King's cousins, and, when they chanced not to be at feud with him, they kept up between them a friendship of a kind. And, so far as Erling understood the matter, the men whom Erlend was shielding were rather to be found amongst the Haftorssöns' party, and among the youngest of the nobles.

Now, as Simon knew, the King was to hold his wedding in Norway this summer. And there might then be a fitting occasion for Magnus to show mildness and clemency to his enemies. And the King's mother and Lady Isabel would doubtless come to the wedding-feast. Since Simon's mother had been Queen Isabel's maid of honour in her youth, Simon might turn him to Lady Isabel, or Erlend's wife might throw herself before the King's bride and Lady Ingebjörg Haakonsdatter with prayers for their intercession.

Simon thought that the last shift of all to try would be for Kristin to kneel to Lady Ingebjörg. Had the Duchess understood what honour was, she had sure long since come forward and rescued Erlend from his straits. But when he had named this once to Erlend, he had but laughed and said, the lady had always so many ticklish matters of her own to see to; and doubtless she was angry, since it now seemed but little like that her dearest child should ever bear the name of King.

7

SPRING was come when Simon Andressön journeyed north to Toten, to fetch his wife and his little son and take them home to Formo. Then he stayed there awhile to see a little to his own affairs.

Kristin would not remove from Oslo. And she dared not yield to her hungry, burning longing for her three sons who were up there in the Dale. That she might still hold out and endure the life she was now living from day to day, she must not think on her children. She held out, she seemed calm and brave; she spoke with strangers and listened to strangers, and bore with their counsels and comfort; but to do this she must hold fast to the thought of Erlend, of Erlend alone! In the stray moments when she failed to hold fast her thoughts in the grasp of her will, pictures and thoughts flashed through her mind: Ivar stood in the wood-shed at Formo with Simon, watching his uncle intently, as he searched out a piece of wood to helve the boy's hatchet, bending and testing the sticks with his hands. Gaute's fair boyish face set manfully as, bending forward, he struggled against the snowstorm that grey winter day in the mountains — his ski slipped back, he sank backward some way down the slope, and landed deep in a snow-drift

— and for a moment his manful mien was all but gone, and he was an over-wearied, helpless child. Her thoughts would turn to the two little ones; 'twas like Munan could both walk and talk a little now — was he as lovely as the others had been at that age? Lavrans had perhaps forgotten her. And the two big ones out in the cloister at Tautra — Naakkve, Naakkve, her first-born — How much did the two big ones understand, and what were their thoughts — how did Naakkve, child as he was, endure the thought that nothing in life now was like to be for him as she and he himself and all men had deemed that it would be?

Sira Eiliv had sent her a letter, and she had told Erlend what was written in it of their sons. Else they never spoke of their children. They spoke not any more either of the past or of the future. Kristin brought him a piece of clothing or a dish of food; he asked her how things had gone with her since he saw her last; they sat hand in hand on his bed. Then sometimes it might chance that they were left alone a moment in the small, cold, dirty, stinking room — and they clung together with dumb, burning caresses, hearing, without marking it, Kristin's woman laughing with the watchmen outside on the stair.

Time enough, when he had either been taken from her or given back to her, to face the thought of their troop of children and the change in their lot — of all else in her life save this man beside her. She could not bear to lose an hour of the time that was left them together, and she dared not think of the meeting again with the four children she had left in the north — so she was fain to assent when Simon Andressön proffered to go alone to Trondheim and, along with Arne Gjavvaldssön, watch over her interest in the settlement of the forfeited estates. Much richer King Magnus was not like to be for Erlend's possessions — the man was more heavily in debt than he himself had had any knowledge of, and he had raised moneys that had been sent off to Denmark and Scotland and England. Erlend shrugged his shoulders and said with a half-smile that he looked not now to reap any return from *them*.

Thus Erlend's case stood much as before when Simon came back to Oslo about Holy Cross day in the autumn.* But he was dismayed to see how worn out they looked, both Kristin and his brother-in-law, and he felt a strange, sinking qualm at his heart when they both had yet enough self-mastery to thank him for

* 14th September.

coming hither at this time of year, when he could least well be spared from his estates at home. But now were all folks' faces set towards Tunsberg, where King Magnus was come to await his bride.

A little on in the month, Simon managed to hire passage in a ship bound thither, with some merchants who were to sail in eight days time. Then one morning a strange serving-man came to pray Simon Andressön to be at the pains of coming at once to St. Halvard's Church — Olav Kyrning waited for him there.

The Under-Treasurer was vehemently stirred. He was holding charge at the castle, whilst the Treasurer was at Tunsberg. And, the evening before, there had come a company of gentlemen who showed him a letter under King Magnus' seal, signifying that they were to inquire into Erlend Nikulaussön's case; and he had had the prisoner brought in to them. Three of them were foreigners, Frenchmen doubtless — Olav had not understood their speech, but the chaplain had spoken with them in Latin this morning, and " 'tis said they are kinsmen of the lady who is to be our Queen — a fair beginning! " They had put Erlend to the question by torture — they had with them a kind of ladder and some fellows used to work such things. To-day he had denied to bring Erlend out of his chamber, and had set a strong watch — for so much he was ready to answer, for these were lawless doings, such as never were heard tell of in Norway before!

Simon borrowed a horse from one of the priests of the church and rode with Olav straightway out to Akersnes.

Olav Kyrning looked a little fearfully at the other's grimly set face, over which stormy waves of red were beating. Now and again Simon made a wild, violent movement, as if knowing not what he did — and the strange horse leapt aside, reared and balked under his rider.

" One can see on you, Simon, that you are angered," said Olav Kyrning.

Simon scarce knew himself what was uppermost in his mind. He was so stirred to the depths that at times he felt qualms of sickness. The blind and wild feeling that struggled in him and goaded him to utmost fury was a kind of shame — a helpless man, without weapon or defence, forced to suffer strangers' fists in his clothes, strangers manhandling his body — it was like hearing of the outraging of women; he grew dizzy with thirst for revenge, with longing to see blood shed for it. No — such things had never been the use and wont of this land — would they accustom Norwegian nobles to suffer such things — ? That should never be!

He was sick for horror of what he was to see — fear of the shame he must bring on another man by seeing him in such a pass over-powered him above all other feelings, when Olav Kyrning opened to him the door of Erlend's cell.

Erlend lay on the floor, stretched out aslant from one corner of the room to the other; he was so tall that only thus could be find room to stretch out at full length. Some straw and clothes had been laid under him on the thick layer of filth that covered the floor, and his body was covered over with his dark-blue fur-lined cloak right up to the chin, so that the soft grey-brown marten fur mingled with the curly, tufted black beard Erlend had grown while in his prison.

His mouth showed white through the beard; his face was snow-white. The great, straight-lined triangle of the nose stood out monstrously high above the sunken cheeks, the grizzled hair lay in clammy, separate wisps back from the high, narrow forehead — on each of the hollow temples was a great bluish-red mark, as though something had pressed on or gripped him there.

Slowly, with labour, he opened his great sea-blue eyes; essayed a sort of smile when he recognized the man; his voice sounded a little veiled and like a stranger's.

" Sit down, brother-in-law — " He moved his head slightly towards the empty bed. " Aye — now have I learned somewhat new — since we last met — "

Olav Kyrning bent over Erlend and asked if there was aught he would. There was no answer — doubtless because Erlend could not speak — and he took away the cloak from over him. Erlend had on him naught but a pair of linen drawers and a rag of shirt — and the sight of the swollen and discoloured limbs shook and maddened Simon like some loathsome horror. He wondered whether Erlend had a like feeling — a shade of red came over his face as Olav passed a wet cloth, which he dipped into a vessel of water, down over his arms and legs. And when he laid the cloak over again, Erlend pushed it into place with some small movements of his limbs and by drawing the hood up with his chin, till he was quite covered up.

" Aye," said Erlend — he was a little more like himself in voice now, and the smile on his pale mouth was a little plainer; " next time — will be worse! But I am not afraid — none need be afraid — they will break naught out of me — in this way — "

Simon felt within himself that the man spoke the truth. Torture would not force a word out of Erlend Nikulaussön. There was naught that he might not do, might not reveal, in anger or in recklessness — he would never be moved a hair's breadth by force. And Simon felt that the shame and insult that he himself suffered on another man's behalf, Erlend scarce felt at all — he was filled with an obstinate joy in defying his torturers and a contented trust in his hardihood. He, who ever broke down so pitifully when he came up against a firm will, who might himself doubtless have been cruel in a moment of fear, rose above himself now that in this cruelty he scented an opposer weaker than himself.

But Simon's answer, growled through his teeth, was:

" Next time — I trow there will be none! What say you, Olav? "

Olav shook his head, but Erlend said, with a shadow of his old reckless flippancy in his voice:

" Aye, if I could but — believe it — as firmly as you! But these gentry will scarce — be content with this — " He grew ware of the working of Simon's heavy, sinewy face: " Nay, Simon — kinsman! " — Erlend would have raised himself on his elbow; the pain forced from him a strange muffled groan, and he sank back in a swoon.

Olav and Simon ministered to him clumsily. When the swoon was over, Erlend lay a little with open eyes; he spoke then, more gravely:

" See you not — it means — much — for Magnus — to get on the track of — what men he would better not trust — farther than he can see them? So much unrest — and discontent — as there has been — "

" Aye — if he deems that this will quench the discontent — " said Olav Kyrning threateningly. Then said Erlend, in a low and clear voice:

" I have dealt so in this matter — that few will deem — it matters much how it goes with me — I know that myself — "

The other two men reddened. Simon had thought that Erlend saw not this himself — and never before had Lady Sunniva been so much as hinted at between them. Now Simon broke out desperately:

"How could you have borne yourself so recklessly — so madly?"

"Nay, I understand it not either — now," said Erlend simply. "But — in hell's name! — how could I have thought she could read writing? She seemed — most unlearned —"

His eyelids drooped and closed, he was nigh swooning once more. Olav Kyrning muttered about fetching something, and went out. Simon bent over Erlend, who now again lay with eyes half opened.

"Brother-in-law — was — was Erling Vidkunssön with you in this?"

Erlend shook his head a little, with a slow smile:

"By Jesus, no! We thought — either he would not be bold enough to join with us — or else he had kept all things in his own hands. But ask not, Simon — I will say naught — to any — so only am I sure not to let aught slip out —"

On a sudden Erlend whispered his wife's name. Simon bent over him again — he looked the other should ask him to bring Kristin to him now. But he said quickly, as if in a flicker of fever:

"She must not hear of this, Simon. Say order has come from the King that none is to come near me. Take her out to Munan — to Skogheim — hear you? — these French — or Moorish — new friends — of our King's — will not give up yet! Get her out of the city before it is noised about! Simon?"

"Aye." How he was to bring this about he knew not.

Erlend lay a little with his eyes shut. Then he said, with a kind of smile:

"I thought last night — of the time she bore our eldest son — she was in no better case than I — if a man may judge by her crying. And if she has been able to bear it — seven times — for the sake of our joys — I trow that I can —"

Simon was silent. The fearful shrinking he felt — from looking into life's deepest secrets of torment and of joy — Erlend seemed yet to have no touch of. He played with the worst and the loveliest things as simply as a guileless boy, whose friends have brought him with them to a bordel, drunken and curious. . . .

Erlend shook his head impatiently:

"These flies — are the worst — Methinks they are the foul fiend himself —"

Simon took his cap, and smote high and low at the thick cluster of blue-black flies, so that they flew up in the air in buzzing noisy clouds — and trampled furiously into the mud of the floor those that fell stunned. It could not avail much, for the window-hole in the wall stood open — the winter before, it had been closed with a wooden shutter with a bladder-covered port-hole, but that had made the room too dark.

But he was still at this when Olav Kyrning came back with a priest bearing a drinking-cup. The priest lifted Erlend's head, and stayed it while he drank. A great deal of the liquor ran out into his beard and down his neck, and he lay quiet and untroubled as a child when the priest afterwards wiped it away with a cloth.

Simon felt his whole being in a ferment; the blood thumped and thumped in his neck below the ears, and his heart beat strangely and unsteadily. He stood a moment gazing back from the doorway at the long body outstretched beneath the cloak. The flush of fever came and went now in waves over Erlend's face; he lay with half-open glittering eyes, but he smiled to his brother-in-law, the shadow of his strangely boyish smile.

The next day, as Stig Haakonssön of Mandvik sat at the breakfast-board with his guests, Sir Erling Vidkunssön and his son Bjarne, the hoof-beats of a single horse were heard in the courtyard. The next moment the door of the hall was flung open, and Simon Andressön came swiftly towards them. He wiped his face with his sleeve as he came — he was splashed to the neck with mud from his ride.

The three men rose to meet the comer, with little outbursts, half of greeting, half of wonder. Simon answered not their greetings — he stood leaning on his sword, both hands upon the hilt, and said:

"Would you hear strange tidings? They have taken Erlend Nikulaussön and stretched him on a rack — some foreigners the King sent to put him to the question — "

With a cry the men gathered round Simon Andressön. Stig smote one hand into the other:

"What has he said — ? "

At the same moment both he and Bjarne Erlingssön turned, as though unwittingly, towards Sir Erling. Simon burst out into laughter — he laughed and laughed.

He sank down on the chair that Bjarne Erlingssön had drawn forward for him, took the ale-bowl that the youth proffered him, and drank greedily.

"Why laugh you? " asked Sir Erling sternly.

" I laughed at Stig." He sat a little bent forward, with his hands resting on his muddy thighs — yet once or twice again little bursts of laughter came from him. " I thought — we are sons of nobles, all of us here — I had looked that you would be so wroth that one of our fellows should be so dealt with, that you would have asked first how such things can be. . . .

" I cannot say that I know to a hair how the law stands in such matters. Since my lord King Haakon died, it hath been enough for me that I owed him that came to his throne my service when he listed to call for it, in war and in peace — else have I dwelt in quiet upon my estates. But I cannot see aught else than that in this case against Erlend Nikulaussön there have been unlawful doings. His fellows had sifted his case and given judgment in it — with how much right they doomed him to death, I know not — then was he offered reprieve and safe-conduct till he could be brought to a meeting with the King, his kinsman — that perchance he might grant Erlend grace to make his peace with him. . . . Since has the man lain in the tower of Akers Castle nigh on a year, and the King has been abroad well-nigh all that time — some letters have passed to and fro — naught has come of it. Then he sends hither some varlets — Norsemen they are not, nor of the King's guard — and dares to put Erlend to the question in such wise as none ever heard that a Norseman with a Guardsman's rights was dealt with before — this while there is peace in the land, and Erlend's fellows and his kinsmen are gathering at Tunsberg to honour the King's wedding. . . .

" What think you of this, Sir Erling? "

" I think — " Erling sat down on the bench over against him. " I deem that you have set the matter forth clearly and plainly, Simon Darre, as it stands. I see not that the King can do aught but one of three things: Either must he let Erlend pay the penalty according to the doom given at Nidaros — or he must choose out a new court of Guardsmen and have the case against Erlend set forth by a man who bears not the knightly name, and they must doom Erlend to outlawry with such respite as the law allows for him to remove himself from King Magnus' realm — or he must grant Erlend grace to make his peace with him. And that would be the wisest thing that he could do.

" This matter seems to me now so plain that whomsoever you will lay it before at Tunsberg will join with you and take up your cause. Jon Haftorssön and his brother are there. Erlend is their kinsman no less than the King's. And the Ogmundssön brothers must see that this is injustice and folly. 'Twere best you went first to the Lord Marshal — move him and Sir Paal Eirikssön to call a meeting of the sworn King's-men that are in the town and that seem fittest to take the matter in hand — "

" Will not you and your kinsmen go with me, my lord? "

" We mean not to go to the wedding-feast," said Erling shortly.

" The Haftorssöns are young — and Sir Paal is old and ailing . - and the others — You know best yourself, my lord, — they doubt-less have some small power, through the King's favour and such-like, but — Erling Vidkunssön, what are they all beside you? You, sir, you have such power in this land as no other chief has had since — I know not when. Behind you, sir, are the old houses that folk in this land have known man by man, so far back as record goes of evil times and good times in these our country-sides. On the father's side — what is the birth of Magnus Eirikssön or Haftor of Sudrheim's sons beside yours — are their riches worth naming beside yours? These counsels you give me — all this will take time, and these Frenchmen are in Oslo, and you may stake your soul that they will not give over. . . . Olav Kyrning has sent letters, and all gentlemen he could find to join with them, the Bishop promised he would write — but all this unrest and strife, Erling Vidkunssön, *you* could end it, in the same hour you stepped forth before King Magnus. You stand foremost among the heirs of those that ruled this land in the old age — the King knows that you would have us all at your back." . . .

" I can scarce say that I marked as much some time back," said Erling bitterly. " You speak out warmly for your brother-in-law, Simon — but can you not understand? *Now* I cannot move. It would be said: the very moment they put such duress on Erlend that a man might fear he would not be able to keep his tongue between his teeth — that moment I came forward! "

There was silence for a while. Then Stig asked again:

" Has — Erlend spoken? "

" No," answered Simon impatiently. " He has held his tongue. And I trow he will go on holding it. Erling Vidkunssön," he said beseechingly, " he is your kinsman — you were friends — "

Erling breathed short and heavily once or twice.

" Aye. — Simon Andressön, have you fully understood *what*

Erlend Nikulaussön had undertaken? To put an end to this sharing of our King with the Swedes — this way of rule that never has been tried before — that seems to bring more and more hardships and troubles on this land with each year that passes; to bring us back to the kingship that we knew of old, and that we know brings welfare and good fortune. See you not that this was a wise and a bold counsel — and see you not that this counsel can now hardly be taken up by others after him? He has ruined the cause of Knut Porse's sons — and other men of the kingly house there are none for the folk to rally round. You will say, mayhap, had Erlend carried through his intent and brought Prince Haakon to Norway, then had he played into *my* hands. Much further than the boy's landing had these — young boys — scarce been able to carry forward their plans without having need of prudent men to come forward and work out what remained to do. So it is — I dare avow it. Yet God knows that I gained nothing — rather had I to set aside the care of my own affairs — in those ten years when I lived in disquiet and toil and strife and troubles without end — some few men in this land have understood so much, and with that I must e'en be content." He struck his hand hard against the table. " See you not, Simon, that the man who had taken on his shoulders such mighty plans that none knows whether the welfare of us all in this land and of our children for long ages to come was not the stake in them — and flung it all from him with his breeches on a harlot's bedside! — God's blood! — he would be full well served with the measure that was dealt to Audun Hestakorn? "

He went on in a little more quietly:

" Yet would I be fain that Erlend should be saved; and believe not that I, too, am not angered at the tidings you have brought us. And I deem that, should you follow my counsel, you will find men and enough to join with you in this matter. But I believe not that my company would be of such great help to you that for the sake of it I should do well to come uncalled before the King."

Simon rose, stiffly and heavily. His face was streaked and grey with weariness. Stig Haakonssön went over and took him by the shoulders — now he would have some food brought; he had but bided till they had had their talk out before having serving-folk in. But now Simon must strengthen himself with meat and drink, and must sleep on top of it. Simon thanked him — he must ride on in a little while, if Stig could lend him a fresh horse. And would he give shelter to his man, Jon Daalk, to-night? — Simon had had to leave the man behind on the road, for his horse could not keep up with Digerbein.* Aye, he had ridden the most of the night — he had thought, for sure, that he knew the road out hither well enough — but yet he had gone astray more than once.

Stig bade him stay till to-morrow, and he would ride with him himself — at the least a part of the way — aye, and he might as well go on to Tunsberg with him too. . . .

Simon said:

" Here is naught more for me to stay for. I would but go over to the Church — seeing that I am here once more, I would yet fain say a prayer where Halfrid lies — "

The blood rushed and tingled in his weary body; his heart beat deafeningly. It was as though he must drop down headlong; he was as one but half awake. But he heard his own voice say, calmly and evenly:

" Will not you bear me company, Sir Erling? I know she held you dearest of all her kinsmen."

He looked not at the other, but felt him stiffen. In a little he heard, through the rushing and singing of his own blood, Erling Vidkunssön's clear and courteous voice:

" That will I, willingly, Simon Darre. — It is rough weather," he said, as he buckled on his sword and threw a thick cloak about his shoulders. Simon stood still as a stone till the other was ready. Then they went out.

Without, the autumn rain poured down, and the mist drove in from the sea so thickly that they could scarce see more than a couple of horses' lengths over the fields and the yellow tree-clumps that bordered the path on each side. It was no long way to the church. Simon fetched the key from the chaplain's house near by — he was glad when he saw they were new folk, come since his time, since so he was spared much talk.

It was a little stone church with a single altar. Unheedingly Simon saw again the same pictures and ornaments he had seen so many hundred times, while he knelt by the white marble tomb a little way from Erling Vidkunssön, saying over his prayers, and crossing himself where 'twas fit — without knowing what he did.

He understood not himself that he had been able to try this. But now he was in the midst of it. Of what he should say, he had no

* Digerbein = Big-legs.

guess — but, sick with horror and shame at himself as he was, he knew that he would make the trial at all costs.

He remembered the ageing woman's white, suffering face deep in the half-darkness of the bed, her lovely gentle voice — that afternoon when he sat on her bedside and she told him. It was a month before the child came — and she herself looked that it should cost her life — and she was willing and glad to buy their son so dear. The poor little soul that lay here beneath the great stone in a little coffin by his mother's side — No, no man could do what he had meant to do. . . .

But Kristin's white face. She knew what had befallen, when he came home from Akersnes that day. Pale and calm she was as she spoke of it and questioned him — but he had seen her eyes in one short glimpse, and he had not dared to meet them after. Where she was now, or what she had done, he knew not — whether she had stayed in her lodging or was with her husband, or whether they had prevailed on her to go to Skogheim; he had left it in Olav Kyrning's and Sira Ingolf's hands — he could do no more, and he deemed that he must lose no time. . . .

Simon knew not that he had hidden his face in his hands. Halfrid — there is naught in it of shame or of sin, my Halfrid. — And yet — what she had said to him, her husband — of her sorrow, and of her love that had made her stay on under the old devil's roof. Once already had he killed his child under its mother's heart — and she had stayed on with him because she would not tempt her dearest love. . . .

Erling Vidkunssön knelt, his colourless, clear-cut face showing no sign. His hands he held close in to his breast, with the palms pressed together; from time to time he crossed himself with a quiet, supple, gracious gesture, then brought his finger-tips again together.

No, thought Simon. This was so hateful a thing that no man could do it. Not even for Kristin's sake could he do it. — They rose together, made obeisance to the altar, and went down the nave; Simon's spurs jingled a little at each step he took on the stone pavement. As yet they had spoken no word together since they had left the manor, and Simon knew not at all what would now come.

He locked the church-door; and Erling Vidkunssön walked ahead through the graveyard. Under the little roof of the lich-

gate he stopped. Simon came up; they stood a little in the shelter
before going out into the pouring rain.

Erling Vidkunssön spoke quietly and evenly, but Simon felt the
dull, measureless rage muttering deep within the other — he dared
not look up.

" In the devil's name, Simon Andressön, what mean you by —
devising — this? "

Simon could not answer a word.

" Think you that you can threaten me — force me to do your
will — because, maybe, you have heard some lying rumours of
things that befell when you were scarce yet weaned from the
breast — ? " His rage growled nearer the surface now.

Simon shook his head:

" I thought, my lord, when you called to mind her who was
better than the purest gold — mayhap you might take pity on
Erlend's wife and children."

Sir Erling looked at him — he made no answer, but began strip-
ping moss and lichen from the stones of the churchyard wall.
Simon swallowed, and wet his lips with his tongue:

" I scarce know what I thought, Erling Vidkunssön — maybe
that when you remembered her that suffered all those evil years —
without other comfort or help than God alone — that then you
would help these many unhappy beings — for you can! — since
you could not help her. If you have repented at any time that you
rode away from Mandvik yonder day and let Halfrid remain behind in Sir Finn's power — "

" But I have not! " Erling's voice was piercing now. " For I
know that *she* never did — but this I trow *you* could not understand. For had you ever understood for one hour how proud she
was, the lady you won to wife " — he laughed in his wrath — " then
had you not done this. I know not how much you know — but you
may as lief know this. They sent me — for Haakon lay sick then —
to fetch her home to her kindred. Elin and she had grown up together as sisters — they were well-nigh of an age, though Elin was
her father's sister; — we had — things had come about so that, had
she come home from Mandvik, we had been forced to meet daily
and hourly. We sat and talked, a whole night through, in the balcony of the dragon-house — every word that was spoken both she
and I can answer for to God on the day of doom. And then let *Him*
answer *us*, why it should have been so — "

" Though, indeed, God rewarded her holiness in the end. Gave her a good husband to comfort her for the one she had had before — a whelp of a boy like you — who lay with her serving-women in her own house — and had her bring up your bastards — " He flung away the ball of moss he had kneaded together.

Simon stood motionless and dumb. Erling peeled off a flake of moss again and flung it away:

" I did what *she* bade me. Have you heard enough? There was no other way. Wherever else in the world we might have met, we had — we had — ' Adultery ' is no fair word. ' Incest ' — is yet uglier — "

Simon moved his head in a stiff little nod.

He felt it himself — it would be laughable to say what he thought. Erling Vidkunssön had been a man in the twenties, courtly and gallant. Halfrid had loved him so that she would fain have kissed his footprints in the dewy grass of the courtyard that morning in spring. *He* was an ageing, hulking, ugly farmer — and Kristin? Never, for sure, would the thought come in her head that there would be peril to the soul of either, should they live under one roof for twenty years. Surely he had learnt to understand that well enough. . . .

So he said in a low voice, almost humbly:

" She had not the heart to suffer the innocent child, even though 'twas her woman's child by her husband, to fare ill in the world. *She* it was that prayed me to do it right and justice so far as lay in my power. Oh, Erling Vidkunssön — for Erlend's poor innocent wife's sake — She will grieve to death. Methought I could not leave any stone unturned in seeking help for her and all her children — "

Erling Vidkunssön stood leaning against the gate-post. His face was calm as it was wont to be, and his voice cool and courteous, when he spoke again:

" I liked her well, Kristin Lavransdatter, the little I have seen of her — a fair and stately woman she is — and I have told you already, Simon Andressön, I deem full surely that you will find help if you will follow my counsel. But I understand not rightly what you mean by this — strange device. You surely cannot think that because I had to suffer my father's brother to rule the matter of my wedding, being then in my nonage, and because the maid I liked best was betrothed elsewhere when we first met — And so innocent as you say, I trow Erlend's wife is not, either. Aye, you are wedded to her sister, I know it; but you and not I have brought about this — strange parley — and so you must suffer that I name it. I mind me there was talk enough about it, the time Erlend was wed with her — 'twas against Lavrans Björgulfssön's counsel and his will that that bargain came about; but the maid had thought more of having her own will than of obeying her father or guarding her honour. Aye, she may be a good wife none the less — but she *won* Erlend after all, and they have doubtless had their time of joy and mirth. I trow that Lavrans had never much joy of that son-in-law — *he* had chosen another man for his daughter ere she came to know Erlend — she was promised in marriage, I know — " He stopped short, looked at Simon a moment, and turned his head aside in some confusion.

Flushing red with shame, Simon bent his head on his breast, but he spoke, none the less, low but firmly:

" Aye; she was promised to me."

For a moment they stood, not venturing to look at each other. Then Erling Vidkunssön threw away the last ball of moss he had gathered, turned, and went out into the rain. Simon was left standing alone — but when the other was some way off in the mist, he stopped and beckoned impatiently.

Then they went back together, as silently as they had come. When they had well-nigh reached the manor, Sir Erling said:

" I will do it, Simon Andressön. You must wait until to-morrow; then we can ride in company, all four together."

Simon looked up at the other — with a face all drawn with pain and shame. He would have given thanks, but could not; he had to bite his lip hard, his lower jaw trembled so violently.

As they were passing through the door of the hall, Erling Vidkunssön touched Simon's shoulder, as it were by chance. But each knew that neither of them dared look at the other.

Next day, when they were making them ready for the journey, Stig Haakonssön pressed Simon to let him lend him clothes — Simon had brought no change of garments with him. Simon looked down at himself — his man had brushed and cleaned up his dress, but it had suffered past remedy in his long ride through foul weather. But he slapped himself on the thighs:

" I am too fat, Stig. — And I go not thither to be a guest at the feasting."

Erling Vidkunssön stood with one foot on the bench, while his son buckled the gilded spur on it — it seemed as though Sir Erling tried to keep his serving-folk at a distance to-day as much as might be. The knight laughed in an oddly vexed fashion:

" 'Twill do no hurt, I trow, if it should show on Simon Darre that he has not spared himself in his kinsman's service, but bursts right in from the high-road with his bold and subtle speech. He is no tongue-tied loon, this one-time kinsman of ours, Stig. One thing only I fear — that he may not know himself when he should stop — "

Simon stood there, flushing darkly, but he said no word. In all that Erling Vidkunssön had said to him since the day before, he marked a grudging mockery — and a strange, unwilling kindness — and a firm will to see this matter through — since, once and for all, he had taken it up.

So they rode with him north from Mandvik, Sir Erling, his son and Stig, with, in all, ten fairly clad and well-armed yeomen. Simon with his single follower thought now he could have chosen to come to the meeting more fittingly attended and equipped — Simon Darre of Formo had no need to ride with his former kinsmen in the guise of a small franklin that had sought their aid in his helplessness. But he heeded not much. He was so weary and so broken with what he had gone through the day before, that almost it seemed to him now he cared not what the outcome of this journey might be.

Simon had ever averred that he put no faith in the ugly rumours about King Magnus. He was no such saint but that he could suffer a gross jest amongst grown-up men-folk. But when people stuck their heads together and muttered shudderingly of dark and secret sins, he ever grew ill at ease. And it seemed to him unseemly to believe or to hearken to aught of the kind about the King among whose sworn men he was counted.

Yet was he filled with wonder when he stood before the young King. He had not seen Magnus Eiriksson since the King was a child, and, in spite of his disbelief, he had looked to find something womanish, soft or unhealthy about him — but this was one of the properest young men Simon had set eyes on — and he looked manly and kingly too, despite of his youth and slender fineness.

He wore a flowing robe of light blue shot with green, falling

to his feet, and girt about his slim waist with a gilded belt, and he
bore his tall, lean body with exceeding grace in the heavy dress.
King Magnus had light hair, which lay smoothly on his well-
formed head, but was cunningly curled at the ends, so that it
seemed to toss and wave about his neck's broad, free-standing
pillar. His features were fine and boldly cut, the hue of his skin
fresh, with red cheeks and a yellowish tinge of sunburn; he had
clear eyes and an open look. He bore him fairly and with winning
gentleness as he greeted his liege men. Then in a while he laid
his hand on Erling Vidkunssön's sleeve and drew him some steps
apart from the others, while he thanked him for his coming.

They talked together awhile, and Erling let fall that there was
a special matter wherein he had to crave the King's grace and
bounty. The royal ushers then set a chair for the knight in front of
the King's high seat, showed the other three men to places somewhat further down the hall, and then went out.

Without effort Simon seemed to have found again the mannerly
and courtly bearing he had learned in his youth, and, since he had
yielded and taken from Stig the loan of a long brown dress of
state, in outward looks, too, he differed in no wise from the other
men. But as he sat there he felt as though he were in the midst of
a dream — he was and he was not the same as yonder young Simon
Darre, the quick-witted and *kurteis* son of a noble knight, who had
borne napkin and taper before King Haakon in Oslo Palace an
endless tale of winters agone — he was and he was not Simon, the
esquire of Formo, who had lived a life of freedom and cheer
away north in the Dale through all these years — free from care,
after a fashion, though he had known all his days that within him
lay this glowing ember — but he turned his thoughts away from
it. A dull and threatening humour of revolt rose up in the man —
it was no willed sin or fault of his that he knew of, but fate, that
had blown the embers into a blaze, so that he must strive and make
no sign while roasting over a slow fire.

He stood up when all the others did so — King Magnus had
risen:

" Dear kinsman," came his young, fresh voice, " methinks the
matter stands thus. The Prince is my brother, but we have never
tried to keep court together with a common guard — the same men
cannot serve us both. Nor does it seem that Erlend had meant
that things should continue in such wise — even though for a time

he did hold his Wardenship under my hand, while at the same time he was Haakon's sworn man. But those of my men who would liefer follow my brother Haakon shall have leave from my service and freedom to seek their fortune in his house. Who they may be — that I mean to learn from Erlend's mouth."

"Then must you, Sir King, try if you can come to agreement with Erlend Nikulaussön in this matter. You must keep the promise of safe-conduct that you have given, and grant your kinsman an audience — "

"Aye, he is my kinsman and your kinsman, and Sir Ivar moved me to promise him safe-conduct — but *he* kept not his oaths to me, and *he* remembered not the kinship betwixt us." King Magnus laughed a little and again laid his hand on Erling's arm. "My kinsmen seem to be faithful to the byword we have in this land: None so unkind as kin. Now is it my full will to show my kinsman Erlend of Husaby grace for the sake of God and Mary Virgin, and for my own lady's sake; life and goods and leave here to abide, if he will make his peace with me — lawful respite to remove him from my lands, if he would betake him to his new master, Prince Haakon. — The same grace will I grant to every man who has been leagued with him — but I will know who they are, and which of my men dwelling up and down this land of ours has been a false servant to his lord. What say you, Simon Andressön? — I know that your father was my grandfather's trusty henchman; you yourself served King Haakon with honour — think you not that I have the right to make inquiry in this matter? "

"I think, my lord King " — Simon stepped forward and again made obeisance — " that so long as your grace rules according to this land's law and custom, mercifully, you will surely never learn who the men may be that had planned to have recourse to lawlessness and treason. For as soon as the people of this land see that your Grace will hold fast to the right and justice that your forefathers have set up, of a surety no man in this realm will think of troubling the peace. And those will be silent and will bethink them again, to whom for a time it may have seemed hard to believe that you, my Lord, young as you are, could rule two great kingdoms with wisdom and strength."

"It is so, my lord King," put in Erling Vidkunssön. "No man in this land has thought of denying you obedience in aught that you may command rightfully — "

" Have they not? Then you deem, maybe, that Erlend has not been guilty of disloyalty and treason — when we look more closely into the case? "

For a moment Sir Erling seemed at fault for an answer, and Simon took the word:

" You, Sir, are our lord — to you each man looks to punish law-breaking by the law. But if you should follow where Erlend Niku-laussön has led the way, it might well befall that the men whose names you now so hotly seek to know should come forth and name them aloud, or other men who may begin to ponder over the rights and wrongs of this matter — for much talk will there come to be of it if your Grace should deal as you have threatened with a man so well-known and so high-born as Erlend Nikulaussön."

" What mean you, Simon Andressön? " said the King sharply — he grew red as he spoke.

" Simon means," Bjarne Erlingssön broke in, " that it might do your Grace an ill service if folk should begin to ask why Erlend must suffer such dishonour as the law warrants all men against, save thieves and nithings.* They might come then to think on King Haakon's other grandsons — "

Erling Vidkunssön turned sharply on his son — he looked angry — but the King only asked dryly:

" Count you not traitors and rebels as nithings? "

" None *call* them so, sir, if their plans speed well," answered Bjarne.

For a moment all stood silent. Then Erling Vidkunssön spoke: " Whatever Erlend should be called, my lord, it beseems not that you should override the law to come at him — "

" Then should the law be mended in this matter," said the King vehemently. " If 'tis so that I have no power to get me by all means the knowledge of how folk mean to keep faith with me — "

" Yet can you not act upon a mended law before it is changed," said Sir Erling doggedly, " without oppressing the folk of the land — and that folk has ever found it hard to use itself to oppression from its Kings."

" I have my knighthood and my sworn King's-men to back me," answered Magnus Eirikssön with a boyish laugh. " What say you, Simon? "

" I say, my lord — it might well prove that that was no such sure

* See Note 18.

backing — to judge by the measure the knighthood and the nobles of Denmark and Sweden have dealt their Kings when the commons had no strength to back up the kingly power against them. But if your Grace be set upon such counsels, then would I pray that you will loose me from your service — for then would I liefer be found among the common folk."

Simon had spoken so calmly and soberly that it seemed as though the King at first understood not his meaning. Then he laughed:

" Is this a threat, Simon Andressön? — Is it so that you would throw down your glove to me? "

" That must be as you will, my lord," said Simon as evenly as before; but he took his gloves out of his belt and held them in his hand. Then young Bjarne bent forward and took them:

" These are not seemly wedding-gloves for your Grace to buy! " He held the thick, worn riding-gloves in the air and laughed. " If it should come out, Sir, that you are seeking for such gloves, you might well have proffered you all too many of them — and all too cheap."

Erling Vidkunssön uttered a cry. With a sharp movement he seemed to sweep the young King to one side, and the three men to another; and he drove the men down the hall toward the door:

" I must speak with the King alone."

" No, no! I would speak with Bjarne! " cried the King, running after. But Sir Erling pushed his son out with the others.

They loitered about awhile in the castle yard and on the hill outside — none of them spoke a word. Stig Haakonssön looked doubtfully, but held his tongue as he had done throughout; Bjarne Erlingssön went about all the time with a little, hidden smile. In a while Sir Erling's weapon-bearer came and prayed them from his master to wait for him at their lodging — their horses were in the castle yard.

Afterward they sat in the inn. They were shy of speech about what had just befallen — at last they fell into talk of their horses and hounds and hawks. The end of it was that Stig and Simon sat far on into the evening telling stories about women. Stig Haakonssön had always great store of such tales, but with Simon the worst was that most of those he called to mind Stig straightway began to tell, and 'twas ever so that either the thing had happened to himself, or it had befallen of late at some place near Mandvik

— even if Simon remembered having heard the tale in his boyhood from the house-carls at home at Dyfrin.

But he chuckled and laughed as heartily as Stig. From time to time it was as though the bench rocked beneath him as he sat there — he was afraid of something, but dared not think what it was. Bjarne Erlingssön laughed quietly, drank wine and munched apples, fiddled with the hood of his cape, and told now and then a little snatch of a tale — they were the worst of all, but they were so cunningly veiled that Stig did not understand them. Bjarne had heard them from a priest in Björgvin, he said.

At last Erling came. His son went to meet him and take from him his outer garments. Erling turned angrily on the youth:

" You! " He flung his cloak into Bjarne's hands — and there flitted across his face, as though against his will, the shadow of a smile. He turned to Simon:

" Aye — now you must be content, Simon Andressön! I make no doubt that now you may safely hope the day is not far off when you shall sit in peace and comfort together on your neighbouring manors — you and Erlend — and his wife and all their sons."

Simon had grown a shade paler when he stood up and thanked Sir Erling. — He knew now what the fear was that he had not dared to look in the face. But now there was no way out. . . .

About fourteen days after, Erlend Nikulaussön was set free. Simon, with his two men and Ulf Haldorssön, rode out to Akersnes and fetched him.

The trees were almost bare already, for it had blown hard the week before. A black frost had set in now — the earth rang hard under the horses' hoofs, and the fields were wan with rime, as they rode in towards the town. It looked as though snow were coming — the heavens were evenly overspread with cloud and the daylight was sullen and chilly grey.

Simon had seen that Erlend dragged one foot a little, as he came out into the castle yard, and he seemed somewhat stiff and unhandy in mounting. He was very pale, too. He had had his beard taken off and his hair cut and made trim — his upper face was now a dull yellow, and, below, the blue of his shaven beard showed against white cheeks and chin; there were hollows beneath his eyes. But he made a stately figure in his long dark-blue robe and cloak, and, as he said farewell to Olav Kyrning, and made gifts of money to the men who had guarded him and brought him food in prison, he bore him like a chieftain parting from the house-folk at a wedding-feast.

At first, as they rode, he seemed to feel cold; he shivered more than once. Then a little colour came into his cheeks — his face lighted up — it was as though sap and life were welling up in him. Simon thought: sure it was Erlend was no easier to break than a willow wand.

They came to the lodging, and Kristin went to meet her husband in the courtyard. Simon tried not to look thither, but he could not forbear.

They gave each other their hands and exchanged some words, in quiet, clear tones. They managed this meeting in the sight of all the people of the house in fair and seemly wise enough. Only that both flushed red, looked at each other a second, and then both dropped their eyes. Then Erlend proffered his hand again to his wife, and they went together towards the loft-room where they were to dwell whilst they were in the city.

Simon turned towards the room where he and Kristin had lived till now. Then Kristin turned at the lowest step of the stairway and called to him, in a wonderful ringing voice:

" Will you not come, brother-in-law? — get you some food first — and you, Ulf! "

She seemed so young and supple as she stood there, turned a little from the hips, and looked back over her shoulder. As soon as she came to Oslo, she had begun to fasten her head-gear in another fashion. Here in the south it was only small farmers' wives who wore the linen head-dress in the old-world way she had used ever since she was wedded; tight round the face like a nun's coif, with the falls fastened cross-wise over the shoulders so that the neck was quite hid, and with many folds on the sides and over the knot of hair at the back of the head. In Trondheim it was accounted, so to speak, a token of piety to set up the coif in this fashion, which Archbishop Eiliv praised always as the most fitting and modest way for wedded women. But so as not to be too much marked out, she had taken up now with the fashion of these southern parts: the linen cloth laid smoothly over the crown of the head and hanging straight down behind, so that the front hair showed, and the neck and shoulders were free — and then it was the proper thing that the plaits should be but tied up so that they did not show under the edge of the coif, while the linen fitted close above, throwing out the form of the head. True, Simon had seen this before and deemed that it became her well — yet he had not seen before how young it made her look. And her eyes shone like stars.

Farther on in the day many folk appeared to greet Erlend — Ketil of Skog, Markus Torgeirssön, and later in the evening Olav Kyrning himself, Sira Ingolf and Canon Guttorm, a priest of St. Halvard's Church. When the two priests came it had begun to snow — a slight dry fine-grained drizzle — and they had missed the path and come in among some burdocks — their clothes were full of the burrs. Everyone set to work to pluck burrs off the priests and their followers — Erlend and Kristin rid Canon Guttorm of his — from time to time their faces flushed, and their voices were strangely unsteady, as they jested with the priest and laughed.

Simon drank much in the first part of the evening, but he grew not at all light-headed with the drink — only a little heavy in the body. He heard each word that was said with unnatural sharpness. The others soon grew free-spoken — none of them were friends to the King.

He was heartily sick of it all now 'twas all over. Foolish prate it was that they babbled forth as they sat there — loud-voiced and heated. Ketil Åasmundssön was somewhat simple, and his brother-in-law Markus was none too wise either; Olav Kyrning was a right-minded and sensible man, but short-sighted — neither did the two priests seem to Simon too clear-witted. They all sat there and listened to Erlend and chimed in with him, and he grew more and more like himself as he had ever been, wild and reckless. He had taken Kristin's hand now, and laid it over his knee, and sat playing with her fingers — they sat so that their shoulders touched. Now the deep flush showed clear through her skin, she could not take her eyes from him — when he stole an arm about her waist, her mouth trembled, so that she had much ado keeping her lips shut. . . .

Then the door opened and Munan Baardssön stepped in.

" Last came the great bull himself! " shouted Erlend, laughing, and leapt up to meet him.

" Help us God and Mary Virgin — I believe you care not a straw, Erlend," said Munan in vexation.

"Aye, deem you, then, it would help aught to whimper and sorrow now, kinsman?"

"Never have I seen the like of you — all your welfare have you cast away —"

"Aye — for I was never the kind to go unbreeched to hell, to save my breeches from the burning," said Erlend, and Kristin laughed softly and dizzily.

Simon laid him down over the table, his head between his arms. If only they might think he was so drunken already that he had fallen asleep! — he would fain be left in peace.

Nothing was otherwise than he had looked that it would be — should have looked it would be, at the least. Nothing — not even she. Here she sat, the only woman amongst all these men — as gentle and bashful and fearless and secure as ever. Even so had she been yonder other time — when she betrayed him — shameless or innocent, he knew not which. Oh, no, 'twas not so either; she had not been so secure, she had not been shameless — behind the calmness of her bearing she had not been calm. — But that man had bewitched her — for Erlend's sake she would gladly tread over redhot stones — and she had trodden over him as though she knew not he was aught but a cold stone.

Oh, all this was folly — her mind was set on having her own way, and she heeded naught else. Let them have their joyance, he need not care a jot. What mattered it to him if they had seven sons more, so that there would be fourteen to part betwixt them the half of Lavrans Björgulfssön's estate? It looked not as though *he* would need to be careful and troubled for his children — Ramborg was not so quick at bearing children as her sister — but as though in due time he would leave behind his children and children's children in riches and power. But 'twas all one to him — to-night. He would fain have drunk more — but he knew that to-night God's gifts would not cheer him — and then he would have had to raise his head and perhaps to join in the talk.

"Aye, you think, I trow, *you* were the man for Regent of the realm," said Munan scornfully.

"Nay, surely you must know we had meant that place for you," laughed Erlend.

"In God's name, heed your tongue, man —" The others laughed.

Erlend came over and touched Simon's shoulder:

" Are you asleep, brother-in-law? " Simon looked up. The other stood before him with a goblet in his hand. " Come, drink with me, Simon. You I have to thank most of·all that I came off with my life — and, such as it is, 'tis dear to me, lad! You stood by me like a brother — had you not been my brother-in-law, I trow I had lost my head for sure. — And then could you have wed my widow — "

Simon sprang up. A moment the two stood looking at each other — Erlend grew white and sobered, his lips parted in a gasp. — With his clenched fist Simon struck the goblet out of the other's hand — the mead splashed on the floor. Then he turned and went out of the room.

Erlend stood there alone. Without knowing what he did, he dried his hand and wrist with the skirt of his coat, then looked behind him; the others had not marked aught. With his foot he thrust the goblet in under the bench — he stood still a moment — then went quietly out after his brother-in-law.

Simon Darre stood at the foot of the stairway — Jon Daalk was leading his horses out of the stable. He made no movement when Erlend came down to him:

" Simon! Simon — I knew not — I knew not what I said! "

" You know it now."

Simon's voice was toneless. He stood quite still, not looking at the other.

Erlend looked about him, as at his wit's end. The moon showed dimly, a pale patch, through the veil of cloud; small hard grains of snow showered down on them. Erlend made a shivering motion.

" Where — where are you bound? " he asked dully, looking at the man and the horses.

" To seek me another lodging," said Simon shortly. " Maybe you can understand that *here* I care not to be — "

" Simon! " Erlend burst out. " Oh, I know not what I would not give if it could be unsaid — ! "

" Nor I either," answered the other as before.

The door of the upper room opened. Kristin came out on the balcony with a lanthorn in her hand; she bent over the railing and threw the light down on them.

" Why stand you there? " she asked in a clear voice. " What would you without the house? "

"I felt I must go out and see to my horses — as 'tis the courtly fashion to say," answered Simon, laughing up to her.

"But — you have takén your horses out," she said, in laughing wonder.

"Aye — a man will do strange things in his cups," said Simon in the same tone.

"Well, come back now," she broke in, brightly and gladly.

"Aye. In a moment." She went in, and Simon called out to Jon to take back the horses. He turned towards Erlend — the man was standing there, strangely helpless in looks and bearing. "I shall come in a little. We must — try to bear us as though this were unspoken, Erlend — for our wives' sake. But so much maybe you too can understand — you were the last man on earth that I would — would have had know of — this. And forget not that I am not so forgetful as you!"

The door above was opened again; the guests came out in a troop; Kristin was with them, and her woman, bearing the lanthorn.

"Aye," tittered Munan Baardssön, "the night is well worn already — and these two good folks would fain to bed, I trow —"

"Erlend — Erlend — Erlend!" Kristin had thrown herself into his arms the moment they stood alone within the loft-room door. She clung close and tightly to him. "Erlend — you look so sorrowful —" she whispered in fear, with her half-open lips close to his mouth. "Erlend —" She pressed the palms of her hands to his temples.

He stood a little with his arms laid loosely around her. Then, with a soft moaning sound in his throat, he crushed her to him.

Simon went across to the stable — he would have said somewhat to Jon, but he forgot it on the way. For a while he stood in the stable-door, looking up at the light-haze of the moon and the tumbling snow — it had begun now to fall in great flakes. Jon and Ulf came out and shut the door behind them, and the three men went together across to the house where they were to sleep.

THE MISTRESS OF HUSABY

P. 277.   1. *Husaby (see Sketch Map)*

THE old manor of Husaby, comprising some thirty greater and smaller farms and homesteads, lies about twenty English miles southwest of Trond-hjem (Nidaros). The head-quarter buildings are on a broad mountain slope above a little lake, about ten English miles from the nearest point on the Trondhjem Fjord (Birgsi), and between the great valleys of Guldal and Orkedal, which stretch southward up to the Dovrefjeld. The journey from Husaby to Nidaros would ordinarily be made by horse to Birgsi and thence by boat. The path followed by Kristin on her pilgrimage ran across the hills to the estuary of the Gula River, and thence across Bynes, the high promontory which shoots into the fjord between the Gula and Nid estuaries.

P. 278.   2. *Hall at Husaby (see Plan)*

The hall at Husaby was a large, ancient stone building, in the style of the Saga-times, when the chieftain and his house-carls dwelt and slept under one roof — the serving-women being quartered in a separate women's house (the "little hall" of this book).

Two rows of wooden pillars supported the roof. Between the line of pillars and the wall on each side was the sleeping-accommodation — two box-beds with doors at one end of the hall, and two broad fixed benches running the rest of the length of the hall. These benches were divided into sleeping-places for the warriors (originally called "rooms"), and were wide enough to admit of each man's keeping his belongings by him, while his weapons hung on the wall above him. As in the "hearth-room house" of the later mediæval manor, the room was heated from a hearth in the middle of the floor, and the only daylight came from the smoke-vent above this or from the door; but the hearth was much longer, and several fixed fires were ordinarily kept burning on it, when artificial heat was required. On festival occasions long tables were set up — otherwise each man ate his meals sitting in his "room," with his porridge-bowl or his meat in his lap; or drank his beer sitting on the floor by the hearth.

In later times, when a separate house was assigned to the servingmen, the "rooms" in the hall were left free to be used, when necessary, as sleeping-places for the family or guests. The high seat was moved up to the east end of the hall, and temporary tables were put up daily for the chief meal of the day (supper).

Later, yet further changes were, of course, made. Thus the plan shows the hall as arranged for the banquet described in Part I, chap. iii. By this time, it will be seen, a smaller table has been put up across the hall, before the high seat, with a loose outer bench for the servants.

Above the "outer room" and the "closet" at the lower end of the hall, there was, at Husaby, a loft-room (Margret's bower) reached by a ladder leading up from the hall.

P. 330.   3. *Gunnulf's Song*

Master Gunnulf must evidently have come upon an early version of the old English ballad, "The Falcon," and have adapted it freely, with an eye to edification.

P. 331.   4. *Lady Midwives*

The Church laws, as well as the custom, of mediæval Norway (and Denmark) made it the duty of all married women to act as midwives to the women of their neighbourhood. The housewives living in the neighbourhood (*grannekoner*) were bound to come, each accompanied by a serving-woman (*gridkone*). Professional midwives were unknown, but any woman who gained a name for skill in midwifery was bound to go wherever she was sent for within half a day's horseback journey. No fee could be claimed for this assistance, but custom required that the father should send the ladies and women away with gifts when they left his house. The value of the gifts was proportioned to the importance of the event — in the case of a first-born son the father would be expected to show special generosity.

When an heir to an estate was expected, the father should, months before, have prayed every neighbouring housewife of social standing to come to his wife's assistance. This was a matter of practical importance, as the ladies' evidence might be required to settle questions of inheritance. For instance, if the mother and child both died, the ladies could testify whether the child had been born alive and been christened, and whether it had died before or after its mother. In the former case the wife's family inherited her share of the joint estate; in the latter the husband inherited from the child. A conclave of *sages femmes* of quality would always be a guarantee as to the identity, etc., of an heir, if doubts of any kind arose.

Thus Erlend's failure to invite the ladies of the country-side to his wife's lying-in was a culpably rash, as well as a scandalous, omission.

P. 371.   5. *Trondhjem Cathedral*

In the steep sand-bank by the River Nid, where King Olav's body had lain buried the first winter after his death at the battle of Stiklestad (A.D. 1030), a spring welled up, the waters of which were credited with healing powers. On this site, first marked by a small chapel, a Bishop's Church, completed about the year 1075, was erected, in honour of Christ and St. Olav, the shrine containing the saint's remains being transferred to it from the wooden church in which his successors had lodged it.

In 1152 Norway was organised as an independent ecclesiastical province, and the Archbishopric of Nidaros created, by Cardinal Nicholas Breakspeare, afterwards Pope Hadrian IV. Shortly after, the building of the great Cathedral was begun, on the site of the existing Bishop's Church. "The man who had the most far-reaching influence on the work," says Professor Nordhagen, "was Eystein Erlandson, the imperious and highly gifted third Archbishop (1161–1188)." The work was begun in the Norman style, but, on returning from a three years' exile in England (1180–1183) — a result of his quarrel with the no less imperious and forceful King Sverre — Eystein brought with him the new ideas in architecture which had shortly before reached England and were even then being put into practice in the building of the choir of

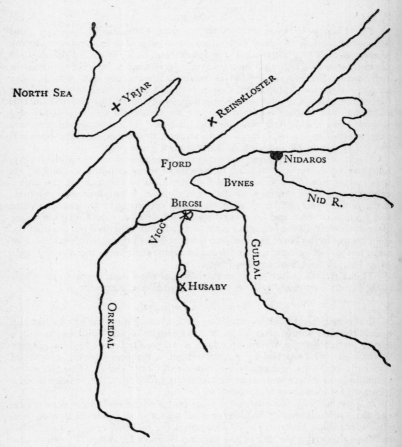

NORTH SEA

✝ YRJAR

✗ REINSKLOSTER

FJORD

NIDAROS

BYNES

NID R.

BIRGSI

VIGG

GULDAL

✗ HUSABY

ORKEDAL

SKETCH MAP SHOWING HUSABY

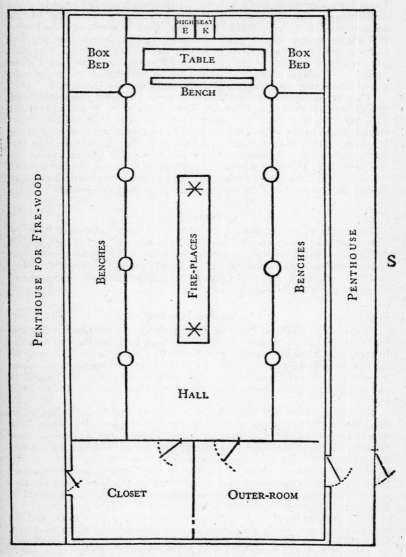

Canterbury Cathedral. Later, the work continued to be influenced by the contemporary developments of Gothic in England. Completed, in its first form, in the fourteenth century (about the period of this book), the Cathedral was the wonder of the North, and was sought by thousands of pilgrims, come to visit the shrine of the saint and the wonder-working well. The press was greatest at the time of the great Olav's Festival — the 29th July. *Feginsbrekka* — "The Hill of Joy" — was the hill on the pilgrims' route from the top of which they first caught sight of the city and the Cathedral.

The first of numerous fires from which the Cathedral has suffered was that of 1328, referred to in this book. It was again swept by fire in 1432 and 1531, yet even as it stood half destroyed in 1567 it is described by a Norwegian writer of the period as "the crown, the flower and ornament of the kingdom." There were further visitations by fire in 1708 and 1719, so that in the eighteenth and nineteenth centuries its original glories were much obscured. Very elaborate schemes of restoration were put in hand towards the end of the nineteenth century, and have in great part been carried out; though the renovation of the west front remains to be completed.

P. 381.   6. *Court of Six*

Practically all nobles, and a great part of the landed gentry of Norway, were *hirdmænd* (in this book, translated "Guardsmen" or "King's-men"); that is to say, had at one time or another served in the King's household. Suits at law between such *hirdmænd* were referred, not to the ordinary *Things* (see Note 9), but to a special Court of Six (*seksmandsdom*), composed of six of the parties' fellow-*hirdmænd*.

P. 381.   7. *Norway, 1319–1335*

Magnus VII. (King of Norway 1319–1343) was the grandson of Haakon V., being the son of Haakon's daughter Ingeborg by Duke Eirik of Sweden. In 1318 Duke Eirik was murdered by his brother, King Birger. The party of the murdered Duke rose and drove away the King, making the baby prince Magnus King of Sweden in his place. The leader of their army was the gallant and handsome Danish knight, Knut Porse, who had been the Duke's loyal vassal.

Since Magnus was heir to the throne of Norway also, King Haakon on his death-bed foresaw a union of the two Crowns. He appointed eight Norwegian lords as a Council of State for the minor King, and made them swear solemnly to rule according to the laws of the country, and to keep out foreigners from all posts of influence, especially from the strongholds of the Crown. When, on the death of Haakon in 1319, Magnus became King of both countries, an agreement was entered into by the Councils of the two realms, providing for their independent relations and respective duties. The King's mother was given a very influential position in both countries.

She very soon began to abuse her power in favour of Knut Porse, and the attachment of the young widow to her champion became much talked of. Knut Porse's plan was to bring the then Danish province of Skaane (Scania in southern Sweden) by conquest under the Swedish Crown, and win a Dukedom for himself, so as to be in a position to marry the Lady Ingeborg.

When, in 1321, King Magnus' little sister Eufemia was betrothed to a son
of Duke Henry the Lion of Mecklenburg, in the presence of members of both
the Swedish and Norwegian governments, a secret compact was made between the Duke and Sir Knut, by which the Duke pledged himself to furnish
soldiers in support of the Skaane enterprise. Some Norwegian noblemen,
among them Sir Munan Baardssön, who was an intimate friend of Sir Knut
and Lady Ingeborg, attached their seals to this compact. And Lady Ingeborg,
who had unlawfully carried the Great Seal out of Norway, tried by all means
to raise funds for the war.

But in the summer of 1322 the Swedish lords met in parliament at Skara,
and by a *coup d'état* took all power out of the hands of the lady; and in
February, 1323, the Norwegian nobles, under the leadership of Archbishop
Eiliv, gathered at Oslo and followed the Swedish example. A young lord of
the highest descent in the land and of great wealth, Sir Erling Vidkunssön,
was made Regent of Norway, with the title of *Drotsete* (here translated High
Steward), with the Council of nobles to assist him.

As a result of the union of the two Crowns, Norway had been dragged
into the wars between Sweden and Russia, and for some years from 1323
onwards the Russians made a series of destructive raids on the coasts of
Northern Norway, coming as far south as Haalogaland (the modern Nordland's Amt). Sir Erling took measures to defend the country, and achieved
some success, but he wanted money badly, as Lady Ingeborg had left him an
empty treasury. He sought assistance from the Bishops, as the Russians were
accounted heretics or worse; the Archbishop stood by him, but Bishop Aud-
finn of Bergen refused help. In the years following, Erling had several quarrels with this Bishop, who was a staunch partisan of Lady Ingeborg. In par-
ticular the Bishop defended the lady's rights to some estates in his diocese,
when, in 1326, she further enraged her native country by marrying Knut
Porse, who, by one of the vicissitudes in the struggle between the Danish
King, Christopher II., and his nobles, had now become a Danish Duke. Knut
Porse, however, died in 1330, leaving his widow with two little sons, Haakon
and Knut.

In 1326 peace was made between Norway and Russia, on terms not
unfavourable to Norway.

In 1330 King Magnus, now sixteen years old, was declared to be of age,
and Erling Vidkunssön resigned. King Magnus took up his stepfather's plan
of winning Skaane, stayed on in Sweden, and made an old antagonist of
Sir Erling's, Paal Baardsen, his Chancellor for Norway and bearer of the
Great Seal. But when, in 1333, Paal was chosen Archbishop in succession to
Archbishop Eiliv, Magnus failed to appoint a new Chancellor; and, as the
King still stayed on in Sweden, always in want of money and demanding
supplies, and leaving Norway without any lawful government, a party
among the Norwegian nobles, headed by Erling Vidkunssön and the King's
young cousins, Jon and Sigurd Haftorssön, rose against him. The matter was,
however, settled the same year without bloodshed; the leaders of the revolt
were forgiven, and kept their position and titles, King Magnus appointed
Sir Ivar Ogmundssön *Drotsete* and Chancellor for Norway, the Council's
powers were strengthened, and Norway once more had a working government. This seems to have been all that was aimed at by Erling Vidkunssön.

whom history represents as an upright, honourable, brave and sensible man, though somewhat lacking in the vigour which achieves great things.

Erlend Nikulaussön's subsequent attempt to separate the Crowns of Norway and Sweden by placing Lady Ingeborg's son Haakon on the Norwegian throne has escaped the notice of history, which, however, records the wedding of King Magnus at Tunsberg in 1335 to the Countess Blanche of Namur.

P. 386.   8. *War Levies*

The word translated "levy" or "war levy" is in the original *leding*. All landholders were bound to pay to the Crown an annual contribution (*leding*) towards the defence of the country. This was due in time of peace as well as in war-time; but they might be called on for additional voluntary assistance in emergencies.

Failure to pay the tax rendered the defaulter liable to fine. Lavrans undertakes to pay any fines that may be imposed on his tenants owing to their refusal to comply with the illegal demands made upon them under colour of the enforcement of the contribution.

P. 399.   9. *Things*

At the period of this book there were three classes of *Things* (popular assemblies):

I. The parish Thing (held ordinarily at regular intervals, but which could also be specially summoned) for the transaction of all sorts of local business. Appeals from its decisions could be taken to:

II. The county Thing (*Herreds*, or *Fylkesthing*), which was held in each *Fylke* (county) twice a year — in the middle of Lent, and three weeks after the return of the county representatives from the *Lagthing* (see below). These county assemblies were known as *sysselmandsthing*, as they were convened by the *sysselmand* (warden) of the county (see Note 12, *Wardens*). Lawsuits which were to be brought before a *Lagthing* must be announced at these county *Things;* and their sentences and decisions (arrived at by a jury, not by the *sysselmand*, who had no judicial functions) were appealable to the *Lagthing*.

III. The *Lagthing*. Norway was divided into four sections called *lagdömmer*, each of which had its annual *Lagthing*. These were known as *Frostathing, Gulathing, Eidsivathing and Borgarthing*, and, at the time of the story, all met on the same day, St. Botolph's day (17th June). The *Frostathing*, which represented the northern section of the country, met at Nidaros.

Each of the four *lagdömmer* was a complete legislative and judicial entity. The *Lagthing* was composed of representatives chosen by the *sysselmænd* from the members of the various county *Things*, and was attended by all the *sysselmænd* of the section, whose duty it was to follow the cases from their several counties, and to report the decisions, and any new legislation, to the county *Things* summoned by them to meet three weeks after their return from the *Lagthing*.

The chairman of the *Lagthing* was known as the *Lagmand*. His functions corresponded roughly with those of the Speaker of the early House of Commons in England.

P. 413.   10. *Fourteenth-Century Rome*

Master Gunnulf had, of course, visited Rome during the so-called " Baby-
lonian exile " of the Popes at Avignon, which began in 1305.

P. 425.   11. *Land Measurements*

The words here translated " half a hide " are in the original *to maaneds-
matsbol*, meaning literally " two months'-meat's-area " — *i.e.* twice as much
land as will feed one man for one month.

P. 448.   12. *Wardens*

The word translated " Warden " is in the original *sysselmand*. The
sysselmand was a high official in charge of a district, roughly correspond-
ing to a county in England, his duties being those of a chief administrator, mili-
tary commander and chief police officer. The appointment was made by the
Crown from among gentlemen of distinction — at the period of the story a
sysselmand would be usually, though not always, a knight. He had to maintain a certain number of armed men and subordinate officials. His remunera-
tion varied in different cases — he might be paid directly by the Crown or
remunerated by a share in fines and fiefs.

Among other duties, the *sysselmand* had to hold each year in Lent a
" wapinschaw " (*vaabenting*), at which he reviewed the weapons in the
possession of the men of his district, to make sure that each man had the
weapons he was bound by law to possess, according to his station. He had
also to choose the delegates from his district to the annual *Lagthing* of his
section of the country (see Note 9, *Things*), and to attend at the *Lagthing*
to follow all cases relating to his district. Within three weeks from his return
home he had to call a *sysselmandsthing* and there communicate to the people
all decisions and sentences of the *Lagthing* affecting his district, all new laws
passed, etc. He had to account for the fines and other dues of the Crown to
the Treasurer of his section of the country (see Note 15, *Treasurers*).

P. 491.   13. *Veöy*

A little island near Molde, where in the Middle Ages there was a small
market town, with a couple of churches and a royal mansion.

Pp. 527, 543.   14. *Grace to Criminals*

When a man had committed any offence punishable with outlawry (such
as manslaughter or the abduction of a woman), he might, on making a
payment to the Crown, be given leave to remain at his home under the
protection of the law till his case was judged.

P. 529.   15. *Treasurers*

For purposes of financial administration, Norway was divided into four
Treasury Districts (*fehirdsle*), each under a Treasurer (*fehirde*). The
Treasurer of the district which had its head-quarters at Tunsberg was a sort
of Minister of Finance, supervising the whole.

P. 601.   16. *Safe-Conduct*

As a *Hirdmand* (Guardsman — see Note 6), Erlend has the right to be
tried by a court of his peers within the boundaries of the *lagdömme* (section

— see Note 9) where he is domiciled. Having appealed against the finding and sentence of the court on the ground of the illegality of its composition, and claimed a fresh trial, he is granted a safe-conduct in order that he may be taken outside the bounds of the *lagdömme* to be brought before the King. The effect of this is that, if he fails to make his peace with the King, he is entitled to be sent back in safety to his own *lagdömme*, there to be given a fresh trial or to suffer the execution of the sentence of the original court, according as his appeal is or is not admitted.

P. 601.   17. *Baagahus*

Now Baahus in Sweden, near Gothenburg. The boundary between Norway and Sweden at this time was the Göta River, and Baagahus was the Norwegian frontier town.

P. 635.   18. *Immunities of Freemen*

This passage, translated as literally as possible, would run: "why Erlend must not enjoy such personal immunities [*mandhelg*] as are the right of all men save thieves and nithings."

By the ancient laws every free man of Norway was guaranteed *mandhelg* — *i.e.* immunity from dishonouring bodily punishments and outrages against his person and honour. This involved, in Saga-times, his right to avenge himself and his kin.

DESIGNER'S NOTE

A PAGE of "old style" type (Linotype *Janson*) furnished with a running-title of "modern face." Quite irregular. For what reason? To be perverse, and shock the typographically pure? No. The purpose is to cut the running-head quite away from the text—to put the two parts of the page in two different regions of historic time almost—as though you had the old chronicle complete in a compact type sympathetic to the narrative, and added the running-title notations in script for your own convenience. To keep the story moving at its own pace, in its own atmosphere, without interference from merely *indexing* details. Whether or not the project is a success the reader will have to say. He will see that the flourished blackletter initials aim to contribute a faint tinge of old time.

The book was set in type by the Plimpton Press, Norwood Massachusetts, and the printing and binding are by H. Wolff, New York.

W. A. DWIGGINS